THE
DRAGON
LORDS

FALSE IDOLS

All around him, everything was collapsing to ash. Why shouldn't the people of Kondorra believe he had as well? A martyr would be as good as a living prophet. Better perhaps.

So he staggered away, through the tattered ruins of his tent, past the scurrying guards just coming alert to the chaos at the heart of their camp, and off into the night to find somewhere he could bleed in private for a while.

By Jon Hollins

The Dragon Lords

Fool's Gold
False Idols

THE
DRAGON LORDS
FALSE IDOLS

JON HOLLINS

www.orbitbooks.net

ORBIT

First published in Great Britain in 2017 by Orbit

1 3 5 7 9 10 8 6 4 2

Copyright © 2017 by Jonathan Wood

Map copyright © Tim Paul

Excerpt from *Kings of the Wyld* by Nicholas Eames
Copyright © 2017 by Nicholas Eames

The moral right of the author has been asserted.

A CIP catalogue record for this book
is available from the British Library.

ISBN 978-0-356-50766-8

Printed and bound in Great Britain by CPI Group (UK) Ltd, Croydon, CR0 4YY

Papers used by Orbit are from well-managed forests
and other responsible sources.

Orbit
An imprint of
Little, Brown Book Group
Carmelite House
50 Victoria Embankment
London EC4Y 0DZ

An Hachette UK Company
www.hachette.co.uk

www.orbitbooks.net

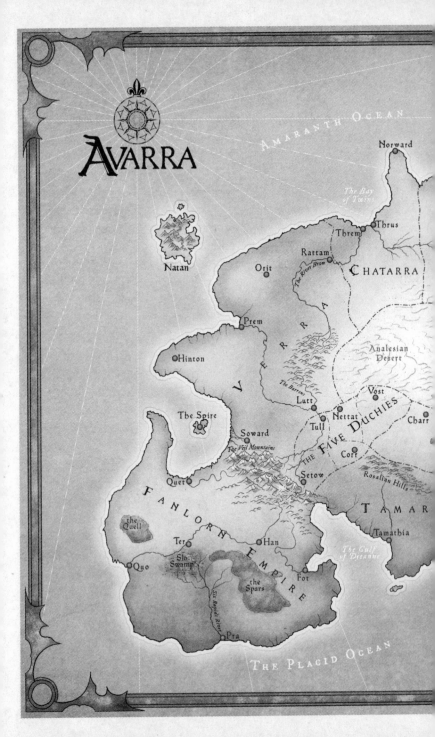

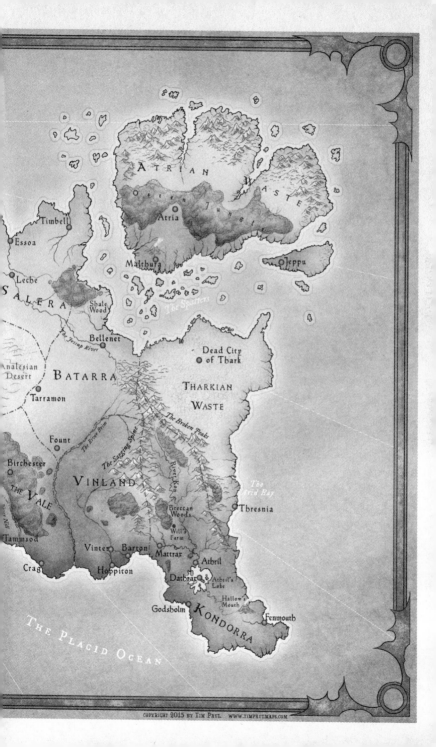

"Come not between the dragon and his wrath."

—*King Lear*, William Shakespeare

PART 1:
DRAGONS RISING

1

Big Thaumatobiologist
on Campus

Quirkelle Bal Tehrin dreamt of fire. It kindled in her sleep, licked at the feet of her desires and fears, then rose—wings spreading—to the sky, tearing through her subconscious. It was a roiling ocean of flame, obliterating everything in its wake. She would come awake in the cot she kept in her garret above the Tamathian University, sheets soaked with sweat, her palm prints scorched into the sheets.

She had yet to work out if the racing of her heart was a symptom of terror or pleasure.

And yet, despite this confusion, there were some things Quirk was certain of in life. That she knew more about dragons than anyone else alive. That such knowledge made her position at the Tamathian University more secure than a princess's chastity belt. And that the Tamarian Emperor's palace was not quite as impressive as he thought it was.

She sat now at his dinner table, two seats away from the man himself, flanked by his daughter and the Empress.

The Emperor was a small man, in his late fifties, balding, and with his remaining hair cropped to short gray stubble. He was wreathed entirely in gold. Great swirls of fabric encircled his arms, his torso. A great gold neckpiece—that probably weighed almost as much as the birdlike Empress—wreathed his neck. His deeply lined face, emerging from its depths, appeared somewhat inadequate in comparison. Religious iconography dangled from him. A medallion inscribed with the scepter of Lawl, king of the gods, bobbled over the neckpiece. The open palm of Klink, god of commerce, was etched into his broad earrings. The wheat sheaves of Toil, god of fertility and the field, was upon his rings.

He had invited her here, as was now his weekly custom, to dine with his family, several highly esteemed courtiers, and a smattering of visiting dignitaries. At first she had served more as a conversation piece than as a source of conversation. Still, over time she had managed to become something much more integral to the gatherings.

At that precise moment, his eminence was attacking a small roast partridge and coming off the worst of the two combatants. More than once he had needed to signal for a bodyguard to throw an elbow into his sternum so he could hawk up whatever bone had lodged in his throat. On the plus side, he had not yet called for the beheading of the chef. He knew now that Quirk did not like that.

"So," the Emperor said around a mouthful of gristle, pointing a partridge thigh at her like a miniature rapier. "What is it that you make of this business with the elven king?"

Quirk felt thirty pairs of eyeballs come to rest on her. Nobles, lords, ladies, the Emperor's cousin, two of his bastard children, three ambassadors, and a visiting dignitary from Verra. They all watched her and they waited.

The truth was, of course, that her limited knowledge of the world made her woefully inadequate to answer the question. She had, for most of her life, lived in seclusion, first as the personal weapon of a murderous demigod, and then as a hermit-like academic lost in the warrenlike tunnels of the Tamathian University. The one time she had ventured out into the world she had witnessed the death of seven dragons and just over ten thousand of the inhabitants of Kondorra. It was not a period in her life she would necessarily describe as successful.

And yet, they all waited. They all wanted to know what the world's leading thaumatobiologist and expert on dragons would say.

She wondered if any of them had actually read her papers. Had attended her lectures. She could not imagine the Chancellor of the Exchequer really getting to grips with the inner workings of *Varanus draconis*'s digestive tract. He was having enough trouble getting anything other than alcohol into his own.

On such things, she thought, *the fate of nations fall.*

The specific matter the king was referencing was the death of a white hart at the hands of several of his huntsmen. The hart had wandered from the forests of the Vale—which the Elven Court claimed as their own—and into the path of the several huntsmen looking for boar in the Emperor's abutting forest. Not being the sort of men to question providence when it stood in the way of a full purse, the huntsmen promptly shot the hart, skinned it, and sold the hide for a profit that would make even a city merchant blush. Which was all well and good until the elven king delivered a message stating that the hart was his sovereign property, that the huntsmen were thieves, and that unless they were handed over to him for execution, the consequences would be dire.

Well…that was if she paraphrased the specifics of the elven dialect. More directly the message had read: "So-called Emperor of the so-called empire of Tamar: give me the round-ears who stole my hart, or I shall come and fuck you. His highest eminence, master of the bowstring, slayer of the round-ears, commander of the Vale forces, fine-aspected Todger IV."

"Well," Quirk said, as delicately as it was possible to, "given the tone, and content of the letter, I do not honestly believe that King"—she hesitated—"Todger," she managed as gracefully as she could, "should be entertained in this manner. And furthermore, I do not believe that he can necessarily follow up on his threat to, erm"—she hesitated over this one—"to violate you."

"So screw him," said one of the nobles, and brayed with laughter. Several other followed suit. There was much stamping of feet, and pounding of golden goblets on the red velvet tablecloth.

Quirk winced, and not just because she was being reminded of the red velvet tablecloth. Sometime she really did need to speak to the Emperor about that particular detail. She raised a delicate finger to indicate that she was not quite done.

"However," she said, but no one was listening anymore.

The Emperor coughed loudly. All noise stopped. All attention returned to the richest, most powerful man in the room. He glared around at them, then looked back to Quirk. "You were saying?" he said.

Small he might be, but it was rumored that the Emperor had personally throttled two assassins after they had killed the rest of his personal guard.

"However," Quirk said again, "there doesn't seem to be much point in purposelessly angering King…Todger. And while he cannot…violate anyone here, his forces can certainly make things difficult for your border patrols, and nobody wants to actually go to war with the elves."

"I wouldn't mind," said one lord, who then seemed to realize people could hear him.

"Truly, Lord El Sharred?" said the Emperor. He had a harsh, nasal voice. "You would like to take your cavalry into thick forest, and have arrows rained down upon you, while you chased men who disappeared like ghosts among the branches?"

Lord El Sharred appeared to vacillate momentarily between whether he should capitulate to his lord's greater wisdom, or if he should attempt to preserve face in front of his peers. He chose wrong.

"We should burn the place down around their ears," he said defiantly.

There was more pounding of goblets. The Emperor rolled his eyes. Quirk smiled at him. A question about fire, she could answer.

"Have you ever tried to burn living wood, Lord El Sharred?" she asked. "To be honest, I doubt you've even tried to burn dry wood. You have people to do that for you, after all." She smiled sweetly and watched as the insult passed over the man's head. "Living wood does not burn like the fire in your hearth at home. It is slow, and smoky, and reluctant. If you were able to get one tree to burn before the elves turned you and your men into novelty pincushions, I would count you very good at your job."

Now finally the Emperor laughed. And when he laughed, everyone laughed. Even Quirk. Lord El Sharred turned very red, and nodded, and managed a quick "I daresay I am" before retreating to his goblet.

"As ever," said the Emperor once the general mirth had died down, "you have proven yourself of greater wisdom and experience than many of the men who sit here, Professor Bal Tehrin. I ask again, and pray that you can answer without interruption, what would you advise?"

"Merely to send him ten of our own harts, slain, and ready for roasting so that he may feast at our expense. Lives will be spared, and honor will be satisfied."

The table held its collective breath as the Emperor considered this. Finally he clicked his fingers. Instantly a servant was at his side, eyes angled obsequiously low.

"Tell the huntsmen to kill ten harts and prepare them for delivery to King Todger along with a message expressing my deepest regrets at the unfortunate situation."

The servant nodded and backed away. The Emperor picked up the last of his partridges, looked at it distastefully, and cast it over his shoulder. "Let's just get to the gods-hexed dessert, shall we?"

This time no one disagreed.

After the meal there was of course music, and dancing, and the overwhelming desire to get away.

Quirk knew well that it was an honor to be invited to the Emperor's palace so frequently. She was aware that many looked upon her with envy, if not outright jealousy. She knew that she ate here better than she could ever hope to eat at the university, and that her opinions could have significant sway in the way the country was run. But she also knew that what she truly desired was a quiet night with her scrolls, and her notes, and a full pot of ink.

Unfortunately, though, the visiting Verran dignitary had managed to trap her in a corner. What was worse, he seemed willing to keep her there—by force if necessary—until she managed to vomit up an opinion on his proposed trade agreement.

"But, don't you see," he pressed, "that a two-point-six percent reduction in the import surcharge on Verran cotton could significantly change the landscape of the entire textile export industry here?"

"No," said Quirk, who was by now well past the point of pretending polite confusion.

"Oh," said the dignitary with a genial grin, "then I better explain again."

Quirk wondered if the Emperor's favor would be enough to acquit her of murder. Then she reminded herself she was a pacifist.

A pacifist partly responsible for the death of seven dragons and approximately ten thousand inhabitants of Kondorra . . .

Fortunately, just as the Verran was sucking in a lungful of air that would put a foundry bellows to shame, a disturbance at the stairs distracted him. He turned around, and virtually squealed with pleasure. "It's here!" he told her, a grin spreading across his face like a wine stain across a tablecloth, and he skittered away.

"Your eminence!" the dignitary called to the Emperor, in breach of all kinds of decorum. "Your eminence! It's arrived!"

The Emperor squinted at the Verran. Quirk didn't think much for the chances of his trade accord.

Four servants were shuffling down the stairs, staggering under the weight of some vast burden shrouded by a purple sheet. They just about made it down to the ballroom floor, stumbled right three paces, then set their burden down with a crash.

"Careful, you dolts!" hissed the Verran.

The Emperor rolled his eyes.

The Verran struck a pose of significant pomposity beside the shrouded bundle. It was almost as tall as he was. Asymmetrical protrusions thrust out, lumpen beneath the folds of fabric.

"May I present to you," he said in grandiose tones, "a token of Verra's esteem." He bowed deeply.

He meant a bribe, of course. *I give you this, and in return can you make it cheaper for me to import my cotton? And let's neither of us talk about the large number of cotton plantations that I have back in Verra, and instead pretend this is for the good of all.*

The one good thing about the Emperor's gaudy display of wealth, Quirk thought, was that it reassured her that he would be very difficult to bribe.

The Verran tugged on the curtain shrouding the object. It got stuck on one of the protrusions. He yanked again. There was a ripping sound, the snap of fabric pulling taut, and then the sound of the Verran stamping his foot. He heaved again, realized it wasn't going to work, and went to fix the snag. His smile had become something of rictus. Finally he worked everything free, tugged again, and revealed the...

What word best summed it up?

Obscenity?

"May I present to you," said the Verran dignitary, with another deep bow, "*The Conception of Cois.*"

The statue—cast in gold—depicted Lawl, king of the gods, lord of law and order, bending his son Toil over, and plowing him like a field. So, the popular legend went, Toil—god of fertility and the field—became pregnant with his father's seed, and later gave birth to the hermaphroditic god(dess) of love, Cois. A burst of pearls where the two deities conjoined graphically indicated that this was indeed the exact moment of conception.

Love, lust, violence, betrayal, and rape, all wrapped up in a tasteless, ostentatious display of wealth and power. Quirk supposed it was as relevant a way to attempt to seal a trade agreement as any other that had occurred to her.

She, along with the others, had just turned to see the Emperor's reaction to this masterwork of depravity when their collective silence was shattered by the sound of slow hand claps coming from above.

Every eye turned.

A man stood at the top of the stairs that slowly swept new arrivals down into the ballroom. He wore a simple but voluminous brown robe, the hood pulled back to reveal a bald head and a face lined like a cartographic map. His skin bore a dark tan, but he still seemed pale among the sea of Tamarians. He wore gold earrings, and a sinuous curving tattoo unfurled over his forehead, coming to a point between his eyes. The Emperor's guards flanked him, but instead of appearing confined, the man stood as if he were the one in command.

Quirk's childhood at the hands of the barbarous demigod Hethren had bred into her an immediate and violent suspicion of all strangers. As part of her long rehabilitation, she had learned to push that suspicion away just as instinctively. And yet, looking at this man, she found she did not like him.

"What is the meaning of this interruption?" snapped the

Emperor, though Quirk suspected he was as glad as any of them for a chance to ignore the Verran dignitary.

The court marshal bustled forward, looking harassed and put out. "My most sincere and humble apologies, your eminence. May I present—"

But the man interrupted him. "I am Ferra, emissary of Diffinax, and I come to beseech your fine court."

Diffinax.

While Quirk would be the first to admit that there was still much about dragons that she had yet to learn, she knew enough to recognize one of their names when she heard one.

What sort of man would give himself a dragon's name?

The sort of man, she supposed, *who would have an emissary who thinks it's all right to burst into an emperor's ballroom and interrupt a private dinner.*

But Ferra was still talking, even as he started down the stairs, the court marshal flapping ineffectually in his wake.

"And I see," the emissary continued, "that I arrive only just in time. I arrive as the filth, the depravity, the *chaos* of the so-called pantheon attempts to worm its sordid fingers around your heart more tightly. I arrive as your senses are assaulted and insulted by this…" He paused mid-stride to regard the Verran dignitary's sculpture with a look of disgust that bordered on hatred.

Obscenity, Quirk filled in silently.

"Vileness," said Ferra.

Impertinent ass, he might be, Quirk thought, *but I can't question his taste in art.*

The Verran dignitary had different ideas, however. "Who *are* you?" he spat. "How dare you enter here—"

"How dare *you*?" Ferra spat back. "How dare *you* hold up this wantonness, and worship it? How dare *you* call this desecration sacred? How dare *you* insult this man, this emperor, by telling him this is what he should emulate? Is this what you think of him? That he is a rapist? That he is a sodomizer? That he is the father of hermaphrodites?"

"Nothing wrong with a little bit of sodomy," commented the Emperor's cousin, with a shrug.

Ferra visibly twitched.

The Emperor, who had been watching with increasing interest, leaned forward, head cocked to one side. "And you," he said, "you are one who would dare to speak for me? You are one to presume my opinions of sodomy and hermaphrodites?"

Quirk was almost completely sure that the word *obsequious* had never once entered Ferra's mind. She was not disappointed.

"I am one," he said, "who sees a man beset by a world of filth, a man born into a world of excrement. I see a man with the power to lift his people out of the slurry. I see a man who can elevate a whole world. I see a man Diffinax wishes to save."

The Emperor leaned back. "So," he said, with a slight curl of contempt to his lips, "you are a man who presumes to speak for a man who presumes I wish to be saved."

"He presumes nothing," said Ferra. "Whether or not you desire it or not, you need to be saved."

"He dares presume my situation now?" The Emperor's smile was spreading. Quirk, though, had the distinct impression that it was the smile a cat gave a mouse.

"He dares presume the situation of the whole world," said Ferra without hesitation. "There is nothing he does not dare."

The Emperor chewed on that like a mouthful of partridge bones.

Ferra was on the ballroom floor now, leaving the still-spluttering court marshal and Verran dignitary behind him.

"Your master is a daring man, it seems," said the Emperor at last.

"My master," said Ferra, with a smile to rival the Emperor's, "is no man."

And that brought a pause to the conversation. The Emperor was caught flat-footed, suddenly uncertain.

As she spoke, Quirk thought her voice sounded small and timid in the large room. "Diffinax," she said, "is a dragon's name."

Ferra turned to her, and graced her with a smile as thin as a stiletto blade. "Quirkelle Bal Tehrin," he said to her. "Your reputation precedes you."

Inhaling seemed to take forever.

The Emperor looked at them both, back and forth, hesitated, then chose to address Ferra. "Your master, is he a dragon?" He did not sound tentative. Recent years of bloody civil war had ensured that no emperor of Tamar would dare show temerity for generations to come. But neither did he sound anxious to know the answer.

"My master," said Ferra, yanking his attention away from Quirk like a man twitching a blade out of a wound, "is the solution to the madness of this world. My master is a balm to this world's wounds. My master is the answer to all the prayers that the gods have ignored for too long. My master—"

"Your master is fire and domination." Again, Quirk's voice seemed too small in the large room. But she could see it in front of her. That ocean of fire that haunted her dreams, spreading across the world.

"My master," said Ferra with savage intensity, eyes not leaving the Emperor for a second, "is peace. Long sought after. Long fought for."

"He is a dragon," the Emperor repeated, less of a question this time.

"He is many things. One of them is a dragon."

There was a quiet gasp from the assembled nobles, all but forgotten in the heat of the exchange.

"Dragons kill," Quirk said, quietly, almost to herself. "They dominate. Dragons are…no, *cruel* is not the word. That's a human emotion, and they do not have those."

She had interviewed hundreds of women and men who had lived under the rule of dragons in Kondorra. She had witnessed firsthand the squalor in which they had been forced to live.

Ferra shook his head. A look of something like sadness crossed his face. It seemed out of place on his harsh features. "Oh, Ms. Bal Tehrin, how misled you have been. How much you have led others astray. For what? Personal fortune? For the favor of powerful men?"

For a moment, Quirk truly did not understand what the man was saying. The implications were utterly foreign to her thoughts.

"You...I...What?" was all she managed.

"But how can I blame you," said Ferra, voice dripping with false pity, "when all the gods in the heavens themselves do is mislead us? When no one sets a better example? When you have not yet accepted the wisdom of Diffinax into your life and your soul?"

"These," said the Emperor as Quirk still reeled, "are serious accusations."

Ferra waved a hand dismissively. "I do not deal in accusations. Diffinax has taught me to be above such things. I deal in truths. I deal with the world as it is, not how I wish it to be. I see it, accept it, and I question, what will change truly require? How can I leave a legacy of change? How can I make the people look up and remember me with love?"

It was shameless pandering. It was a low, craven pantomime of political seduction. And from the look upon the Emperor's face, Quirk could see it was working.

"You think I am here for *fame*?" she said. It was not the right way for her to start her argument, but she could not help herself. Ferra's accusation was too brazen, too *false* to ignore.

Ferra finally turned to look at her. His look was one of utter contempt. "I truly do not care why you are here, Quirkelle Bal Tehrin. Maybe it is for the self-aggrandizement. Maybe it is so you can feel superior to your colleagues. Maybe it is so you can impress some dark-eyed student with tales of the Emperor's table. Maybe it is simply that you enjoy the food. All I know, all I care for, are the lies you use to poison the Emperor's ear, to keep him turned from the truth and the light of Diffinax."

Quirk almost laughed in the man's face. "I do not beg him to worship a dragon, and therefore I am the one clouding his vision?"

Ferra's mouth twisted in a smile. "And you ask nothing of him? You do not try to steer him toward one course of action over another? You do not stand there and try to use your influence to turn him away from my master?"

"I try to turn him away from enslaving himself to the teachings of an inhuman beast with a psychotic desire for power and wealth."

She could, she felt, go toe-to-toe with this man. He had caught her off guard at first, but he was as petty, and stupid, and poorly informed as all the other ambassadors and dignitaries, too caught up in his own agenda. He had caught the Emperor's attention with his boldness, but she had long ago won the Emperor's respect.

Ferra took a step toward her. It was a move designed to intimidate. Instead she stepped toward him, closed the distance.

He leaned toward her, lowered his voice. "Did you tell him?" he asked. Almost conversationally. Almost intimately. She suppressed a shudder at the thought. "Did you tell him about how you came about your knowledge?"

"Everybody knows how—" she started, not seeing the angle of the attack, because everybody knew of how she had gone to Kondorra. It was why she was famous.

But Ferra continued. "Did you tell him of the people you burned? The women you left as widows? The children you left as orphans? Did you tell him of your dreams of fire?"

Quirk's breath caught in her lungs. Suddenly the vast ballroom felt too small, too tight, everything pressing in on her.

An ocean of fire, spreading from horizon to horizon.

And no dragon stood at that ocean's heart. She did. Flame poured from her hands. Her flames wiped men, and women, and children from the world. Her flames stripped the flesh from their bones.

She remembered a night in Kondorra, in a cave, standing before a dragon, flame streaming from her palms, and killing, and killing, and killing.

No. No, she had not told the Emperor about that. She had told no one about that. No one outside of her companions in Kondorra had known about that.

How in the Hallows had this man known that? This ugly, twisted, shit of a man.

"You want to burn me now, don't you?" Ferra continued, his voice still lowered in that ugly parody of intimacy. "I know you do. I have spent my life with dragons. I know creatures of fire, Quirkelle Bal Tehrin. Part of you wants to watch us all burn."

"No!" she shouted. She couldn't help it. Because she had to. She had to deny it. She could never let herself acknowledge the fact that he was right.

The Emperor was staring at her. His Empress. His daughter. His court. All of them. Even poor, golden Toil—captured bent over and humiliated forever—was staring at her. All of them sharing that same look of horror. Because they knew. As soon as she had shouted they had known. She was a liar.

She turned and she ran.

She checked her flight at the palace gates. Servants were staring at her. Guards were looking around for some sign of disturbance. Her hands were smoking.

She breathed, long and shaky, pulling the chill night air into her, trying to get the coldness to sink into her core.

Arsehole. She couldn't believe what she'd just let happen. But how had he known? How could he have known?

She should go back there. She should show him just how afraid she was of him.

She should make him burn.

No.

She was too worked up, too close to the edge to plead her case tonight. She would only make things worse. She should go back to her garret, to her cot, to her papers, and her ink. She should find her calm again, her peace.

Be the surface of the lake. Tranquil. Unmoving. She ran through the old meditation techniques the priestesses of Knole—goddess of wisdom—had taught her.

She couldn't even picture the gods-hexed lake right now.

With a grimace, she pushed out into the night.

The Tamathian University was a reassuring bricolage of stone, mortar, and wood all rammed together in a myriad of disparate architectural styles. Flying buttresses crashed into sterile cliffs of brick. The gentle curves of domes were punctured by angular spires of jutting stone. The gas-filled observatorium bobbed above the dining hall, caught in its mess of tethering ropes.

The gatehouse, one of the oldest structures in the place, was done in the early Brutalist style. A forbidding mass of iron spikes and disruptive stone tumors, making the entrance look more like a wound than a gateway, yet the light that spilled out of it was soft and yellow, and the sight of it filled her with the warmth of home.

Tamper, the doorman, was sitting on a stool inside the gate holding a cudgel that was almost as old and gnarled as he was.

"Mistress Quirk," he said with a touch of his finger to his forehead.

"Tamper," she said with a nod and a smile, and the simple ritual of it stilled the trembling that yet touched her hands.

"Mistress Afrit was looking for you." Tamper's voice sounded like a door creaking open.

Quirk sighed. That was the last thing she needed. And then, as if summoned by the utterance of her name, like some fairy-tale genie, there was Afrit, bustling across the grass of the courtyard, calling, "Quirk! Quirk! You're back!"

Quirk closed her eyes, turned to Tamper. "Thank you," she said to the old doorman. He nodded in return. Possibly off to sleep.

Then Quirk turned to Afrit and assembled her face into something that was as close to a smile as she could manage. "Yes," she said. "I am back, and it is late, and you are still up."

Afrit smiled. "I've been grading papers," she said, "and despairing about the youth of this nation." She was young, dark-skinned, her hair worn long and pulled back into thick braids. She favored the same sort of loose robes that Quirk wore, though whether that was a recent affectation, or simple coincidence, Quirk wasn't sure. Honestly, she and Quirk had never exchanged more than a few words before Quirk's fateful trip to Tamathia. But since her return, and the publication of her folio on dragons, Afrit had flocked to the light of Quirk's flame like a peculiarly suicidal moth.

"How was the Emperor's this evening?" Afrit went on unabashed, asking the question Quirk had least wanted to answer.

"Exhausting," Quirk said. It seemed her best bet for escaping the situation.

"Of course," Afrit said. "I'm sorry. I forget how late it is." She smiled and stepped back a little.

For a moment, Quirk dared to hope she would be left alone. But then Afrit pushed on.

"No papers to keep you up late tonight?"

Quirk tried to avoid sighing audibly. "The Chancellor gave me another month off teaching. My lecturing schedule is still quite full though."

Afrit smiled more broadly. "I shall have to become famous

myself one day. It seems to be full of perks. Though I think perhaps I would miss teaching. Don't you?"

Quirk shrugged helplessly. "Mostly I am just finding fame to be simply tiring right now."

Afrit had the decency at least to look embarrassed. "I'm sorry. You have needed to tell me twice. I shall let you get to bed."

Quirk shook her head insincerely. "I'm sorry. I am sure I will be much better company in the morning."

Afrit nodded. "And I shall do a better job of picking up on obvious social cues."

Quirk's smile was at least half-genuine at that point. "Tomorrow," she said, albeit grudgingly.

"Tomorrow," Afrit agreed, and a moment later Quirk was finally alone.

Quirk's garret was long, low, and smelled of dust and paper. She sighed as the door closed behind her. In the darkness she went to where she knew her tinderbox lay, and lit the first candle.

Finally, as she slowly went through the ritual of lighting the garret's other candles, Quirk felt the last vestiges of her encounter with Ferra sloughing away. Her own space. Where she could be herself without judgments. Where she was not famous, or aloof, or wise, or anything but a thaumatobiologist. The candles by the door lit, she pulled off her cloak and the tall, uncomfortable boots that were popular in the Emperor's court. She pushed the pins out of her hair, collecting them on a table where a hairbrush and small piece of polished tin lay.

She could have a larger room, she knew. The Chancellor had offered one to her. But this was *her* home. This was the refuge she had longed for all the time she had been in Kondorra. Now that she had reclaimed it, she could not give it up for all of Avarra.

In the shadows, something creaked.

She looked up, the sound unexpected, not fitting into the

usual concert of creaks and moans that filled old space. It came from somewhere near her desk, in among the piles of papers and notes, down at the unlit end of her garret.

"Pettar?" she called. Sometimes a gray feral cat would wander in and beg for scraps. But it preferred the daytime hours, when the light came in through her windows and puddled on the wooden floor. "Pettar, is that you?"

Silence. Enough of it that she thought she was making a fool of herself.

And then the misplaced creak came again.

She stepped toward the darkness.

"Pettar?"

Silence.

But then—

"Not exactly."

She knew that voice. Knew it clearly and well. Had listened to it only an hour before as it insinuated and berated, as it revealed secrets she had not shared.

Ferra.

Fire burst out of her before she knew what she was doing. An instinctive, blazing rush of fear and hatred. Her hand slashed the air. A ribbon of fire ripped out of the cage that she pretended kept it locked up in her soul and coursed across the room.

For a moment, everything was illuminated. She saw candles catching fire, wax running free. She saw pages of her notes curling. She saw the dragon's talon she had brought back from Kondorra and had yet to mount on the wall, glistening warmly. She saw her desk, its shadow racing up the wall trying to flee the scene. And she saw Ferra, wreathed in his robes, hood pulled high, about to die at her hands.

All this, she glimpsed in the moment it took the fire to race across the room. All this, and just time to think, *How will I explain this tomorrow?*

Ferra drew his hand up in a vicious slashing motion. There

was a crackle and fizz. White and cold filled the far end of the garret. Her ribbon of fire smashed into a dazzling spire of sparkling white.

Her fire died.

"No," she breathed as much in disbelief as in shock, as Ferra stepped toward her and flung out his own hands.

She saw icy hands form in the air in front of her, massive replicas of Ferra's own, knuckles bulging, and thick, ropy sinew standing out on the backs of the palms.

The fingers closed around her arms, her chest. She gasped at the cold, driving into her, penetrating her. They clenched and she gasped again as the breath was driven out of her by the force of their pressure. Her vision blurred.

Ferra was advancing down the length of her garret, hands still outstretched, still squeezing. "As much fun as it is to watch you squirm at the Emperor's court," he was saying, "I am afraid I shall have to end our acquaintance now." She could barely make out the words over the sound of her own rattling breaths.

Cold was taking her. She could hardly feel where the fingers pressed into her anymore.

She grasped for fire. So eager to race out of her a moment before, now it was cowed and cowering inside her.

Fight back! she roared at it. *Do not capitulate to this thug. This bully.*

Flame quivered. She roared at it. *Burn his world!*

Flame flared once more, a corona cocooning her. The icy hands sprang apart as if scorched, already melting. Ferra grunted, staggered back, arms flung wide. Quirk sucked down lungfuls of warm air.

With a roar, Ferra slashed his hand through the air. Something frozen and savage smashed into Quirk's left side. She reeled across the room. But her corona of fire protected her from the worst of the cold.

She had almost recovered when Ferra's next blow came from

the right, batting her back across the garret like some child's plaything. Her cocoon of fire quivered. She stumbled into his next blow. She staggered. He hit her again. Again.

Fuck explanations. Fuck Ferra. Fuck dragons. Fuck fear. This man was going to burn.

She lowered her head, bull-rushed him. The corona of fire stretching out in front of her, becoming a lance, a battering ram.

She heard him yell, made contact with...no, not with him. With a grinding wall of ice that pushed back, held her still.

She grit her teeth, poured all her power into the space in front of her. Her feet slipped on the floor, skidding over the rough wooden grain. She fought forward one step, two. She drew level with the old dragon talon. Icicles lined its surface.

Ferra redoubled his defenses. She felt his wall of ice stretch up, thicken. She felt her forward progress grind to a halt.

And then, slowly, inexorably, he began to push her back.

He was stronger than her. That was the detestable, unavoidable truth. He had chased her out of the Emperor's palace, chased her back to her garret, and trapped her here like a rat. And now he would overpower her, and he would kill her. It was as simple as that.

Quirkelle Bal Tehrin was the world's leading thaumatobiologist, the foremost expert on dragons in all of Avarra. She had been present for the Kondorran uprising, and played a critical role in the death of seven dragons. She had been a living weapon for the demigod Hethren, and had killed more men, women, and children than she could count. And all of it counted for naught in this moment.

But she would not give up and die for this man.

She dropped her defenses, her assault, let it come crashing down. And for a moment she felt Ferra hesitate, thrown off, searching for the next lance of heat.

It didn't come.

Quirk threw herself to the left, rolled across the floor, through the scorched ashes of her research notes, skidding over patches of freezing ice.

She came up beside the dragon's talon, scavenged from the blasted waste that lay before the Hallow's Mouth volcano. A treasured possession. A source of awe and fear. And without ceremony she grabbed it and launched it at Ferra.

She could see him, in a beam of moonlight that streamed through a window. Could see the outline of his hooked nose as it turned in the direction of her grunt of effort. But she could not see his eyes, could not see if they went wide, or narrowed with concentration, as the talon smashed into his side.

There was a gout of blood. A yell.

She didn't care for the rest. She was already charging, balling fire around her fists.

There was a flash of white light, a flare of freezing wind, the sound of glass breaking. Quirk threw up an arm to protect her eyes. Wind lashed at her face.

When everything cleared, she was alone. Ferra was gone. Only ice and a broken window showed that he had ever been there.

Her fragmented research notes shuddered across the floor, and Quirk pulled her robes tightly around her as the night's cold air rushed in.

2

Shedding His Skin

Balur had the very strong urge to bite someone's face off.

To be fair, this wasn't an entirely unusual state of affairs for him. Back in the Analesian deserts where the lizard man had spent his formative years, faces were considered a delicacy, peeled from the skull and roasted over an open fire. Admittedly, that was how the Analesians cooked everything. They were desert nomads. It wasn't as if they had an abundance of cooking options available.

Now, though, he sat in the heart of the grassy plains of Kondorra, his scaly posterior balanced upon a throne carved from a dragon's skull, set at the center of a vast tent made of swooping red cloth. Outside, birds whooped and called, and horses stomped. And yet still he imagined the taste of blood on his tongue.

Also, in his defense, the Vinlander ambassador standing in front of him at that precise moment was being very insulting. Or condescending. Or both. Balur still wasn't entirely sure about all the nuances of human interaction.

Further compounding the issue was the fact that Balur had about twelve inches and three hundred pounds on the ambassador. Plus, the ambassador was entirely lacking a skin of stony scales to protect himself. Or a tail for balance. Essentially he was asking to have his face bitten off. He might as well have come in with a silver platter and a napkin in hand to make the process that much more civilized.

But he hadn't done that. He'd come in here with an enormous army at his back instead.

"We recognize"—the ambassador slurred on, with…was it disdain perhaps?—"the great service the people of Kondorra perceive you, their so-called prophet, to have gone about doing when you killed off the Dragon Consortium. But the weight of those actions ends at your borders. Extant trade agreements do not stop there. Quite the opposite. Kondorra made some promises to Vinland—regardless of its rulership—and we expect them to be honored." The ambassador burped.

That was, Balur suspected, staggering bullshit. He had spent enough years in mercenary armies, working for corrupt barons, earls, and lords, to know that nobody expected a new ruler to honor the agreements of the old one.

He also knew that the ambassador didn't give a shit. Kondorra could muster a fighting force of about fifteen thousand warriors. Vinland could throw more than ten times that number at him. The math was simple: He was Vinland's bitch.

It didn't help that the ambassador was staggeringly drunk. The scent of alcohol reeled off the Vinlander in thick waves. Every time Balur licked the air he could taste it, heady and intoxicating—both an insult and a call to battle. Still, his advisors had told him that drunkenness was to be expected. The ambassador was from Vinland, after all, an entire nation dedicated to the worship of Barph—god of drunkenness, excess, and revelry. Being sober was a great religious offense in their eyes.

Balur would like nothing better than to be drunk. Unless possibly he could be drunk and arse-deep in concubines. But if he was drunk he suspected the few restraints he placed upon himself to stop him from removing the man's face and slurping it down raw would be severed. And in doing that, he would condemn the entire nation of Kondorra to becoming so much fermentation materials in the Vinlander brewing pits.

So instead, he rumbled, "And if those trade agreements are lacking any paperwork, and are seeming to be incredibly detrimental to my nation, and are being brought to me on the hearsay of..." He chewed on a number of insults before reluctantly selecting "...you."

"You question the divine word of the Vinland High Priesthood, dribbled down from the slack jaw of Barph into the waiting ears below? You question the slurry of his wisdom written large upon this world by his holy bartenders?" There was fire in the ambassador's voice. He was, Balur had to admit, an incredibly high-functioning drunk. If the man hadn't pissed himself halfway through the discussion, Balur would almost have been impressed by him.

When Balur had seized control of Kondorra it hadn't seemed like it was going to be this way. He had been at the head of an army of sixty thousand, the apex of an uprising of the people. They had screamed his name, screamed for the prophet, and they had sworn their lives to his rule. He was going to forge them into a force red of tooth and claw. He was going to take them sweeping through the world, burning, and pillaging, and forging a new empire in his name.

Except what they had actually done was sober up from their bloodlust, gone back to their farms and forges, their shops and their sheep, and they had tried to rebuild the lives that had been stifled by thirty years of oppressive rule by the Dragon Consortium. And while the people of Kondorra still worshipped him with a near-religious fervor, the true pantheon of Avarra had not set a great example for what religious fervor meant. A nod of the head and a tip of the cap seemed to have been sufficient obeisance for most of the gods in the pantheon. At least for all of them, it seemed, except bloody Barph. How the drunk god was the only one who managed to elicit slavering zeal out of his followers was beyond Balur.

There again, a lot was beyond Balur these days. Like how in the Hallows he was going to deal with this Vinlander bullying.

He could go to war, of course. Part of him wanted to do that. It would mean the annexation of Kondorra and the death of tens of thousands, but it would be an absurdly impressive way to be killed. To wade into battle heinously outnumbered, to kill until he was walled in by the dead, and then only finally be overwhelmed when they collapsed the walls of his own kills upon him. Bards would sing some really epic ballads about that. They would use them to pick up a considerable number of attractive young people with self-esteem problems. It would be everything Balur had ever dreamed his death could be.

Really the only thing stopping him was that he suspected it was exactly what the Vinlanders wanted him to do. Drunk they might be. Idiots they were not. So he could either suck up a trade deal that would bankrupt him, or march into a war it was impossible to win.

The trade deal would at least buy him a few months to figure everything out.

He actually found himself wishing Will was there. Will liked all this thinking nonsense. He was the one who planned everything.

In fact, truth be told, Will was the prophet Balur was pretending to be.

Or...well, he wasn't the prophet. There was no prophet. It was bullshit they'd sort of used to deceive the Kondorrans into rising up against their dragon overlords, and then he'd perpetuated the lie to stay in power. Not that any of that troubled Balur. He didn't see the lie hurting anyone. Plus, he'd killed a dragon single-handedly, riding its corpse out of an exploding volcano. He'd *earned* everything he got.

Except what it had gotten him was a morose populace and this belligerent, drunken ambassador.

"Fine," he sighed. "We'll—"

"Piss on your deal! To the Hallows with your deal. With your lies! You swaggering stain on the britches of humanity! The prophet spits at you and sprays a lot of people standing around you! That little fine spittle that gets everywhere!"

Balur sighed even more heavily. Because the other thing posing as the prophet had gotten him was his very own High Priest. Firkin, the old farmhand who had grown up with Will, who had ruined pretty much everything from beginning to end with his huge, drunken mouth.

If the alcohol fumes were a fugue around the ambassador, they were a full orchestral composition around Firkin. Balur could taste them, redolent on the air. The old man half-fell across the room, waving a wineskin at the ambassador and shouting incoherently.

"...and...piss...and...fucking with...twelve well-bred sheep... some chicken feathers...ate a stew...your mother!" was about as much as Balur could make out.

The Vinlander ambassador reeled around to face his verbal assailant.

"And who," he said, trying to look down his nose and going a bit cross-eyed, "is this human arse-sore supposed to be?"

Balur braced himself before he said it. "My High Priest, advisor to the throne, the most vaulted Firkin, esteemed by all." The people for some gods-hexed reason loved Firkin. They hung on his every word. And it hadn't taken Balur long to realize that keeping Firkin happy was an expedient way to get things done. And what made Firkin happy this week was stupid, stupid titles.

"He's a dick," said the ambassador.

"Yes," Balur agreed.

"Must be why I was in your mum last night," said Firkin with regrettable clarity.

The ambassador visibly bristled.

"Firkin," said Balur, through gritted teeth, "don't you have a speech you should be delivering?"

"No," said Firkin, taking time out of a violent bout of flatulence to answer.

Balur wondered if he could kill Firkin, blame it on the ambassador, and use the ensuing outrage to rile up the populace enough to give the Vinlander army a proper fight. He gave the ambassador a contemplative stare. *Would the people be believing that he had been biting Firkin's face off?*

He decided against it.

"We are agreeing," Balur said as loudly and as quickly as he could. "We are agreeing to the whole stupid deal. It is being fine. Whatever. You are having the bigger dicks today. We are congratulating on the might with which you are swinging them."

"The piss we are!" Firkin roared. "We are cramming the deal very, very, very, very—"

"Shut up!" Balur roared. Everything had been far simpler when he hadn't been a ruler.

"You!" Firkin yelled. "You can take your 'shut ups' and cram them very, very, very, very—"

Balur finally rumbled out of his throne and advanced on Firkin. "I shall be removing your spine from your body and shoving it very, very, very, very—"

"I shall be shoving myself into your mum very, very, very—"

"Oh be quiet!"

Both Balur and Firkin turned to stare at the Vinlander ambassador, who was looking at them with distaste and swaying slightly as he pulled a flask from his robes and tipped it down his throat.

"Bunch of nattering biddies," he muttered to himself. "Get your shit sorted out and get me an answer before I make it back across the border to Vinland or I'm coming back with an army." He made several hand gestures that his bearing would suggest were usually beneath him, and staggered back out of the tent.

"Oh that is being brilliant." Balur threw up his hands.

"I was wondering"—Firkin stabbed a finger at him—"have you seen your balls anywhere?"

The taste of just one delicious face...

Except the problem was, Firkin was right. Running a nation was a constant exercise in emasculation. He was confined by this absurd need to look out for the well-being of others, by the need to keep them alive so that he could...what? Look out for their well-being some more?

He was getting old and soft. And in no way was that more evident than in the fact that he didn't eviscerate Firkin on the spot, but merely head-butted him into unconsciousness, and then went off to blame it on the drink so no one would get mad at him.

Hours later, Balur watched the fire die disconsolately. His personal tent was smaller than the one in which he had met the Vinlander ambassador, though still large enough to contain several small houses. He could hear his horsemen outside, settling the camp. He had assembled them when he was still planning to sweep across the plains carrying out lightning raids, taking what he could, burning the rest.

It was hard to raid somewhere that welcomed you as a conquering hero. It took all the fun out of burning a building to the ground when everyone just stood around and clapped.

He reached for his flagon, took another swig, and found that he'd emptied it again. He considered calling for another but the obsequiousness of the boy who came bearing them was grating on his current mood. He flung the tankard away, picked himself up, and stumbled toward his cot. The ale already had the tent spinning around him at a good rate. He didn't need more ale anyway. Piss on ale.

Gods...Piss on ale? What was he thinking? Ruling Kondorra really had gotten him turned around. What he was needing was a fight. A good old-fashioned fight.

At that exact moment, a blade slipped six inches between his ribs.

Despite this staggering coincidence, Balur did not take any time to appreciate the irony of the timing. Instead he roared and twisted away from the violent flare of pain.

The blade was razor sharp, and the tip was barbed. A professional's weapon. It tore at the skin as he pulled away, and the wielder twisted the blade, opening the sides of the wound, trying to maximize the damage and the blood flow. On any normal man it would have been an incapacitating blow, quite possibly fatal. Given what the blade told Balur about its owner's professionalism, he guessed that the blow was meant to drive him to his knees so that his throat could be cut more easily.

Which meant that they had underestimated him.

As it was, the blade had only made it a few inches through his thick armor-plated skin, and at worst had nicked the edge of his lung. Infection was a concern, but not until long after he had crushed this fool's skull. Free of the blade, he lunged and punched.

He struck nothing.

A shadow moved in the dying light of the fire. Another blade stuck him in his other side. Either his assailant was inhumanly fast, or he had friends.

Balur changed tactics. He didn't want to be bleeding from too many wounds. Two was not too many, but it was the start of a bad trend.

Before his attacker had time to twist and remove the blade, he stepped into the attack. He felt a satisfying "oof" as his greater bulk collided with their lesser one. Balur dropped to one knee, feeling the smaller figure caught beneath his weight. There was a satisfying scream as the attacker's pelvis shattered beneath him.

I am still having it.

Then he felt the whisper of the first attacker's movement, closing in while he was still off balance. He felt the edge of the knife click off a thick scale where his chest met his neck.

Maybe not having all of it . . .

He lunged out with an open palm even as the blade skittered toward the more delicate flesh of his throat. He felt the whoomph of air as the attacker folded around his hand.

Balur grunted, heaving himself to his feet, but even as he did, his attacker slashed again and again at his arm. Ribbons of flesh curled between hacked chunks of scales. Balur roared.

Then another knife. Lancing into his back. A throwing blade from the weight and the penetration. He'd been hit with enough of them to know. Considering the second assailant was still screaming on the floor trying to work out what parts of her arse still held together, that meant a third knife wielder in the fight.

Who in the Hallows had he pissed off this much?

The answer, he supposed, was obvious. *The Vinlanders.* Which was insane because he hadn't even put up resistance.

No. *Firkin had.* Lawl's black eye upon that little shit stain. The old man ran his mouth, and now lunatics with knives were trying to kill *him.*

He reached back, snagged the knife from his back, and flung it back in the vague direction it had come from. There was a distinct lack of a satisfying grunt.

That was always being Lette's trick anyway.

He satisfied himself by stamping down at where the first attacker had fallen, but the figure had rolled away off into the shadows.

There are being too many gods-hexed shadows here.

He needed more light than a dying fire could provide. And grabbing a log to use as a torch would just ruin his night vision further. He needed something, something to shift the balance of this fight.

Gods, three men with knives and they were having him on the back foot. He truly was going to seed running this armpit of a nation.

Someone came at him again, from the left this time. He let them come, felt the blade go in and out once, twice—

Be coming on. Be getting greedy.

—a third time. He grabbed his attacker bodily, crushed her to his bleeding side. A grunt of surprise. Balur seized her by the back of the skull and squeezed. She died with a scream.

Two down.

Someone else came at his right side. Gods, he could not keep this pincushioning bullshit up.

Just as he grabbed the attacker's wrists another throwing knife landed in his back.

There were being four of them now?

Fuck this. Balur knew exactly where he could get some more light.

Dragging his yelling attacker by the arms, Balur ignored the next two knives that landed in his shoulder blades and hurled the man into the last embers of the fire.

The man leapt up with a yell, but it was already too late. Fire was creeping up his arms and legs.

Why you should not be using pitch to be blackening your clothes, thought Balur. *Not so professional after all.*

The man, now a scribbled stick figure of flame, staggered across the room. Balur could see his remaining attackers clearly. Three of them arrayed around the room, two men and one more woman unless he missed his mark. But they did not look like Vinlanders. They did not sway drunkenly. They held themselves tall and alert.

One of the men held a fistful of throwing knives. "For Theerax," he said, cocking an arm.

And that whoreson, Balur decided, would be the first to die.

Then the red came, and occluded his vision for a while.

When it cleared he was hacking in the smoke of his flaming

tent, holding a loop of gut that was threatening to spill out of his midriff, and he had the unmistakable taste of someone's face in his mouth.

It is still being as good as I was remembering at least. This is not being a total waste of a day.

Just a total waste of a life.

The flaming attacker had managed to tangle himself in the wall of the tent before he died, and the canvas itself was on fire. Balur was breathing heavily, though. Too many cuts had gone too deep. Too much blood was running down his sides.

Old and fat. Slow and dead.

What had he even been fighting for? The Vinlanders—or whoever it had been—would just send another attack. And another. He would post guards, and that would stop some of it, but not all of it. And then eventually he would live long enough to see the Vinlander army coming to smash him into oblivion.

And that was it, in the end. He was achieving nothing here but his own slow death. It had tried to come at him more quickly tonight and he had almost allowed it. Allowed it through his maudlin, pathetic attitude. He was Balur, slayer of dragons, prophet of the Kondorra valley. He was an Analesian. He seized life by the throat and he shook it. He did not wait timidly for it to dole out its next beating.

All around him, everything was collapsing to ash. Why shouldn't the people of Kondorra believe he had as well? A martyr would be as good as a living prophet. Better perhaps.

So he staggered away, through the tattered ruins of his tent, past the scurrying guards just coming alert to the chaos at the heart of their camp, and off into the night to find somewhere he could bleed in private for a while.

3

Happily Never After

Willett Fallows—once heralded as the prophet of Kondorra, the architect of the downfall of the Dragon Consortium, mastermind behind one of the most lucrative acts of thievery in Avarran history—was knee-deep in pig shit.

"It's all right, Mr. Fallows," called one of the farmhands, a thick-limbed young man who seemed at ease in his skin in a way Will had never managed. "We've got them."

Will waved the man off. This was his farm. He'd grown up raising and slaughtering animals. Instead he focused on the piglet. It needed branding and it was going to get branded, whether it wanted to or not.

"Really, Mr. Fallows…" the farmhand started again. Will thought his name was Joelep.

Will made a grab for the piglet. It darted left. He lunged after it. Then his foot flew out from under him, tipped his arse up in the air, and for a moment he was completely free of the ground, heels kicking up great soaring arcs of brown filth, before he landed down in it with a thick, wet splat.

It probably wouldn't have stung his pride quite so much if he hadn't heard Joelep's groan.

"Here, Mr. Fallows, let me help you up," he heard. And strong arms were grabbing him, hauling him up. The filth let go viscously.

There were three or four farmhands with him now. He shook

them off. They backed up as he spattered muck around him. "Fine," he muttered. "I'm fine."

He could have done anything he wanted with the coin he had stolen from the Dragon Consortium. He could have become anything he wanted. And he had chosen this.

It had seemed such a glorious thing. A proper farm. Bustling and full of life. Home to others, and with a kitchen that fed them all. A life of warmth. Of family. A life made with his own hands.

Right now his hands were full of mud and shit.

"Course you're fine, sir," said Joelep with almost painful deference. "But why don't you go and wash the worst of that off you. Me and the boys have this."

"I'm—" Will started. Then he looked around. The degree to which he wasn't wanted was painfully apparent.

"Just trying to help," he muttered.

"And much appreciated it was, sir," said Joelep. Will had to hand it to the man, he was an impressively good liar.

"Okay," he said, trying to muster what little pride he had left. "Looks like you all have a good handle on this. I'll leave you to it."

He went to stride away. Joelep caught him as his foot went out from under him again.

"Careful there, sir."

Will walked stiffly away. He tried not to hear the mutters that followed him.

Will stood in the center of the farmhouse, and stared at the bottle of wine on his kitchen table. It was, he had been informed, a very good vintage. The wine merchant had been very insistent on that. There had been a whole backstory about the vineyard, and the vintner. A child was involved, and three lambs, as he recalled. It was very touching.

It was also, he had been informed, strong enough to peel paint off walls.

She, was the one who had told him that.

He popped the cork and poured himself what was far from being the first glass of the day.

He thought about Joelep's groan. But…gods, who was the pissing farmhand to judge anyway? He paid the man's wages. He could do what he liked on his farm. *His* farm.

He could command them, he thought. He could force them all to come into eat with him. To share his hall. People used to beg to eat with him. He'd commanded an army of sixty thousand. He'd had the love of the people.

But then he'd given it all away.

He'd given all the love away.

You couldn't tell people to love you. Even this wine—and *she* had been right, it was particularly strong—wasn't enough to make him think that. It had to be earned. People had to be seduced.

Stew. He could make stew. A huge pot of stew. It would steam and bubble all afternoon, and the scent of it would draw them to him.

The cook had quit two months back. Said she felt bad taking his coin, when no one came in for the meals. Said, it was lonely just cooking for herself and him. Said it hurt to see so much food going to waste. And then she'd left too.

But he could cook. He'd cooked for himself for years.

And it felt good, that afternoon, cutting the mutton, slicing the vegetables, stoking the fire. The cauldron bubbled and frothed, and the wine helped the time slip by as good strong smells filled the room, and wafted up through the chimney out into the surrounding fields.

The stew was thick and strong as darkness rolled in over the fields.

Will poured himself a bowl, cut himself a thick slice of bread from the loaf baked in his oven, made from the flour ground from the wheat that grew in his fields, and sat down at the long table, and waited for company to come.

He waited a long time. Cold stew sat heavy as a brick in his stomach.

He thought about the others from Kondorra. Not *her*. But the others. Balur. Quirk. Firkin. What were they doing? Had they bought happiness? Should he have let Balur take over? Would *she* have stayed if…

He threw the thought away. He wasn't thinking about that. He didn't want to think about anything. He would open another bottle of wine.

He found one stashed in a cupboard, stood by a window, looking out onto the empty farmyard, listening to its merry glug as he poured it into an ale tankard, and tried to capture some of its cheer.

The farm was still tonight. Even the animals seemed quiet. Normally there was someone running back and forth on some late-night errand or escapade. There was always life here, at least. Some sort of bustle. He may not be able to find a way into it, but at least he was surrounded by it. Sometimes it muffled things as much as the wine did.

But not tonight.

But then… A shadow shape flickering just out of the reach of the firelight. He peered. Something about the half-glimpsed silhouette nagged at him. Something furtive. Something familiar. And a nag of fear that he hadn't felt in eight long months strummed at the base of his gut.

Without exactly knowing why, he opened a drawer and pulled out a long-bladed knife.

Behind him, a fist pounded on the door.

The farmhands didn't come here. As much as he wanted them to, as much as he tried to make the space inviting…they didn't come. And it was late, and dark, and everyone should be asleep.

He looked down at the knife in his hand.

But what if someone needed help? Or company? Or a shoulder

to cry on? Anything that could allow him to ingratiate himself with them.

What if he greeted them with a knife in his hands?

The pounding came again. Harder. Louder.

Assailants didn't knock. Assassins didn't ask politely to come in. He was being paranoid.

Slowly, aware for the first time just quite how much he'd drunk that day, he slipped the knife between his belt and britches in the small of his back, drew back the bolt and unlatched the door.

It flew open. Will stumbled back a half step. A massive bulk pounded toward him.

He genuflected, throwing up a hand, the knife forgotten. And—

Wait...

"Balur?"

"Yes, yes," said the lizard man. "Come in," he rumbled impatiently. Wind blustered and blew, whipping Balur's cloak about him. The lizard man clapped his massive hands. "Be shutting the door," he said. "It is being cold enough to be freezing a lizard's balls off out there."

"Balur?" Will couldn't...He...He tried to put it together. Balur. *Her* old companion on the road. *Her* old tribe, as she would have said.

So if he was here...

"Is *she* with you?" he said. He could hardly dare hope. But he had to.

"Who?" Balur looked at him puzzled.

The wind from the open door stroked Will with icy fingers as his heart sank. "Lette," he said, voice barely audible above the wind.

Balur's brow creased. "Is she not being with you?"

Hope died. It curled up and rotted right there in Will's chest. "Never mind."

Balur chewed on that. "Are you going to be shutting that door or not?" he said eventually.

* * *

They sat at the end of one of the long empty tables, sharing the bottle of wine.

"That," said Balur smacking his lips, "is being the good shit."

Will was still having trouble with the reality of the situation. Balur was from a life left behind. From a dream abandoned. One that had seemed like a nightmare at times. And yet it was from that place and time that *she*...that Lette had emerged. And Balur was her oldest friend, her long-time traveling companion. If anyone might be able to figure out where the hell she had gone.

"So," Balur started, his only preamble being him emptying his first glass of wine down his throat and immediately pouring himself a second, "how were you fucking it up then?"

"I...I don't...She didn't..." Will had been over it so many times in his head, but this was the first time he'd been asked to say it out loud, and he stumbled over how to begin. "Everything was fine," he managed. "There was no warning. We came out here to Batarra, we bought this farmstead. We invited people to come and make a life with us, and they came. We had so much gold. It was so easy to buy animals, and crops, and equipment. Farming has never been so easy. Everyone lives well. The crops have been incredible. Breeding season was great. And she was by my side, and we...we..."

Memories bubbled up unbidden. Laughter, and love, and the embrace of her skin. Everything he failed to drown out on a daily basis screaming louder in his ears than ever.

"We were so fucking happy," he said, taking a sip to try to hide the shaking in his hand, spilling wine down his chin. "And then one morning I wake up and she's gone and there's just a note saying she couldn't take it anymore, and not to follow her."

He looked up at Balur for the first time. The large lizard man appeared largely unmoved, but given the sometimes striking similarities between Balur and a cliff face, it could often be hard to tell exactly what he was thinking.

"You were going after her," he said. It wasn't a question.

"Of course I did," Will spat.

"So you are not being a complete idiot." Balur nodded.

Given that he had just opened the wound in his heart and let the contents spill, bloody and raw over the table, Will thought that was a touch harsh.

Balur saw his expression and rolled his eyes. "Truly? Truly you are telling me this story and are not expecting me to be calling you fucked in the head. *Breeding season went well?* Were you talking with her about the excitements of crop rotation as well?"

Will hesitated. "I...yes...well..." Why was he being defensive? "We're farmers," with a little more vigor.

"No." Balur put a hand on his shoulder. "Let me be stopping you right there. *You* are being a farmer. Lette is being a cold-blooded killing machine who is looking for a way to be spending her life with less blood on her hands. I would be giving Lawl's left nut to be knowing why, but I am not possessing that, and so I am taking it how I must."

Even through the wine haze, Will was starting to see Balur's point. "You think that she wasn't interested in crop rotation?"

"I am thinking that if she was managing to be manifesting any semblance of interest then she must have been truly loving you."

That word. *Love.* It hung in the air like an accusation. Because if it had been real, if he did allow himself to believe that she had truly loved him, and not just used his body while it was convenient...then it was his fault. He had driven her away.

Which, in the end, was exactly what Balur was saying.

"Oh Gods," he said, letting his head sag and hit the table.

"How long was she managing?" Balur said as if his former ally wasn't repeatedly beating his head against a wooden surface.

"She's been gone four months now."

"So she was making it four." He patted Will on the shoulder. "That is a surprisingly long time for her."

Will looked up sharply. "She tends to leave men often?"

Balur shrugged. "After the first night usually."

"And you didn't think this was useful information to tell me before I hitched my ride to hers, and built a life around the future we were promising each other."

Balur shrugged. "You seemed happy enough with how things were."

"Because I thought my life was built on a solid foundation!" This sort of conversation, Will thought, was exactly why he had snuck out of the whole being-a-prophet thing.

"You would not have been listening to me, if I had been telling you." Balur gave a resigned shrug. "Lovestruck idiots are being that way."

The other reason he'd walked away from Kondorra, Will went on to think, was because his companions had no qualms about beating him about the head and neck with ugly truths.

"So," he managed to conclude, "I screwed up my life, and now you're here." He chugged his wineglass. Balur handed him the bottle. "How can I help you?"

Balur shrugged. "I was not looking for you."

This, Will thought, seemed disingenuous, and not entirely respectful of his bitterness. "You came to my bloody farm," he pointed out.

"I was thinking Lette was here."

"Oh." Will chewed on that. It was, he decided, unreasonably reasonable. "Well she's not."

"No," Balur agreed. "There is only being the drunk wreck of the man you used to be being. It is being very warming to the cockles of my heart." He did not appear to be being very genuine.

"Well," said Will—there was no warmth left in him to buoy his voice, "it looks like we've both been left in her wake doesn't it?" He sighed, poured himself another drink. Balur retrieved the bottle and did the same.

The silence between them grew.

"Why are you even looking for her anyway?" was all Will could finally muster by way of conversation.

"Oh," Balur shrugged. "Some assassins were coming a little too close to killing me, so I was abandoning the whole prophet thing, and was hitting the roads again. And at first I was thinking that perhaps the assassins were from Vinland, and as Lette and I share history with Vinland that is predating our meeting you then perhaps—if the Vinlanders are feeling murderous—they may be sending assassins after her as well, and that I should be telling her that. But then I was realizing they had been saying a dragon's name. But Lette and I are sharing that history too. So I thought I should still be telling her about it. But now she is not being here, so"—he chugged his wineglass again—"I am thinking whatever."

"Wait…" Will said, struggling to parse Balur's torturing of Avarran grammar. For the first time in a long time, he wished he wasn't quite as drunk as he was. "Assassins?" he said. "Vinland?"

"Yes," Balur nodded. "A while ago, Lette and I were hearing of an artifact in the Sacred Section of Vinter." He looked at Will. "The Vinland capital," he added.

"I am knowing…" Will shook his head, corrected himself. "I know what the bloody capital of Vinland is," he said irritably.

"Well, we were hearing about this cup that used to belong to Barph, and how it was always being full of sacred liquor. So we were thinking to be lifting it and be selling it for so much gold we would be able to be making a life-size sculpture of my genitals. But things were going rather awry, and we may have been burning down a significant portion of Vinter. Which was why we were heading to Kondorra in the first place and met you. But they have been having a death warrant out for us for quite some time."

"Death warrant," Will repeated. "Assassins." An idea was coming to him. Emerging from the soup of the night.

"It may have been being to do with the trade dispute," Balur went on, oblivious to Will's slowly building epiphany. "But quite frankly, as soon as plots around trade disputes are being involved, I am considering disemboweling myself."

And then finally it came to Will. Like a light descending from the heavens. Knole, goddess of wisdom, reaching down a single glowing fingertip and pressing it to his forehead.

"We have to go after her," he said. He felt a smile spreading across his face. "We have to find Lette and warn her that her life is in danger!"

Balur's brow furrowed. "Why?"

"Because her life is in danger!" Will stood up. He swayed slightly but he felt more clearheaded than he had in months.

"And how will knowing about them be making her more capable of killing them?"

"She'll be able to hide her tracks. To live more safely." His grin threatened to split his face. "She'll be *grateful*."

Balur shook his head. "Have you even been meeting Lette?"

But Will wouldn't be stopped. He turned around. "We'll leave this whole place. This whole fucking farm. Leave it in our dust."

"Weren't you being the one who was insisting on the farm, and driving off the love of your life with it?" Balur looked thoroughly confused.

"Yes!" Will shouted at him. And it felt good to just say it. To just finally say it and know it was true, and that it didn't matter, because finally, finally he had a way back. A way to reunite with *her*.

"I fucking hate this farm!" he yelled.

The farm, taking offense, caused him to step in some cold, spilled stew, and sent him flying to the floor, where he smacked his head against the flagstones. But he was still smiling, even as the sense was knocked out of him.

4

The Open Road

Even the cataclysmic headache that came the next morning could not dampen Will's spirits. Balur had bound his head inexpertly, largely making it look like Will had been savagely attacked by some bloodthirsty bedsheets, and now the open road beckoned. Will's wanderlust had him out of bed early and chastising Balur to ready his pack and be on his way.

"Are we not taking horses?" said Balur, confused. "Are you not being a wealthy farmer or some shit?"

Will scoffed at him. "This is a return to my roots, Balur. I got out of touch with myself."

"Yes," Balur deadpanned. "You were a farmer. Then you were leading a revolution. Then you went back to being a farmer. I can be seeing how that would be being the total opposite of a return to your roots."

"I mean a return to being one of the people," said Will, purposely ignoring Balur's sarcasm. "I want to be someone down in the dirt again. This separation from the people—that's what was wrong."

"So it was not being the whole chasing off of Lette and lapse into drunkenness then?"

That was a little harder to ignore, but Will managed it.

After three days of aching feet, a continually pounding head, vomiting, loose bowels, constant rain, sleeping in barns, and utterly failing to come across any sign of Lette, Will was beginning to think he was as full of shit as Balur had suggested.

He also finally decided that he would be able to live with Balur's smug satisfaction.

"Fine," he said into Balur's silent judgment, "tomorrow we'll hire pissing horses, and gallop about like the poncey arseholes we apparently are."

Balur clapped him on the back. Will staggered and Balur laughed heartily. "Do not be thinking of it as going soft, Will. Be thinking of it as never actually being anything but soft to begin with."

Will tried to not regret his decision. And another hour later, as they passed through the fortified walls of Pekarra, a small market town, he was glad that he had climbed down off his high horse.

The Pekarra gate guards wore the colors of the Batarran High Council—green and yellow emblazoned with the Coin and Keys. They were lighting torches, and preparing to bar the gates for the night. One poked a pike tentatively in Balur's direction. "He going to be trouble?"

Balur grinned. "You be wanting trouble?"

Will massaged his brow. "No," he said as definitively as he could. "An idiot, yes, but trouble, no."

"Oh good," said the guard, who looked rather glad. Balur was about the same height as the man's pike itself.

Such niceties dealt with, Will stared about. Pekarra's gates opened onto a broad but shallow square of buildings. Most were dark now, but in one lights blazed, and a fiddle and pipe played a jaunty tune.

"All right," Will said, "how's about this for a plan? We go in there, we pay whatever obscene amount it is they demand to put you up for the night, we sleep until the sun is high in the sky, and then we finally hire those gods-hexed horses?"

"There?" Balur nodded toward the inn. It was four stories tall and draped all over with red bunting. A festive place, in Will's opinion.

"It looks nice," he said. He was surprised Balur showed any hesitation at all.

Balur shook his head. "I was not thinking of it as being your sort of place."

Will tried to work out if he was being insulted or not. "What's wrong with it?" he asked as they crossed the square. His legs ached, and the blisters on his heels were approaching the point where they were close to screaming. He pulled open the door to the inn and, in a moment of confused largesse, held it for Balur. "Why are you being such a cryptic bugger all of a sudden?" he asked.

Balur hesitated, filling the door. Music and tinkling laughter pushed out around his massive frame. "Cryptic?" He looked as puzzled as Will felt. Then realization must have dawned, because he smiled, and clapped a heavy hand on Will's shoulder. "Ah," he boomed, as he dragged Will bodily through the door, "you are not understanding what the red flags are signifying."

Slowly, but with irresistible force, Will's mouth formed a perfect O.

The doors opened up onto a massive space, more than half the full footprint of the sprawling tavern and stretching up to the rafters. The space was packed with round tables, and each table was packed with men. And the space between each table was packed with women. Women and lace. Though significantly more women than lace. Indeed, it seemed the town was under a significant lace shortage given what the women seemed forced to wear. Everything was sheer fabric, and soft curves, and jiggling, jiggling flesh. The place stank of sawdust, sweat, ale, and lust.

A bordello.

A long bar stretched the full length of one long wall, and on either side broad oak stairways led up to walkways that circled the room. Upon the walkways paraded yet more women. And behind each woman was a door. And through each door was the glimpse of a soft, warm, red bedroom. Three tiers of walkways looked down upon the room, each one lined with women and doors.

Will watched as a man so drunk he could barely walk was escorted by two women, both half his age, through one of those doorways. The door swung shut. It was not the only closed door.

He swallowed hard.

It was not as if he were unaware such places existed. He was in his twenties, after all, and he had more than a rough idea of how to keep Lette entertained on lonely nights. And yet, to be confronted with it all so abruptly, so...much all at once.

"I always wondered why the farmhands were so eager to take a three-day journey just to sell corn," was all he finally managed.

Balur slammed his palms together in an echoing clap. "Two rooms for the night!" he bellowed. "The Emperor's package!"

Will turned to him. "The Emperor package? You've been here before?"

Balur shook his head with an expression of mixed exasperation and fondness. "No, of course not, but if I ask for an Emperor's package then they shall either give me the closest thing they have, or they will be making something up, and it shall be as glorious as it is expensive."

"Expensive?"

"He's paying!" Balur roared, thrusting a finger at Will just before they were enveloped in giggling women.

Without quite understanding how, Will found himself sitting at a table with a woman on each arm and a mug of ale in each hand. The girls kept asking him inane questions, and even answers such as "Erm?" and "Pardon?" seemed fit to send them into gales of giggles. And each giggle seemed an excuse to press ample flesh against him.

Some part of his mind could see the artifice of it all. He could glimpse the professional hardness that leaked out behind the airy giggles. And part of him knew that he did not want to be here, that bedding whores while you claimed to be looking for your great love was hypocritical at best, and hazardous to the continued health of one's nethers at worst.

And another part of him yelled, "Titties! Titties! Titties!" And every time he took a sip of ale to try to work out what he should do, it got louder.

He leaned his head back, trying to shake himself free from the moment, from the press of delicate hands on his chest, from the buzz of alcohol in his mind, from the sinuous rhythm of pipe and fiddle, from the cheers and laughter of the men, from the smell of perfume and sour ale. He looked up at the tiers of balcony and tried to lose himself in the abstract pattern of wooden railings and doorjams.

One girl, who seemed drunker than the rest, though he couldn't be entirely sure if that was true, leaned in and licked his face.

It was as her tongue reached his cheekbone that the door he was staring at dispassionately opened and...

No.

No, it couldn't be. It mustn't be.

A divine pissing comedy.

She emerged. *She*, laughing. *She*, smiling. *She*, without a care in the world.

Two girls were with her, and two boys. All young. All very pretty. And at first he wanted to scream. Because some great tragedy had befallen her. Something awful that had condemned her to this life, selling her body instead of her sword. She had been robbed and broken. That must have been it, because there could be no other explanation for Lette being here, in this place.

But there was, and as the whore's tongue arrived in Will's ear, and began to make slow circles, he saw it. He saw it in the way the girls and boys fawned on her, laughed too hard with her, in the way they touched and stroked her. He was not looking at an employee, but a patron.

Together, Lette and her entourage stumbled down the corridor. She was holding a wineskin, slopping drink over the railing to fall like red rain on the hall below. One boy and girl were on either side of her, propping her up, laughing so hard they could barely support her.

She was coming down. She would see him. She would . . .

He didn't know. But, gods, he didn't want to find out.

He stood up fast. The whore with her tongue in his ear fell away with an irritated gasp, which then dissolved into another gale of giggles. More hands pawed at him.

He stood, trapped by table and bodies, pinned by events and emotional paralysis. *She would see.*

And then she did.

Their eyes met across a crowded room.

And then a whore grabbed his arse, and he flinched just as he saw Lette mouth a single word.

"Shit."

"Will?" Balur was shouting. "Will, you are being ready for a room then? Because I am wanting to swap my blonde here for your . . . Will?" And then he saw what Will was looking at, and trailed off.

A moment of perfect, silent stillness. Lette avoiding his eye. The whores still fawning around her, not feeling the change in the temperature of her emotions yet. The patrons of the bordello utterly oblivious to this tragedy of the heart playing out around them.

"Lette!" Balur's bellow was a war cry that silenced the room. Everyone in the place froze, a primal fear rising in them.

Balur took off, bulldozing through the table, chairs, patrons, whores, and serving girls. People flung themselves out of his way. Will watched it all. Watched Lette staring at this oncoming monstrosity, eyes wide, as she braced for the impact of her oldest friend.

"Lette!" Balur roared again, catching her up in his massive hands and tossing her into the air. She didn't flail, just rose straight as an arrow. It was not an elegant maneuver, just one of blunt efficiency. It was utterly her. Will's heart tremored in the cage of his ribs. Balur caught Lette, spun her around. "We have been finding you!" the lizard man roared. "Will is always finding a way. It may be being a rough road but it is getting you there in the end."

Lette said something. Will could see her lips move. But the words escaped him. The hubbub of the room was rising once more. Outrage and amusement in equal measure, though none of the irritated parties seemed interested in pressing their point with a creature capable of ripping them in two.

Then Balur was setting Lette down, and pointing to the table, and they were walking through the remnants of Balur's wake back to where Will was standing, back toward his table. *She* was walking toward *him*.

"Will." One of the whores pawed at him. "Come and sit down, Will. I want to have more to drink."

Toward *him and six whores*.

"Get out," he said, trying to keep his voice steady.

"Wiiiilllll." A wheedling pleading in the whore's voice.

"Get out!" he snapped. He wheeled on all of them. "Leave. Now. Go and ply your trade with someone else. You are not welcome at this gods-hexed table."

Confusion. And again that hard glint beneath the softness of their eyes. Perhaps even desperation. This was, after all, how they earned their suppers and paid . . . gods, half of them probably had families at home.

"But Will," one of them started, puffing out her ample chest.

"You still get paid," he said, an edge of desperation creeping into his voice.

And like that they were gone.

And *she* was here.

"Will." Lette's voice was like a cold blade dragged down his spine.

He turned, and he didn't know what he was going to do when he saw her. Weep? Scream? Rush forward to hold her? To kiss her? To throttle her?

And then he was facing her, and he had no thoughts left.

"Lette," he heard himself say.

"Let us sit!" Balur was still shouting. "Let us drink!" He clapped them on the back, sent them staggering toward seats.

Will sat. He didn't know what else to do. He had lived this moment over and over in his head, had rehearsed what to say a thousand times. But none of those imaginary meetings had quite managed to take this particular set of circumstances into consideration.

He couldn't quite meet Lette's eyes. He watched her hands exploring the deep grooves in the wood of the table.

He had to say *something*. Something more than just her name. Some acknowledgment of what they'd had. What she'd taken away. What he'd been through.

Balur was standing a yard away, yelling for more ale. This was as good an opportunity as he was going to get.

"I—" he started.

"I—" she said at the same time.

An embarrassed pause. His hands smothered each other in tiny acts of silent murder.

"You go," he said.

"No—" she started.

"Please," he pressed. This would be easier perhaps if she just explained, just told him what had been going through her head.

She shrugged. "It's just . . . I've got to tell you—"

He leaned forward.

"—I'm fucking hammered right now. So, you know, if it's

important, you might want to wait until morning. I can't guarantee I'll remember anything right now."

"The fuck?" It was out of him before he could stop it. Irresponsible, ill-timed frustration. And yet...? Gods, there was only so much of a beating his heart could accept. "A fucking whorehouse, Lette?" he said. "Of all the places?"

This was not how the conversation had gone in his head.

She burped into her cuff. "Yeah," she said. "And were you planning to pine for me just before or after you went nuts-deep in a whore?"

"I wasn't..." Will shook his head. "That's not why..."

Lette laughed. "Well, why not, Will? Why not grab life by its balls for once? Why not be the man you were in Kondorra? Because I liked him. Not this boring, stunted fuck that dragged me off to the arse-end of Batarra."

That had not been in Will's imagined conversations either.

At that moment, Balur crashed back down at the table beside them. He wrapped an arm possessively around Lette. "So," he said, "what are we talking about?"

Will's mouth was open, but no sound was coming out. There was nothing to come. Or too much, perhaps—everything jammed in his throat. He looked about desperately for a bottle of wine, another jug of ale, but the whores had swept up everything in their departure.

He could feel Lette's eyes on him. Balur's. Waiting to see what he did. And what did she want out of him? What did she expect? And right now would he even give it to her, if he figured it out?

The bordello, he realized, had fallen silent again, as if his own paralysis had crept out to swallow the whole room. A few voices still rang out momentarily, their owners too drunk to pick up on the mood of the room, but one by one they died. And even Will managed to tear himself out of his own navel-gazing enough to notice where the attention of the room was focused.

A man wearing a long brown travel-stained robe had

mounted a table. The hood of his robe was pulled up, his face buried in shadows. He carried a long oaken walking staff and was thumping its steel-shod base against the table's surface.

With each blow, purple sparks rose into the air, and a sound like a gong rang out. The noise mounted, each blow louder than the last. The ringing filled the vacuum left by the voices, rose to dwarf it. The air vibrated against Will, blew at his hair as the figure tap-tap-tapped. No one moved.

Magic, Will thought. A curiously dispassionate appraisal. The encounter with Lette had left him hollow, it seemed.

A tiny fraction of a noise made him glance down at Lette's hands, still resting on the rough surface of the table. Three throwing knives were balanced between her knuckles.

The man ceased his tapping. The depths of his hood surveyed the crowd. "A moment of your time," he said, and his voice was deep, and coarse, with a quality that made Will think of gnarled wood, but it rang out clearly in the quiet room. A voice everyone would hear. "A moment," he went on, "for your eternal souls. That is all I ask. Not much to ask for such a thing as eternity, is it not?"

He turned around, his robe billowing out, yet still nothing of his figure was revealed.

"Fuck off, preacher!" yelled some brave soul from the back of the crowd.

"Fuck a whore!" yelled another.

The robed man beat down with his staff. There was a quiver in the air. Nothing visible. No burst of light. But somehow a sensation of overwhelming disapproval was suddenly thick in the air. Laughter died before it even rose to lips.

"Preacher," said the man, turning once more. "Preacher?" He tested the sound of it. "As if I am here to preach for the gods. As if I am going to tell you about the fine examples they have set for you. As if I am going to tell you to pour libations for the morally decrepit, whoring, raping deviants we have chosen to worship?" He stared around the crowds, eyes blazing. "Do they truly deserve that? The so-called gods? Do they truly deserve people who preach in their names? What have they done to deserve our worship? What do they promise us?"

Silence. Will was not sure if no one dared speak, or if it was simply an issue no one had ever considered before. He knew he hadn't. Why did he worship the gods? Because his parents had. Because everyone else did. Because they were there. It was expected. Under the gaze of that shadowed hood, none of those felt like very good reasons all of a sudden.

"What even is our reward for worshipping them?" asked the robed man. "The Hallows? An eternity under the thumb of Lawl? Toiling for him in the land of the dead? Our will robbed from us? That is what we build toward, strive for? That is why we honor them?"

The man started to laugh, an awful, wet, rotten sound that creaked up out of his dry throat.

"They're the gods!" someone else yelled. "We worship them because they're massive, all-powerful beings who can crush us if we don't." And then, as an afterthought, "You fucking idiot."

The man nodded slowly. "Fear," he said. He whispered. And yet everyone heard. They could feel the menace of the word. "Fear. Yes. Exactly. That's at the heart of it, isn't it? You worship the gods because you fear what will happen if you don't. You fear how bad the Hallows could be. You fear their intervention in your lives." And then, sounding as if he were almost licking his chops as he said it, "You fucking pussies."

It was a bold claim in a room full of men awash in adrenaline and alcohol, but nobody shouted back at that. Will could feel it too. His own chagrin. His own inadequacy.

Why? asked a voice in the back of his head. *Why in all the Hallows do I care what this man has to say? I just had my heart eviscerated by a woman I traveled leagues to find and spent months pining over. Why do I give the slightest shit what he has to say?*

The memory of those purple sparks rose.

Glamour. Magic.

Shit.

He wanted to reach out, to grab Lette's hand, and shake her. Make her see what he had just seen. But he couldn't touch her. Not after what she had said. He just couldn't.

"What if..." the man whispered as seductive as any whore in the place, "there was someone who could stand up to the gods? Someone who could fight for you? Someone who could promise something more than the chaos of uncaring deities? Someone who could throw them down from their vaulted heavens, grind them into the dirt, and take their place. What if there was someone who deserved your worship?"

One or two men made scoffing sounds but nobody dared more than that. Will dared do no more than that. He could feel the tension in him, like a physical force pressing on his chest. *Some sort of suppression?* He wished he knew more about magic. He wished Quirk were there. Even with the level of condescension she brought to almost every conversation, she might have at least known what was going on, and how to fight against it.

"Balur," he hissed, not daring to raise his voice above the thinnest of whispers. "Balur."

The lizard man ignored him.

"You doubt me?" said the man upon the table. "My truth? My words? Well, they are not my words. I am merely a prophet. Merely the shadow of that which is to come falling upon this nation, with the sun at his back."

"Who?" rose one tremulous voice. "Who comes?"

The man paused, pushed back his hood. His head was bald and horribly burned. Flesh gathered in rivulets, twisting and pulling at the musculature beneath. His mouth was tightened in a permanent leer. One eye was milky white. The other was sharp and black as it stared out across the room.

"Theerax." The word was almost a whisper, almost a moan,

almost a prayer. "Theerax comes to this realm. He comes to liberate you all. He comes to tear down the gods."

And just like that, the spell was broken for Will. He could feel the pressure on his chest shatter. A sudden lightness filled him. He felt almost giddy with indignation at this man's ludicrous bullshit.

Theerax. A dragon's name. That, he recognized. And he knew that the only thing dragons liberated was the coin in your pocket.

"What the actual fuck?" It was not the most elegant way to begin his counterpoint, but the urge to shut this man up was overwhelming, and if he had learned anything from Balur at all, it was that hitting hard and fast counted for a lot in a fight. "I mean," he went on, "I'm a farmer, and I've seen a lot of bullshit in my life, but that's an impressive load even by my standards."

The man on the table wheeled round, fury writ large in his lone dark eye.

"A dragon?" Will asked, then hawked and spat. "Like the ones the folk in Kondorra had to kill? One of those fat, flatulent, lazy lizards is going to save us from ... what again? The fact that the gods leave us alone and let us get on with our lives? Yeah, that's terrible that is."

He could feel the energy in the room balancing on a knife edge. Because truly he was just saying what half or more of the room wanted to say. Wanted to say but couldn't. This man's glamour holding their will in check, pressing back against them.

The man raised his staff again, held it high, then brought it crashing down on the table. Wood splintered. A sound like cannon fire. A wave of purple erupted out from beneath the staff's steel cap, flooded the room like a tidal wave. Will felt it break against him. Felt the force of it as it rushed around him, felt it blow his hair back. And yet he was left untouched. He walked toward the man easily.

The man snarled.

"What?" asked Will. "Don't know what to do with a man whose spirit you can't break by force? Don't know how to mount a proper argument? Did Theerax not give you anything but lies and empty promises to sow?"

But the energy in the room was different this time. An ugly growl emitted from the crowds. And while Will seemed immune to this prophet's powers, they did not.

"Who are you?" The man on the table was leaning forward. He seemed genuinely interested. "A Kondorran, I suppose. A fool, certainly. Someone who fought against his own best interests."

Will tried to work out how to play it. How much time could he buy and what could he do with it? He was far too far from the exit, and there were far too many people in the way.

He glanced back toward Lette and Balur, the lizard man emerging like a pillar of yellow stone in a desert of angry faces. Will tried to read his expression. Was he under the man's power? Was Lette? Did he have *any* allies here?

"Me?" Will shrugged as carelessly as it was possible to do while caring very much about appearing careless. "I'm just the voice of reason." Mentally he added, *and it's a pretty messed-up day when I can say that.*

"I'm the voice of experience," he went on. "I'm the voice that's going to rise up every time you open your stupid mouth."

He was twenty yards away. Too far. And he wouldn't call his current course of action a good plan, but at least it was a plan. He kept walking slowly. If only he could keep piquing the man's curiosity.

"You pretend to be an enigma?" the man smiled. "You will beg to tell me everything before the end."

Eighteen yards.

Will nodded. "Maybe. But I'm not the only reasonable man. I'm not the only one who will resist."

"Resisting Theerax is a fool's errand. Not even the gods will stand up to Theerax."

"In my experience dragons can't even stand up to a rabble of disorganized farmers. I think the gods will swat the dragons like the overgrown bugs that they are."

Twelve yards now.

"You think angering me will make me sloppy." The man twisted his head. "Will it make all of these other men sloppy?"

Ten yards. *Come on. Come on.*

"You assume I give a shit what a bug-worshipping turd like you actually thinks."

He was actually proud of that one. And proud that his voice didn't shake when he said it. It sounded like the sort of thing Lette might say. If she wasn't too glamoured to pay attention.

Eight yards. He could probably rush him from three—close the last gasp of distance at a run.

"I will enjoy watching these men tear you apart."

It was pretty tricky to think of a snappy comeback to that. It was probably true after all. Will went with just ambling quietly forward. Six yards now. Five. Four. He tensed the muscles in his legs.

And stopped moving.

He pushed hard, trying to force his legs to move. But something held him in place. He grunted with effort.

The man laughed. Slowly he raised his staff, and Will felt himself leaving the ground. He was floating.

"What did you think to do? Rush me? Wrestle my staff away? Did you think that would save you?"

"Well…" Will would have shrugged if he could. "Pretty much."

The man sneered. "You know, perhaps I shall enjoy killing you myself rather than handing you to these men. Maybe I shall—"

He stopped talking abruptly, pivoted around with a cry, and collapsed to one knee.

Will flailed, landed in a pile. His vision flexed. He shook his head.

The man stood with a snarl. He was clutching at the hilt of a throwing dagger that emerged from one shoulder. He opened his mouth—

—and promptly let out a gasp as he took a step backward. A second hilt had appeared, this time protruding from his other shoulder.

"You know," said Lette, and her voice was low and conversational, "you probably would have had me if you didn't keep up with this whole 'men' shit. I really didn't want to be left out of tearing him apart just because I'm not packing the right equipment in my britches."

It was not, Will reflected, the most reassuring speech to deliver when you were saving someone.

The man let out a snarl, phlegm spraying from his mouth as he barked, "Kill them!"

That wasn't overly reassuring either.

The room quaked. Will felt the pulse of movement in the floor, the air. A mass inhalation. A mass tensing of muscles. A mass bunching of legs.

It was all the time he had to react.

He flung himself forward as the crowd clenched around him like a fist. Hands scrabbled at his kicking heels as he put two hands on the edge of the robed man's table and hauled himself up onto it.

The robed man was still on his knees, struggling to rise through his obvious pain. Will grabbed him by both shoulders, heaved against the force of the hands grabbing his shirttails, and for good measure slammed his knee into the man's chest. The man brayed in pain, then began choking for air. Will pushed him off the table and down into the crowd. Then Will spun around and kicked the shirt grabber in the face.

Where was Lette?

He scanned quickly, caught sight of her, a tiny whirling dervish, surrounded by a blur of steel and blood as she beat drunk men back. But as warming as that sight was, it would only be moments before she was overwhelmed.

Which was approximately the same time frame he was on. He kicked another three men in the face. Someone grabbed at his ankle. He only just twisted away before being hauled off balance. He couldn't keep this dance up much longer. Someone was grabbing the table and starting to tip.

Across the room, a roar crashed out like a meteor coming to earth. Ripples of reaction spread out through the crowd, people taking a momentary break from their desire to surge forward and rip him limb from limb, so that they could see what in the Hallows was making that noise, and were they in its way.

It was Balur, and he was charging.

This time there was nowhere for people to fling themselves to avoid the oncoming lizard man. The press of bodies was too tight. Balur bludgeoned his way through the crowd like a mace into a man's skull. Blood and destruction was left in his wake.

Well, Will had time to think, *this has been particularly disastrous.* And then his table was turned over and he was sprawling forward into the savage fury of the crowd. As he sailed through the air he saw Balur reach the edge of the circle where Lette was hacking apart her assailants. *Odd,* he added, taking advantage of the curious time dilation such moments seemed to thrust on him, *I thought he would have come to kill me first.*

Then he landed. Hands grabbed at him. Fists and feet beat at his sides. He screamed, and couldn't hear himself. He tried to pull himself into a protective ball, to get his hands up over his head, but too many people were pulling at him. He tasted his own blood, his own fear.

This is a shitty way to die, he thought, though he had no examples of better ways at hand at that particular moment.

Someone had him by the hair and was managing to drag him

backward through the crowd, while he yelled (for some reason that he could not entirely fathom), "The hair, you childish bastards? Seriously, the hair?" when it happened.

He was, at first, convinced it was divine intervention. Some thunderbolt cast down by Lawl, slamming into the bordello's stained and warped floorboards, sending bodies and splinters flying into the air. Then he realized his mistake.

It was Balur.

It was Balur with Lette astride his back. His fists shattering bones and ending lives. Her knives lancing out with more accuracy than any mere deity could hope to achieve.

Retreating hands dropped Will. Bodies dropped to the floor around him. Howls of rage became gurgles of guttering breath.

Balur grabbed Will by the front of his old work shirt and heaved him bodily over his shoulder, buttons popping, peppering the crowd.

"Now," Balur growled, "we are fighting!"

A blast of purple light lanced across the room and smashed into Balur's chest. Roaring, Balur skidded back, feet digging splintered trenches in the floorboards. Smoke wafted up from a black scorch mark on his chest.

Across the room, the man from the table stood, staff aimed at Balur, purple smoke drifting from its tip.

"No, you stupid bastard," Will heard Lette say, "now we run for our lives."

"I am being an Analesian!" Balur growled. "I am not running!"

"Gods," Will heard Lette groan, "how many times do I...?"

Will was still draped over Balur's shoulder, staring directly down the lizard man's muscular back.

"Look," Lette went on, "don't think of it as a retreat. Think of it as a way of not dying as stupidly as the rest of your fucking race."

A man charged them screaming. Balur's fist ended the scream, quickly and bloodily.

"If they can be taking us, then they are deserving their victory," Balur insisted. "That is being the way of life. You cannot be crawling and hiding from the truth of the world. It will be finding you, and it will be clawing your guts from your chest."

"Look," Lette tried again, "we've had this talk. The mightier thing totally works when you're dealing with roughly equally numbered sides, but when you're outnumbered, say... two hundred to one at the best, then it's a really, really stupid philosophy."

Another blast of purple light struck Balur, sending him skidding back. He was pressed up against one wall of the bordello now. The angry crowd had spread out in a crescent before him, slowly closing in, bloodlust overcoming trepidation.

"How about," Will tried, "we don't think of it as a retreat, but instead—"

A man, braver than his peers, ran forward. Balur punted him toward the back rows of the assembled men. The crescent drew back a little.

"—instead think of it as more of a tactical regrouping. Aiming for a strategic advantage on the battleground. Not so much a show of cowardice, but rather outwitting them. Mental might, so to speak."

Balur let out a deep rumbling. It could have been a considering hum, or a bloodcurdling growl. Will always found it hard to tell with Balur.

Their assembled foes took it as the latter, and finally found their spine. They let out a yell, their collected voices bursting over Will, Balur, and Lette like a tidal wave.

"All right," Balur said. "I can be living with mental might."

He took a roaring step toward the crowd.

They charged.

So did Balur. Backward. Spinning on his heel and heading pell-mell toward the wall of the bordello, shoulder lowered.

Will heard wood give way. He felt the rush of cold night air embrace him after the sweat and stench of the bordello. He heard the change in the timbre of the crowd's yell. And then the three of them were running through the town night, he and Lette still clinging to the lizard man's massive shoulders.

"So," he said to Lette, finally shifting his weight and facing her, "was that more what you had in mind?"

She stared at him incredulously, and then, finally, grimaced. "Yes," she said despondently. "I suppose it was."

5

Master of His Own Domain

It had taken Firkin about a week to realize that Balur was not coming back.

There had been panic at first, of course. Their prophet missing, the charred tents, the blood, the dead bodies. But Balur's massive body itself had not been found. And so after much pleading and cajoling, Firkin had been able to convince the populace that this was not a disaster of epic proportion, nor the death knell of their hopes and dreams, but was instead a moment of transition, of becoming.

"Like, you know, one of them...oh fuck it, flappy things," he had screamed to the assembled crowds. "See a shit ton of them in the summer."

He had been standing on a hillside, in a natural amphitheater, the rock at his back amplifying his words.

"Bird?" someone had yelled back.

"No." Firkin shook his head.

"Duck?"

"No." Firkin knew that wasn't right.

"Swan?" checked another soul.

"These are all just birds!" snapped Firkin. "I said it wasn't a gods-hexed bird."

"Butterfly?" someone in the front rows yelled out.

Firkin pointed. "Yes! One of those bastards. That's it. We're like one of them. Just before they're one of them. When they're the fat little grub things. Not," he corrected himself, taking a swig from his wineskin, "that we're a fat little grub." He shook his head violently, watched the world wobble in front of him. "No, no, no. We *were* one of them. But now we're in the in-between state."

"Chrysalis?" yelled out the same helpful voice in the front row.

"Shut up!" Firkin barked. "Who's the voice of the fucking prophet here?" You had to keep the rabble in line, he'd learned. That was a big part of it.

He returned his attention to the crowd. "We're a chrysalis!" he yelled.

There was an inhalation of breath, a vast nod of understanding. It had all been pretty easy after that. He just kept on saying things that Balur would say, without all the bothersome chore of listening to Balur actually say them. It was a marked improvement.

And then, finally, he realized that Balur was just not coming back at all ever. And then things became significantly more fun because Balur had had a way of saying boring, tiresome things like "No, that is being completely insane," and "No, that will be leading to mass starvation, and the death of everyone," and "No, you will be causing a war, and our bloody slaughter," and "No, the human body cannot be fitting that much wine inside itself, you will be causing parts of yourself to rupture," and things of that ilk.

Now there was no one to say, "No," and it was glorious.

To be fair, there were a number of deaths, and a lot of ideas that in retrospect were somewhat regrettable. That said, Firkin was generally of the opinion that they were funny enough to be excusable.

Still, things were getting dicey by the time the Vinlander ambassador came back. Firkin met him in the second-best Kondorran tent. The first best was still in ashes where Balur had left it. Nobody seemed to want to clean the area up and it had taken on an almost religious quality. People gathered there now. At least in part to avoid his dictates.

"Wotsit?" Firkin slurred at the ambassador.

"Issa trade deal," the ambassador managed after a few false starts. He was noticeably more drunk this time around.

Firkin had vague memories of Balur telling him to send people off after the ambassador the last time he was here so they could agree to things. Firkin hadn't bothered to do that. Balur should have known better than to trust him with things like that. So really, whatever was about to happen was Balur's fault. "Iss Balur's fault," he said. He thought it was important that people know that.

He took his feet off the kneeling man he had decreed should become his footstool and leaned forward.

"I think," he said, then hiccupped and lost his train of thought. "I think...I think..." He rummaged through mental closets looking for the errant words. "I think you can piss off."

Despite himself, the Vinlander looked impressed by Firkin's audacity.

Pleased by this reaction, Firkin warmed to his theme. "No trade," he spat as vehemently as possible. "No agreements. None of your namby-pamby, bullying bullshit. We won't have it. We are Kondorra. We are proud. We are defiant. We are..." He paused and tried to think of something else they were. "Are... proud!" He said it louder this time. That should do. "We don't bend to bullies like you. We don't capitulate. We fight! We struggle and we succeed. It's the, er...the, er..."

"Way?" suggested the ambassador.

Firkin shook his head.

"Stuff?" the ambassador hazarded.

Firkin shook his head. "No. That's not what I mean. Where we are." He pointed at the ground. "Here."

"Tent?" asked the ambassador.

"No. Begins with a *K*."

"Kondorra?"

Firkin smiled and nodded. Then spat at the ambassador's feet. "It's the Kondorran way!" he screamed at the top of his lungs.

The ambassador nodded sagely. "Bloody fine then," he said.

The ambassador turned his back and Firkin felt a surge of divine, prophetic power thrum through him. That would put bloody Balur in his place. Never back down. Never surrender.

"Of course," said the ambassador as he reached the tent flap, "this does mean war."

He pulled back the flap and a stream of soldiers poured into the tent. Ten, twenty, thirty of them. They surrounded Firkin, swords drawn.

"Oh," said Firkin in what felt like a small voice. "Well, you know, in that case..." He shrugged. "We surrender."

6

Round Two

The morning after her disastrous evening with the Emperor, Quirk returned to his palace to warn him about the magic-wielding assassin currently trying to worm his way into his eminence's favor. She strode through Tamathia quickly, feet tap-tapping on the cobble steps. It was early and the sun was just breaking over the yellow stone of the city's skyline, shining down into the streets in blinding shafts, illuminating straw and cobbles. Despite the sun, though, the day was still cold, and her breath misted in front of her as she bustled past clerks and storekeepers scurrying off to work.

She could have taken a carriage, of course. Her jaunt to Kondorra had been profitable, to say the least. But her wealth was of little interest to her. She used what little she needed to fund her research, and the rest she let the Chancellor and Bursar of the university freely pilfer. Still, in return they had offered to let her use the university's carriages whenever she wanted. But having worked so hard to become one of the everyday citizens of Tamathia, it seemed foolish to remove herself from the streets and to shutter herself away from the people she had so long aspired to mimic.

Afrit had tried to talk her out of this visit at the university gates. The woman had been there collecting her mail from the gatekeeper. And it was just coincidence they bumped into each other again, of course. Quirk could hardly assume she had been waiting for her all night…

"Where are you off to so bright and early?" Afrit had asked, as eager as ever.

And then somehow it had all spilled out of Quirk. Every detail. Everything she had planned to say to the Emperor. Every accusation, every plea. Afrit had listened, eyes growing wider and wider.

And then at the end of it, "You can't go."

Quirk had gaped at her. She had to go. She had told Afrit as much, though perhaps not as politely.

"What proof do you have?" Afrit had asked. "Assassination is not a slight charge."

"The Emperor knows I do not shy away from the truth, however distasteful," she had replied. "That is why I am in his good graces. My word will be enough." And she had finally felt confident then, because that *was* true. She had built her reputation at the court on firm foundations.

Afrit had had more to say, but Quirk hadn't stayed to listen for it.

Now the palace guard nodded to her as she passed through the gatehouse. She was well known to them. She strode across a gravel courtyard and up the stone steps to the ornate double doors, which were opened for her by a pair of footmen who seemed blind to the presence of the woman they were helping. Inside, a butler—clad entirely in the same ghastly velvet as the table she had been eating at last night—led her to a seneschal, who in turn led her to the court marshal, who was still standing before the ornate double doors that led to the ballroom. Gray circles hung below his eyes.

"Mistress Bal Tehrin," he said, "it is so good that you return to us." From his demeanor, you would never have known that he had last seen her running from this place halfway to tears.

This whole palace was like a carriage, she thought, insulating the emperor from the reality of the city around him. She should talk to him about that too, once the business with Ferra was dealt with.

"Is his eminence available for an audience yet this morning?" she asked, cutting through the social niceties. Small talk was something she had mastered late in the recovery from her childhood and the skill was usually the first to abandon her when she was stressed.

The court marshal pursed his lips and exchanged a minute glance with the seneschal. Quirk flicked a glance at the woman, just in time to see the fractional nod.

"His eminence has yet to retire from the evening's revelries," the court marshal said.

Which was an impressive level of debauchery even for the Emperor. It also meant that if she went into the ballroom, she would probably not be the only woman there, but she might well be the only one wearing a blouse. Still, she had no desire to wait.

"Is he receiving guests?" she pressed.

Another pursing of the lips. This one so hard, Quirk thought he could have cracked a walnut.

Another glance at the seneschal preceded his nod. "I shall announce your return, Mistress Bal Tehrin."

He knocked upon the ballroom doors once with his gilded, ceremonial staff and then opened them wide. Quirk, who had been expecting to be buffeted by the dubious sounds and scents of revelry, was surprised by the quiet. Just the low whisper of two voices.

"Mistress Bal Tehrin!" bellowed the court marshal, shattering the silence.

Quirk stood at the top of the ornate staircase leading down to the ballroom. The dinner table was still there, still clad in velvet. A few plates of grapes remained. The Verran dignitary's statue had been pushed off to the side of the room and covered back up with its sheet.

The Emperor sat where he had during the meal, leaning forward on the table with both elbows. His head was cocked to one side, resting on his golden neckpiece. An expression of rapt attention was on his face. It was a look with which Quirk was intimately familiar. She had enjoyed it on many occasions as she regaled the Emperor with stories about dragons and Kondorra, and gave him her opinion on political philosophy and the aesthetics of the court.

But today, she was not on the receiving end of that gaze.

Sitting across from the Emperor, bathing in the warmth of his rapture, sat Ferra.

The man turned his bald, hawk's head upon her and smiled broadly. Hate and fire flared in her. Where had this man come from? *Where had he gotten his information?* Who did he have spying on her? Her mind flicked quickly to Afrit, back at the university. The young professor's insistence that she not come here and confront Ferra. Was she protecting him?

"Mistress Quirk!" Ferra interrupted her thoughts, speaking before the Emperor could. "You return to us! And we are so glad to see you."

Quirk hesitated. How could the Emperor have been with Ferra all night? Ferra had been at her rooms trying to kill her. She had injured him. Gods, how could the Emperor have sat here all night listening to this man's drivel?

She was still standing at the top of the steps. She had her mouth open. She had been ready to burst in full of bluster, and import. She had been ready to dismiss whores, and shake the Emperor by the lapels. And yet now she looked like a fool. Ferra had made her leave looking like one, and now he made her enter like one. He had her entirely wrong-footed.

She stopped. She breathed. She pictured the surface of a still lake. She had learned to control her emotions. That had been the crux of her recovery. She would not lose all that progress to this man.

She walked down the steps slowly.

"Ferra," she said, and she was pleased that her voice was calm. "I'm surprised to see you here."

"While the Emperor and I both expected your return." Ferra's smile didn't falter for a moment. He was prepared for this war. She needed to collect herself quickly.

"Well, I suppose that given that you had failed to kill me earlier, this was a touch predictable." Still not a tremor in her voice, or her smile.

Be the surface of the lake. Be the stillness of the wind. Repeating the mantra in the back of her head.

The Emperor, who had seemed happy to watch them spar, abruptly lost his aura of stoicism. His head jerked quickly back and forth between the two of them.

"I must assume," he said in his rough tones, "that you are speaking in a metaphorical manner."

Ferra just watched her. She had unsettled him, she thought. He had not expected her to attack so quickly.

"I wish I did," she told the Emperor. She kept her voice even, her tone almost demure. She did not meet his eyes. She was the perfect subject. It hurt to cast away the months of growing familiarity and trust, but this was more important than pride.

"A serious accusation," said the Emperor. His eyes flicked for a moment to Ferra. The dragon's emissary still hesitated. She pressed forward.

"Indeed, and yet one I must make. Several hours ago—"

"Hours ago?" The Emperor cut her off sharply.

Quirk permitted herself only a hair's breadth of a pause even as she felt the ground she was basing her argument upon shifting beneath her feet. "Yes," she said. No room for uncertainty. She would use the truth like a club. "I was in my rooms—"

"This, then," the Emperor cut her off again, "is not some slight from years gone by?"

The time for demureness was gone. Quirk let herself meet the

Emperor's eyes. She let a tongue of flame uncurl in her chest. And she let the Emperor see that it was loose. "I would hardly call slipping into my chambers at night and assaulting me with magic a 'slight,' your eminence."

Behind her, she heard the court marshal draw a sharp inhalation.

The Emperor looked to Ferra once more. And for the first time, Quirk felt a stab of the emotion that she suspected had struck all the Emperor's old advisors and diplomats when her star had become ascendant at court. Fear mixed with jealousy.

Ferra nodded his head slightly.

"That," the Emperor said, "would have been difficult, given that Ferra has been with me all night."

And suddenly the ground on which Quirk's argument stood was not simply shifting, it was a mess of rotten planks tumbling down into the void.

Ferra let himself smile. All his confusion had been a feint. And she was still a fool.

"All night?" She was scrambling at straws and she knew it. "He didn't step away for even a moment?"

"A thirty-minute constitutional hardly provides enough time to get to the university, let alone attempt to kill you in your chambers and return here, Bal Tehrin," the Emperor snapped. Ferra didn't even have to lay it out for the Emperor. The man was already convinced of the answer.

Quirk had lost academic debates before. She knew when defensive maneuvering was called for, but this man was a killer, and he sat at her emperor's right hand.

"He is a mage of unknown power, your eminence." She tried to keep the desperation out of her voice. "Who knows how long it takes him to get anywhere?"

The Emperor sighed, no longer exasperated, but just sad. "Quirkelle, please. For a great deal of time you have given me trusted advice. This is unbecoming. Master Ferra warned me that your prejudices would lead you to try to discredit him. Though I don't think even he expected your attack to be so desperate or so pathetic. I spoke in your defense. I am beginning to regret that now. Leave us now." He gave her a kind smile.

She hated that smile. And for a moment the desire to burn the room and bring the roof crashing down around all their ears was almost overpowering.

"If I leave you," she said, her desperation laced with exasperation now, "then I leave you with an assassin."

"Gods!" the Emperor roared. "You try my patience. This man has come here to try to save us all from the anarchy of a pantheon gone mad, and whether you agree with him or not, that is a noble goal, and speaks of a noble heart. I know you have prejudices against dragons, colored by your experiences, and your past. But I shall not allow my ears to be stoppered by your bigotry. Maybe the time has come for the gods to fall. Maybe a new pantheon is required. And while I have valued your opinion in the past, that does not excuse rudeness or impertinence now. I am your Emperor. You exist in this nation because I permit it, Bal Tehrin. Do not forget that. Not ever. Not one single time."

The room quivered with the Emperor's rage. Quirk could feel it thrumming about her. She could hear the anxious panting of the court marshal behind her, and his feet scuffing on the rich carpet as he attempted to scuttle behind the door and out of sight. She could see the Emperor's body shaking with it, hands gripping the edge of the table, where he had stood up in his anger. She could feel it in the racing of her heart.

Only Ferra looked at ease, leaning back in his chair, smile spreading like a sickness. He had done his work well. Had not even needed to fight his own battle. She and the Emperor had done it all for him.

But this was only another skirmish. There would be more and she would be better prepared.

Quirk turned, and made a tactical retreat.

7

Money Talks

Not for the first time in her life, Lette wondered what in the name of all the gods she was doing. As she stared into the inn's mirror, the closest thing she could come up with was *indulging my chronic addiction to idiotic life choices*.

Then she checked to see how her profile looked.

She regretted it instantly.

I left him.

One week. It had been one week since Will had found her in the bordello. One week on the road together. One week with him staring accusations at her. One week of not knowing if she felt guilty or indignant. One week of asking herself what in all the names of the gods she was doing.

Fighting, she told herself. Because it was an answer she liked. Even if she wasn't sure it was true.

There was, at least, a fight to be fought. Word of the dragon Theerax was spreading throughout Batarra faster than the clap through a whorehouse. She, Will, and Balur would arrive in a town, and already the air would be abuzz with talk of dragons. A dragon that had come to save them from the gods.

There were even rumors of dragons in other countries. One called Gorrax in Salera. Diffinax in Tamar. Jotharrax in Verra. All of them equipped with the same mad promise: that they would tear the gods out of the heavens. That they would replace the debauchery of the current pantheon with law and order. But if Lette knew one thing, it was that if you saw a dragon making promises, you tore out its tongue and throttled the beast with the thing.

Not that there had been any sightings of actual dragons yet. Which was odd considering most of them were large enough to be judged part of the geography in several small countries. And so while technically it was a fight, there was nothing for her hit. Which left her with the unfortunate fact that she had nothing but her thoughts about Will with which to while away the time.

Oh gods...

Will did look good still. There was that. Some of the muscle was gone, but there was a darker look about his eyes too. And that was definitely working for him.

And he still wanted her. Gods, that much was obvious too. In between the accusations, his desire was as raw as ever. And there was some flattery in that.

But she had walked down that path. She had tried. She had buckled down and committed. She had birthed lambs and scythed wheat. And Will...Will had been just so cursedly happy. So satisfied. And she had...

Gods, what could she truly have done except leave? What could she have asked of him? To accompany her back to the life she had sworn to leave behind?

So she hadn't. Instead she had simply left. And the thing that had really hurt, if she was honest, here in a tavern's bathroom, examining her reflection in a piece of polished tin, was that it had felt like cowardice. Will had made a coward of her.

So fuck him. And fuck his accusing glances. She had tried. He had failed.

Except, of course, here she was examining her reflection in a piece of polished tin.

To save what scraps of her pride remained, she left the mirror and headed down to the tavern's common room. Balur was there, right where she had left him, slumped over a table. A barmaid swept fresh wood shaving onto the floor around him, with the look of a woman asked to declaw a lion.

And Will, of course. Will was there too.

Will opened his mouth to speak. Quickly Lette picked up one of the stale tankards the barmaid had not dared to remove from Balur's table and slammed it down hard next to the lizard man's ear. He came awake shouting, "—said fourteen donkeys, you b—" Then his gaze settled on Lette, and he said more morosely, "Oh. You."

"Breakfast," Lette said to the barmaid. "Something that used to bleed, and now looks like ash."

Unfortunately, the time it took for Lette to make sure the barmaid had comprehended this allowed Will to get a word in edgeways. "So," he said, coming over, holding a bowl of steaming oatmeal. "I scouted out the village square. It sounds like most people will be passing through in about an hour, so we should secure a good spot for our talk soon."

Lette decided that it would probably be good for both her and Will if she reached over the table and slapped him. So she did.

In retrospect, she should have waited until he swallowed his mouthful of oatmeal.

"What in the name of Lawl's black eye?" he spluttered.

"Talks," she said. "I have had it up to fucking here with talks." She demonstrated the height by slapping Will again around the head and neck.

So far on their travels, Will had given three separate talks about the dangers of dragons in three separate villages. The best-attended one had had five people in the audience. Four if she didn't include the chicken. But to be honest, the chicken had seemed a little more engaged than most of the others.

She had been behind the idea at first. The dragons were waging a war of ideas. Surely they should do the same. But the problem was that the dragons were having fun making grandiose, groundless promises. Will was stuck with the truth. And the truth was boring at best, and downright depressing most of the time.

So now, she reasoned, the time had come to help Will recognize that fact.

"Get your shit together," she told him matter-of-factly. "We all know you've been a lucky bastard with plans in the past but this one isn't working."

For a moment there was nothing but hurt in his eyes, and that look made her chest ache like a blade had slid between her ribs. But then her anger flared higher, because that sort of shit was exactly the problem. That he should somehow feel entitled to have a shit plan, and entitled to use it to screw up her life.

He opened his mouth.

She slapped him again for good measure. "Shut up," she told him. "I've changed my mind. You are actually banned from coming up with gods-hexed plans until you extract your head from your arse. Now it's my turn."

The barmaid arrived with Lette's formerly alive, now burnt thing. Lette hacked a chunk of it free and chewed. It was awful, but in the pleasantly familiar way that most tavern food was awful.

"The dragons want the will of the people," she said, ignoring the wounded looks Will was shooting at her. "Well, fine, let them have it. In this world, your opinion only actually matters if you can afford to have a servant who's dedicated to wiping your arse on sheets of gold leaf. Money is power. Not how pleasing peasants find you. Why bother working from the bottom up? Screw the little people. Let's go to the capital, march up to the Batarran High Council, knock some heads together, and get them to kick some sense into everybody. They have an army."

She hacked off another chunk of burnt whatever. She chewed some more. Overall, she thought, it was acceptable.

Balur nodded. "I am liking the part where we are knocking heads."

Lette glared at him. "I don't give a shit what you like, you lump of iguana meat. We're doing it."

Will opened his mouth again. Balur laid a hand on his arm. "Now is not being the time. Unless you are particularly wanting to carry your balls around with you in a small purse for the rest of your life. But I am finding that having both hands free is more helpful for fending off further attacks." He shrugged. "It is being up to you."

Will hesitated, considered his oatmeal. Then he got up and walked away.

Lette thought about it, but she didn't go after him. Along with the new plan, it made her feel considerably better.

It was eighty leagues to Bellenet, capital of Batarra. Ten days of travel across fields and plains. Sheep and cattle grazed around them. Farmers hacked at browning wheat and corn. Windmills waved their arms in lazy circles. Starlings chattered and taunted in skies ragged with clouds.

They passed through farmsteads, villages, and towns. They slept beneath hedges, in tavern rooms and stables. They set campfires and exchanged small talk so diminutive it could hide in a gnat's arsehole. They murdered two groups of would-be bandits, and that raised Lette's spirits further.

But everywhere they went, word of Theerax had already been. Men gathered around tavern tables and griped about the gods, about how libations had not helped with blight among the potatoes this year. About how old mistress Novak had sacrificed her prize bull to try to save the rest of her herd, but that disease had still taken them all. Women pumped water in village squares and told how all their prayers to Cois had still left them disappointed on their wedding nights. How Knole had disdained to make their children any smarter. And those idiot children played "chase the gods" in between market stalls, one with arms spread, roaring, hunting the others who dashed about squealing and laughing.

And then, on the tenth day, Bellenet appeared on the horizon, like a vast ship rising out of a sea of cornfields. The roads slowly clogged with farmers' carts. A bard stood in the back of one juggling and singing a bawdy tune. He winked as Lette approached, and added red hair to the song's female lead. Lette tossed her knives, and knocked his juggling balls out of the air one by one. The bard decided to take a break from entertaining the crowd.

The oozing traffic finally congealed into a clotted mass at the city gates. Soldiers inspected wagons with painful thoroughness. Will, Lette, and Balur queued with increasing impatience for their turn to pass through the massive oak doors and under the yellow stone arch of the city walls.

And then they were through and into Bellenet proper. Noise enclosed them. Carts crammed into whatever space they could find, their owners not even pulling back their covering cloths before they started hawking their wares, mostly to the men and women they'd been queuing with only moments before.

Lette saw Will staring around wildly, trying to take it all in. It was probably the first city he had been in. Fields were what he knew. This place was more foreign to him than some rice paddy in the Fanlorn Empire might be.

For herself, Lette had grown up in Essoa, the Saleran capital. Her childhood had been a thrum of noise and energy. Family after family packed into a single house, meals a mess of siblings and cousins, the streets outside always bursting with life and sound.

She still liked cities. Their energy. Their potential. That she could always find a certain type of room containing the certain kind of man who always had the certain kind of job that required her particular talents. In a city there was always someone whose death would profit you.

Though, of course, she was still trying to leave that part of herself behind, trying not to be the woman who had plotted eight escape routes from these crowded, cluttered streets, or who had prioritized its occupants in the order of whom to kill first.

The question was, what to do instead? Four months after she had left Will, the best answer she had managed to come up with was pissing away all of her not-inconsiderable wealth on hedonistic pleasures. Which was all well and good until your ex wandered in on you in the arms of four whores. Which, no matter how stonily you set your face, couldn't help but be a touch embarrassing.

They pushed on through the clog of warehouses, wagons, and horseshit that made up the city's outer layer. They entered streets where children ran back and forth between slumping houses, and the smell of shit was no better than it had been back among the horses. Those led them to cobbled streets, strung with flowerpots and small market squares like beads on a merchant wife's necklace. And then, at last, the streets truly opened up, and the buildings stretched for the heavens. City guards wandered the streets greeting the populace with deference instead of suspicion. And that populace didn't scurry or bustle. Instead it took slow, refined steps, usually either to or from a carriage that waited, gilt gleaming, horses clicking their freshly shod hooves on sharp flagstones. The horses defecated here, just as they did at the city's limits, but their dung landed in baskets lined with rose petals, and there was an air of elegance to the whole business that Lette had never really anticipated before.

At last, with the sun slowly dipping toward the horizon, they arrived at the High Council buildings. They were a series of blunt limestone boxes set off from the streets by a high, wrought-iron fence. The gates were ostentatiously elegant. It was the first time Lette had seen filigree used as a weapon.

Just in case that didn't work to deter people, a squad of eight soldiers had been posted inside the gate, though how they were supposed to fight under the weight of all the braiding that decorated their costumes, Lette wasn't entirely sure. Fighting one of them would be like fighting a particularly well-coiffed sheep.

She hitched their horses to some posts outside a goldsmith's a few yards down the street.

"We'll need a plan," said Will. "Some sort of distraction to pull the guards away. And we'll need to be high up to go over the fence. Probably to one of the sides. And—"

While Lette was happy to see Will taking an active part in things again after ten days of sulking on the road, this was also a horribly misguided active part.

"Listen, you poorly educated child," she said and ignored his hurt expression. It was time to viciously assault Will with some knowledge. "We don't need a plan. Batarra is a meritocracy—"

"It is?" Will looked genuinely shocked.

Balur shook his head. "How long were you living here?"

Will shrugged. "I'm from Kondorra. I'm used to a government that takes ninety percent of everything I own every winter. Being able to ignore them here has been a luxury."

"Be quiet and listen," said Lette. "I'm educating. Meritocracy sounds like it means some sort of egalitarian paradise, but what it actually is, is another word for horrendously corrupt haven of bribe-mongers. So if you want into the corridors of power, you just need to have passed one of the entrance exams."

"But—" Will started, pointing at the guards.

"And if you want to pass one of the entrance exams," she went on, "you just have to pay the entrance fee."

Will's eyes suddenly narrowed. "What's the entrance fee?"

Lette smiled. Now he was catching up. "A thousand golden bulls minimum."

Will's jaw dropped. "A...a thousand...That's outrageous. That's utter hogshit. Who can afford that?"

Even naïveté, Lette reflected, *could lose its appeal over time.* She reached out and slapped Will full in the face. "We can, you ignorant arse!" She threw up her hands. "We robbed the dragons of Kondorra. We are obscenely rich. And we are in the heart of a country that is outrageously and preposterously corrupt. This is our fucking playground. We don't need a plan."

She turned to the guards at the gate. "A golden bull to whoever opens the gate for me first."

The guards fell over each other in their rush.

They spent another five hundred golden bulls between the front gate and the doors to High Council's chambers.

Will tried very hard to hide his disappointment, but in the end he just wasn't up to it. And there had been a time when she found his wide-eyed hope regarding Batarra so charming. After Kondorra, she knew, he had seen this as a place of hope and opportunity. He had told her about how free from persecution and crushing poverty it seemed.

And she hadn't had the heart to tell him.

Now...Now she still felt bad. But maybe it was what he needed. Maybe a few short, sharp shocks to his hopes and dreams would wake him up a little.

The particular official they were bribing at the moment finished counting his coins. He leered at them and pulled a vast ledger from a drawer in the desk where he sat. He was the last gatekeeper. He wore a blue velvet suit, buttoned tightly over a white shirt that seemed to consist entirely of ruffles. Behind him a pair of double oaken doors led into the High Council's chambers.

"All right," he said in a voice that Lette couldn't help but equate to that of a weasel, "let's see when I can pencil you in for."

From what Lette knew of Batarran power structures, this pompous plutocrat had paid in excess of ten thousand gold coins for the privilege of writing things in this particular ledger. It was one of the worst obscenities she knew. Apart from possibly the one involving a goat, two pigs, and a saltshaker.

"All right," said the man again, licking the nib of his quill. "I should be able to get you some time with the council for a month from now."

And that, Lette decided, was the point at which she was pretty much done with bribery.

But then, before she could get the blade into her hand, Will was stepping forward, face red, cords standing out in his neck. "A month?" he bellowed. "A fucking month?"

The man looked at them like he was regarding a trio of turds he had just found in his sandwich. "If you have an urgent matter," he said, "then you could always pay the expediting fee, though I hear that it has just gone up"—he glared at Will—"substantially."

Lette almost heard Will's patience snap.

He stepped forward, seized the man by the back of the head, and bounced his forehead off the surface of his absurd, ostentatious desk. He let go, and the man slumped to the floor. Without looking up, Will took the man's quill, found the date in the calendar, and wrote them down on the entirely empty page.

He straightened and shrugged. "Looks like we're in."

And there it was. Something of the old Will that she recognized. The purity of his outrage plucking at some deep resonance in her chest.

Balur clapped Will on the shoulder, making him stagger. "It is being good to have you back," he said.

Even as she strode toward the Council Chambers' double doors, Lette found she suddenly wished she had a mirror to check her reflection in.

8

Yes, Minister

As one, the Batarran High Council fell silent as Will, Lette, and Balur pushed into the room. They were, as far as Will could tell, in the middle of a card game. Most of the chairs on the chamber floor—usually reserved for plaintiffs and witnesses—had been pushed aside to make room for a large circular table topped with green felt, gold coins, and strong alcohol. The High Council sat around it holding fistfuls of cards. The stakes of the game, it seemed, were the councilors' clothes.

A large woman in her fifties, hair piled lopsided above her head, and with her unbuttoned dress half falling off her shoulder, looked about in confusion.

"Did we have any appointments today?" she said, slurring slightly. "I didn't think we had appointments."

A man, naked except for his underbritches and a cravat still knotted around his neck, leaned forward, attempted to prop himself up on his elbow, failed, fought not to collapse, and managed to thrust a finger at the woman. "Don't think this gets you out of it, Jocasta. You lost that hand fair and square."

The woman—Jocasta, Will supposed—looked from the half-naked man, to Will, to the other councilors. Then she shrugged, and started tugging the dress off her other shoulder.

If Will really thought about it, he supposed the only truly surprising thing was that she didn't have someone to help her do it.

"Sod off, would you?" said another man, wearing a mustard shirt, who had managed to retain at least one of his shoes.

Balur rolled his shoulders. Inhuman anatomy cracked audibly.

"Or," said another councilor who had a better view of Balur, "you know, you could stay."

"Deal the redhead in," said a man who had to be in his eighties. "She looks like she's got spunk."

"If she's in, then he's in." The woman who had taken off her dress, Jocasta, was pointing at Will.

Batarra, when Will had come here with Lette, had felt almost magical. The sun had felt different on his skin. The wind had sung a different tune between the trees. No dragon rode on its currents. No soldiers came and beat up his farmhands to remind him what would happen come tax season. There were no screams of livestock as savage claws lifted them to the heavens.

This had been his escape, his happily ever after. And then his love had left him. Dragons had come here to wreak their savagery upon everyone. And now all his hopes for good and just rulership were being savagely torn out from beneath his feet. Dispiriting did not do the experience justice.

And quite frankly, Will had had it with useless, overprivileged arseholes.

"Shut up!" he bellowed. "Shut up, all of you! Don't you know what's happening?"

This approach seemed to catch the High Council off guard. They blinked at him owlishly.

Behind him, Will felt Balur shifting his weight. "Maybe be taking it down a notch," the lizard man said in as much of a whisper as he could manage. "I am thinking that I am in there." He thumbed at a painfully thin woman, with hair stacked a foot high above her head. She was looking cross-eyed in their direction.

Will took a calming breath. It didn't really help.

"Dragons are going to steal this nation from you!" Will shouted. Though now that he saw who was in charge, it was a little harder to get worked up about it. He took firmer hold of his hatred of dragons. "Theerax has preachers in every corner of this city talking about the ills of the gods, and slowly convincing people they should be worshipping him."

Still the only response from the council was blinking. Will resisted the urge to tear out great chunks of his hair, so he could stuff them down their throats and choke them all. Finally one turned to another and said, "Is he talking about permits? Preachers without permits?"

Will advanced on the man, who was in his thirties and, if his chin was anything to go by, the product of several generations of inbreeding. "All this," he said, sweeping his hand at the table, and the alcohol, and the cards, and the coins, "is going to be taken away from you."

The man looked at him dubiously. "By priests? Don't be silly. You can't fit this table out the door. They had to build it in here. No knowledge of woodwork, priests. It's all chanting and writing with them. Obsessed with it, they are. Funny buggers, if you ask me."

"By a fucking dragon!" Will roared into the man's face.

"Don't we have guards for this sort of thing?" said someone else.

"Oh don't make them go yet," said another. "I think this is rather fun. I mean, look at how angry he is."

"I think he's an actor," said the woman who had been giving Balur the eye. "I think I saw him in a performance of *The Rape of Themalee.*"

"Oh I haven't seen that yet," said a third. "Is it any good?"

"He was quite good in it," said the cross-eyed woman, thumbing at Will. "The rest of them were a bit amateur."

"I wasn't," Will said through gritted teeth, "in any gods-hexed play."

"Are you sure?" a fourth councilor chipped in.

Will looked to Lette. "I thought you said they had to pass exams to get here."

Lette shrugged. "I don't think they're very hard exams."

"Be suggesting that you will be pulling their intestines out through their mouths," Balur suggested. "It is usually being quite effective when Lette is suggesting that."

"Do you juggle?" called another councilor.

"Whose hand is it?" said yet another, who didn't seem to have noticed the interruption to the card game yet.

"We're not seeing anyone today," said the woman Jocasta, putting a finger to her chin. "I remember it quite distinctly. I said to Fredricks outside that either that door stayed closed or my legs did. I was very clear on the whole issue."

Will had had enough. He got up on the table and started kicking things over. As drinks spilled and coins went flying he felt he was finally getting their attention.

"I," he said, "am Willet Fallows, prophet of Kondorra. I have led an army. I have organized the death of dragons, and you will fucking listen to me, or I swear by Lawl's black fucking eye, Batarra will not have a council tomorrow."

"Are we getting a day off?" asked someone from behind him.

"No," Will snapped, "you are getting your shit together. There is a dragon at the gates, and he is telling how he's going to steal the heavens from the gods. And along the way he's going to take your country from you. So you are going to organize. You are going to get your military together and you are going to kick him and his preachers out of here. Because otherwise he is going to kill you. Each and every one. He is going to take all your wealth, all your power, and keep it only for himself."

He turned in a slow circle, fixing each of them with his gaze, one by one.

And he was angry, and his heart was racing, and his breath was coming fast, and his fists were shaking, and he felt hot, and as if his shirt neck was slightly too small, but gods, he also felt fully alive for the first time since...since Kondorra.

Jocasta held his gaze. "You, sir," she said, "are a bully."

And abruptly it was Will's turn to blink.

"You come in here," she went on. "You shout at us. You threaten us. You demand you have your way. You say someone is talking against the gods. Let them talk. This is Batarra. People can say things you don't like. That's allowed. We're not going to hunt them down for you. You can't bully us, sir. Not you. Not your devilishly attractive companion, nor your pet monkey-lizard. Though if your devilishly attractive companion would like to join me and Fredricks later, then she is more than welcome."

Will was still reeling a little. A bully? Him? He suddenly felt absurd, standing up on the table and throwing a tantrum at them all. How in the Hallows had that happened?

"It's a dragon," he said, pleading. "It's not a someone. It's a dragon. And it doesn't matter what he says. He wants to take this kingdom over and force it into slavery. It's what they want. They're animals."

"Says you," said Jocasta, still bristling. "I don't know who you are. You don't have any proof you're even from Kondorra. We need someone like that expert...what's her name. That one from Tamar. Begins with a *Q*..."

Will threw up his hands. "I know Quirk! She's a personal friend."

Jocasta rolled her eyes. "Prove it."

"Ask her," said Will with a certain amount of heat.

"Will," said someone else, "she's three hundred leagues away." It was Lette, he realized. He turned and looked at her.

"Look," Lette said, ignoring the council's blather, "the way I see it we have two options. One, we can kill all of these fools." She indicated the council with a sweep of her hand. "Take control. Fight off all those that resist the coup, and take control of the rest of the army."

Neither Will nor the council seemed to be a big fan of this option. Balur looked hopeful, though.

"Or," said Lette, "we could find someone they do trust, get him to accompany us, and show that person. Then they report back, and these people remove all their fingers from their arses and do something."

"Of the two," said no-chin, "I think I like the second one more."

"Is there any way," asked the cross-eyed woman, "that we can get to keep the big monkey-lizard as some sort of hostage?" She winked at the room in general.

"Just so you know," said Balur, "I am being fine with that."

Will was looking at Lette. She shrugged and a knife appeared in her hand as if by magic. A couple of the council members still capable of paying attention started backing away from the table and toward the door.

And part of Will did want to take option one. He did want all of these arseholes to die. They were small, and petty, and awful. He wanted to end them the same way he had ended the dragons. He wanted to be the man Lette had thought he was.

But of course, if he did that, then really he would be small, and petty, and awful. And murderous to boot.

He looked at all the smug, overprivileged faces staring at him.

"An observer then," he said.

Then he tried to pretend that part of him didn't regret it.

9

Home Sweet Home

Quirk cast furtive glances about the Tamathian University as she made her way through it. Striding down its familiar corridors and past its once-comforting courtyards, she felt as if every eye was on her. Expressions curdled. Boisterous conversations died. Whispers slithered back and forth. She tried to control herself, to keep her shoulders straight, hold her head high. She had nothing to apologize for. This was her gods-hexed home.

It just didn't feel that way anymore.

In her sleeve, her pamphlets felt heavy.

Diffinax was a landslide in Tamar now. No one had seen him, and yet still his name was on every set of lips. His message was echoed on every street corner. Order had been lost from the world. The gods were to blame. Diffinax was their savior.

In its worst extreme, groups calling themselves Diffinites would patrol the street, setting right the things they saw as wrong. Exactly what definition of wrong they used depended on the makeup of the group. Some hated sodomizers. Others hated those with pale skin. Others found those who hewed to a particular god especially offensive. Diffinax's message was significantly lacking in details. It simply required dissatisfaction. Hatred was an added bonus.

One day she had found a boy called Eyter lying in a pool of his own blood outside one of Toil's temples. He had had the temerity to question the wisdom behind a dragon threatening to overthrow the gods. Some Diffinites had taken offense. Quirk had helped him to safety, helped bind his wounds, and then helped him make his way home.

It turned out Eyter worked at the university printing press. It turned out Eyter had not been cowed by the Diffinites. It turned out that this caused several nebulous ideas to condense suddenly in Quirk's mind.

So now Quirk wrote pamphlets protesting Diffinax's presence. Eyter laid them out after-hours at the printing press and left her the copies to pick up. Each time she had searched for the magic combination of words that would unlock the truth in people's minds. Each time it had felt like the stakes had grown higher.

Distribution was the worst part, though. Walking about with a stack of pamphlets hidden on her. She could not simply hand them out at a street corner. It would be like handing out invitations asking the Diffinites to come and beat her to death. And no one wanted to be seen taking the pamphlets, lest they offer the same invitation. Instead she had to find the right places to leave them. Where they could be stumbled over, and taken without attracting attention.

She knew it was working, though. She had heard her words discussed in the quad. Never flattering words. But discussed all the same.

Let that be enough. Please Knole, let that be enough.

She finally made it through the gauntlet of unfriendly corridors and reached the door to the stairs to her garret. Breathing a sigh, she pulled it open and stepped into the welcome shadows.

"Quirk."

She felt as if she had been gut punched. Afrit's voice hissed out of the stairwell, soft and urgent.

"Quirk, we have to talk. This can't wait."

Flame leapt in Quirk's heart.

"No!" she heard herself shriek, more at the impulse to burn

than at the woman who was stepping away from the wall to block her passage up the stairs. She pushed bodily past, sending Afrit staggering, and started up the stairs.

"I have to warn you!" Afrit called after her. "You can't go up there!"

Quirk kept her head down. She did not trust Afrit. Ferra had gotten his information somewhere, and no one had showed more interest in her than Afrit.

She could hear the young professor running up the stairs after her. "I don't know what I have done to offend you," Afrit was calling inanely. "But you can't. You mustn't."

Suddenly a new fear gripped Quirk. That Afrit was there to delay her intentionally, to buy someone else time. Was Ferra up there now? In her rooms?

She redoubled her pace, made the top of the twisting staircase, looked down the long wooden corridor. It was dark, and smelled musty, the far wall truncated as it reached the slope of the eaves.

Men were at her door. Three of them. Two had the bulk of soldiers, or whatever sort of all-purpose thug Ferra hired. The third wore robes and was stooped, fiddling at her door.

This time Quirk let the fire rise in her of her own volition. She felt her palms growing hot.

"Get the fuck away from my door." She cursed not for Ferra's benefit, but for her own, to pump the boiling blood through her system faster.

The two heavies turned. The robed figure straightened abruptly, started striding toward her. Quirk set her feet.

And then stopped, caught off guard.

It was not Ferra.

"Chancellor?" she said. The head of the university was walking toward her, a stern expression on his face. "I didn't...I'm sorry. I...What can I do for you?"

Chancellor Trillidunce was a tall man with an athlete's build, belying the fact that he was in fact one of the foremost experts on empirical law in the country. She had seen him debate with the skill and grace of a fencer. It had been he who had agreed to house a rabid wastelands wastrel who had burned and raged her way through a hundred lives before her sixteenth birthday. And while he had never taken a personal role in her recovery, he had always existed in the background of her life—a smiling benefactor; the university's own kind god.

Now he looked ready to launch a thunderbolt.

"Is it true?" he said without preamble.

Quirk felt her brows furrow, even as her gut lurched. She had absolutely no idea what Trillidunce was talking about. There were too many things he could mean. Behind her, she heard Afrit make the top of the stairs. Gods, she did not want that woman observing this.

"Is what true?"

She was trying to picture the still lake. To become its surface, smooth and calm. It was about as much use as pissing on a forest fire.

"That you're writing this filth?" He reached into his sleeve, and for a moment Quirk had the absurd idea he was going for a knife. Flame pulsed inside her skull.

Trillidunce pulled out a sheaf of papers, flung them at her. Her own flyers piled about her feet.

She felt Afrit stepping down the corridor toward her. "Can we talk about this in my rooms?" she said. Trying not to snap at him. Trying not to plead.

"Search her," snapped Trillidunce.

"What?" Quirk managed to say, but then the two university guards had her by the arms, were pinning her against the wall. One held her, while the other ran his hands lightly over her frame.

Burn him. Burn him. Burn him.

She closed her eyes, breathed slowly through her nose.

"If we find nothing on you," said the Chancellor, sounding as if he was speaking through gritted teeth, "then we search your rooms. If we find nothing there, then you may talk."

The guard's hand went up her sleeve, fastened on the sheaf of papers she had hidden there.

BURN HIM!

This is my home...

The guard ripped the latest set of pamphlets free from her grasping hands, shoved them toward the Chancellor. He looked them over, quivering with silent rage.

Back at the stairs, Afrit turned and ran away. No doubt gone to report to her secret masters.

Trillidunce looked up from the flyers. "So it's true." His voice was flat but there was cold fury in his eyes.

"Why are you doing this?" It made no sense to her. Trillidunce had a brilliant mind. For more than three decades he had fostered the Tamathian University's long history of academic brilliance and helped forge the place into a modern intellectual and financial powerhouse. He had a magpie's eye for valuable minds, gathering them up regardless of appearance, or political leaning.

"Because I will tolerate a lot, Bal Tehrin, but I will not tolerate..." He sputtered for a moment. "Filth!" he finally spat.

He was literally frothing with rage, she realized. Only just holding it together. And the flame inside her quailed for a moment at that realization. That anything, let alone her, could have inspired so much rage and hatred in someone. Maybe before...back when she had been Hethren's tool. But now?

"You would censor me?" She couldn't believe it. Not even as it was happening.

What in the Hallows *was* happening?

"Censor you?" Trillidunce was still stuck a thought behind her. He had a look of horror on his face. Not, she thought, that he had been accused, but that it was she who had accused him.

That someone as low and craven and her should dare. That was what had held him up.

"You can publish whatever filth you want, Bal Tehrin." Her name was a stain upon his tongue. "You just can't do it here."

"What?" She didn't understand. She was too caught off guard to process what he was saying. She struggled against the hands of the guards holding her to the wall, but they didn't release their pressure.

"You are no longer a professor here, Bal Tehrin. You are no longer housed here. You are no longer spoken of. You are excised from this university. Your possessions will be burned, your rooms scrubbed. Your students will be told to forget your teachings. You do not exist to us. You are nothing to us."

And like that, fire died.

"What?" Quirk managed. "What?"

But Trillidunce wasn't listening to her. "Get her out of here," he said to the two guards.

And so they did. They dragged her down the corridor by her arms. Dragged her down the stairs and past the courtyards. They dragged her past staring, whispering students. Past the classroom where she had taught her first class. Past the lecture hall where she had received a standing ovation after her first talk about the dragons of Kondorra. Past the spot where, unable to contain her excitement until she was back in her room, she had opened her first invitation from the Emperor. Past the sunny spot in the corner of a courtyard where she had composed most of her first folio. Past the temple of Knole, where she had discovered the first peace she had known in seventeen years. Past the corner where she had conceded a kiss to a student ten years her junior and discovered that it meant nothing to her. Past the spot where she had lost her temper in an argument about the vestigial thumbs of Fanlornian Murk Apes and almost roasted a professor alive. Past the spot where she had tentatively started to carve her name into the stone of the college with a knife, and stopped after the letter Q because it felt like sacrilege, and she realized that this was now her home. Past the place where Trillidunce had told her that she could move her things up into the abandoned garret she'd been bothering him about. Past the gatehouse that had seemed so forbidding and cruel when she had first been taken across it. Past Tamper, the old doorman, sitting there, nodding to himself with a look of grim satisfaction on his face.

And then she landed on the street, in a pile of her own limbs, and tears, and confusion. Around her, pedestrians were shying away, staring down in confusion and mild disgust. Not a single expression of pity met her there on the street.

She looked back at the university. Tamper was pushing the door shut for the first time she could remember. The guards stood behind it, hands on thick black coshes tied to their waists. When had the university guards started carrying those?

She stood only slowly, staring at the uncaring wood of the university door. And she could ... could ... what?

She couldn't burn it. Even if the fire was raging in her, she couldn't burn it. It was too precious. She loved that wood. Even in this moment as it rejected her. She loved that institution with everything she had. And it was lost to her. She was a widow. This was grief.

She stumbled away. She *had* to get away. That was all she knew in this moment. That she couldn't even look at the university. She had to ... to ... to ... She didn't know. She couldn't know. The wound was too fresh in her mind.

She wandered. She found herself facing the south wall of the university. She walked away, cursing at herself. She ended up at the blank east wall. The city had become a labyrinth, the university her own personal lodestone. She could not escape.

"There she is!" A rough shout that only punched through her confusion because it was so obviously aimed at her. She reeled round as if she had been in her cups all day.

A group of youths. Their heads shaved almost clean, except for "dragon tails" of hair plaited down their necks. They held wooden staves.

Diffinites.

"No," she muttered. Not now. She couldn't deal with this now. She was too off balance. And this felt timed. Ferra's hand behind everything. The sly conductor to all events. She shook her head, trying to clear it.

The Diffinites approached, whistling to each other, twirling their staves. "Not now," she said out loud, thoughts still feeling sluggish. "Come back during my office hours."

They were laughing at her. A crowd was gathering.

"Fuck off!" she screamed. And there were tears on her face. "Leave me alone!" People jeered. They crowed.

The first stave caught her in the gut, doubled her over. She gasped as the world came into sharp focus. As the pain grounded her deeply and sharply in the now. Spit sprayed from her lips. She tried to stand straight, couldn't.

Another stave in the middle of her hunched back, knocked her to the floor. And she was angry. So very angry all of a sudden. That this was happening now, of all the times it could happen. And it was an absurd reason to be angry, some part of her knew, but it didn't stop her anger.

And her anger was always hot.

Another stave, this one to her face. She felt her lip split, felt blood flow. She felt the heat of it on her face. She raised a shaking hand to her face, pulled it away smeared with red. She was gasping, her breath coming in short staccato bursts.

The Diffinites pulled back, stood in a circle around her to admire their handiwork. She managed to get to her knees, sat back gasping, blowing bubbles through the blood streaming down her chin. She could see men and women standing around staring, half-fascinated, half-horrified, none of them doing anything except watching.

One of the Diffinites, a woman who could be no more than twenty-two or twenty-three, stepped forward. She twisted, her stave grasped in both hands, poised to torque her full body weight into the blow she was aiming at Quirk's face.

Quirk didn't even remember stretching out her hand. But the woman simply disappeared. There was no longer a torturing, leering figure in front of her. There was simply a pyre, a torch blazing against the radiance of the sun high above. Defying it.

This is the gods, she thought. *This is their lack of a shit for all your posturing bullshit. They reached down and they touched* me. *They gave* me *this power.*

The Diffinites were recoiling, confusion and horror raging through them, still not sure what was happening.

Quirk set them ablaze one by one. She took her time. And gods, it felt good. Watching their eyes go wide as they realized what was happening, what she was doing.

This is how you fight back, the fire whispered in her ear as it rushed up and through her. *This is how you teach the world a lesson and bend it to your will.*

The last of the Diffinites was running, screaming. She stretched out a palm toward him. Around her, the other Diffinites were writhing, slowly going still. She exhaled slowly. Flame burst from her palm. A thick lash of it that raced out and filled the space between her and the running Diffinite. For a moment she could clearly see the thin yellow strands she wrapped around him in a tight embrace, then they blurred together in a yellow smear of fire. The Diffinite dropped and howled.

Quirk let the fire die. Felt the cool air of Tamathia's afternoon on her smoking palm. The screams around her were very clear.

The screams.

And then she realized what she had done. Then she saw the crowd staring, and screaming, and screaming, and screaming. She smelled the burning flesh.

Again.

Oh gods. Oh no. Oh what had she done?

She sank to her knees, buried her face in her hands.

There were footsteps. She heard a voice. "Come on. Come on. You have to get out of here." Someone pulled at her arm. She ignored whoever it was. It was too much. Everything was too much.

Then there were other footsteps, heavier, accompanied by the sharp clank and clap of steel. City guards. Whoever was pulling at her arm melted away.

They struck her from behind, a short, hard blow to the back of the neck, and then she knew nothing more.

10

Alcoholics Go to Meetings

The headsman's block, Firkin decided, was not a good sign.

That said, he really did have to hand it to the High Priesthood of Vinland. If anybody was looking for interior decorating tips on how to achieve the opulent dictator look, these were the guys to know. It made him think that everything he'd achieved in Kondorra was a bit paltry.

Though, to be fair, these bastard priests hadn't really given him the time to develop his themes in Kondorra. He'd still been preoccupied with the process of consolidating his power base. Before he'd had time to really grapple with the aesthetic of his rule, they'd come and stolen his nation from him.

It had been three weeks since Vinland had annexed his fledgling nation. Three weeks that he'd spent on the road in a prisoner's cart, hands and feet chained. He could not be allowed to remain among his people, he was told, lest he become a rallying point for resistance. Firkin had tried to explain they didn't need to worry about that sort of shit. His whole using-a-servant-as-a-footstool thing seemed to be fresh in a lot of people's minds. But they hadn't listened. And, truth be told, spending three weeks out of his gourd in a wagon hadn't been too bad. That was the nice thing about being captured and taken as a hostage of war by the Vinlanders, at least: not much food, but plenty of drink.

But now, for perhaps the first time in his life, he found himself wishing he was perhaps just a hair more sober.

They'd been passing through vineyards for days, drunken farmhands looking up from reeling through their fields to watch the procession of soldiers on the road, when finally the walls of Vinter had lurched onto the horizon. They had looked exactly like what they were—the efforts of the religiously inebriated. They slouched around the city, sprawling, exploding into tumors of creative masonry, then lapsing into sections that appeared to be little more than heaps of piled stones. Guards stood upon the wall, most of them fast asleep, snoring loudly, heads pressed to their poleaxes.

Inside its walls, the Vinland capital was vast. An expanse of stone and mortar that boggled Firkin's already well-boggled mind. He had been to Vinland a long, long time ago, had loved it even, but had not seen it in…what? Decades? When had he been here last? It all seemed very hazy. But he knew he had never conceived that the city could grow so large.

The whole place stank of yeast and fermentation, stale beer and spilled vomit. It was a fetid, dirty, redolent city. His cart had rolled past men and women fighting, and singing. Street sweepers had waved brooms laconically at the tides of filth. A heavy, misty fug seemed to hang in the air. The light was diffuse and red. Every other building was a temple. Statues of Barph rose at every street corner. Preachers stood shouting the tenets of his worship, and pouring out libations into the mouths of worshippers slumped around them.

It was so beautiful, Firkin had thought he might actually weep. He'd felt like he'd come home.

And now this headsman's block bullshit.

He was still in his chains, on his knees now, in the highest temple of them all. A vast edifice of red brick, the same color as day-old vomit. The High Priesthood were assembled on a dais before him, sitting on gold-encrusted thrones, wearing robes of chardonnay yellow and claret crimson.

"Firkin," intoned one, and then stopped. "Wait...what's his title?"

"Do they have kings in Kondorra?" said another. She attempted to lean on the armrest of her throne, and missed. She swayed dangerously in her chair.

"They have dragons," said another, nodding sagely.

"He doesn't look like a dragon," said the third.

"Maybe he's in disguise."

The fourth just stared at him.

"Are you a dragon in disguise?" asked the first High Priest.

Firkin looked around. One of the guards shook a spear in Firkin's direction.

"Answer his inebriatedness!"

Firkin blinked. "No," he said.

The priests all nodded. All except the fourth, who was still staring.

"That's good," he heard one of them mutter. "All be a bit fucked if we'd brought a dragon back here."

"Do we really need to know his title if we're just going to kill him?" asked the third. "Seems kind of pointless."

"Yes!" shouted the second, waving her goblet around, while the poor servant attempted to fill it. "Of course we do. Protocol is very...it's very...what's the word?"

They stared blankly at her.

"Important?" Firkin hazarded.

"Shut up!" screamed spear-enthusiast guard.

"Oh hush," said the second High Priest, flapping her hand at the guard. Then she smiled at Firkin. "Important, exactly. Protocol is important. It's nice to have a prisoner who recognizes that."

Firkin bobbed his head. "Good to appreciate the little things," he said. Then added as an afterthought, "and the big things too.

People always go on about the little things, but big grand gestures deserve love too, I say."

"That's a good point as well," said the second High Priest. She sampled her freshly filled goblet and smiled happily.

"Wait..." said the first. "So what do we do if we don't know his title?"

"Well," said the woman, "we'll just have to ask him what it was. Find out."

The first High Priest turned to Firkin. "All right then," he said. "What was your title back in Kondorra?"

Firkin thought about that. "Just to be clear," he said, desperately fighting for clarity in his foggy thoughts, "you can only kill me if you know my title?"

The spear enthusiast quivered. "Do not question—" he started.

"Shut up!" yelled the third High Priest. He rolled his eyes. "Can't get the staff these days."

"Well..." Firkin gave a sheepish grin. "Doesn't lend me much incentive to tell you."

"I could torture it out of him," said the spear enthusiast, almost vibrating out his boots. His level of energy was really starting to irritate Firkin.

It also made him suspicious. Firkin turned accusing eyes on the guard. "Are you even drunk?" he asked.

The guard looked horrified. "I took my prescribed three shots of whiskey along with everyone else in the barracks. You ask any of them."

"Torture would probably be a pretty quick solution to everything," said the third High Priest.

The fourth kept up his dead-eyed stare.

Firkin thought desperately. "Wait!" he shouted. Then he tried to think of something that they should have waited for. He turned back to the guard. "So you had your three whiskeys, because that's the rule? Because that's what you were told to do? Because Barph just loves slavish following of rules. That's what

Barph is all about. Lawl's little lapdog, isn't he? Doing whatever he's told!"

He glared daggers at the guard, while appreciating the way his voice bounced off the temple's stone walls. The acoustics really were excellent.

"I..." the guard spluttered. "That's not..."

"He does have a point," said the first priest, who seemed interested in the whole exchange. "When I was in the guards I was always stealing other folks' whiskey. Start off the day with a good buzz. If I had trouble tying my laces, I knew I was in a good spot."

"I've got a buzz!" said the guard.

Firkin thought he smelled blood in the water. "I don't think you do," he said, as viciously as he could manage. "I think you've built up a tolerance. I think you're almost entirely sober."

"It's a lie!" screamed the guard. "A vicious, ugly lie!" But his hand on his spear was shaking.

Three of the four High Priests looked at each other. The fourth remained resolute in staring at Firkin.

The first priest pursed his lips. The other two shrugged. The first turned to the guard. "You," he said, "say the alphabet backwards."

"What?" the guard looked confused. "You want me to... erm... Z, Y, X." He looked about for help. The servants were all staring at their feet and shuffling. "W, V, U, erm, T, S."

"Shut up," snapped the priest. "I've heard enough."

The guard sagged against his spear in relief.

"Come into this fucking chamber, and you're so sober you can say the alphabet backwards. I can barely even remember what a letter is right now. You sicken me. Take him to the headsman's block."

"What?" said the guard!

But two of the other guards around Firkin sighed and grabbed their companion. He kicked and screamed, and the third smashed him in the mouth with the butt of his own spear. The guard sagged, then was unceremoniously dragged to the headsman's block and held in place. The headsman gathered up his axe and quietly did his job.

The first priest clapped. "Lovely," he said. "I love that part."

The second priest was less easily distracted. "We still don't know his title," she said, pointing at Firkin.

"Weren't we going to torture him?" said the third.

And the fourth stared.

"Is he all right?" Firkin asked, pointing.

The other three looked at the fourth. "Oh by Barph's hairy balls," said the second.

"Not again," said the first.

"Somebody shake him," said the third.

A servant ran forward and shook the priest. He slumped stiffly to the floor. The servant screamed.

"If they refuse to check their livers before they promote people," said the second to anyone who would listen, "this is going to keep on happening."

The first sighed. "Someone take him away and tell the clerics we need a fourth High Priest again."

"Good spot," said the third, nodding to Firkin. "The last one started to smell before anyone noticed."

"What were we talking about, again?" said the first, who seemed distracted by the group of servants fussing around the dead priest.

"Torture, I think," said the second, who was far more persistent on the subject than Firkin had hoped.

"My title," he said, trying to ride over her.

"That was it." The first clicked his fingers. "We don't know it, and we're going to torture it out of you." He smiled. "It's all coming back to me now."

Firkin's mind reached speeds that he usually tried to avoid.

He could feel a violent hangover coming on. "What if..." he said, playing for time. "I...I didn't have a title?"

The three surviving priests looked perplexed by this statement. "But you were in charge of Kondorra," said the first. He sounded irritated. "Of course you had a title."

Anger was not the reaction Firkin had been aiming for. He tried to steer them more toward sympathy, affecting a mournful air. "My lack of a title was a great tragedy," he said, bullshitting wildly. "It was about to be enacted, but unfortunately—and I know you didn't intend this—but you invaded before we could come up with a title."

The three High Priests looked momentarily horrified.

"Well," said the first, staring tragically into his empty cup. "That's awkward."

"Don't think that's happened before," said the third.

"Men always say that," said the second priest, waving her cup at more servants.

"I am terribly sorry," said the third, addressing Firkin directly. Firkin shrugged, trying to suggest he understood, and felt bad that he'd raised such an awkward subject. But honestly it was getting increasingly difficult to work out what in the Hallows was going on.

He flailed for a plan. "What if," he said, "you gave me a title?"

The priests looked at each other. "Us?" asked the first.

"Just something lowly in the priesthood," Firkin suggested.

"Well that would be pretty decent of you," said the second. "Help us out a lot."

"Does that mean there won't be any torture?" The third sounded sad.

"We could make him, erm..." The second drummed her fingers. "What do altar attendants do?"

"Blow me mostly," said the first priest, with a bored look.

The third roused himself from his despondency long enough to nod.

"Maybe not that," Firkin hazarded.

The second nodded. "Maybe something clerical. In the Third District?"

"That's a shitty district," said the third. "What's wrong with an altar attendant?"

"Do you really want to be blown by him?" The second priest nodded at Firkin, who smiled, showing his haphazardly placed, browning teeth.

The third priest blanched. "The Third District then."

"Seconded," said the first priest.

The second priest nodded. "And so it is writ." They all went to take a sip from their glasses. Then there was a pause as servants rushed to fill them. Firkin shuffled a little more toward the back of the room.

"So," he said, once the High Priests were settled, "I should probably be off to the Third District then."

The second priest narrowed her eyes. "Why?"

"Oh," said Firkin as nonchalantly as possible, "I'm a cleric there. It's a shitty district. Lots to sort out there. Wouldn't want to trouble you with all the things going on there. Breakouts of sobriety. That sort of thing."

The priests blanched. "Sobriety? Gods."

The first shuddered. "I can't even." He drank deeply again.

"So I'll be off then?" said Firkin. He grinned hopefully at his surrounding guards.

"Yes," said the first. "Sobriety? Barph be pissed upon. Deal with that now. And wear gloves."

"But weren't we—" started the third.

"Sobriety, man!" shouted the first priest. And drank again. The second was still working through her recently filled glass and seemed on the verge of falling out of her chair.

Firkin took the opportunity to quietly step away.

11

Substandard Subterfuge

Lying on his stomach in the soft Batarran grass, the sun stretching lazy fingers over the horizon, Will wondered which God hated him so much.

Next to Will, lay Cyrill.

Cyrill was the independent observer that the Batarran High Council had provided to himself, Lette, and Balur. Cyrill was the man they had determined best suited to accompanying them on a mission to infiltrate the ranks of the Theerax worshippers and to elucidate whether the dragon had nefarious plans to take over the country.

Cyrill was approximately eighty years old, and it was not the good eighty years. It was not the spry, leather-skinned eighty that came with a dry wit and knowing ways. Not even the slightly delirious, flirtatious eighty that came with the joyful knowledge that here one had finally arrived at the stage of life where one no longer had to give a shit. Cyrill was the sort of eighty that looked like it had been arrived at through slow erosion, until all that was left was a papery rag of a human being. Internal structures seemed to be subsiding, the man collapsing in on himself, achieving a strangely bent and bloated configuration. And honestly, if Cyrill managed to actually observe anything at all, Will would be shocked. He peered out at the world through rheumy eyes mostly hidden behind thick, bulbous lids.

What was more—indeed, what was worse—Cyrill loved

only one thing in life. And that thing was not task of observing the world. In fact, in the three days he had known Cyrill—and when Cyrill had not been rhapsodizing on the object of his desire—the old man had filled in the silences by talking about how much he disliked being an observer. "Sixty years of being passed over for promotion," uttered in Cyrill's dry, creaking tones, was a refrain that played in Will's dreams now.

And still, so very much worse than this was Cyrill's great love.

"You're going to be observing Theerax!" Will had shouted at the old man back in his cramped office in the Batarran council buildings.

"Theerax?" Cyrill had whispered back, his voice drawn taut.

"He is being a big dragon arsehole," Balur had explained. "He is trying to convince everyone else to be an arsehole too."

Balur had been crammed into Cyrill's office like a lion in a dog kennel. But Cyrill, it turned out, didn't have much of a sense of self-preservation. Instead, at Balur's pronouncement, Cyrill had begun to show signs of life Will had been worried simply weren't present.

"You take that back!" he had screeched, waving a finger threateningly, and squinting. Because—and Will really had to take a moment to appreciate this—he was having trouble picking out the only eight-foot-tall lizard man in the room.

"Theerax is a prophet!" Cyrill had gnashed his teeth as he talked. "He is a glory! A masterpiece of scale and muscle!" He had waved his finger again. "You willfully ignorant Philistines!"

Looking back on it, that had probably been the point when Will had probably been most tempted to murder every Batarran in the Council Chambers. But his sanity had finally emerged—beaten and panting hard—to rein him in.

"Look," he had said, imitating a placating voice. "You get to come with us and observe some people who are just like you. Who believe exactly what you do. It's basically just socializing."

Cyrill had sneered at him. "You think I'll share anything with you? That I'll take you to where Theerax himself has landed in Batarra? Where his worshippers are gathering at this very moment?" He stared at them defiantly.

And finally Will had smiled, because it turned out that when the gods shat on people, they at least shat on everybody equally.

"You know what?" he had said to Cyrill. "Now I do."

And so with a little light encouragement, and with Will working out several of his anger issues, the old man had. And now Will lay in the grass, next to Cyrill, and Balur, and Lette, and he looked down on the encampment where Theerax was amassing his worshippers. And he had the distinct impression that the gods were not done messing with him.

He had known that Theerax was popular, that his followers were legion, but the scale of the encampment still caught him off guard. A city of white tents lay before them. A stockade had been raised around it, which meant that somewhere else a bunch of people must be wondering where their forest had gone. Guards in uniforms of black and red stood outside thick gates.

There's a dragon in there, Will thought, and for a moment the world seemed to retreat as a scrim of red fell before his eyes and a roaring started to fill his ears. He was possessed by the urge to charge down the street, scale the walls, and go hunting. That victory was impossible without an army or two at his back seemed like a negligible concern.

He was brought back to reality by Lette's hand on his arm. "Don't make me have to go and find stones for your cairn," she whispered.

Which was actually the sweetest thing she'd said to him in a while, and made him feel a little better about everything.

The road they had abandoned two miles back led to the gate a few hundred yards to their right. As they watched now, a wagon laden with a family's worldly possessions rumbled toward the encampment. A couple sat at the front, she leaning her head on his shoulder as he held the reins. Two children sat on top of the piles of possessions, waving their arms and shouting happily. A third child scampered after the cart, while a dog yapped at her heels. The couple waved to the guards, who waved cheerily back. They pushed open the gates and the wagon rolled in.

"Very sinister," Cyrill said, the sarcasm palpable.

"All right," Balur said, nodding thoughtfully to himself. "Lette will be throwing her knives and taking out the guards, while I am charging the gates directly. We will be breaking through and carving a path—"

He cut off as he checked Will's expression. On the other side of the lizard, Cyrill was turning unusual shades of purple and mauve.

Will grinned inanely. "He's just joking." And then, because he hadn't even convinced himself: "You're here to observe Theerax, remember. No need to observe us." He hoped his smile was more winning than it felt.

Lette sighed. "Just…" She shook her head. "What's the actual plan, Will?"

Will had not, he decided, been born with deceptive sweat glands. His heart and mind were willing and able when it came to subterfuge, but his sweat glands were scrupulously honest. The wind and weather were brisk, and yet as their cart rolled toward Theerax's waiting encampment, he was slowly pickled in his own brine.

There were three guards at the gates, each holding a tall pike, each topped with a vicious-looking blade. But their faces stood in contrast to their weapons, broad and open, plastered with the sorts of smiles Will associated with the mothers of small children and village idiots.

"Welcome!" called one.

"May the wind of Theerax's wings fill the sails of your life," called another.

"And his flame warm your heart," called the third.

From inside the cart and under several blankets, Balur snorted derisively. Which did nothing for Will's sweat problem, and made Lette grind her teeth audibly.

"You are the thermals beneath his wings." Cyrill surprised them by calling out to the guards. He seemed to have forgotten a lot of his trepidation as they had drawn closer and closer to the encampment. Perched on blankets in the back of their wagon, he was virtually giddy. Though perhaps that was just knowing that if he shifted his weight inappropriately, Balur would bite his balls off through the fabric.

"You are well met on the sky flight of your life," said the tallest of the guards, apparently their leader, as they pulled up outside the gates. "Do you seek to open your lives to the glory and order of Theerax into your lives?"

"Yes!" Cyrill blurted, while Will shrugged and muttered, "Sure."

"Not really," Lette said, sotto voce. Will nudged her. She should be taking this more seriously.

"Then welcome to our humble encampment," said the tall guard. His smile was so unmoving that Will was beginning to wonder if the man was seriously intoxicated.

Cyrill leaned forward and asked, "Is it true that Theerax himself is here?"

The guard's smile widened, which Will would not have guessed was possible. There was something vaguely nauseating about the expression.

"All secrets will be revealed behind these walls," he said with a dangerously delusional twinkle in his eye. Will started to question if the man was wholly sane.

Cyrill, independent observer that he was, clapped his hands in delight. Meanwhile the other two guards pushed the gates of the camp open.

"Lax security," Lette muttered as she twitched the reins and their wagon rolled forward. And for the first time since his departure from the brothel in Pekarra, doubt entered Will's mind.

Then the gates slammed shut behind them. Will looked around, startled by the volume of the sound. The gates, which had looked like loosely knit pilings from the outside, were bound with thick bars of black iron on the inside. Three great, iron-shod poles of wood now barred it. Twelve guards in full armor, wielding their pikes with significantly more menace than the ones outside, were leveling their weapons at them.

Or alternatively, Will thought, *I've been right about all this from the start.*

"Off the wagon!" screamed one of the guards.

Will hesitated for at least half of half a second, a look of bewilderment on his face. The guard lunged at him with the pike. Will flinched, as the guards must have known he would, and the guard smashed him in the temple with the flat of his blade. Will tumbled arse over elbow off the front of the wagon and down into the mud of the encampment. The impact echoed hollowly through his skull.

He picked himself up, staggering slightly. Lette was on the floor, looking remarkably at ease given the amount of weaponry being thrust in their direction. Cyrill was on his knees, bent forward with his nose in the dirt and his hands covering his head.

"Up against the wall!" shrieked another guard, and Will received another smack on the back of the head, sending him stumbling toward the stockade wall. "Know your place!" the guard went on. "The key to truth is order! The key to happiness is acceptance! Accept your place in the dirt beneath my heels!"

Will felt his fist ball up, even as spots danced in front of his eyes. Then he felt a grip on his arm, pulling him back. He jerked his arm away but the grip was firm.

"Stop being a fucking idiot," Lette hissed, closer to his ear than he expected. "We're not here to start a fight."

"Move the wagon!" barked another of the guards, and two men jumped up into the seat of the cart.

"Hey!" Will snapped. "That's our—" Then he cut off. *That's our place where we hide our giant lizard man friend* didn't sound like the right thing to say at that moment.

The butt of a pike hit him in the stomach before he had time to think of a better way to end the sentence.

"All property belongs to Theerax!" yelled a guard with zealot fervor. "You belong to Theerax. All will be distributed as he sees fit. All will be distributed according to the great design. Your will is nothing. Your wishes are nothing. You will submit and you will be grateful!" The pike butt made a second—and unnecessary, in Will's humble opinion—trip into Will's appendix.

"All hail Theerax!" yelled the guards.

"We are the thermals beneath his winds!" rang out Cyrill's reedy voice. He received a pike butt in the face for his troubles. He dropped to all fours, mouth streaming blood.

"Shut up, maggot," snapped a guard.

Will thought that was probably enough independent observation for Cyrill now. They could probably get onto the bit where they escaped and told the Batarran High Council what a bunch of shits these people were. Except Cyrill was picking himself up, and nodding fervently to the guard.

If there was one good argument for the current pantheon, Will thought, it was that they didn't inspire this sort of lunacy.

"All right," said another of the guards, "take the woman."

"What?" said Will. It felt like he was saying that a lot.

Apparently one of the guards thought so too. He stepped in close to Will, his face inches away. "Are you not getting the fucking message, worm?" he yelled, his spit flecking Will's face. "You don't matter anymore. All the rules you have been taught are important, they mean nothing here. This is Theerax's world. This is the world as the dragons envision it. Free from all the shit the gods forced upon us. All their false hierarchies and hypocrisies. All their corruption and bullshit. This is life in its pure fucking form. And you are nothing. You are less than nothing. You are property. You belong to me. And I belong to Theerax. And he belongs to the dragon kin. And they belong to the great design. And you are so fucking small and petty it makes me taste bile in the back of my throat. If I killed you here, now, no one would care. It would be meaningless. So I fucking dare you, I challenge you, to ask me, 'What?' one more hexed time."

Some part of Will, really, really wanted to say, "What?" But Lette was looking at him, even as two guards led her roughly away. And her eyes echoed her sentiment of a moment before. *Don't be an idiot.* So for once in his life, Will wasn't. And he held his tongue. And he waited to see if this dragon that pretended to divinity would treat him any better than the current gods usually did.

The guards pushed them away from the wall and started them marching through the maze of white tents.

"Still happy you joined in with this cult?" he hissed at Cyrill, who was still bleeding openly from his split lip. "You see what sort of fucking monsters you've thrown your lot in with?"

Cyrill managed a quivering shrug. "All I've observed," he huffed, "is a little boyish enthusiasm."

Will half-lunged at Cyrill, lost his footing, and ended up knee-deep in mud and filth. In the moments before a guard hit him again, he looked to the heavens.

"I am trying to defend you bastards," he muttered.

They didn't appear to be listening.

12

A Tamathian Roast

Quirk came around to the sound of voices approaching. She heard metal shoes scuffing against stone steps.

Where was she?

Stone walls. Bars. Mold on the walls. Dirty straw on the floor. No windows. And she was tied to a chair. And the chair was buried in a barrel of water.

I've been here before.

Because this was how you kept a fire mage from harming people. This was how you imprisoned them either for their own good or for yours. This was exactly how she had spent most of her first five years in Tamathia after being rescued from the demigod Hethren.

She would never forget the feeling of smother rags either. Honestly, she could have lived without the reminder. They were wrapped tightly about her submerged hands now. But they bound more than mere flesh. She could feel the intrusion of them, worming into some ineffable part of her, binding her magic. Her thoughts felt sluggish and awkward.

Gods. Quirk didn't know if Ferra had orchestrated everything or if she had just played into his hands entirely of her own volition. But she had killed those Diffinites in broad daylight. Not just killed them. She had burned them. Quite deliberately. She had reached into herself, pulled out fire, and hate, and rage, and done everything she had sworn she would never do again.

And yes, circumstances had conspired against her. And yes, she was in fear for her life. And yes, some cackling cruel part of herself that she could never fully silence was insisting that the little fuckers had deserved it, and she was only truly alive when the world burned to a crisp before her. But she was better than that. That was the whole foundation of her life. That she could be better. That there was a good person inside her that could be salvaged.

She looked around the sad, familiar cell. She deserved to be here. She had done this to herself.

She was pulled back to reality, by the owners of the voices and the footsteps coming into view at the base of a set of spiral stairs that led down into the dungeon that held her. Her cell was at the end of a short corridor, and if she twisted her head she could see other sets of bars marking the entrances to other cells. Whether they were occupied or not she could not tell.

One man, dressed as a guard, held two torches. He set them in sconces in the wall. The other—a jailer—carried a sack. She saw him reach into it, pull out a dry hunk of bread. He chucked it between the bars of one doorway.

"Eat," he said. His was a thickset man, the sort who seemed to have been made from parts twice the size as the ones used to build Quirk. Fat fingers and thick lips, with a curiously aquiline nose in the middle of his broad, blunt face.

The jailer then turned to her, and as he approached, he seemed to sink down to a deeper level of revulsion. Without taking his eyes off her, he reached into his sack, pulled out a crust of bread, and threw it between the bars of her cell door. It landed on the floor six feet in front of her barrel, skidding through dirt, rank water, and rat shit.

"Eat," he said in the same gruff growl.

Quirk just stared at the filthy crust of bread from the confines of her barrel.

The jailer turned to his companion and barked a short laugh. The guard grinned, but it was a nervous look.

"She can't hurt anyone, you pussy." The sneering jailer dropped his sack on the floor and fiddled with a ring of keys on his belt. While he set about the lock to Quirk's door, the guard drew his sword. His eyes were slowly going wider and wider.

Quirk tried to smile at him. "It's okay—" she started.

"Shut the fuck up," snapped the jailer. "You start casting any spells and I'll hold your head under that water until you stop kicking. Then I'll piss in it."

After a moment's consideration, Quirk kept her mouth shut. She did not think this man would be open to reasoned debate.

"There you go," said the jailer. He turned to the guard, who was still clutching his sword. "I've got a way with women, I do."

He opened the door to the cell, and the pair stepped in. The jailer, bent, picked up her scrap of bread from the ground. He reached out to give it to her, then hesitated. Then he bent again and, with one finger, collected the dirt between two of the prison's flagstones. He smeared the black filth over the surface of Quirk's bread. "Talking shit about our lord Diffinax," he said. "As if some cunt-eater like you had any right to have his name even in your mouth." He spat into Quirk's barrel. Then he held the bread out to her. "Eat," he said.

She shook her head. She didn't know how long she'd been down here, how long she'd been unconscious, but her stomach was crying out for food. And yet the sight of that filthy bread...No.

"Eat it, or I will force it down your throat." The guard spoke quite slowly and deliberately.

Trying not to show any of the disgust she felt, Quirk opened her mouth.

"Bite my fingers," the guard told her, "and I'll break every bone that still leaves you alive."

He crammed bread into her mouth. His companion watched with sick fascination. She waited to chew until his hand was away. Her stomach roiled.

The jailer gave her a mirthless smile. "Good girl," he said, and patted her head. He turned to his companion. "You can train them good," he said, "if you know how to talk to them."

Gods, she would like to see him burn. She closed her eyes. *No,* she told herself. *No you would not. Not even him. You must not. You are not that person.*

The jailer tossed the remaining scrap of bread into the barrel with her. It began to sink. "Eat up," he said, smiling, as he turned his back.

"Quirk!" A voice hissed through the dungeon. "Quirk, that's you, isn't it?"

The jailer and his friend were gone. Quirk felt nauseous and stupid. She lolled against the edge of her barrel.

And then she recognized the voice. And how . . . Was this some sort of divine torture? Had she gone about trying to defend the gods all wrong, and this was their petty revenge?

"Quirk, please!"

Afrit. It was Afrit's voice in the darkness. Afrit her constant shadow at the university. Maybe Quirk was losing her mind.

But she had seen the jailer toss bread into that other cell . . .

"Afrit?" she whispered back, incredulous.

"Oh thank the gods." The relief in Afrit's voice was palpable. "Oh Knole, thank you. Thank you." Relief edged toward hysteria.

"What are you doing here?" Quirk whispered. Was she still spying for Ferra? Did they think giving her a friend in this hellhole would trick her into confessing some great secret?

"Looking for a way out." Afrit did not sound as if she was doing very well in her cell. "But you're here. Oh, thank Knole."

"I don't know what you think I can do..." said Quirk, still hedging, still searching for Afrit's angle.

"You can burn your way out," said Afrit. The woman sounded almost delirious. "You were god touched. I thought...I mean you could just melt your bars. Couldn't you? You could melt that...that...fucking..." And there was a world of spite and hate in that word, that made Quirk's suspicion waver. That was not hurt that someone could fake. "That jailer. You could kill him. You could just..." There was an indecipherable noise from Afrit's cell, some choked emotion.

"No," said Quirk, still against her better judgment. "They have smother rags on me." She shook her head, even though Afrit couldn't see it. "And I don't do that. Not anymore. That's not who I am."

"But you could get the rags off. Cut them. Something. There's got to be some rough surface in your cell. Even if it takes a day or two." Afrit either wasn't listening or didn't want to listen.

"It doesn't matter," Quirk said, speaking slowly and loudly. It was important both that Afrit hear this, and that she say it. "If they took these rags off, I would wait, patient as a lamb. I am not going to burn anyone or anything ever again."

She pictured the lake. The still surface. And even despite everything, it felt calm.

"What? What the fuck?" She had apparently finally gotten through to Afrit.

"That is not who I am." Quirk was pleased with the steadiness of her voice.

"Then...Then..." Afrit was breathing hard. "Why do you even fight? Why do you write those pamphlets? Why do you try to inspire people to fight if you won't fucking do it?"

Quirk drew a breath. So Afrit *had* known about the pamphlets. But before she could decide whether to accuse Afrit or defend herself, Afrit was barreling on.

"You *have* to fight! It's hypocrisy! It's worse. It's cowardice. And

I know, I know, I know you are not a coward. You went to Kondorra. You faced down dragons. You were there. You're my... my... Fuck!" There was an edge of hysteria in Afrit's voice now.

"Calm down," Quirk hissed. She didn't want to bring the guards back. Anything but that.

"You have to get us out of here!" Afrit snapped.

"I can't." Quirk aimed for matter-of-fact over helpless.

"You won't." There was bitterness in Afrit's voice. "Because... Because..." But there was a precipice of anger that Afrit seemed unwilling to plunge over. She heard the woman drawing deep breaths.

And *why* was Afrit here?

"You *have* to escape," said Afrit, sounding a hair calmer now, if no less urgent. "You above all people. You're the voice of the resistance. You give shape to everyone who stands against Diffinax. Without you, everything is going to fall apart."

And that brought Quirk up short. Because of all the things she had expected to hear, that was not one.

"What?" she said, trying to process Afrit's angle. Did she aim to flatter her?

"Your pamphlets," Quirk said. "We have meetings. We read them. We talk about them. We disseminate them. They give us structure. They inspire us. They keep the fight alive. They are necessary, Quirk. You have to get out. You have to keep on writing."

"What?" Quirk repeated again, feeling stupid. It had to be the smother rags. She was misunderstanding something basic. "Who is we?"

"The resistance," said Afrit. She sounded almost as confused as Quirk. "Those of us who stand with you against Diffinax."

"Who?" Quirk repeated.

"You didn't know?" Afrit sounded winded by the news. "You didn't... Oh gods, that explains... Oh... Oh, I thought. Oh gods..."

"What?" Quirk tried to parse the emotion she was hearing. Was it...humiliation?

"I'm...Oh gods." Afrit let out a little mirthless laugh. "I'm your *fan*, Quirk. You're my academic hero. You have been ever since I was sixteen and one of my teachers read our class your paper on the breeding habitats of wendigos. That you brought all of that to life. That someone could know so much about something, and render it...I don't know. It's stupid. But *you* were why I applied to the Tamathian University. *You* were why I stayed on to teach."

"But..." Quirk felt blindsided. She had written that paper more than fifteen years ago. "You teach practical politics," was all she could manage.

"It's not..." Afrit managed a laugh that actually sounded halfway genuine. "It wasn't your *subject*. It was...Gods this is embarrassing. It was *you*. Your drive. Your personality. Your past. Everything you'd overcome. Everything you'd become. The way you approached your subject. Your teeth bared, you know. Some of that...fuck, you must hate the word...but something of the savagery of your upbringing in the way you just took down a subject. Just broke other people's arguments apart. I wanted to be that sort of academic. After you came back from Kondorra...I've been petitioning the Chancellor for a chance to go to the Fanlorn Empire, to observe their bureaucracy in action." Another laugh. "No chance of that happening now."

"You're my...fan?" Quirk was still back at the beginning of the story. She was trying to put years of history back in context.

"I thought you knew," Afrit said helplessly. "I don't know... I thought somehow that made it okay to pester you. And then when word of Diffinax arrived. And you were so adamant about what his true goals were. And, of course, I'd read everything you'd written about dragons, and been to all of your lectures. So it made complete sense to me. And I just assumed that you'd know that I must agree with you. And when I saw the pamphlets, I just…Gods, I'm such an idiot. You'd left a pile on the table in the library where I always sit. And, of course, I recognized your style right away. I knew it had to be you. I mean, this was back before everybody knew—"

"Everybody knew?" So much of Quirk's world was falling down. So many assumptions collapsing.

"Of course." Afrit sounded almost amused. "You're Quirkelle Bal Tehrin. You're the most famous thaumatobiologist in all Avarra. You were raised by a demigod barbarian, and were present in Kondorra when the dragon syndicate was brought down. You dine nightly with the Emperor. You're kind of a big deal. Someone like you doesn't just start publishing screeds against the dragon whose cult is sweeping the nation, and have it go unnoticed."

Quirk was just left blinking in her water. She'd had…No, it just…Could this all be true? And yet, it did all make sense as well. The way Afrit had treated her…

Could she have been such an entitled fool?

"So," said Afrit, "I thought you'd left the pamphlets for me. I thought you knew I sat there. That I'd agree with you. I thought we were…" Another chuckle. "Gods, I thought we were conspirators. And you must have…Gods know what you thought. But I helped pass them out. And I organized meetings. And we talked. And other people wrote responses to your pieces. And we distributed them. And we organized. Because of you. We preached against Diffinax. Because of you. You were the core of everything. You were our rallying cry. We need you. There is no resistance without you."

"No," Quirk said. Denial was the only recourse left to her. This had to be some trap. Some appeal to her vanity. Some… thing. Gods, she didn't know. "No, that's not true."

There was silence from Afrit. Quirk waited. Nothing. "Hello?" she said.

"What?" asked Afrit. She sounded defeated. There was a

new note of resignation in her voice. "I don't have any proof. I'm chained up in a cell. I can't go and get a witness. You either believe me or you don't. You either have the will to get out of here or you don't. I can't...I'd love to say I picked the wrong hero, but I don't think I did. I just...I don't know if I screwed it up, or something else did. But..." She sighed. "The world is waiting for you, Quirk. For you to burn it down, or build it up, or...something in between. I don't know. But I can't make you do it. That's up to you."

"No," Quirk said. And she felt that it was suddenly very important that she convince this shockingly earnest young woman of that truth. "It's not up to me. That's the point. It should never be up to one person. It should be the group. When one person decides, then despotism happens. I won't be that. My youth was defined by a despot, and everything I have done has been to avoid that."

The silence that greeted her went on so long, she thought Afrit wasn't going to speak again. But then finally the other woman said, "I was a professor of practical politics. I know how despotism happens. I just...I wish the world was as pure as your intentions."

And after that, the silence did last.

Quirk woke, limbs aching. Her chin was soaking wet, and she could smell the water going stagnant. She blinked, trying to work out what had woken her.

Steps. Metal-clad feet on stone stairs. The jailer was coming back. When he appeared, the guard was with him. They went to the door of Afrit's cell. Afrit let out another short, shrill scream. The jailer unlocked the door.

The screaming went on for a long time.

When Quirk heard the door of Afrit's cell swing shut, she also heard sobbing.

Burn them, whispered a muted voice.

She opened her eyes. The jailer was walking toward her

grinning. As he reached for the keys at his belt, she could see that his knuckles were covered with fresh blood.

Burn them.

"You don't have to do this," she said, as keys rattled in the door to her cell. "You can reject Diffinax. You can see through his lies. You can look at history. You can look at biology. He is a beast driven to dominate. A beast driven to control. To consume and burn."

The door to her cell swung open and the jailer crossed her cell in a few short strides. He smashed a gauntleted fist into her mouth. She reeled backward. For a moment her barrel rocked backward, teetering on its rim before settling back down. Her lip was broken, blood smeared across her face. "I told you to shut your whore mouth!" the jailer shouted.

And the lake was not calm. And the lake was full of fire.

No, she told herself. *That is not me. I am not a god. They judge life. Not me. I do not decide.* All the old lessons. She repeated them all to herself.

The jailer looked to his companion, then back to her grinning. "Not so lippy now, are you?" he said.

She ground her teeth. She could feel something breaking inside of her. Some rage she had not known she possessed.

"What's that?" he said, cocking his ear toward her. "Want to say something?" His grin widened. He cavorted toward her—a parody of a jester's step. The guard had his sword drawn, but managed a nervous laugh.

Quirk's teeth worked. She flexed her arms in the water. And the smother rags were bound tight. And at her straining the fog grew in her mind. But was there a fraction of give in her bonds? She strained and she strained.

"Got some sweet nothing you want to whisper to me?" said the jailer, still grinning. He was walking around her now. He reached out and stroked her cheek. "Oh I bet your tongue could be so pretty."

Rage and frustration and hate were screaming inside her. They were a fire obliterating all her resolve.

She opened her mouth.

"Come on." He leaned closer still. His face an inch from hers. She could smell his breath.

And she fought it down. She fought through the rage, and she triumphed. She emerged on the other side. And the surface of the lake was calm.

And then she remembered Afrit's sobbing. And the lake, calm as it was, was full of fire.

And Quirk made a decision. She came to a realization of who she was. Who she wanted to be.

"Come on," breathed the man.

Quirk closed her mouth. Hard. Directly onto the fucker's nose.

He screamed, writhed. He tried to pull away but she held on tight, ripping and shaking, fighting against her gag reflex as his blood filled her mouth.

She could hear the guard yelling. Felt something jar against her barrel. The man's sword surely.

She bit harder, deeper. Her teeth tore. The man squealed, and shook, and screamed. She wrenched her head backward. And she ripped half of his nose free from the mooring of his face.

The jailer reeled away. Blood was fountaining from his ruined features. He clutched at the ragged wound, letting out high-pitched screams. The guard was just repeating the word *fuck*, over and over again.

She spat the man's nose out of her mouth. It slapped wetly against the wall, slid to the floor, leaving an obscene crimson trail behind it. She grinned redly at them.

"Bet you wish you had a god you could pray to now," she said.

The noseless jailer let out an inarticulate gurgling scream of rage and came at her, braying blood. His massive gauntleted fist came back.

She braced for the blow. She knew this was coming. She knew this was necessary.

His fist landed like a sledgehammer. Her head slammed back. Pain rattled inside her skull. She rattled inside the sloshing barrel of water. The barrel rattled on the floor, rocked back under the momentum of the blow, of her weight slamming back. It rocked back on its rim. Quirk fought to hold on to her senses, to throw her weight in that direction.

The barrel teetered. The barrel fell.

Water sluiced across the room. Quirk went with it, sloshing out of the barrel in a sodden spilling mass of limbs and hair. The chair cracked beneath her, sodden wood no longer up to the task of holding up to strain.

"Oh fuck!" the guard shouted. "Oh fuck!"

A life of academia had not been kind to Quirk's muscle mass, but she had always been limber. She curled her legs up to her chest in a tight ball, swung her bound hands over her arse. For a moment she thought that she wasn't going to manage it, that she was going to be caught there, hands jammed in her own arse crack, and skewered by some blinkered slackwit. Then with a wrench her hands were in front of her.

"Fuck!" screamed the guard again, but then he managed to gather himself enough to lunge at her with his sword. Quirk rolled desperately sideways. Even as she moved she was bringing her hands up to her mouth, tearing at the smother rags with her teeth.

She heard the guard's sword clatter against stone, another bellowed curse. She rolled more, hit the bars of her cell, cursed herself. She looked up, saw the guard coming at her again. She bunched her legs, kicked out, pushed herself beneath his swing.

Which whoreson tied these cursed wraps so tightly?

The jailer was straightening, blinking around the room. Blood soaked his chin and shirt.

She scrambled to her feet, then immediately danced left as

the guard swung his sword once more. It was increasingly clear that he'd been given it in the strict understanding that he'd only have to use it against people bound hand and foot.

Come on. Come on. Come on. She bit and bit and ripped at her bindings. *You can bite a man's nose off but not some simple rags?* And then on the heels of that thought. *Gods, I bit a man's nose off.*

And then finally, as the guard took another swing at her, she felt some give in the rags. *Thank you,* she muttered to the heavens.

And the guard swung his sword again. Quirk danced away. But she had misjudged the space, bounced off one of the cell walls, and then was suddenly screaming as the sword bit into her arm.

The guard yelled too, almost as surprised as she was. For a moment they stood there staring at each other, the side of his sword slicing into her arm. "Gods," he said, eyes wide, and then jerked his sword free. Quirk bellowed, her arm spasmed, and blackness swam at the edges of her vision. But there was a ripping from her wrists. In a moment of hope she looked down. But she was not free yet. She tried to pull her arms apart, but the pain in her bicep almost made her drop to her knees.

"Get her!" screamed the noseless jailer, barely articulate through the film of blood still dripping down his face. The guard set his feet, prepared a lunge. She bit at her wraps again. The guard closed his eyes.

Frayed cloth parted in Quirk's mouth. Fabric and fog dropped away. Pain rushed in to fill the void. She gasped, barely able to focus in the cold shock of it.

She blinked desperately, heard a howl from the guard as he drove his sword forward in a savage lunge.

In desperation she flung out a hand toward him.

And the world filled with fire.

13

Sacrilege for Fun and Profit

"That Lawl chap. He's a bit of a bastard, isn't he?"

Silence. Someone coughed. Someone else shuffled her papers. Others scuffed their feet.

Firkin cleared his throat and looked out at the small crowd.

The temple was cramped and smelly and appeared to be mostly constructed from sweat stains. How, Firkin was not entirely sure, but he admired the ingenuity. That, though, was pretty much all he admired. The crowd was lackluster, the holy wine was sour, and he was confined in so many reams of fabric that he could barely move. The whole religious getup he'd been wrapped in seemed antithetical to his brand of preaching, and, what was more, didn't seem to match his recollection of Barphist priests' brand of worship at all.

To be fair, Firkin's recollection of Barph worship was hazy at best, but Firkin was used to describing pretty much everything as hazy—from yesterday to his current view of his own feet. Still, as he stood upon the temple altar and cast his memory back, it was as if he felt something stir inside his mind. An almost-physical presence shifting inside his skull. And memories flaked from it like silt stirred by some vast aquatic presence.

So, standing there, unsettled as he was, he did suddenly quite clearly remember a group of Barph's priests standing in a circle, stark-ball naked, soaked in blood and wine. No robes required.

When had that happened? Had that happened to him?

He had not actually intended to get embroiled in the Vinland priesthood. Saying he would had just seemed like a convenient excuse to get out of the High Priesthood's presence. But the guards he'd been with at the time seemed to know the shit he'd been pulling even if the High Priests didn't, and they were of a mind that if he had made a bed, he should lie in it. So off to Vinter's Third District it had been. There the guards had told the altar attendants that Firkin was to be given clerical duties.

Unfortunately, it turned out that the last priest had been set upon by a drunken mob after one of his sermons had taken a lecherous turn, and so Firkin had received a rapid promotion.

Now here he was, watching an ugly crowd get uglier. He took a pull on a bottle of the sour wine he'd grabbed from the temple's altar.

"Lawl," he tried again, shaking his head. "All those rules and restrictions." He pointed at them with the wine bottle, and he found himself saying with far more vehemence than he had expected, "Enough to drive a good god to drink. Am I right?"

Somewhere, miles away out in the wilderness surrounding Vinter, a cricket chirped.

Firkin considered a moment, then drank from the bottle again. He was decidedly off his game.

There was a disgruntled rumble from the crowd. Someone smacked their fist into an open palm. Apparently, while disparaging Lawl was not a favorite pastime in the Third District, priest beatings were.

Firkin shuddered. Screw this. He started scrabbling at his priestly wrappings. He needed to get away from this confining bullshit, get back to that unexpected memory of naked dancing priests. Back to blood and wine. The desire was sudden and urgent.

"Can't blame you for being more boring than a drunk uncle," he said, thinking more freely as the fabric dropped away. "All this bullshit that surrounds you."

District Three was not even the armpit of Vinter. It was the sweaty, diseased crotch of the place. The part even a whore would think twice before touching. When the rest of Vinter had finished gathering up all the shit from last night's bender, District Three was where they dumped it all.

Vinter generated a lot of shit.

These people had grown up knee-deep in the filth of the rest of the city, and waist-deep in its scorn. And everyone who lived here knew it.

And here he was, foisted upon them, come to tell them to be better than who they were. Come to tell them, yet again, that they weren't good enough.

No wonder a man had just pulled out a club with nails driven through it.

He managed to get the top half of his robes off, stood there bare-chested, scratching his navel, and contemplated the room.

"Look at you," he said again. "Just look at you."

The man with the club stood. He was not the only one. They were surprisingly well armed. Firkin admired that.

"You're a bunch of magnificent bastards," he said in the same tone. The people standing hesitated. They had not, it seemed, expected that. Then again, he wasn't sure that he had been either. Again there was that sense of detachment, of not being fully in control.

And gods it felt like fun.

"All this shit," he said. "All around you. This city. A giant wobbling testament to a god who never gave a shit for giant wobbling testaments. For a god who just wanted to kick shit over. And you hate it. You absolutely hate it." He nodded. "That's brilliant," he said.

They had, he noted, still not clubbed him to death. He took that as a good sign.

"Because you get it," he went on, developing this theme now. "Of all the million souls in this sweaty arse crack of a city, the only ones who really get it are you." And they seemed to like that too. That struck a chord.

Firkin had never been one to plan out what to say. It was hard to prepare a speech when you couldn't remember you were meant to give one. The words just tended to come when he needed them. But for the first time, standing there, he wondered where it was they came from.

There again, he was still alive, and momentum seemed to be of the essence right now. Self-reflection could wait perhaps until he had time to take a breath and scratch his nuts.

"They crap on you, all these other idiots, don't they? They talk about District Three as if it's worthless. As if it's lost its way. But it's the only place that has held on to the right way of doing things. This is the only district with a true Barphian ethos. Fuck this! Fuck that! Let's get drunk, and piss on the rest of it!"

"Preach!" yelled a voice in the crowd. Some people looked around in surprise, but others nodded their heads.

"You!" Firkin shouted. "You grab life by the balls, and you shake them. You shake them hard. Just like Barph would have done. You spit in life's eye. Because your hands are busy with all that grabbing. Because life has a sizable pair and you need both of your hands. But you spit. You're the sort of people willing to hold on with both hands if that's what it takes. You're the sort of people who don't care about sweat, or rashes, or dangerously contagious infections. You're Barph's people. Ball grabbers!"

"Ball grabbers!" yelled a few people at the front. Someone else whooped.

"These others..." Firkin took a slug of wine, then spat it into the corner. He felt drunker than he had in ages. "These high-and-mighty priests who sit on their high thrones casting down judgment on folk. Did Barph judge people?"

"No!" someone yelled out, and which Firkin was suddenly sure was the wrong answer, but he didn't think now was the right time to point it out.

"No!" he yelled. "Which is why we're judging them. I think." He waved a hand. "They're arseholes, just go with it."

And that did get a laugh, and a cheer. Firkin grabbed one of the bottles of holy wine off the altar and tossed it into the crowd. Someone caught it, whooped.

"Worship." Firkin spat. "They tell us how to worship. How to commune."

There was a scuffle at the edge of the altar. Firkin looked round. One of the altar attendants was shaking his head violently and making stopping motions with his hands.

Firkin started to walk toward him. "We worship how we like!" Firkin yelled, yanking free of the last of his priestly wraps, standing before them in just his moldering yellow loincloth. And that felt right. And he felt the thing in his head stir again, and there was pain with that, but joy too.

Blood and wine.

"They shout chaos at us like it's an accusation. We..." He lost his train of thought. The attendant was drawing his finger across his neck in a cut-throat gesture.

By this point, Firkin wasn't exactly sure what his message was meant to be, but he did know he didn't like someone breaking his flow. He grabbed the attendant by the hair. He had a lot of it, loose, curly, and blond. Given the uniformly shaven heads in the crowd, Firkin suspected he wasn't a local lad. The attendant yelped and twisted in Firkin's grip.

"They shout chaos at us," Firkin said again. "We tell them to fuck off."

Yes, a voice seemed to whisper in his ear. *That's it. This is right.*

Firkin began pulling the boy toward the front of the altar. "We worship how we like. Our church. Our district. Our rules." Another cheer. "We want to drink? We drink!" Another cheer. "We want to shit on their doorsteps? We shit on their doorsteps!" Another, louder cheer. He tossed another bottle into the crowd. The altar attendant jerked in his grip, and Firkin yanked back hard, sending the young man to his knees. "We want to fight? We fight!" Firkin yelled. "We want to knock the shit out of something? We kick its shit into next week."

The man with the spiked club drove it into the pew, and it was Firkin's turn to cheer. He'd forgotten how much fun preaching could be. You could wrap pretty much any old shit in a holy robe, tell people it would make them feel better, and they'd eat it up with a spoon.

Blood and wine, whispered the voice in his head. *The old ways.*

And Firkin found he was grinning.

"We want to get some good old blood sacrifice going?" Firkin asked the room.

The cheer was deafening.

"Yeah," he said, "that's what he thought."

He tossed the altar attendant to them. The clubs went up, and the clubs went down.

And something inside Firkin's head smiled.

14

The Loss of Cyrill's Innocence

Will wondered if he wished he was dead.

Some priests reported that Lawl welcomed everyone to the Hallows with open arms, inviting them to lives of rest and pleasure. However, a lot of priests seemed to agree that the quality of one's rest and pleasure depended on how much one donated to a particular god's temple. Will had always been too cynical to accept that idea, but he did find himself a little concerned about the message—more common among the po-faced priests of Knole, Klink, and Toil—that one's afterlife was actually spent in constant labor, furthering the great work of the gods. *If labor is the best thing death has to offer,* Will thought, *then death can go fuck itself with a rusty shovel.*

Theerax's guards had had him digging latrines all afternoon. His arms felt ready to fall off, his heart was still thundering in his chest, and he was covered in human excrement from head to toe. And yet as bad as he felt, he knew Cyrill was in an even worse state. The old man was unconscious on the cot beside him, and Will was fairly sure that he had suffered a pretty substantial systemic failure. Before he had collapsed, Cyrill's limbs on one side of his body hadn't seemed to be working properly, and even now his skin was the sort of white that made fresh snow appear a little dirty.

It did not bode well for the evening Will had planned.

Outside, though, night had fallen, and the guards had finally left them alone. And even though sleep clawed at Will, and even though he was half-convinced Cyrill had suffered a stroke, he knew this was the moment they had been waiting for.

He leaned over and nudged Cyrill. The older man jerked awake with a noise like an ejaculating pig. "Yes, your...what?" he shouted.

Will clamped a hand down over his mouth. "Shut up." Cyrill's eyes slowly reduced in size from full-on saucer to more of a toy dishware size. Slowly Will removed his hand.

"Does Theerax need us?" Cyrill asked. He sounded eager.

Will wondered what the punishment for murdering stupid old men was in the encampment. Probably a beating, since that was the punishment for everything else in the camp, from refusing to work to breathing at a volume a nearby guard found annoying.

"No, you sycophantic moron," he hissed at Cyrill. "I need you to spy with me so we can find all the incriminating shit."

Cyrill pouted. "I don't think that would fit into the grand design."

"The grand design," Will said, fighting to keep the volume of his voice below that of a murderous howl, "is to grind humanity beneath Theerax's bootheel. Now you are here as an independent observer, not as a bootlicker. So get your arse in gear and independently observe me revealing something that gets the Batarran High Council on message."

Cyrill lay obstinately in bed.

"Look," Will said, fighting for leverage, "I'm pretty sure the council said you'd be promoted to a collator if you did a good job with this."

Cyrill sat up, as if someone had yanked his puppet strings. "Collator?" he said. "You heard them say collator."

And no, of course Will had not. "I think Theerax would be really impressed knowing he had a full-fledged collator among his faithful," he went on blithely.

"You think so?" Cyrill seemed the sort of man who was flattered so infrequently, he was unlikely to recognize whether it was genuine or not.

Will nodded enthusiastically, and thus motivated, Cyrill scraped himself off his cot and accompanied Will to the back of the tent, where they clawed a few pegs free and snuck out into the chill night air.

Crouched low, Will edged along the row of tents trying to spy a place that looked like it contained compromising information. Unfortunately, everything in this gods-hexed place looked the same. Starched white tent was lined up next to starched white tent. The same design for each. No flags. No ostentatious displays of color. Apparently Theerax's grand design didn't involve a very sophisticated grasp of color theory.

"Screw it," said Will, pulling back the flap to the next tent he passed. It was difficult to make things out in the dark, but it soon became apparent the place was full of tools. Shovels and ropes of a disappointingly innocent aspect.

The next ten tents were similarly unhelpful.

"Very suspicious," said Cyrill, demonstrating a hitherto hidden capability for sarcasm. Will weighed the merits of ramming the ability back down Cyrill's throat.

They pushed on, deeper into the camp. From time to time patrols would send them scurrying down a side path, or between two tents. The deeper into the camp they went, the more frequent the patrols became. Will's exhausted nerves sparked. Surely they must be getting closer to something Theerax wanted to hide.

They had just finished sticking their noses into a tent full of sacks of vegetables when they heard a patrol approaching, shockingly close. Will grabbed Cyrill by the arm and dragged him back into the tent.

"His nibs is in a bit of a mood tonight," said a gruff female voice.

"Watch your mouth," hissed a younger woman. She sounded

alarmed. "Theerax is our lord and deliverer and demands our respect." She paused. "Plus, someone is always listening in this place."

Well, thought Will, *she was right about one of those two.*

The older woman laughed. Their footsteps started up again. "I tell you," said the older woman, "this gig got a lot less fun since Theerax actually showed up."

At this utterance, Cyrill let out a very high-pitched squeal. Will, not thinking clearly, grabbed the nearest thing to him, and attempted to murder Cyrill with a carrot.

"Shut up!" he whispered.

"He's here!" Cyrill said, hopping up and down and hyper-ventilating. "Theerax is actually here!"

Will closed his eyes and attempted to count to ten. He got as far as three and then replaced the remaining numbers with expletives. He listened for the sounds of guards running to investigate. He couldn't hear anything over Cyrill's feverish hyperventilating.

After a moment of not being accosted by angry guards, Will grabbed Cyrill by the back of the neck and thrust him toward the entrance of the flap. "Come on," he said. "Let's get out of here before you attract any more attention."

He stepped out after Cyrill. Unfortunately the old observer was in the process of letting out a squeal of fright and stop-ping short. Will built on this inauspicious continuation of their adventures by bumping straight into Cyrill's arse, and grabbing for a sword hilt that wasn't at his belt.

"Hello, boys," said Lette's voice. "Fancy meeting you here."

Will found that he wasn't too busy disentangling himself from Cyrill to sigh in relief. "Lette," he said. "Oh, thank the gods." Without thinking he went to wrap her in his arms, then caught her look and checked himself.

"Hey!"

And then Will found out that he had more things than social

awkwardness to worry about, because the two guards had heard them after all, and had turned around, and had pulled out their swords.

"Balls," he muttered. Because this was always the part where his plans went horribly, horribly wrong, and tended to involve people's insides becoming their outsides.

The older guard stepped toward them, lowering her blade into a fighting stance as she came. But as she approached she passed into a patch of shadow between the intermittently posted torches. There she suddenly jerked to a halt. Then she let out a sputtering wet noise and convulsed. Then she stood absolutely still.

Everyone, Will included, stared at the guard, who was now staring dumbly at the ground.

The guard's younger companion was the first to find her voice. "What—" she started.

Suddenly the older guard's body convulsed again, shaking back and forth, limp head flopping obscenely in and out of the light.

"Doo-bee-doo-bee-doo," said a growling voice in the shadows. "I am being a big bossy soldier. Be listening to me. Doo-bee-doo-bee-doo."

"—the fuck?" finished the younger guard.

Then Balur stepped into the light. The fingers of his left hand were buried in the back of the lead guard, puncturing lungs, liver, and heart. He wielded the dead body, which he had been flopping like a puppet, and brought it down savagely on the head of the remaining guard.

There was a lot of blood.

Cyrill was quite noisily sick.

"Hello," Balur said cheerfully. Will couldn't be entirely sure, in the flickering light of the guards' dropped torches, but he thought Balur's teeth were stained red.

"Holy shit, Balur," Will said, then found he didn't have much else to say. What did someone say after that?

It turned out that if you were Lette you just sighed and said, "Oh come on. We are attempting to be subtle here. This is meant to be a quiet infiltration."

Balur licked the air with a narrow tongue. "Quiet?" he said. "Really? Because"—he thumbed over his shoulder—"I was killing, like, thirty of them back there."

"Thirty?" Will's voice headed for the higher registers.

Balur shrugged. "I am being a little out of practice."

Lette snorted. "False modesty doesn't suit you, you big bastard."

Balur grinned wickedly. "It was being more like forty-five. I was thinking Will might object."

Will threw up his hands. "But that I'd be okay with thirty?"

Cyrill was sick again.

"Is he being all right?" Balur said.

"I don't think we give a shit," said Lette.

Which, Will reflected, was probably pretty accurate. He tried to ground himself, ground this conversation. "We need him to see something that convinces him that this place is a threat to everybody in Batarra," he said. It sounded pleasingly rational to his ear.

For a moment Lette and Balur appeared suitably impressed by this pronouncement. It was spoiled by the sound of yells in the distance. Words like "Intruders!" and "To arms!" came over the night air.

Will turned to look pointedly at Balur.

"Never can be pleasing some people," Balur groused.

"No," Will agreed. "You can't."

"Perhaps," Lette suggested, "we should be moving instead of pinning blame?"

And while Will felt there was plenty of blame to be pinned at that precise moment, Lette had a point. So they moved, pushing deeper into the camp, away from the shouts and stomping boots.

The groups they skirted around now were different. There were no longer patrols of soldiers, but rather ragged groups of

them, helmets off, laughing and lounging. There were lone figures in hooded robes, walking with purpose, heads held high.
There was a sense of happy industry.

The tents they ducked into were smaller here too. No longer
did they store vegetables, ropes, or shovels. Instead they held
the beds for two or three soldiers. Or they were someone's personal study. And the few storage tents they did come across
held not work tools but weapons. Balur found two long blades
that were at least passably balanced and shoved them through
his belt. He threw a third to Will.

"Be taking this," he said.

Will arched an eyebrow at him. "Me?" he said.

"Reach," Balur told him. "You do not need to be knowing
much to just hold it out and be keeping someone farther away.
And it is being better for blocking blows than your forearm."

"The idea is to avoid combat," Will said. But he shoved the
sword into his belt while Balur laughed in his face.

"These people are surprisingly well stocked." Lette looked
around the tent. "This is of the scale of an invading army. Someone has been planning this for a very long time."

Will looked pointedly at Cyrill. "You're writing this down,
right? That bit about an invading army?"

Cyrill blinked up at him. "Theerax is an organized being," he
said defensively. "Everything is organized to the scheme of the
grand design."

"Except," Lette cut in, "it isn't just Theerax. There are other
dragons all over Avarra. That's been the news for weeks now.
They're all over the place, all preaching the same crap. That the
gods are anarchic and awful—"

"They are!" broke in Cyrill. "My prayers go unanswered. I
kowtow to corrupt dilettantes who do nothing but swindle and
diddle each other all day long. If that is the design of the gods,
then I am ready to embrace the alternative."

Lette waved a hand dismissively. "Look," she said, "no one

here is arguing that the gods have done a great job. What we're arguing is that the job they've done is still better than some totalitarian bullshit. Which, by the way"—she prodded Cyrill in the chest—"is exactly what we're seeing here. I hope that's going in your gods-hexed report."

"I," said Cyrill self-importantly, "am here to find threats to Batarra, and so far I have seen none."

Lette cocked a fist at him. "Does this look like a threat to you?" Cyrill flinched back. "That's what this encampment is," Lette went on. "This camp is Theerax cocking a fist at all of Batarra."

"He's here," Will said quietly. He was still trying to mentally digest the idea.

Lette turned to him sharply. "Who?"

"Theerax," Will said, truly feeling the weight of the word this time. "He's in the camp."

Lette puffed out her cheeks, then started pacing in short, controlled circles. "Oh, it is go time then." She nodded to herself. "Theerax's move is surprise. Make this all seem peaceable enough. And then when he mounts his coup, the populace already wants him. So if he's here we're in the endgame."

And Will had known it. He'd just not wanted to admit it.

"This," said Cyrill, "is all wild supposition on your part. I have seen nothing to corroborate any of it."

Will thought about using the sword Balur had just given him.

Balur himself was still stuck a few moments back in the conversation. "A dragon is being here?" he said.

Lette sighed. "Oh put your murder boner back in your pants. You killed one dragon once, by luck."

"*Two* dragons." Balur was indignant.

Lette wheeled back on him. "One was drugged unconscious."

"Still counts," Balur snapped back. "And the second I was in its mouth, murdering it in a volcano. That is not luck. That is being magnificent skill."

Lette considered this. "Okay, I'm not willing to concede

magnificence, but I will acknowledge maybe more than just luck was involved there."

"Magnificent," Balur repeated.

"How about," Will said, "we do this at a time when we don't have about ten thousand better things to do? The most pressing being not being murdered by a dragon's zealot army!"

"Fine." Balur held open the tent flap for them all in a poor imitation of graciousness.

"Hey!" A man stood framed by the open tent flap. He had a helmet under one hand and was clearly halfway through unstrapping his steel breastplate.

For a moment they all stood and stared at each other. Then several things happened at once.

The man yelled, "Guards!"

Cyrill yelled, "Save me!"

Balur and Will drew their swords.

Lette flung a knife across the room.

The man collapsed with a blade protruding from his neck. Balur flicked an irritated glance at Lette.

"Get quicker," she said, as the lizard man hauled the dead body inside the tent. But already there was the sound of running and shouting, and then three guards were pushing into the tent, and even Lette wasn't that fast.

"Move!" Will yelled, which Balur did, but he moved to grab two of the men by the necks and shake them. The third he just bit in the face. This saved Lette from using her knives for deadlier work, however, and allowed her the time to slash a hole in the back of the tent.

Less fortunately, the space behind the tent was full of guards.

The next ten seconds were a blur of blood and fear. Will's world rang with steel on steel. The harsh clang of his desperate parries. The sleek whistle of Lette's blade gliding through her opponent's guard. The cacophonous crashes of Balur's blows knocking his opponents' weapons aside.

Then it was over, and Will was clutching a gash in his arm, and Lette was bleeding from her cheek.

"Come on," Will panted. It seemed like fewer shouts were coming from their left. Will started pushing that way.

"Do I have to be explaining about retreating again?" Balur threw his arms up in the air. "Gods, are they removing people's pride from them at birth outside of the Analesian Desert?"

"Oh shit, Balur." Lette was staring at the lizard man's side. And then Will saw the blade jammed hilt-deep in Balur's flank.

"Is nothing," Balur told them. He yanked the blade out of his side and pinched the gushing sides of the wound together.

"Gods." Will blanched.

"Oh crap," Lette said. Then, "Cyrill, take off your shirt."

"What?" Cyrill looked up alarmed.

"I need your gods-hexed shirt, Cyrill. And you're either going to give it to me or I'm going to take it by force."

"Aren't we running away?" The old man was panting.

"I am not running away." Balur seemed to be far more concerned about that than he was about bleeding out.

"Tactical regrouping!" Lette snapped. "Tactical regrouping!" Then she removed Cyrill's shirt by force.

Balur pressed the wad of shirt to his streaming wound while Lette bound the second half of the shirt around his midriff.

"That'll have to do," she told him.

"Livers are good at growing back," he told her with a shrug.

"Fuck, Balur." Will saw there was genuine concern in Lette's eyes.

"You are going soft," Balur told her. "It is making me feel nauseous."

"No," she said. "That's the toxins from your liver."

Balur hesitated, then nodded. "That is being a fair point."

Then another shout. The guards had found them.

"Move!" Will yelled, at the same moment Lette screamed the word, and then they were moving. Will led them down haphazard twists and turns, praying that neither Cyrill nor Balur collapsed.

Predictably, the old observer disappointed him first. He almost tripped over Cyrill. The man was on the floor letting out great rasping pants.

"Shh!" Will hissed at him. He looked around trying to get his bearings. He'd totally lost track of where they were. They were between two large tents. One resembled some of the barracks tents they had peered into, large, and long, and low. The other...

The other was more like a circus big top. A massive dome of white fabric. And... did Will feel heat coming from the fabric?

Lette was trying to look at Balur's wound, but he wasn't paying attention.

"Eurk," said Cyrill. He was holding his chest.

"This place is a gods-hexed maze." Will looked left, looked right. He tried to formulate something resembling a plan. "I think we wait for everything to die down, then make a dash for it, half an hour before dawn. Hopefully they change the guard around then, and we can take advantage."

Lette nodded. "That—"

She was interrupted by a sound like a landslide. Like rocks splitting, and earth subsiding. Like mountains pushing up through rock. She was interrupted by a voice.

"Are they dead?" it said.

It boomed out from confines of the massive tent. A voice as large as that fabric space.

On the floor, Cyrill let out a strangled "Hurk!" and struggled to sit up.

It was—could only be—the voice of Theerax.

Will was aware of a slight shaking in his hands. The edges of his vision seemed to grow hazy. A sense of unreality setting in.

Inside the tent, someone answered Theerax indistinctly.

Yellow light flared briefly. There was a wave of heat, and a very, very short scream.

The last time Will had been this close to a dragon, it had been chasing him across the plains of Kondorra. An army had been on the verge of turning on it.

Balur drew his two swords. His lips were peeling back in an uncontrollable grin.

Lette placed a hand on the lizard man's arm. "Put those down, you mad bastard."

And this was not the moment where a battle would be won. Not quite. But maybe it could be just as decisive. Maybe, just maybe Theerax would say the words that would turn the might of the Batarran military upon him.

"Does anyone else need to be reminded of the stakes?" Theerax roared, his voice like the crashing of a storm. Will could feel Theerax's voice reverberating in his chest. Balur was growling, his deep baritone still a higher-pitched counterpoint to the dragon's bass roar. But the lizard man was not putting his swords away.

"Diffinax already has Tamar in the palm of his hands," bellowed Theerax, his derision like a punch to Will's solar plexus. "Gorrax will ensure Salera falls within a week. Verra will be Jotharrax's inside a month. And all you have to do is rip Batarra from the incompetent hands of the High Council. And now you fail to kill four idiotic intruders."

For a moment Will thought his heart had stopped. He thought perhaps he would rip through the wall of the tent and go and embrace Theerax. "Finally," he breathed. "Finally. You just went and said it." He turned to Cyrill. "You cannot deny that that was completely incriminating."

But Cyrill wasn't listening to him. Cyrill wasn't even listening to his great love, Theerax. Because Cyrill was on his back, clutching at his left shoulder and turning purple.

"No!" Will gasped. Because surely...surely... "Not now, you bastard!" he almost howled. "Don't you dare die on me now!"

"And once we have Batarra," boomed Theerax, "once this

whole country is on its knees, bowing its head, and chanting our worship, we shall have all Avarra in our hands. And then we shall ascend to the heavens, and tear it from the gods. And we shall cast them down, and we shall rule utterly. This whole world will be ours. Every act shall be done according to our bidding. Every word uttered will be the words we wish to be uttered. Every piece of gold will be ours."

"Holy shit!" Will threw up his hands. "You have to be hearing this! You have to be. You have to report this. This is everything!" He grabbed Cyrill and shook him by the shoulders. "Observe this, you fucker."

Will was no medical expert, but he was pretty sure from the noises that Cyrill was making that the shaking wasn't helping matters after all.

He looked around desperately. "Help me!" he begged Lette.

But Lette, like Cyrill before her, wasn't paying attention to him. She was instead looking at Balur. Because Balur stood, almost quivering, his swords shaking in his hands, staring at the massive tent. The blood still flowing down his side shone in the torchlight.

"Balur," Lette said quietly, but with unquestionable authority, "sit the fuck down."

"No," Balur growled.

And Will knew that something very bad was playing out right next to him. And yet, right there, in front of him... "He's dead," he said. And he knew he sounded outraged, and he knew that was a monstrous thing, and yet. "He's actually bloody dead," he said again. "I don't believe it."

And then from inside the tent came a human voice, quite close. It said, "Do you hear...voices?"

And Will looked up from the tragedy at his feet, and really took stock of the one playing out at his side.

Because then, with a howl, Balur slashed through the fabric of the great tent and, teeth bared, flung himself inside.

15

Run, Lettera, Run

"Oh, you stupid, silly bugger." Lette made a grab for the back of Balur's belt, and missed by a hair's breadth. It was probably a good thing. She had about as much chance of stopping him as she would have stopping a landslide. And being literally dragged into a fight with a dragon was not high on her wish list for tonight.

There again, neither was Cyrill's turning into a cold, limp corpsicle, but that hadn't made much of a difference.

Not that she was completely convinced that his testimony would have been worth much. All over Avarra the dragons had stated that their mission was to steal the heavens from the gods, and the collective reaction had been an enthusiastic thumbs-up. Certainly, taking Batarra was perhaps a bit closer to home for some of the councilors, but if you believed the bit about the heavens, why was the bit about Batarra so hard for them to believe?

It was all idiocy. All of it. Theerax claiming he was going to make all of Avarra worship him as if that weren't just evidence of ferocious dragon inbreeding. The High Council pushing the boundaries of corruption as if daring the populace to get involved in the popular-uprising business. Balur running into a tent full of dragon as if he weren't bleeding heavily from his liver. All pure idiocy.

Balur was through the ragged hole in the side of the tent now, roaring madly, whirling his blades in complex arcs. In some ways it was nice to see him with the swords. He was an exquisite swordsman, though he didn't usually show it, too happy to let his bulk do the work for him. A dull flicker of ill-placed pride briefly flared in her.

Then the world around Balur exploded into fire.

The lizard man threw himself sideways. Crates and tables piled near the side of the tent, detonated, became so much ash and waste. The tent caught fire. Lette saw Will hurling himself backward, raising an arm against the heat. Balur was on the ground, clothes smoldering.

"End them!" shrieked Theerax. The sound was so loud, Lette's legs almost buckled. But she fought on, pushing toward Balur. She ducked through the flaming hole in the tent. Balur rolled onto his back, stared at her groggily.

Five men in black robes were approaching. And beyond them…

Gods she had forgotten how big dragons were. She had… gods…

Theerax was a cathedral of muscle, scale, and horn. He was an epic poem composed to Lawl's foulest moods. He was a rocky crag of rage. Eyes of liquid fire glinted golden in a field of slate-gray scales. A ridge of wicked horns bisected his broad, snub face. He had a mouth that could swallow lives whole, two fangs the length of halberds protruding up from the lower jaw. He had his wings half-spread, great sweeps of midnight swallowing the world, coming to end everything.

For a moment, Lette blanched. And gods, for a while she had been excited by life back on the road. She had looked forward to days where adrenaline thrummed through her again. But she had forgotten about this. She had forgotten the terror dragons inspired. She had forgotten how small and helpless her fear made her, in a way she could hide but never deny. But now, staring Theerax in the face in the absurdly tight confines of this tent…gods, she was so close to death, she could feel Lawl's fingers stroking her thigh.

Her hesitation was all that one of the approaching robed men needed to fling out an arm toward her. Magically summoned winds smashed into her like a fist, hurled her across dusty ground. She hit flaming tent fabric, collapsed.

Gods, she hated magic. And part of the terror evaporated in the heat of her fury.

Five of them, whispered a quiet voice in her head. *Five of them that can move as fast as thought. But how fast can they think? With a tent on fire? With their dragon-god raging at them? There are a lot of things to pay attention to...*

Battles were not just skill, and brawn, Lette knew. Fights were strategy. And strategy was just another word for trickery, for sleight of hand. And Lette had fast hands.

She flung three knives at once, a great wild, sweeping motion. The men saw them coming, managed to throw up their hands in time. The knives whipped away, battered by the magical winds.

But Lette was moving too, running low and hard. And she moved faster than the robed men. She jumped, grasped the hilt of one deflected knife as she spun through the air, grasped another. Two out of three was good enough. She started to descend, still spinning, whipping her legs out to increase her speed, to catch their eyes. Then her arms chased her body around, and the blades sang through the air once more.

Two of the fives mages screamed. Which was a shame, because if they were screaming, they were still alive, but it was the best that Lette could manage in a pinch.

She had landed next to Balur. She reached down to slap his face. "Get up, you—"

A blast of wind sent her spinning through the air. She fought for control, skidded to a landing, barely keeping her feet.

"Your mothers were whores," she spat, as loudly as she could with wind and fire roaring around her, "and you were conceived by bastards who had to tie sticks to it to keep it up."

Again, it was the best she could manage for now. And it at

least captured their attention long enough for Will to sneak up and stab one of them.

Why the fuck he stabbed the mage in the leg, she had no idea. Surely even a farmer knew to stab someone in the head or chest? The principles of homicide and animal slaughter couldn't be that different, surely?

Still it was another man down and screaming. And it had the other two turning to look at him so she could throw knives at them properly. They went down without screams, with the air whistling out of the new vents she had carved in their lungs.

She would have liked to have finished off the others properly but at that point she heard Theerax rumble, "If you want something done properly..."

And then there was a noise like billows the size of the world inflating. "Will!" she yelled. "Cover!"

Except the only cover she could see were several screaming men in robes.

Again, the best she could manage in a pinch. She dived into a roll as the world filled with fire.

It was brief, but long enough for the kicking and screaming man she was holding to become a flaky, brittle thing that crumbled beneath her scorched palms.

She flung the incinerated man's flaming robe away and scrambled back to Balur, who was scorched but largely still whole.

"What?" he asked her confusedly.

"You're a fucking idiot and we have to move."

"So pretty much the same as usual?"

"Move!" she screamed. And she was not proud of it, but there was a dragon pacing toward her, and the ground was shaking, and gods she would not soil herself in front of these two. Would *not*. Would *never*. But gods, she wanted to just a little bit.

"Will?" Balur said, dragging himself to his feet far too slowly.

"Fuck!" Lette's voice was definitely too shrill, and honestly, if she was actually good at this—the way she used to actually be good at it—she wouldn't be giving a flying fuck about Will. She would be cutting her losses and running like...well, exactly like a dragon was on her heels in fact. But she stopped and she looked.

Where in the Hallows had farm boy got to now? And she was surprised at the hollowness she felt as she realized that one of the piles of charred flesh on the floor was probably him.

The ground shook under Theerax's advancing footsteps.

"You," he said, and Lette felt the full force of his attention upon her. "I know you."

A blackened corpse flopped obscenely. Roasted flesh sloughed away from smoke-stained bones. Will emerged, staggering.

"You!" roared Theerax, and Lette heard him inhale.

And then she was running. Gods she was running. And if the gods had any love for her, or for what she was doing on their behalf they would speed her flight. Balur was loping beside her. And Will...gods she really did hope he was running too.

Despite herself, she looked back over her shoulder. Will was right there, legs pumping, arms pistoning. And behind him—

She dove to the ground, slid through slick mud, felt it spattering up over her.

Flame roared through the world. A shrieking stream of it. She rolled desperately. The heat was searing, unbearable. She was screaming.

Then someone was grabbing her arm, hauling her to her feet. Balur, looking dazed, side slick with blood still.

"That is being fucking toasty," he said.

Her whole side felt raw. But she was moving still. Balur was moving still.

"Will?" she managed.

Balur grinned. "I knew you were caring."

Lette didn't have the time or the energy to punch him. There wasn't time to do anything but move. She could hear Theerax howling, "Stop them!"

And then there was another voice, Will, half the hair on his head scorched short, screaming, "This way!" and beckoning down between two lines of tents.

Then life dissolved into blurs of motion, and battle madness. It collapsed into mud paths, and faceless junctions, and knives flung at guards. There were shouts, and roars, and the sounds of flame. And Lette kept her ears open, waiting, waiting, waiting for the sound of wings, of death mounting to the skies.

Is this why you went to the farm with Will? part of her asked. *Because you never wanted to go through this again? Were you just running away?*

And then another part of her asked, *What in the Hallows? Is this really the time for self-reflection?*

But she had not been afraid like this in a long time. Even back in Kondorra, with the dragons in the skies chasing after her, she had not truly felt this way. It had been in the weeks afterward. It had been lying in bed at night beside Will. That was when she had started to relive it all.

Maybe stopping was the mistake.

Shut up! Shut up and run!

She didn't know. She couldn't. All she knew was that she had wanted to be a better person, someone who wasn't defined by killing anymore. And she had achieved that. She had been a farmer's wife, then a dilettante, and now she was…a freedom fighter? A voice of reason? She wasn't sure. But she was doing the right thing. Even now, scrabbling through the muck, desperate to get to her feet. Even punching a guard in the throat and plunging a knife between his ribs. She was doing the right thing.

Was fear the price of that?

Gods, if any of the divinities could get her brains to shut up, she might even start worshipping them while she was trying to save them.

There was a knot of soldiers by the gate. They knew what was about to happen. They had readied spears and halberds. Others had swords drawn.

Balur lowered one shoulder, let out a roar.

But then she was tearing past him, a knife in each hand. And they would not stop her, could not stop her. She would not be taken prisoner by them, by fear, by questions. She would defy it all. Fuck these people. Fuck this dragon. Fuck her fear.

She tore into their ranks, pirouetting, whirling, ducking, leaping. She arced through trails of blood. Her knives rose and fell, rose and fell, stitching out a pattern of violence, of defiance, of escape.

She stood panting, in a circle of bodies.

Balur was standing nearby, head cocked to one side. Will was standing, bent double, hands on his knees, sucking in air.

"Damn," Balur said.

"Shut up and just get those gods-hexed doors open."

He didn't even bother removing the bar, just kicked five times, until it split. Cold air rushed in, and they rushed out.

16

Some Like It Hot

Quirk's stomach rumbled. Of everything, that was probably the worst of it. That the smell of cooked flesh filled the small cell, and her stomach rumbled.

Two corpses stood before her. Silhouette sketches of men. One had a sword held out toward her, clutched in ashen fingers. The other stood farther back, pointing at her. Then, slowly, they fell apart. The sword clattered to the floor as the finger that clutched it flaked to ash.

She was alone in a room of dust and smoke.

A noise left her. Something like a sob. Something like a laugh. Something like horror and something like ecstasy. She had done this. She had. And they had deserved it. Gods, they had deserved it...But...Had she?

Had she been worthy to be their judge? Their executioner? How could anyone? Wasn't she in this moment as bad as Diffinax himself? Her unilateral decision to simply end a life. Who had given her that right?

And yet, even as her head reeled, her heart sang. She had done it. She had unleashed herself, been truly herself for the first time in years, in decades. She felt...complete. As if this was meant to be. As if she had been born for this.

"Gods." She put her head in her hands. Her stomach growled again. She felt her knees giving way.

Something was rising out of her, and for a moment she didn't know what it was. And then she was screaming, howling out all of her fear, and her rage, and her hate. She was storming through the cell, kicking at the swirling ashes, screaming obscenities, until she was left gasping and panting, watching the tears drip from her face to make small craters in the ashes on the floor.

And then she heard another noise. Someone else's sob.

Afrit.

Gods, she was so wrapped up in herself she had forgotten all about the other woman. And with that thought came the realization that this had not—perhaps—been wholly selfish. That she had been trying to do some greater good. That she had been trying to save someone.

Her cell door was still open. Stumbling slightly, feeling as if she were in a dream, she pushed it wide and stepped out into the central hallway. She could smell the damp, and the rot, and the filth—undertones to the stink of roast flesh and hot steel that still emanated from the room behind her. She could feel the uneven flagstones, smoothed by the footsteps of countless souls, slightly slick with algae and mold.

She went to Afrit's cell. The door was sealed by a heavy bronze lock. And the keys were back in her cell, buried in the ash of dead men.

So she took the lock in her hand. And for a moment she hesitated. But Afrit was in that cell. And if she could hang on to nothing else, she could hang on to that. Rescuing Afrit was the right thing to do.

Fire unfurled within her. And it was not a ripping or a tearing this time. It was not a moment of fear or hate. This time she chose to unbind the fire. This time she coaxed it to life. And she felt its warmth spread through her. And she felt strong, and sure, and for a moment she knew that this was exactly what she should be doing.

Then, in a moment of a cresting ecstasy, the heat in her palm rose, and rose, and rose, and then erupted forward.

And then it was over, and the door's lock was just so much slag on the stone floor. Quirk felt spent, and oddly forlorn, as if she had been grasping toward some greater meaning of life and then abruptly veered from the path.

"Afrit?" she said. Her voice sounded small and tentative now. "Afrit, are you there?"

In the shadows, something moved. Quirk caught sight of a chain that snaked into darkness. It tremored. One end was attached to an iron hoop embedded in the floor. She stepped toward it.

Afrit whimpered.

"It's okay," Quirk said. "We're going to get out of here." She knelt, took the end of Afrit's chain, and slowly followed it, hand over hand into the darkness. She stopped moving when she heard Afrit whimper.

"It's okay," she said again. And slowly, slowly, she let the fire uncurl. The metal began to glow, dully at first, but with increasing fierceness. And she could see Afrit's face sketched out in the dull light. The bruises. The pain. The disbelief that she could hope again. Then the chain fell apart in molten spatters.

Quirk opened her glowing hand, let its light fill the space between them. And despite the blood and contusions that marred Afrit's face, she forced a smile onto her own. With the fire thrumming through her, it was not as hard as she had expected. "See?" she said. "Sometimes there is a light in the dark."

Still supporting Afrit's weight, Quirk hesitated just before the top of the steps that led up and away from their cells.

Fill the space with fire, whispered a voice in her mind. *There's no one here who deserves to live.* And for a moment it was Hethren whispering to her, reaching out of her past, telling her to do terrible things.

No. She shook herself slightly. This was *her* voice. That was one of the first lessons she had learned: *Take responsibility for my own actions, for my own thoughts; recognize them as my own, and respond accordingly.*

In some ways, the preemptive strike was the safest thing to do. End everything before it began.

It's not a question of whether I live or die, she thought, *but rather of how I live. Of what I can live with.*

So she balled her courage and rounded the corner without summoning a flame.

And she stared onto an empty corridor. She felt foolish and relieved in equal measures.

The corridor continued the theme of the cells below. Stone, lichen, dirt, and piss. A few torches guttered at the far end. There was little light.

"We're still in the dungeons," Afrit said.

Quirk took stock. "This must be the Northern Barbican," she said. "That has plentiful dungeons. It moves people out of the city center, away from the city's eyes. Out of sight and mind. I had heard they were taking political prisoners there."

Afrit nodded and they carried on shuffling down the corridor. Then a noise made them stop. Quirk felt flame flare in her heart, but Afrit stopped and cocked her head to one side. Then she looked at Quirk. "Did you say prisoners? Plural?"

They moved as a pack now.

Quirk had gone back, gone through all the doorways, checked all the cells. Each one had held someone, sometimes more than one. And so fire had flared in her again and again. Each prisoner had stumbled into this imitation of freedom asking questions, gabbling with them. Shushing them did no good, and so Quirk just moved on to the next door, the next prisoner, and one by one they fell into line. A murmuring pack pacing behind her.

Her blood felt hot. Her arteries were lines of fire striping her arms and legs. Flame had infected her. Her breath steamed in the corridor. And she remembered this. This seduction. She remembered feeling this way. That piece of rogue divinity inside of her infecting her thoughts.

She held on to herself desperately, repeated the mantras. And yet her wrath was righteous. She knew it in her bones. As she walked down the corridor with the others at her back. As they moved as one, with the same deadly purpose, the same anger, the same desperation.

We are getting out of here.

They finally arrived at the stairs, at the dull arc of light that had defined escape for so long now. And they did not sneak up now. They surged.

Burn. Burn. Burn. The word beat through her with each heartbeat.

Be the lake, she whispered back. And she somehow held on to that image in her head. But the rage did not subside. Her calm was murderous.

They burst up from the stairs, from the dungeons, and from their captivity in a silent wave. A guardroom greeted them. Soldiers sat at a table, playing cards. Two carved a roast. Two leaned beside a washbasin arguing together. Another sat on a bench polishing his shoes. Another was working away at a stain on his tunic.

He was the first one Quirk incinerated. Flame shot out from her hand, a thick ribbon of it spilling from her palms. She cracked it like a whip, set their table ablaze. Cards flew like flaming butterflies.

The other prisoners spilled out around her, filling the room to the left and right. Three of them fell upon the guard polishing his boots. They kicked and bit and tore. Others grabbed the two at the washbasin.

She filled the center of the room with a cone of flame. She felt her body become little more than a conduit. The fire was a lake, and she was nothing but a burst dam. The other prisoners grabbed a guard, shoved his head into the fire. His struggles died quickly.

A few guards had more wits, or better reflexes. They flung themselves toward the edges of the rooms. They grabbed swords, slashed into the prisoners. But they were only a handful, and they had locked up so many men and women.

It was all over in a few moments. Blood and bodies littered the floor. Quirk's heart slammed against her ribs like a caged bird. She wrestled with herself, managed to erect once more the walls that kept her fire contained.

So long, she murmured in her head. *How did I go so long without this?*

Then the smell hit her. Ash and roast corpses. And she remembered how. Pieces of limbs had been carved from their owners. Blood lay in great sprays up the walls. Three prisoners were dead. Another was on his knees clutching his guts. Another was sitting desperately trying to stanch a great slash that ran up her arm.

"Shit," Quirk whispered. "Shit."

"Where now?" someone asked.

Quirk looked around trying to find someone to answer the question. Then she noticed that everyone was looking at her.

"I don't—" she started, but Afrit cut her off with a hand on her arm.

That was not what these people needed to hear, Quirk realized. They were traumatized, brutalized, and probably on the edge of collapse. Hope and rage were the only things keeping them on their feet. So she looked around, pointed at the first door she found.

"That way," she said.

They moved. A few grabbed the guards' fallen swords as they went. And she found that she was nodding as they did so, the same way she would at the fast learners in any class.

Gods, what am I teaching them? And then, straight on the heels of that thought, *I'm teaching them? Then we truly are all doomed.*

But there was no time for doubts, because the prisoners were smashing through the door, pushing down a short corridor, and breaking out into a courtyard dappled in faint light. She heard the clash of steel before she made it there. She pushed through the crowd, desperation clawing at her. They needed her protection. She could do so much more damage. Could stop the prisoners from being damaged themselves.

The courtyard was chaos. The guards must have been halfway through some drill or other. They all had weapons in hand. Were all hacking into the escapees.

"No!" Quirk yelled in horror, and then she was lashing out. Fire slammed into one man like a physical blow, sent him sailing through the air, knocking over others.

Revulsion quaked in her as she set a man's head on fire. This was far from the melting of cell bars. This was far even from a momentary burst of violent self-defense. Even the mental shield of righteousness was failing her now. This was moving closer and closer to murder. These men could not stand against her.

And still they fought on. Still they hacked and slashed at the people she was trying to rescue.

"Stop!" she screamed at them. "Stop it! Run from us! Run from me!"

But they didn't hear her, or they didn't care, or they were solely employed for their suicidal tendencies, and so she lashed out again, and again, and again, cutting swaths through their ranks.

Finally a group of guards started to pull back. They were a knot of bristling swords, jabbing tentatively out as the prisoners gathered about them jeering.

"Stop!" Quirk yelled at the escapees. "Let them go! We don't need to kill them! We are the resistance. We have to be better than what we aim to supplant."

And that sort of speech, Quirk thought, *is why the academics are never the ones to actually carry out the revolutions.*

For a moment she thought her voice still went unheard, but then the prisoners did step back. They kept their swords up, but they stopped pressing forward, and they stopped their jeering.

"We just," Quirk said, addressing the group of guards, "want to be let go." There were eight or nine of them, she thought. "We don't want to do any more harm."

There was shuffling in the knot of men, and Quirk prepared a smile for whomever they elected leader.

Then the crossbow bolt lanced out of the mass, thundering toward her skull.

She flinched, but it was far too little, far too late. Instead what saved her was that she had personally immolated a score or more of the bowman's friends, and seeing that sort of thing could put a quiver in a man's hands no matter how hefty his loins. And so the man's aim was just short of true. The bolt glanced off her forehead, scoring a deep gash that screamed with pain, but her skull remained surprisingly whole.

There was a moment of hesitation, of perfect calm. Then the prisoners roared, charged the knot of men. And then they were charging at nothing more than a bonfire.

And for a moment, Quirk was lost. She was ignorant of the prisoners staring at her in awe. She was ignorant of the blood sheeting down her face, reflecting her flames in dull crimson. She was ignorant even of the screams of the guards as their skin cracked, their muscles blackened, and their bones cracked. She was aware of only a single word, a single thought, a single intent.

Burn.

Then she was spent, and the guards were little more than ashes on the ground. She dropped to her knees gasping. The world felt distant, hard to understand. She had the sense of having been somewhere else, some dreamscape that was slipping through her fingers. She was only half-aware of Afrit helping her to her feet and guiding her through the field of bodies. Someone had found the stables, horses were filling the yard. They milled about, seeming the only real things in the smoky haze of torched bodies. Weapons were being recovered, distributed. Someone was helping her up onto a horse. Then the gates of the Northern Barbican were being opened. The great gates that led not into the city, but north and away, out onto the great plains, toward the Rosalian hills and Quirk's childhood.

And then she was riding, out into the grass and the wind, swept up and away, the scent of burnt flesh swirling on the air about her.

17

The Hand in the Puppet

"That Lawl chap. He's a bit of a bastard, isn't he?"

The crowd went nuts. They roared, they whooped, they ate it up like pigs at the trough bowl.

To be fair, Firkin thought, he'd probably sold the line a bit better this time. He'd found some hatred to put into the words. A little fire in his belly and his balls to spit out at the world. Because screw Lawl. That pretentious god pretending that he sat above everyone, that because others were squished beneath the fabulous weight of his arse, he was better than them.

Take him down, whispered a voice in his head. *Show them all what a fool Lawl is.*

Also helping sell the line, perhaps, was his improved location. This was no sweaty little temple he stood in now. The inhabitants of District Three had, in fact, managed to dig up an abandoned amphitheater. To be fair, it seemed as if it also doubled as a midden heap, and most of those gathered here were knee-deep in refuse, but it was far more than Firkin had believed his audience capable of.

A lot had changed since his first appearance in the Third District. He had gotten a feel for his audience, for what they liked to hear, and how they liked to hear it. And his audience had gotten a feel for him. And just as in Kondorra, their feeling for him was now much like their feelings for a whore on Cois's feast day. And so the crowds at his temple had grown and then they had burst its walls and he had preached on the streets. And now he was here. And people shouted his words between sermons. And District Three was still a festering hole of a district, but now its inhabitants held their heads higher, and kneecapped people from other districts. And that hadn't exactly been Firkin's intent, but he was going with it.

The whisper was less enthusiastic about their new location. *Looks like that arsehole Lawl took a shit here and expected us to be happy about it*, it whispered. Firkin decided to use that.

"Look at this place." He swept an arm around the filthy amphitheater. "It's like Lawl took a shit here and expected us to be happy about it."

And the crowd ate that up too. Firkin wasn't entirely sure where the whispering voice had come from, but it did have the most tremendous ideas.

"We are honest," he howled at the crowd. "We are true. We are authentic. When we shit, we know it is rotten, foul, and septic."

That, he thought, was true enough. But the crowd did not disappoint. They came right along with him. He grinned.

"We're not like the High Priesthood, are we?" And that they loved. That they lost their absolute gods-hexed minds for. He could pretty much say anything he wanted as long as he turned it back to the High Priesthood being a bag of dicks.

"They're just like Lawl. Just like that frothing fuckhole that deserves to choke to death on a horse's—"

He caught himself. That was…Had he meant to say that? He shook his head. He'd never given Lawl two spare thoughts before. Or…had he? Something like a memory rumbled in his head, turned over, and was out of his grasp.

The crowd stared up at him expectantly.

"Rules," he spat, trying to regain his flow. "Rules, and laws, and order." He pointed uphill, toward the High Temple. "Demanding that we smile and just go along as they smear their filth in our faces."

And the crowd was back to cheering. And he was back in his expected groove. He reached for a bottle of holy wine, upended it over his face, drank what he could. More cheering.

Give them what they want, said the whisper. *What you need.*

Firkin nodded. It made sense.

"They hear us, those priests!" Firkin yelled. "You know that, don't you?" He pointed again. "They pretend they don't pay attention, but they do." He nodded, found himself staring up at the heavens, at the seat of that so-called king of the gods.

He closed his eyes, focused.

"They sent someone down, those priests," he said. There was no need to shout now.

Whisper it in their ears. That's how you'll persuade them.

"They sent someone with a blade. Sent him to my chambers."

That was a bit of a stretch. The idiot with a knife had made it about three blocks into District Three before a gang of fifteen men had set about him with sticks and then dragged what was left of him to Firkin's chambers. It was also debatable whether the High Priesthood had sent him or not. The High Priesthood's disconnection from the city made them easy to decry, but it also meant that it was very possible for them to not know they were being decried at all. Still, the situation was close enough for Firkin's purposes.

Firkin beckoned to the stage's wings, and a pair of heavyset men heaved the assassin out for all to see. He was strapped hand and foot to a giant wooden X. His bloody head lolled above his spread-eagled frame. He looked small and pathetic to Firkin.

The crowd went completely berserk. There were perhaps two thousand of them and they flung themselves at the stage he was using as an altar. The whole place seemed to pulse with the sound of their cheers. He felt waves of it batter him.

Yes, whispered the voice. *Yes, this is right.*

For a moment Firkin licked his lips. Where did the voice come from? He'd been trying to ignore that question. But there was no doubt that as his popularity rose, the whisper had started to become clearer and clearer. He felt reassured when it spoke. He felt certainty. He felt like something powerful was moving within him. But...was it a memory? Had he felt this way before? Had the voice spoken to him before? So much was a blur. He was sure he'd been to this city before, but when? Hadn't he been born and raised in Kondorra?

Gods, he didn't even remember being a child.

He quickly drank more wine. Those felt dangerously like sober thoughts.

Blood and wine, the voice chanted in his head. *Blood and wine. Wine and blood.*

He showed the crowd the knife. The sounds rose even louder.

Why didn't he remember bringing the knife? Had someone just given it to him?

Blood and wine. Wine and blood. And blood.

He strode to the assassin's side, looked up at the small, broken man.

"This is what we think of the High Priest's laws!" he screamed, and it felt right as he said it. The scream of the crowd felt right. Some deep resonance ringing within him, and he didn't pay attention to the people storming up onto the stage in a frenzy. He just reached out and slit the man's throat. He held the wine pitcher so that the blood flooded into it in a hot spray, flecking his fingers and face.

He raised the pitcher above his head, anointed himself with the mess of blood and wine as the crowd closed around him. They lifted him up cheering. The hot mess flowed into his throat.

He felt powerful. He felt like a god. Like he could spit in Lawl's eye, probably while screwing Betra—Lawl's wife—right in front of him.

Then time seemed to blink and abruptly he was back on the stage, and the crowd were back in the pit of the amphitheater, barely able to contain themselves. And how had he...Hadn't they been carrying him just a moment before?

He shook his head. It was not the first time had skipped for him. Though, at least this time it wasn't a weekend and he wasn't being cuddled by an ogre called Garry.

He found a grin to wear, put it on his face. "How do you feel?" he asked the crowd. They roared back their joy. "Do you feel good?"

They'd do anything for you right now, whispered the voice. *They would give you anything.*

"What would you give me?" he said. And he hadn't meant to say it. The thought had simply come out. What did he even want? Wine?

"A fresh pitcher?" he asked, feeling off-kilter. And the crowd screamed, and roared, and laughed, and yes, yes, yes, they would give him a fresh pitcher. Wineskins arced through the air, landed with wet explosions on the stage where the dead assassin's body hung and dripped.

And then the memory in his head stirred. And it stretched. And suddenly it was everything in his head. It was filling him. And still he could not penetrate it. He could only cower and shiver in the back of his own skull, as it reached out and it spoke.

"Would you give me glory?" His body thundered. *"Would you give me treasures? Would you give me shelter as befits me?"*

He felt his body turn. The controls had been ripped away from him. What the fuck was going on?

"Would you fight for me?" His body thundered, and the crowd thundered back.

"Would you kill for me?"

"Yes!" they screamed.

"Would you give me blood and wine?"

Yes, and yes, and yes.

And in the back of his own mind, Firkin fought desperately for control.

18

The Fine Art of Politicking
at Sword Point

Considering that she had little personal attachment to the city of Bellenet, Lette found the place surprisingly reassuring. It was, she supposed, probably because it wasn't full of arseholes chasing her.

Now ensconced within its embracing walls, she stumbled down the steps of the inn where they had stashed what was left of Balur and into the large common room. Will sat there, staring at a tankard of ale, constipated with worry.

"Balur's resting," she told him. "I had to punch the innkeeper's wife to make it happen, but it happened." She sat down heavily opposite him.

Even after all the time she'd spent with Balur, Lette still wasn't as familiar with Analesian health care as she would like. However, she knew enough that—when taken together—turning eight shades paler, seeming only half-conscious at the best of times, and stopping talking altogether were generally not considered a fantastic set of signs.

It was two days since they had fled Theerax's encampment, marching almost constantly, and only seizing a few hours of sleep in scraggly, rain-soaked fields. Two days of coaxing and cajoling Balur, and desperately pushing ahead of Theerax's pursuing guards. But now they were finally safe, and she was capable of properly regarding the tatters that their plans lay in.

"Cyrill's dead," Will said finally.

"I noticed," Lette said. She took the pitcher of ale he'd ordered and, in the absence of a second tankard, poured it directly into her mouth. She swilled the liquid around and swallowed. "It was the way he kicked about as his heart gave out, and then his corpse was roasted by an angry dragon. It didn't leave much room for doubt."

"We rather needed him to be alive." Will was feigning calm, and yet what he was actually doing was moaning. She had no patience for him in this mood. Indeed for the mood he had been in since Pekarra.

"Without him," Will went on, "there isn't anyone independent to tell the Batarran High Council what's going on."

"While we're pointing out obvious things," Lette said conversationally, "if you carry on like this, I'm going to punch that fucking tankard through the back of your head."

"We're fucked," Will said, setting his tankard down, as if in emphasis. "We've got nothing. This whole experience was essentially an exercise in mortally wounding Balur."

And "mortally wounding" was not a phrase Lette needed to hear at that point. "Pick that tankard back up," Lette advised Will.

"Stop it," he told her. Which was far less advisable.

She leaned forward, because she wanted to be certain that the homicide she was about to commit was justifiable. "What did you say to me?" she asked.

And then, catching her entirely off guard, something seemed to snap in Will, and that glimpse of fire she'd seen in the Batarran High Council flared back to life.

"You," he spat with a force she hadn't expected, "were supposed to love me. Happily ever fucking after. To have a life with me. To find peace with me. We were supposed to be happy. Together. But you shit on that. You ran away. Which is not your right, you understand? You're brave. You're a fighter. Or a mercenary, or whatever. You stand and you fight. I'm the one who runs away. I'm the coward. *I'm a farmer.* And I don't pretend that sitting on my arse and drinking myself into oblivion is any sort of admirable thing to have done, but *I'm a farmer.* And then I find you arse-deep in people in a bordello, and then our lives are threatened, and dragons—who, I want to point out, should be all gone from Avarra—are popping up all over the place and sending people to threaten our lives. And I think I was pretty cool about all that. I even worked with you. And we came up with a plan. And it worked. And we found evidence to get the Batarran council on our side. And a dragon chased us. And I still haven't lost my shit. But we're totally fucked now, and *I'm still a fucking farmer,* and I could really use your help, instead of stupid cursed threats, so if you could just stop it, it would be greatly fucking appreciated."

Then he picked his tankard up.

So Lette did her best to put it through the back of his skull. And while she wasn't entirely successful, he did end up several feet away and it took him three tries to get up, which was fairly satisfying.

But then Will went and ruined her sense of catharsis by daring to ask her, "What in the name of Barph's ball sack?"

And gods piss on him. Let them absolutely drown him in piss. Because could he not...? Had he sat there for six months and not understood why she'd left for even a moment? What a self-involved...

"You were the leader of an army." And Lette found she was actually quivering with rage. "You were a divine prophet. You were the head of a nation. You were a dragon slayer. You were a strategist. You were *brilliant.* So don't you fucking dare tell me you are a farmer. You promised me the world and then gave me pig shit. What did you expect?

"And now my best friend in all the world, maybe my only

friend, truth be told, is wounded so badly he cannot stand. So badly I don't know if he'll live or die, and you are going to pull the same shit on me? The same 'I'm just a pig farmer' crap?" Lette spat, and flung the pitcher of beer away. "Fucking nut up, Willet Fallows. Be the man you really are. The man you're apparently too fucking scared to be. Come up with a plan, and tell it to me. Because I have shit-all interest in anything else you have to say."

She was aware of the other tavern patrons' eyes on her. And normally she would give less than a shit about what plebs like them thought, but she felt unusually exposed right now. She had not meant to let all of that out. Or... not in that manner. Just to state it all baldly and nakedly...

Gods, when had she started caring about this crap? She should just stab every idiot in this place. That way no tales would be told.

The man by the door first. Close off the exit. Then the bartender—a potential rallying point. Picking out a kill order helped her find her calm.

Will spluttered. And still she waited for something to harden into resolve.

Stab that little shit over by the bar in the knees. He looks fast. She took a breath, steadied herself.

She was just considering stabbing Will in the meaty part of his thigh and seeing if that helped him focus a little when finally she saw it. The emotional soup locked down. Resolve set in his jaw.

She fought to suppress her sigh of relief.

"We lie," he said.

She arched an eyebrow. "That's it?" Her sigh of relief felt like a waste of effort now.

Will nodded. "Yes. Why complicate it? We just write down what they need to hear, sign Cyrill's name, and tell them he's dead. That last bit isn't even a lie."

Lette rolled her eyes. "It's what he would have wanted."

Will shrugged. "It's what we've got."

And Lette supposed it was. She had nothing better. But, "We don't have a forger," she pointed out.

"Do you think," Will said, "that anyone in that council room would have the slightest clue what Cyrill's signature looks like?"

"Fair point." Lette shook her head. "Gods, we could have stabbed Cyrill as soon as we found him, written the report we needed, and saved ourselves a lot of bother." And gods she couldn't help but feel a little disappointed that this was what she was waiting for.

But when she looked at Will she saw that scrap of steel that lay within him. And maybe that was what she had been waiting for.

All told, it took them about half an hour to get it ready. They wrote the letter, sealed it with some candle wax, and used a Batarran golden bull to stamp it. The coin had some coat of arms or other emblazoned on it.

Before they left for the council, Lette spoke to the innkeeper in a low whisper. "If that Analesian dies while I'm out, I shall carve out your heart, shit on it, and figure out a way to use the resulting mess to murder the rest of your family." She smiled. He genuflected.

Outside, the streets of Bellenet were quieter than she remembered. She hadn't paid much attention to the city when they staggered in, and so she had missed this change in its temperament. The volume of guards patrolling the streets had more than doubled. Groups of tense young men and women moving in groups of three to five. Many stores were closed, and those that were open were either empty or full of the same muttering groups. They looked as ready for violence as the soldiers.

And she heard Theerax's name.

"If this is not a city on the verge of monstrous rioting," she whispered to Will, "then I have not personally helped put down forty-seven riots by stabbing union ringleaders in the face."

Will looked at her. "You are going to have terrible stories to tell your grandchildren."

She shrugged. "My grandchildren will be badasses. They will love my stories."

The High Council buildings were as quiet as the streets outside. Lette and Will barely even had to bribe their way to the central chambers. The same official in the same blue velvet suit was sitting outside the double oaken doors. His broken nose was new, though, and it went well with his new attitude. At the sight of them, he grabbed his ledger, and with a shrill scream, scampered off to a corner of the room so he could hide behind it.

Will stepped forward and pushed open the door to the council chamber. Much to Lette's relief, the members of the High Council all appeared to be fully clothed. The clothes were generally too tight perhaps, and they certainly belonged on people who hadn't weathered as many decades, but at least they were on. In fact, if she were pressed, Lette would probably have judged the lot of them to be slightly more sober than drunk.

What in the Hallows had happened in Bellenet over the past few days?

The council, however, gave her no time to ask.

"Ah, you're back," said the large woman who had first addressed them last time. Jocasta, if Lette remembered her name correctly. "You have proof that this Theerax and his ilk are all arseholes who need to be gutted and served up on feast days, I assume."

Lette exchanged a glance with Will. He was as clueless as she. And what was going on? Jocasta was treating them as if they were expected. As if this were all a final formality before . . . What?

"Yes." Will held out their forgery slowly. Lette felt like perhaps the ring her tankard had left on it was perhaps a bigger deal than she'd made it out to be. But a councilor picked himself up from his seat, walked briskly to Will, and plucked the paper from his fingers.

"I'll summon General Tout," Jocasta said, and picked herself up, heading for a small door at the back of the room. Other councilors around the table shuffled papers about, and flicked through large ledgers. And still no one had opened their report. In fact no one was paying them any attention at all.

"What's going on?" she asked, mostly so Will didn't ask it before she did.

She was largely ignored, so she repeated the question louder. The councilman who had fetched the note from Will glanced over his shoulder. "Oh, we don't need you anymore. You can run along now."

Lette was distinctly tempted to remove the man's tendons and use them to turn him into a life-sized marionette of a useless arsehole. And yet...hadn't this been her plan: to hand off responsibility for this mess? She, Balur, and Will couldn't handle a dragon and his army on their own. The encampment had proven that. And they didn't have their own troops anymore. And so, what else was left? It was time to hand everything over to this set of debauched social climbers and let them cling with deranged tenacity to the power they'd bought.

Will was now the one attempting to exchange a look with her. "We just leave?" he whispered.

"You trust these people to find a fuck in a brothel?" she whispered back.

Will hemmed and hawed... "Well," he said, "for that specific example, yes, I think most of them probably have quite a lot of hands-on experience, but to put down a revolt...?"

"It's a figure of speech," she said irritably.

"No, I'm aware. It's just..." He shrugged helplessly. "Context."

It was this sort of shit that stopped her from feeling bad about leaving him.

The door on the far side of the Council Chambers slammed open and Councilwoman Jocasta marched back in. She was not alone. By her side strode a short, stout man draped in medals, who stood so straight Lette suspected he could taste the broomstick that had been rammed up his arse in the back of his throat. Most of his hair had migrated from his head to his upper lip, where it had accumulated in a truly monumental mustache. This, she supposed, was General Tout.

Filing in after this pair came fifteen more soldiers in full dress uniform. Lette suspected that the creases in their trousers weren't any less sharp than the curved scimitars hanging at their sides. General Tout had probably examined his reflection in one of their breastplates for optimal mustache grooming.

"General," said one of the councilmen at the table, standing up, his chair scraping, "so glad you could join us. We need to discuss war."

"War?" barked the general. He arched an eyebrow that clearly aspired to the same levels of bushiness as his mustache.

"An invader has quietly snuck into our realm, General," said Jocasta. "He has amassed an army, and turned the people against their rightful rulers."

And that was what had changed, Lette realized. That was the reason for it all. The cult of Theerax had reached critical mass in the streets of Bellenet. The people were more interested in what he had to say than in whatever the High Council was spouting that day. The people in this room were clinging to power only through the might of the city guard.

That was why they didn't even bother looking at our "proof," she thought. *They're not looking for proof anymore. Just an excuse.*

Democracies, meritocracies...they always had far too many rules about going to war. It's why she had always liked petty despots and tyrants. Give her the constant infighting of the five duchies with their autonomous princes, or the warlords of eastern Verra, over a democracy any day of the week.

"A snake in our midst," the general said, at earsplitting volume.

"One poised to sink his fangs into our nation's great bosom," said Jocasta, clutching at her own for no reason that Lette could really elicit. "Which is why we need you to gather your troops and stab it repeatedly about the head, neck, and torso. Is that clear enough?"

General Tout beamed at Jocasta. He had, Lette noted, absolutely terrible teeth.

"Perfectly," said the general. Then he yanked out his sword and rammed it neatly through Councilwoman Jocasta's stomach.

19

Oh Snap

For a second everything was very quiet in the Batarran High Council chambers. Everything except Councilwoman Jocasta, anyway. She was dying very noisily indeed. Then General Tout ripped his sword out, in a great jagged sideways slash, opening her guts up properly, and she passed out as she collapsed to the floor and generally spilled everywhere.

General Tout stepped neatly away from the spreading pool of blood, guts, bile, and shit, and into a roar of shock and outrage.

"What?" and "Why?" seemed to be a general theme, along with a heavy dose of "How dare you?" and the more declarative "You'll hang for this!"

General Tout looked unmoved by this outburst, pleased by it even. "A snake?" he roared, in a voice that would carry over cannon fire. "Poised to strike?" He spat massively. The gob of phlegm landed in the dead center of the council table. "Why, the poison has already rotted the heart of this once great nation!" He reached out and with his blade slashed the throat of a councilman who had possessed the temerity to approach him. "It is time to breathe new life into this pitiful shell of a nation. If there is a snake to kill, it is you!" He lunged forward, speared a councilor, who was slow to pick up on the general "run and hide" vibe that was circulating through the room. "You would have me strike against Theerax? I would have him deliver me from insidious turds like you!"

With that he set about himself properly, hurling himself at the knot of paralyzed, panicked councilors, hacking at limbs and chests, coating himself in a fine spray of bright arterial blood, laughing manically.

"Fuck," said Lette. And then the full weight of it hit her. Because this was the man in charge of the whole city's defenses. This was the man to whom the city guards reported. Which meant that they were not suppressing the populace. They were waiting to hand this city and this country over to Theerax. So again she shouted, "Fuck!"

The soldiers who had accompanied General Tout into the room were spreading out, leaping up onto the table, smashing their blades into the councilors with a force and enthusiasm that spoke of years of pent-up hatred. The High Council had not been spending its drunken, sex-filled sessions making a tremendous amount of friends.

Will spun toward Lette, grabbed her shoulder. "What are you waiting for?" he asked her, eyes wild. "Kill people!"

She reached for a knife, but her hands were slow, her mind racing this time. Because what would it achieve? They had needed the Batarran High Council because they needed an army. But the council didn't have an army anymore. Even if she cut down General Tout now, it would achieve little. His colonels and lieutenants would be loyal to him—and therefore loyal to Theerax—not the council. And they would be out in the city right now. If she cut off this head, another would simply arise and take power. Tout was a general, a strategist. He would only be here—grinning so broadly as he sawed the head off a councilman that Lette could see the blood staining his teeth—if he already had a hundred contingency plans in place.

And she...she was just a foot soldier. A mercenary. A blade in the darkness. She had no contingency plans. She just had Balur out there in a city that was in the middle of going to shit.

She put the blade back in her pocket. Soldiers had not yet

blocked off the door behind her. They were having too much fun in the middle of the room. One stood on the table, spearing councilors in the head one by one. Two others held a councilwoman by the shoulders and feet while a third hacked and hacked at her stomach.

"Balur," Lette said simply, and ducked back toward the door.

"What?" Will stared at her. "But we . . . These people."

Lette grit her teeth, let a blade fall into each hand, and killed two soldiers with an open fling of her hands. Two more looked up at them. Otherwise the slaughter carried on unabated.

"There," Lette said. "Now we have to run. Happy now?"

Will stared at her. "What? No!"

"Well, neither am I, so at least you made two of us."

They had four of the soldiers advancing on them now.

"Can't you . . . ?" Will said desperately.

And that was flattering in an oddly stupid sort of way. "There are four of them," Lette pointed out, "and I just completed a forced march." She took a breath. "I am not semi-divine. Now can we run away, please, or do I have to tell you this is a tactical withdrawal as well?"

Will grimaced. "Gods." But he was turning to run.

Which set the soldiers off, of course.

Lette turned and fled.

20

That Which We Have Come to Fear the Most

Will sucked air as they emerged out of the Batarran Council chambers and into the city of Bellenet proper. Then he glanced around, lowered his head...and hesitated as Lette put her hand on his arm.

She's touching me. Which was not an appropriate thought. Partly because it was a pathetic one, especially after this long together, but mostly because of the whole running-for-their-lives thing.

"Slow down," Lette hissed. "We don't want to attract attention."

"This city is being overthrown by a dragon whom we have openly opposed," Will pointed out. "Speed seems like it would be of the essence."

"Openly?" Lette gave him a look like he had just made an indecent proposal. Well...actually, as Will recalled, there was a time when she had actually been quite open to indecent proposals, but...he wasn't thinking about that.

"We have opposed Theerax to a governing body so far removed from the people it governs that they have chosen a giant fire-breathing monster over them." She started pulling him by the arm, entering the streets at nothing more than a brisk walking pace. "No one here has a clue what we said."

Will felt himself relax. "So we're—"

"No." Lette cut him off. "Of course we're not okay. Not everyone in this city is going to support Theerax and so there is going to be violence. Probably quite a lot of it."

Will stopped relaxing. "I'm coming back," he said, "to the point where I'm fairly sure we should be running."

Lette shook her head. "The city guards are waiting for a signal." She nodded at yet another of the ubiquitous patrols. "And they'll be massively on edge. The last thing we want to do is alarm someone and set this whole tinderbox on fire. No. We just walk briskly and hope we make it back to the Balding Eagle before—"

Suddenly the streets rang with a cacophony of booms. Will ducked, pressed his hands to his ears. When death didn't smash him to the ground, he whirled around and searched for the source of danger. Plumes of smoke were emanating from the roof of the Council Chambers.

"Before," Lette said, grimacing as she resumed, "the guards in the Council Chambers fire the cannons signaling to the rest of the city that the council is dead and the coup has begun."

So they ran.

For a moment Will really thought they might outpace the slow burn of the revolution. In the wake of the cannon blasts from the Council Chambers, there was initially nothing but echoing silence. The city seemed to be second-guessing itself. Everyone looking around, asking, "Are we really doing this?"

Then groups of guards started to shout and chant, rattling the swords in their scabbards, pounding spear butts on cobbled streets. "Theerax! Theerax! Theerax!" Next came the crowds, blooming out of stores like flowers in the warmth of the sun. They raised their arms, cheered, whooped. Some had banners. Others dropped to their knees, hands pressed together, praising the gods.

And still, as Will and Lette pounded down the streets, they were largely ignored. The resistance Lette had predicted seemed curiously absent. Instead everyone was too caught up in their own celebrations to care about two people running—perhaps in joy—through the city.

Then they rounded a corner, and Will almost tripped over a body in the street. A young man... perhaps not even old enough to be called a man yet. He had his throat cut, his life making a crimson mess in the street.

"Next street over," Lette said, backpedaling fast.

"But..." Will could see the fight that had left this body behind a hundred yards up the streets. Bodies tangled, teeth bared. "There are people there struggling against Theerax. We can't just abandon them."

"Those people are going to lose," Lette snapped. "Remember the army we thought we could fight Theerax with? Well, now they're on Theerax's side. Now they're directly opposed to these people. And let's not forget, Theerax is almost certainly coming here, his new seat of power. And what's he bringing with him? Oh yes!" She slapped her forehead. "His own enormous army. So that's two well-armed, well-organized military forces against..." She peered. "Oh gods." She shook her head. "I think there's someone in there trying to use a loaf of bread as a weapon."

Will stood, openmouthed, tried to process. "So we...?"

"Balur is lying unconscious somewhere and this shit is only going to get worse," Lette snapped. "He is where my loyalties lie. Fuck these people. I am finding him, stealing a wagon, and getting out of this shithole."

Will stared at her. "And then what?"

She grabbed him by his shirt, shook him until his head hurt. "You're the one who comes up with the fucking plans! When are you going to start consistently remembering that?"

Which didn't really feel fair to Will. This was a crisis. This was the complete collapse of his plans. This was proof that all he had thought of had amounted to nothing. And now? *Now* Lette wanted a plan? In this moment of utter ruin?

"No," he said, and even felt righteous doing it. "No, I don't come up with a plan just because you snap your pretty fingers and demand one." Piss on it. He hadn't meant to say "pretty."

"Then," Lette said, and there was something in her face that brought Will up short, something that looked a lot like pain, "we use my plan. We survive. And we do it any way we can. And if that means leaving these people to die, then that is what it means. Because we can't fight shit if we're dead. And, honestly, if we lose, then I will fight for Theerax. Because that's what survival will mean." She held his gaze steadily. He felt her eyes boring into him, and he looked away.

Will was pretty sure that Lette's decision for him to take Balur's shoulders while she took the lizard man's feet was wholly driven by the fact that she was still pissed at him.

They struggled down the streets of the merchants' district—loaded down by the unconscious lizard man, and a few wineskins Lette had defined as "provisions"—looking for a wagon to load.

This being the merchant's district, a wagon was easy to find. Finding one that wasn't missing a wheel or on fire was a little harder. Finally they discovered one tucked into an archway off the street. Behind it a yard full of crates and barrels sat waiting for looters.

Apparently they were the looters. Lette started ransacking things while he tried to heave Balur up onto the wagon bed. As she did, his conscience twitched. "These people—" he started.

"Survival." Lette's tone was biting. "Mine. Balur's. Yours. In that order. That's the plan. If you have a problem with that..." But she bit the thought off, stalked back toward the crates and barrels.

"What?" said Will. And then, even though he knew she would hate it, "Please."

She stopped walking but she didn't turn around. Just stayed

still as a statue. Will felt more uncomfortable by the second. What did she expect from him?

"Where is your anger?" Lette didn't sound angry anymore. Just tired, and bitter. "Where is your righteous rage? Where is your hatred?"

And Will found he didn't have an answer for her. He didn't know. Looking about him. Listening to the sounds of this absolute disaster…he didn't feel angry. He felt sad. He felt weak. He felt pointless. But he didn't feel angry. He knew exactly why these people had thrown over their High Council. If the alternative weren't a dragon, he'd probably be encouraging them. How could he be angry at these people for hoping for something better than the shitty deal they had?

So instead he heaved as much of Balur into the wagon as he could. As he worked, Lette loaded chunks of cheese, ham, and other dried meats beside him. Splintered wood lay in the courtyard behind her.

"Hey!" He was torn from his work by a shout from the street. He looked up. A man was there, in his late fifties, gray in his beard, a pitchfork in his hands. He was wearing a yellow cotton work shirt, and braces held brown trousers up over an ample belly. There was a woman of similar age behind him, and a young man of perhaps twenty, only a few years Will's junior.

"Yes?" said Will.

"Get off my cart!" the man yelled. "And get the fuck away from my ham!"

Lette, who was in the back of the wagon with him at that moment, slowly put down the large ham she was holding. Will could feel the tension running through her.

"Don't," he whispered.

"Not if they don't make me," she hissed back.

Will held out his hands, placatory. He did not want this fight. The very idea of it made him sick. "I'm sorry," he said. "We'll put it back."

"We will n—" Lette started.

Then she was cut off.

The sound was low at first, a slow, steady beat. A rhythmic thump, thump, thump building gradually in the sky.

They looked up. They saw.

Theerax burst into the space above their heads. He was massive, titanic. He was an impossibility in the sky. He was the sky. Everything above the street was him. The heavens were simply scaled muscle, rippling and flexing. The wind was just the downdraft of his wings, whipping dust down the narrow street, making the surface of the puddles ripple and dance.

And then he was gone, leaving only Will's thundering heart in his wake. Theerax crashed and clattered his way through the air toward the Council Chambers. His new seat of power. Will was nothing to him. Was utterly insignificant.

Slowly, everyone's attention came back to the matter at hand. Will felt the urge to clench his fists, to grit his teeth. The tension was a living, pulsing thing in the air between them.

He did not want this to end in blood.

Survival. That was what Lette said it was about: survival.

Slowly he raised one fist into the air and pumped it. "Theerax!" he shouted. "Theerax! Theerax!" He turned and looked at Lette. She was staring at him. He made an encouraging motion. "Theerax! Theerax!"

Hesitantly, Lette raised her own fist. "Theerax," she said, without what Will would have called the necessary conviction.

The man with the pitchfork, though, was apparently convinced. Or at least convinced enough to shout, voice raw with emotion, "You fucking people make me sick!"

Will paused, fist in the air. "Wait," he said. "What?"

"Throw over our own council for some beast. Praise him instead of the gods. Steal my goods."

"No!" Will waved his hands desperately. "We didn't mean it. We were just saying that because—"

But the man wasn't interested in why Will had been saying that. Instead he let out an inarticulate bellow of rage and charged at him, thrusting the pitchfork at him as he came.

"No!" Will yelled again.

He heard a thrum in the air beside him, turned, saw Lette standing with her arm extended out, and looked back to the street. Three dead bodies lay there. Knives were in their necks. The man with the pitchfork hadn't even gotten to finish his bellow of rage. His wife and son hadn't even got to step forward to either help or hinder him.

Lette knelt and picked up the ham.

"Why?" It was all Will had. This moment, this action. It felt so empty. So fucking pointless.

"Survival," said Lette. She stacked the ham in a neat pile she'd been making near Balur's head.

And suddenly, Will found his rage. He found his anger. He found his hatred. And, to his relief, it wasn't at Lette. It wasn't at the people in the street ruining their lives, and this country. It was at Theerax, sweeping over them, spreading nothing but pointless, stupid devastation in his wake.

"You want a plan?" He thrust a finger at Lette. She turned, surprise writ large on her features. "I've got a gods-hexed plan." He nodded to himself. "This country. This army. It's a bust. A wasted chance. But it's not the only army out there. This isn't the only country. Not all of them will have fallen to these bastard dragons. Not yet. So we go and we find one that's still standing, and we get ourselves a new army, and we put ourselves at the head of it. We don't trust kings, or emperors, or bureaucrats, or politicians. We do it ourselves. We do it right. And we find each and every one of these dragons, and we paint the sky red with their guts. Is that enough of a fucking plan for you?"

Lette stood staring at him for a moment. Then she nodded, and she smiled. "Yeah," she said. "That'll do."

21

Heavy Lies the Crown

Quirk knew that streaming across the Tamathian plains, fleeing her home and the slaughter she had left there, heading north as fast as she could...that was not the time for profound philosophical contemplation. And still, she couldn't help but wonder, why in the Hallows had anyone ever bothered domesticating the horse?

Her arse felt like it had been paddled for the best part of a day. Her thighs burned as if she were suspended above a fire. And the less said about her nethers, the better everyone would be. At this point, panic was about the only thing still holding her upright. But she had been on the run for the best part of eight hours now, and even panic had its limits. She felt numbness setting in.

She glanced back over her shoulder. The escaped prisoners were strung out behind her on their own purloined animals.

We're horse stealers now, she thought. *We've even given them a legitimate reason to hang us.*

That firmed up her panic a good bit.

But she couldn't ignore the fact that she wasn't the only one flagging. Most of the men and women looked dead in their saddles, hunched low, drooping over the necks of their animals. For that matter, the horses themselves didn't look too chipper. This was less of a flight for freedom than it was a slow trudge.

She pulled slightly on her reins, dropped back next to Afrit, who was riding a few yards behind her.

"I think we should stop soon," she said.

Afrit nodded. "That's a good idea." Quirk thought the woman looked exhausted, though it was hard to tell under all the bruises.

They rode on in silence.

Finally, Afrit said, "So...you should probably tell the others then."

"Me?" Quirk was not at all comfortable with that idea. She didn't even know where they were going. She hardly ever even left the city, and when she did she never headed for these domesticated farmlands. This was grazing land for herds and flocks, not the hunting grounds of the beasts she studied. "I don't think that's a good idea," she said.

"Who do you think these people are following?"

"No one's following anyone," Quirk said. "We haven't formalized any sort of organizational structure yet, and—"

"Formalized?" Afrit let go of her reins with one hand to raise it to the heavens as if beseeching Knole for guidance. "You broke everyone out of jail by melting the bars with your bare hands. We don't have to formalize anything."

And that sat even worse. "Oh," said Quirk. "I wield the biggest stick, so I'm in charge?" That had been her childhood. She knew what that sort of power could do. "No." She shook her head. "I'm not going to enforce a false impression of leadership."

Afrit sighed heavily and wheeled her horse around. "Quirk says we need to look for somewhere to rest," she said loudly.

Quirk found she still had the energy left to be outraged. "What did you say that for?" she asked as Afrit rode up back beside her.

Afrit just rolled her eyes.

Quirk wasn't going to be railroaded into anything. She pulled her horse around. It seemed grateful for the excuse to stop. "Look," she said to the crowd, "does anyone know this land? Does anyone know a place we can hide?" Asking questions seemed a good way to get someone else to step up and share in the leadership responsibilities. Soon they'd pick up on the collective mentality.

"I grew up round here." It was a large man who spoke up, his face bisected by a fearsome diagonal slash that had left dried blood plastered down one cheek and over his chin. "It's all scattered farmhouses. We could hole up in a barn. Farmer wouldn't even know, let alone soldiers."

Quirk nodded and smiled. "So you think we should ride until we see one that's suitably isolated and camp down?" she asked the crowd at large.

There was a long silence while they all stared at her. Quirk's anticipation slowly turned to disappointment.

Next to her Afrit sighed heavily. "Come on," she said with a sharpness that Quirk simply could not muster at this point. "You heard the woman. Let's start looking for a barn."

Which was not what Quirk had said at all. As their steeds staggered to life once more, it took her a moment to catch up with Afrit, her horse was so reluctant to get going.

"I said," she hissed, "that I didn't want to reinforce the idea that I'm the leader."

Afrit closed her eyes. "This," she said, "is an odd time for a lecture."

"Well," said Quirk, "you need one."

Afrit's eyes flashed. "I meant," she said, "that this is an odd time for me to need to lecture you on the nature of power."

Quirk's mouth opened indignantly but Afrit didn't give her a chance to say anything. "Power is about will. And so leadership lies at the heart of it, really. Because all leadership is in the end is the will to wield power. And because it's about power and wielding it, a lot of the time people take leadership by force.

A lot of the political systems we have are about formalizing that struggle, of making it seem civil. But if you boil it down, it's essentially about beating your opponents down, and taking what you want."

Afrit let a little heat out of her voice and offered Quirk a smile. "But it's not always like that. Sometimes instead leadership is forced onto people. Sometimes people want to be led. And those, as you are so very clearly aware, are dangerous times, because it is very easy for absolute arseholes to seize the reins. And it's easy for well-intentioned people to become seduced by power.

"But right now," she continued, looking around, "we're really short on options, and we're really short on time. These people need someone with the will to lead them. Otherwise they'll fragment, and be caught, and be cut down. And the list of options for them is you, and that's about it. But fortunately, I don't think you're an arsehole. And unless you think you're going to let all the power go to your head between now and sunset, then I think we'll be okay."

Quirk pursed her lips. And she knew good sense when she heard it. And she was not too proud to admit when she was being a fool. Yet…it still sat queasily in her gut. "What about you?" she said to Afrit, almost plaintive. Above her head, two blackbirds flitted back and forth whistling to each other.

Afrit managed something like a smile. "I thought you were smart enough to recognize when someone is literally begging you to make a decision for them." For a moment the professorial mask shivered, something broken and damaged peeking out from behind. "I'm so fucking scared, Quirk."

And Quirk's heart broke in this moment for this proud, intelligent, defiant woman. For all she had been through. For what she herself was putting her through now.

"I'm sorry." She reached out, clutched Afrit's arm. "I think I've been very selfish for a very long time."

Afrit shrugged. "You're afraid of power. Which as a student of it, seems a good baseline place to operate from to me."

"Hey!" a voice called back to them. They had dropped back in the group as they talked, and now several riders, holding themselves a little straighter, a little taller, had scouted the land ahead of them. A man at the crest of a small rise in the land was pointing away and ahead. Quirk pushed her horse to trot up beside him. A canter was well beyond it at this point.

A small, sagging barn was outlined at the peak of the next rise, a half-mile away.

"Brilliant." Quirk smiled and clapped the man on the back. "Thank you."

The smile she received in return was as bright as a second sun rising into the skies.

To describe the barn as being in poor repair was generous, to say the least. The doors had fallen off their hinges and were propped against the wilting frame. The roof was more than half-gone, and what remained was more than half-covered in moss. The windows were choked with vines, and the smell of rotting straw was ripe on the air from fifty yards away. And still the place looked wonderful to Quirk.

At least it did until she saw the woman walking out of the doors.

As one her troop of escapees pulled up with a jingle of horse tackle, the woman's head snapped up. For a moment they all just stayed staring at each other.

Gods piss on it, thought Quirk. *This leadership shit sounded far better when Afrit was talking.*

"We ain't got nothing," the woman by the barn said as Quirk rode closer. "We ain't got money, and my daughters is all gone." She had her apron held out in front of her, holding a good few pounds of corn and seed.

"No," said Quirk, holding out one hand to her. "That's not

what we want." Down the slope, she could see a farmhouse. Chickens and geese scrambled around a yard.

The woman snorted. "Come to help out around the house have you?" She spat onto the ground.

"We just want shelter," Quirk said, trying to keep her voice soft, friendly, reasonable. "You won't even know we're here."

She knew what the woman feared. It was only a few short decades since bands of horsemen rode back and forth across these lands, burning and looting, murdering and raping, and taking small girls to be their personal war mages, and setting them to burning the world.

Quirk took a slow, steady breath.

"And what if I say no?" said the woman, mouth twisted in something resembling a snarl. "Will I not know you're here then?"

"If you say no," Quirk said, trying to keep her voice as calm and reasonable as possible, "then we ride on, and you never see us again."

The woman chewed her tongue, eyeballing Quirk.

"It's okay," Quirk said into the silence. "We've already taken up too much of your time." She turned her horse away, called back to the others, "We ride on!"

"Wait," said the woman, and her voice was still rough, but some of the harshness was gone. "Who are you running from?"

Quirk twisted in her saddle. "Who says we're running?"

"I don't lend my barn to people who accuse me of being a fucking idiot," said the woman, without apparent rancor.

"If I tell you," said Quirk, still not turning her horse around, "and you agree with the people chasing us, then you'll point them straight after us."

"And if I disagree with them you get a roof for the night." The woman folded her arms.

Quirk weighed her options. "We're running from the Diffinites," she said.

The woman narrowed her eyes. "Them that's taken the city?" she said.

"Yes," Quirk said, trying to read the woman's impassive eyes.

Then the woman spat again. "Toil's always been good to me and my crops."

From the state of the barn, Quirk wasn't sure about that, but she knew better than to voice her doubt.

"Screw dragons," said the woman. "Get in the barn, bed down. If anyone comes looking for you then they won't hear anything from me." And before Quirk could even thank her, she turned away and stomped back toward her chickens.

The next morning, Quirk lay on rotting boards and moldering straw and wondered what had woken her.

Voices.

Not a few. Many voices. And many more horses, stomping and snorting in the brisk morning air. The other escapees were stirring, looking about. She stood quickly and silently, putting a finger to her lips. When she was sure all had seen her, she crept to the barn's wall and peered between the slats.

Fifteen soldiers sat upon fifteen sleek steeds. Their armor gleamed as the morning sun sliced across the plain. They had come at the farm from a different angle than Quirk and the other prisoners, and stood perhaps thirty yards away. Thank all the gods that the barn door was not facing them or they would have had a clear view of all of them, huddled and waiting for the slaughter.

"Grab everything," Quirk hissed back at the group. "Bridle the horses as quickly as you can. Don't worry about saddles. We lead them away single file and pray to Lawl and every other god that they don't see us."

There wasn't time for qualms about leadership now. Quirk put her eye back to the crack in the boards, as behind her the other prisoners bustled into hushed life. The woman she had seen yesterday was out in front of the soldiers remonstrating at them. A stout man of similar age stood behind her, leaning on a scythe.

Abruptly, the lead soldier whipped out his sword and slapped at the woman with it. Quirk gasped, bit back hard on her scream. And then the woman was picking herself up, howling furiously, and her husband was pointing his scythe angrily. And it had been the flat of the blade the soldier had used. And Quirk breathed again. But even so, she was amazed that the soldier hadn't broken a bone, or knocked the sense from the woman.

"—shall search anything we want!" The lead soldier raised his voice, and Quirk could make out the words now. "And anything you try to stop us searching we shall burn to the ground."

"Godless fucking heathens!" spat the woman. Her husband was trying to help her to her feet.

The soldier dismounted quickly, threw the farmer aside, and planted a gauntleted fist into the woman's face. She collapsed back to the ground in a spray of blood. Quirk bit back another cry.

"Quirk." Afrit was suddenly whispering behind her. "We're ready to go. Come on."

But Quirk couldn't look away. The husband had picked himself up and was about to throw himself at the soldier, when suddenly a sword was at his throat. The lead soldier leaned down, picked up the woman by the scruff of her work shirt, and planted his fist into her face again.

"Come on," said Afrit. "We have to go."

Leadership. Power. The will to use power. That was what it all came back to. Goals, and the will, and the power to achieve them. And what were Quirk's goals? To run. To hide. To find safety for herself and these others.

And what of all the people left behind? What of everyone left to suffer beneath the heel of Diffinax? What about these two farmers, right here, and right now?

Quirk knew she had the power. She had used it to rip through the Northern Barbican.

Blood gleamed on the gauntleted fist of the soldier.

"No," she said. And then again, louder, "No." And she felt all the fire in her soul infusing that word. "No," she said a third time, and she felt the barn quake with it.

She pulled away from Afrit, strode toward the collapsed barn doors.

"Quirk!" Afrit called. "What are you doing?"

Quirk was through the barn doors, was out into the morning sun, its heat flooding her, filling her to overflowing.

The lead soldier had picked the woman up, ready to deliver a third blow, when one of his men saw Quirk and let out a shout. She could hear the other prisoners bustling behind her, the sounds of swords being pulled from sheaths.

They wouldn't be needed.

The soldiers wheeled to face her.

And then they burned.

It was both easier and harder this time. The fire came to her easily enough. It seemed almost eager to do what she asked of it, to curl around each man, to embrace him. It was a simple thing to light a man on fire like a match. But it was harder too, knowing she could have slipped away. Knowing she could have chosen to be someone who was not this murderer.

She wasn't sure how long it took. For a while, individual actions lost their meaning. There was only the flow and weave of the fire, the achievement of her goals.

And then it was done, and she was on her knees, gasping at the sudden shuttering of the fire. She looked about. And it was a wasteland. Fire had scoured through the group of soldiers. The earth was blackened scar. The twisted corpses of horses that had died screaming. Soldiers had run from the place, living torches. One had crashed into the side of the farmers' house. Flames licked up one wall. Crops smoldered.

Everyone was staring. The prisoners. The farmers. Even some of the fucking chickens.

She stood up. Slowly. And there had been, she supposed, some honesty in what she had just done. Some acknowledgment of the self that she had hidden for so long. And being a mage, being a conduit of flame...it didn't feel now the way it had when she burned things for Hethren. Because she had burned this world now for her own reasons. For good reasons. For these people. She had burned down a worse world, so that a better one could survive. And she could live with that.

"There," she said. To all of them. Because now seemed like a time to be honest. A time for acknowledgments. "That's who I am. That's what I am. What I can do. And it's ugly, and it's awful, but right now...right here..." She looked about, trying to judge emotions. Fear? Sympathy? Adoration? Hatred? "This is what I thought this situation needed. This is what I had to deal with it. This is everything I have to offer. So if you want me to lead you, that's what you're following. I don't have a plan. I just have a dream of something better. And I don't know if I can deliver. And I don't know if it'll be worth it. And this won't be the only ugly, shitty thing you'll see me do. And I'll probably end up asking the same of you. And I'll second-guess myself. And I'll worry. And I'll be wrong as often as I'm right. But I will fight. I promise you that. Because I've got that ability even if I've got nothing else left. So I'll fight Diffinax until he kills me. Which he probably will. And then he'll probably kill anyone who chooses to follow me."

She should probably finish, she thought, on something stronger than that. On some great rallying cry. But she was abruptly out of words, standing there on that scorched plain, full of scorched dreams.

To be honest, failing to inspire them, sending them all going their own ways...it would probably be for the best. It would be harder for the Diffinites to track them. More would probably live. And it would be easier for her too. Fewer responsibilities. Fewer lives to worry about.

From the pile of charred soldiers, the woman who owned the barn picked herself up. Her nose was a ruin. Blood coated her lips and chin. The edge of her skirt smoldered.

Slowly, her arm trembling slightly, the woman wiped her face with the back of her sleeve.

"Okay," she said, "so where are you leading?" She spat a mouthful of blood onto the ground. "Because I'm following."

PART 2:
DRAGONS DOMINANT

22

Beauty and Grace
Carven in Flesh

Will knew he should say something. It was getting ridiculous that he hadn't said anything. It was coming up on a month since they had escaped from Bellenet. It had already been far too long to have said nothing.

Without meaning to, he let out a sigh. Lette glanced over her shoulder, back at him. "You better have a really good reason for staring at my arse right now."

"What?" Will blustered. "I didn't…I wasn't…Just lost in, erm…thought."

And that was most definitely not what he needed to say.

"Problem is being," Balur rumbled from the back of the wagon, "if you were lost in thought about Lette's arse."

Which really wasn't helping at all. Though, in fact, ever since he had come back to full-time consciousness, about two and a half weeks ago, Balur seemed to have had "avoiding helpfulness" as his main goal. There was almost no doubt in Will's mind that the big lizard man could have gotten out of the wagon and walked along the road for a little bit by now, but whenever Will brought up the subject he would claim "My wound is hurting me." And whenever Will tried to ride in the back of the wagon he was accused of crowding the lizard man and slowing the healing process. So he walked alongside the wagon, scuffing his heels in broken twigs and leaves, rather than sit up at the front next to Lette, all because he was too much of a gods-hexed coward to say ... to say ...

I love you.

How hard was that to say? It wasn't even like it would be the first time he'd said it to her. It would be more like a gentle reminder than a shocking revelation.

I still love you.

Maybe that would be better. Except of course that the real problem was the word *love*.

I still have feelings for you.

Except she would ask what feelings.

Strong feelings.

And she would know that he meant love.

Complex emotions.

Except they weren't complex at all. Love was brutally, stupidly simple.

Maybe I could hire a bard, Will thought. *Bards are good with words.* He glanced at Lette again, carefully, to avoid both staring and her arse. In the end, he thought, she seemed more likely to derive pleasure from gutting a bard and hanging him with his own entrails than from any sort of sweet song.

Maybe I could get her that?

"I am still saying it's a stupid plan," rumbled Balur, and for a moment Will was so preoccupied that he thought Balur was commenting on the availability of suicidal bards, and he blushed furiously. But then he realized that Balur was hitting a well-worn topic—one that he was more than willing to talk about.

"Well, then," he said, "let's go to gods-hexed Vinland instead, befriend them, and raise an army to defeat Theerax and all the other dragons *like I suggested in the first cursed place.*"

"We can't go to Vinland," said Lette with ill-concealed irritation, "because as we have pointed out before, we are wanted there on pain of death."

"I know!" snapped Will. "Because we have this same pissing conversation every pissing day." He stared daggers at Balur. "Batarra is lost to Theerax. Salera is lost to Gorrax. Chatarra is lost to Callax. Tamar is lost to Diffinax. The Five Duchies have finally been united under Pondrax. Every nation has some dragon at its helm. This we have heard in every tavern from Bellenet to"—he cast about—"around twenty leagues back, where civilization ended. The only holdouts are the elves here in the Vale, and Vinland. And of those two countries, you refuse to go to one, because apparently everyone there wants to kill you. Which I am increasingly assuming is because they spent a month on the road with you."

He increased his pace so that he could stride indignantly in front of the wagon. However, he soon regretted it because he had blisters the size of golden bulls on his heels. Because he was constantly walking alongside the wagon. Because he didn't have the stones to admit his feelings to Lette…

"Look," he said, dropping back beside the wagon and affecting a more reasonable tone, "are you sure we can't get out of whatever you two did in Vinland? I mean, if there's anywhere where a god is most likely to manifest and make a stand against these dragons, surely it's a nation entirely devoted to the worship of one god, right?"

This was met with silence that carried a certain weight. After a considered pause, he risked a look up at Lette and Balur.

Lette was shaking her head. "Gods," she said. "Exactly how backwards was Kondorra?"

Which seemed a little unfair to Will. Because first, Kondorra wasn't really all that backwards from what he'd seen of Batarra, and second, if it had been backwards it was because it had been dealing with the oppressive thumb of draconic rule for far longer than the rest of Avarra.

"Barph," said Balur with the same supercilious tone as Lette. *"The absent god."*

Will's brow furrowed. "He's the god of wine and . . . generally hedonistic nonsense." He didn't remember anything about his absence.

"Barph hasn't manifested in almost eight hundred years," Lette said, as if speaking to an infant. "It's why Vinland is such a pissing joke. At least they would be if they didn't mostly consist of well-armed, fanatical Barph worshippers. Which"—she put a finger to her cheek—"is probably why the dragons' anti-deity message has had such a hard time catching on there."

"Look," Will said rather indignantly, "no gods have manifested in Kondorra since before I was born. They didn't come up much."

"Eight *hundred* years," Lette repeated.

Which, Will had to admit, was kind of a fairly large knowledge gap on his part. "Okay," he said finally, "so Vinland makes no sense then."

"I don't know," said Balur, easing back on the cart. "The more the gods are staying in their heavens, the easier time we will be having convincing everybody to worship them and not dragons. Maybe the Barphists are fanatics because Barph isn't screwing everything up for them?"

Which was a depressing idea. Not for the first time, Will wished he was trying to defend some deities not primarily known for their habits of seducing people and ruining shit.

He also wished he understood the goals of the dragons better. To replace the gods? How was that even possible? And why this intermediary step of conquering Avarra and making everyone worship them? Surely there was some intersection between the two desires, but what it was lay far beyond him.

In the end, as long as the dragons all ended up lying in a heap with lances through their hearts, it wasn't a concern that needed answering. And he had seen sixty thousand men kill five dragons before. His dreams were not out of proportion to reality.

Around them the Vale reached heavenward and rustled. Over

the past few days, the scraggly woods of Batarra had grown progressively larger and denser, ash and oak mixing with the elm. Then the occasional yew, pine, and fir had found their way into the mix. Branches had knit together above their heads, casting everything in shades of yellow and green. The trunks of the trees had thickened, the undergrowth surrounding them spreading more thickly. The world smelled fresh and fecund here. Wildlife seemed to be constantly moving somewhere out of sight.

Then three hours ago, Lette had pointed out the border stone marking the transition point where the road entered the elves' domain. There had yet to be any sign of the elves themselves, though.

"You know what?" said Will, as his thoughts threatened to turn back to Lette again, "I'd actually love to hear *your* plan, Balur. If mine is so awful, what great alternative is it that you are suggesting?"

Balur snorted. "You know what I would love to be hearing? *Your* plan."

"My plan?" Will looked to Lette for support, but her eyes were on the trees. "You were just complaining about—"

"Your plan," Balur said, "is consisting of step one, coming to the Vale, and step three, leaving with an army. There is being a distinct lack of step two, I am thinking."

Which was a point well aimed enough to give Will pause. "Well," he blustered, "it's, erm... contextual."

Balur lacked eyebrows, but the look he gave Will definitely conveyed arched eyebrows.

"What?" Will felt that this really wasn't as bad as they were making it out to be. "We're asking them to rally against a group of dragons that are threatening their national borders. It's not that hard an argument to make. They're probably halfway there or more themselves. We're really just offering information and expertise."

Lette grimaced. "I think you might be overestimating the willingness of the elves to be helpful," she said, glancing around at the forest enfolding them. She lowered her voice. "Elves are not exactly known for being the most open-minded of people."

"They are beauty and grace carven in flesh," said Will. He refused to be treated like some backwards hick. He knew the stories. "They are the most beloved of Betra, her chosen race upon earth."

"Yes," said Balur, which was pretty gratifying. "That was being the case right up until humanity was oppressing the shit out of them."

"What?" *Gods piss on it*, thought Will. He was going to look like a hick again.

"The Century War?" Lette looked at him. "Seriously?"

Will just sighed. "Look," he said, "the schooling system in Kondorra was organized by dragons. Ergo, there wasn't one." He tried not to be embarrassed by the fact that he was just using the word *ergo* to prove that he knew it.

"Okay, then. History lesson. The Century War." Lette shook her head. "It actually only lasted about thirty-eight years, but historians are just as big a pack of liars as everyone else." She pushed her hands through her hair. "Anyway, about two hundred years ago there were bad droughts for five years in a row. All the crops failed. People were dying everywhere. Disease was rampant. Bad shit. So humanity, being the ever-so-enlightened bastards that we are, decided that it was probably because someone had pissed the gods off. And humanity didn't want the blame, so they took it out on everybody who wasn't human. Which meant thirty-eight years of rounding up elves, dwarves, Analesians, centaurs, pixies, and anything else with pointy ears, and then stabbing them in their nethers."

"Elves are thinking that you two are being total dicks," Balur summarized, in case Will had failed to grasp the point.

Will nodded slowly. "Well, based on that history lesson, I think I might agree with them."

"So…" Lette fixed him with a contemplative stare. "Asking the elves to assist a bunch of round-ears like us might pose a few problems."

"And you only thought to mention it now?" Again, Will felt like this problem wasn't entirely his fault.

"I was mentioning this numerous times," Balur said, spreading his hands wide. "But—"

"*When?*" Will was having trouble believing this shit.

"When I was saying that I thought this was a shit plan." Balur seemed confused that this needed to be explained.

"Saying that you think my plan is shit is not exactly the same as saying that for politico-historical reasons you think race enmity may mean that the plan might need some additional thinking."

"Well," Balur said, looking wounded, "I was thinking that that was implied."

"I'm about to imply my fucking fist to your nadgers," Will told him. Which wasn't a realistic threat, but it made him feel better.

Balur shrugged.

"Honestly," Will said, "I still think that the immediate threat of dragons looking to destroy your home kind of outweighs the wrongs done by folk several centuries ago, whom I suspect I would disagree with strongly."

"Well, you are a racially insensitive fuck," said someone who wasn't either Lette or Balur.

Lette yanked on the wagon's reins. Their horse let out a belligerent neigh and stumbled to a halt. Will fumbled for his sword. Then he noticed Balur had his hands up.

"Wait," he said, "are you surrendering?"

"Obviously." Balur rolled his eyes.

"I don't understand what's going on." Will felt that statement summed up most of the past few months really.

"That is because you are being an ignorant round-ear pig-fuck," said the mystery voice again. This time it was followed by a rustling in the bushes, and the leaves, and the branches above them. And then a dozen figures emerged on the road around them. And then a dozen more arrows peeked out of the trees above them.

"Oh," said Will. And then, "Shit."

23

Pièce de Résistance

Five days the journey went on. Five days of walking. No roads. No proper rests. No sign of others. No tents erected. No shelters of leaves made. And when the forced march was over, the elves simply lay down in shifts and slept on the cold earth.

Because, Lette thought, as she had tried to point out to Will, *elves are absolute dicks.*

Then finally, on the evening of the fifth day, she caught sight of firelight through the trees. And as they approached, the glow grew, and spread out, and separated into a hundred points of light, floating in the branches.

And then they stumbled into a clearing, and her jaw dropped just a little more than she was used to.

A whole town square floated in the trees above them. Inns, merchant shops, stalls, butchers, fletchers—she could see them all suspended thirty feet off the ground. Walkways of rope and wood were strung between them, lined with torches like diamonds draped around a noblewoman's neck. Elves scurried back and forth, busy on errands. Children chased back and forth, their cries barely distinguishable from the soft animal noises drifting through the slumbering forest.

Their guide—an elf called Lothell, with sandy hair and lines around his mouth and eyes like whorls in the trunk of a tree—turned to them and gave them an acidic smile. "Welcome," he said, "to Birchester."

She stared around, then checked to make sure she was not playing it any more agog than her companions.

Will caught her eye. "Carven beauty and grace," he mouthed at her.

Lette sighed. Apparently she could drop her britches and start slapping at herself and she would still be playing it cooler than Will.

There was a single structure at the center of the clearing, a large, low hut, perfectly round with a roof of green leaves. Lette couldn't tell if they were just fresh picked, or if the whole structure truly was made of living wood. Whatever the truth of the matter, it was a fairly impressive effect, especially considering what a bunch of total dicks the elves were.

"All right then," said Lette, who was about through with Lothell and his arrogant posturing, "so now you actually take us to someone important, right?"

"Or now," said Lothell, "I tie you to a tree and reshape your ears with arrows."

"You have a strange ear obsession, little man," Lette said. "Makes me think you're compensating for something."

Which was why, when they were forced at arrow point into the low, round hut, she was gagged.

The space was poorly lit, and clogged with slightly fragrant smoke. Lette could pick out fifteen shadowy figures in the gloom. Lothell and his men added another eight.

Basically, she decided, if she started something here, Will would die.

That shouldn't bother her.

It bothered her.

So she went where she was prodded, and ended up on her knees before a throne of branches and green leaves. It looked like the same, living-wood gimmick had been used to create it as the rest of the building. And yes, it was impressive, but Lette was beginning to think that elven aesthetics were a bit of a one-trick pony.

Lounging in the chair, smoking a—quite frankly ridiculous—pipe was an elf dressed somewhere between gigolo and woodsman. He wore the tightest pair of leather trousers that Lette had ever seen. Exactly how he got in and out of them seemed like the sort of topic Quirk would like to investigate, especially considering the roll of fat that protruded at the waistband, before the elf's silk shirt took over. The shirt was heavily embroidered with images of a skinnier man in equally tight trousers killing bears and bedding slender women. The ensemble was finished off with a bearskin cloak, and a circlet of bear teeth and claws that clung to the man's forehead.

"His highest eminence, master of the bowstring, slayer of the round-ear fucks, commander of the Vale forces, fine-aspected Todger IV," intoned Lothell in a voice that made Lette think the man actually believed the title was important.

"Oh yeah," said King Todger, and pumped his crotch slightly.

Was it only total dicks who sought out power, Lette wondered, or did it make them that way? She shrugged. Probably a little bit of both.

The shrug was probably not the right move. Especially not in front of someone as full of self-importance as King Todger.

"Oh?" he said. "Unimpressed are we? Well, we'll see how unimpressed you are when I order your death."

Lette tried to say something through her gag. It was not particularly successful.

King Todger gestured impatiently. The gag was removed. Lette took a breath, worked her jaw, and then made scoffing noises.

Todger leaned forward. "Kill her," he said. He arched an eyebrow.

"Nope," Lette said. "Not particularly impressed."

King Todger scowled. "Okay," he said. "Well, I mean it this time."

Rough hands grabbed her.

"No!" It was Will's voice.

"Oh." King Todger threw a hand in the air with a pained expression on his face. "A round-ear has told me not to. Well, I'd better bow, and scrape, and know my place, I suppose?" He swirled the finger of the hand he was holding aloft. "Now I doubly want you to kill her."

"No!" Will said again, because apparently he really didn't want to learn. "I mean, I'm sorry. I'm not telling you no. I'm telling her no."

"So you're contradicting me now?" asked King Todger.

"No!" Will said for what was surely a fateful, third time. "I mean, well, I suppose yes. But I really apologize for it. And for Lette. We just... we wanted to help."

Lette wished her hands weren't bound, just so she could claw them down her face.

"Oh!" King Todger's expressive eyes were open wide. "Your *help*. I see." He nodded enthusiastically. "Because I'm some slack-witted pointy-ear incapable of making my own decisions, or knowing what's best for me and my people, and I need the help of a round-ear fuckface to tell me what to do. I see. Well, thank you so much. I really appreciate you coming here and condescending to me." He shook his head, almost sadly. "Kill both of them," he said. "In fact, see if you can do both of them with just one arrow. That always looks impressive."

The rough hands holding Lette started to pull her back through the room. A few yards away she could hear Will kicking and screaming. Waves of fragrant smoke wafted between them, obscuring the struggle. For her own part, she just went limp.

She was going to have to time this just right...

The trick would be making sure Will didn't die.

She was almost at the back of the chamber when she heard the door creak open. Bodies coming in. People shuffling for space.

That would do nicely.

She jackknifed her body, flipped her legs up into the air, then brought them crashing down on the skulls of two of the elves dragging her. She wrenched free of their suddenly slack hands.

So far so good.

Then came the yells.

Slip from the bonds you figured out how to untie on your first day in the Vale. Drop the first knife into your palm. Next sow confusion. Fling the blade into the crowd at the door. A lateral slashing. Aim for the heads. You don't need death, you need panic. Next focus on Todger. Cut toward him. He's the only way out of here. Throw two more knives, one ahead to the left, one to the right. Scream. Drop and roll. Slash at hamstrings. Scream again. Keep moving. Keep them searching.

The cold voice whispered in her ear and she obeyed. She ignored Will's screams. She ignored Balur's bellows. She ignored the pain in her wrists. She ignored the slash of a blade along her arm. She focused on the voice. On the plan. On surviving.

Get to Todger. Duck this guard's blade. She favors her right leg. Kick her in her knee. Tread on her instep. Feel the bone crack. Thrust up under her chin as she falls. Spin away. Kick her body into an oncomer. Fade into the smoke.

Someone was yelling at her to stop. She didn't.

Wait for a moment. Take a breath. Now step out into the gap. Stab him in the back. Between the fifth and sixth ribs. Angle the blade up. Step away. Just the knot of shieldmen gathered at the foot of Todger's throne now. Bunched too tight. They're making it easy. Grab the torch.

Lette reached out. Cocked the flaming branch, ready to throw.

And let out a yell.

Heat exploded in her hand. The flaming torch was suddenly a roaring inferno cooking the skin of her hand. She dropped it, bellowing. Even as it fell, though, the fire spread out, became a circle around her, three-foot-high flames fanning back and forth.

She hesitated. The whispering voice was at a momentary loss.

Balur stood in a ring of blades. Someone dragged Will to the foot of the throne. He was still bound and kicking but a sword blade to his throat made him lie still.

And just like that, their chance was gone.

Slowly from his throne, King Todger began to clap. "Okay," he said, "now I'm impressed." He shook his head and whistled. "It will be a shame to kill you."

"Actually," said a new voice, "I'd really prefer it if you didn't."

A shadow stepped out of the smoke.

Lette had seen many things. She had seen a king kill his own family. She had seen a merchant hurling all his wealth from the top of a building to a crowd below. She had seen a disemboweled giant throttle a man with a loop of his own intestines before shoving them back in his gut and limping away. On good days she considered herself hardened. On bad days she would call herself numb.

Her jaw still dropped. And that was the second time today.

A woman stood before her. A ragged, bloodstained bandana was wrapped around her head. Mud was smeared in obscuring patterns over her face and bare arms.

And she was human.

And Lette knew her.

The word formed slowly on Lette's lips, dropped from them almost of its own accord.

"Quirk?"

24

Life Is Preachy

Outside, they were chanting Firkin's name. Inside, Firkin perched his posterior in a chair so comfortable, he had to imagine it was composed exclusively of the soft, squishy dreams of virgins. It had been a luxurious gift. And now it lay within a room full of luxurious gifts. And in his hand was a golden goblet full of a magnificent vintage all of which had been bought with money that had simply been given to him. Even the mansion holding all of these gifts—it had been a gift too.

It was glorious, of course. And it was magnificent. And it was everything he had ever dreamed that preaching could be. But still the hand clutching the golden goblet shook, and the excellent vintage held within trembled against its luxurious confines.

Because Firkin didn't remember asking.

The whisper had asked. And it hadn't asked him to ask. It had simply opened his mouth, and spoken for him. He had felt its presence stretch out, expand, fill out his mind, and then… he had spoken. It had spoken. For a moment the two had been indistinguishable.

Was he sober? He couldn't be sober. He was drinking more here than he had done in years.

He couldn't get rid of the feeling that it was something about this place. About Vinter. Everything seemed somehow rooted in its walls, its wine. It tasted of memories. It smelled of them.

How long had he been drunk again?

Sometimes he thought about leaving. This house. This city. And yet when he did, something inside him seemed to rebel. But where did that feeling start? With him, or...

He shuddered.

He'd interrogated the whisper. He'd screamed at it. He'd thrown a full bottle of wine at the polished tin mirror that hung in the mansion's bedchamber. But the whisper did not seem to operate on any schedule he controlled.

He drank again. And again. He leaned back and tried to enjoy all the fine things life had brought him. Outside they were still chanting his name. Sounds of violence had yet to punctuate its lulls. The crowd could wait a little longer. He did not have to go out there yet.

There was a knock at the door. He jerked and spilled some of his wine on the floor.

"Piss off," he mumbled. Company might stop him from being a maudlin bugger, but on the other hand it might hamper his plan of obliterating all coherent thought.

In defiance of his holy command, the door opened.

A small, scruffy child came in, dressed in a loincloth of yellow silk and clutching a wine pitcher almost the same size as his own skinny frame.

"I am sorry your—" he started, then someone kicked him from behind and he went flying across the room, pitcher spinning away, wine spilling everywhere.

The High Priesthood of Vinland marched into Firkin's presence. Three he recognized vaguely from his confrontation with them a month or so before: two wrinkly old men in yellow and crimson robes, and one wrinkly old woman. The fourth was younger, a swarthy fellow who Firkin suspected spent too much time caring for his beard.

Firkin felt his eyebrows scramble up his forehead. He tried to marshal his few thoughts, then remembered he hadn't wanted them a minute ago. He spent a moment questioning his own motives before realizing he should probably say something. "To what—" he said, then belched. "Sorry. To what do I owe the pleasure?"

"Pleasure?" said the first priest, sounding interested. "Where?"

"I'll have some," said the second. She produced a goblet from a pocket in her robes and waved it vaguely around the room.

"It's not a fucking pleasure," said the third, pulling out his own hip flask and unscrewing the top. "We're the High Priesthood, and we are not high right now. We are down low in scum and shit, with this good-for-nothing merchant of turds." Then he pointed at Firkin, which Firkin thought was quite rude. They were chanting his name outside after all.

"I'm sorry," said Firkin, even though he wasn't. He felt like he should probably get out of his chair for this. He struggled briefly but it really was far too comfortable. "So...why are you here?" Somehow he'd missed that part.

"To kick your arse," said the fourth High Priest. He cracked his knuckles. The effect was slightly offset by the fact that he followed it up by stroking his overly luxurious beard.

"Kick my arse literally or figuratively?" he checked.

"Both," said the fourth priest.

"It very much depends," said the third, "on what assurances you are willing to make us."

Firkin contemplated this. He realized he was half-expecting the whisper to answer the question. That was a habit he shouldn't be encouraging. The whisper was an unreliable body-stealing bastard and was to be actively discouraged.

Unfortunately that meant trying to think up something by himself. "I assure you," he said, playing for time, "that I shall refrain from having coital knowledge of your mothers." He thought about that. "Unless I don't know who they are. Or it already happened in the past." Important caveats.

"Well," said the first, "that's not at all relevant, but I personally find the gesture of good faith to be a positive sign. I too shall refrain from knowing your mother in the coital sense."

Firkin shrugged. He honestly didn't remember his mother.

Cantankerous bitch.

Oh gods. It was awake. Oh Barph. Please smash his thoughts to pieces and bring him sweet oblivion.

The whisper laughed at that.

"Look, are we going to kick his arse or not?" said the third priest, who seemed offended by Firkin's distracted look. "I didn't come down here to talk about whose mother is or isn't going to get fucked. I could have happily stayed in my chair to talk about that."

"I still don't understand why we didn't summon him with guards," said the fourth, with something resembling a pout.

"We sent guards," said the third with a snap. "Two converted to become his followers, and his followers set upon the other three and scattered their limbs about the city."

"They can be a little rambunctious." Firkin hedged. He didn't want to piss off either the priests or the voice in his head. Everyone needed to stay really gods-hexedly calm.

"Look," said the fourth, "if there aren't guards, am I expected to do the arse-kicking myself? Because I thought I didn't have to do that anymore. Clean hands was very high on my list of demands when I was negotiating this job."

"Shut up," snapped the second High Priest. "You're new, and abruptly terminal cases of cirrhosis have been rampant of late." She pointed a finger at Firkin. "I think this one's about to come down with it."

The whisper stirred. And it felt different this time, spiky and jagged in his head. And it was coming to the fore, he realized. It was demanding to be heard. And he had to shout it down.

He thrashed his way out of his chair. "Lawl!" he spat. "You're Lawl." It was all he could think of. The whisper hated Lawl. Or he did. Or...Everything was confused and mixed up in his head. But maybe, just maybe, if he said what the whisper might say itself, if he anticipated it, it would stay quiet.

"This is about order," he managed. He sloshed wine about himself. "This is about rules and bullshit. This is about you betraying everything."

Gods, in his desperation he even sounded like he believed it. He slugged wine desperately. But thank Barph, the whisper was quiet.

The third High Priest, however, was not. "No!" he spat, literally as well as figuratively. Phlegm landed on Firkin's cheek. "This is about you and the extravagant amounts of bullshit you have been pouring into the ears of our citizens," he shouted. "This is about the fact that you are wildly off message, sowing seeds of chaos in our city. This is about the fact that there are more people coming to your turding sermons in District Three than there are coming to the High Temple. We were very clear when you first came about the importance of hierarchy. A hierarchy is a stack. Layer upon layer. Like some sort of delicious people cake."

"Sounds grisly," commented the second priest.

"It's a metaphor, you ass," snapped the third priest. He turned back to Firkin. "It's about balance," he said. "The stack has to be well balanced, not stacked like some idiot toddler has been swiping bricks out of it." He stared pointedly at Firkin. "Because then it gets all wobbly, and it falls down." He nodded fiercely. "I saw it at my daughter's house just the other day. The exact same thing."

Firkin was at a loss. "I have not been playing with any building blocks," he said slowly. At least not that he remembered.

The priest stepped forward, pulled back his arm, and slapped Firkin full in the face. "A!" he yelled. "Fucking!" He slapped Firkin again. "Metaphor!" He delivered a third slap for good measure.

Firkin reeled. The whisper in his head reeled. This was not how it should be treated. There were people outside chanting their name. And they were getting louder.

"Vinter," said the priest, speaking slowly, "is *like* the stack of bricks. *Like* it. Not it. But *like* it. And you are like my ass of a grandson knocking it all down and clapping his chubby little hands like he doesn't need a slap in the face. And we"—he circled at the gathered High Priests—"are like the grandfather about to punt that little turd of a child out of the window."

Firkin looked around. "Can't," he said with a little more petulance than he would have liked. "There aren't any windows."

And that was when the priest produced a knife.

"Wait," said Firkin, somewhat hopefully, while also backing up quite fast. "Which part of the metaphor is the knife?"

"I was going to kill you because you're a subversive turd in the toilet bowl of my life," said the third priest through gritted teeth. "Now I'm going to kill you because you're deeply irritating."

"Actually," said the fourth priest, "I didn't follow the knife bit either." He had the decency to look embarrassed.

The first priest, standing next to him, now produced his own knife, turned around, and stabbed the fourth in the neck.

Blood geysered around the room in a thick spray, while the fourth priest dropped to the floor, thrashing like a grounded fish. Slowly he flopped to a stop.

"Sorry," said the first priest, looking at everyone's slightly shocked expressions. "It's just he was really getting on my tits."

The second priest shook her head. "This cirrhosis epidemic is really getting out of hand."

The third priest was not keen on being distracted. He pointed his own knife at Firkin again. "I blame this bastard. Let's stab him a lot and see if that fixes everything."

The whisper pulsed, grew. Firkin felt himself slip-sliding out of control. He desperately tried to hang on to something.

They were chanting his name.

He held on to that scrap of identity. He closed his eyes. He listened. A rabid edge had entered the sound. A few screams punctuated the sound. There was the creak of staging being put under increasing strain.

"Look at me when I'm stabbing you, you fucker," snapped the third High Priest, still advancing.

Firkin took a long, slow breath. He planned. And he promised the plan to the whisper. It did not answer. But it did lie still.

He opened his eyes. "Wait," he snapped.

The third priest cocked his head to one side. "Why?" he said, looking genuinely perplexed.

"Because..." Firkin said, and thought about how best to put it. "Because I need to buy time." It wasn't subtle, but it was true.

"Not good enough," said the priest, who raised his knife once more. Firkin braced.

The door behind them all flew open. All eyes went to the door. It was, Firkin realized, the houseboy that the High Priesthood had kicked into the room earlier. The child must have scampered off somewhere among all the posturing and amateur dramatics. Now he was back.

"Firkin! Master!" he said, breathing quickly, voice sounding reedy. "Please, you must come quick."

"Sorry, gents," Firkin said to the priests. "We'll have to wrap this up later." He took a step toward the boy.

The point of a knife pricked at his throat.

"I don't think so," said the third priest.

"This is taking a terribly long time," said the second.

A very distinct tremor ran through the room.

"What," said the first priest, "in the name of Barph's prodigious wang, was that?"

But Firkin just smiled. He had bought the time he needed.

His houseboy broke the silence. "The crowd is growing..." He hesitated, seemed to finally take in the tableau before him.

The dead priest. The whole knife-to-throat affair. "They're restless, master."

There was a scream from outside like the doors of the Hallows creaking open.

Blood, whispered the voice.

The High Priests exchanged glances that, if they were sober enough, might have been called nervous.

There was a feeling like a fist hitting the house. Or possibly more like a hundred angry people being thrust at it by four or five thousand angrier people behind them.

"They're a rambunctious lot," Firkin said again. "Should probably be getting out there." He wasn't sure if he was grimacing or grinning.

The house creaked under the impact of another wave of humanity.

"So..." said the third priest, reluctant to leave his murderous train of thought.

"If Master Firkin don't go out there," said the houseboy, who was at least old enough to prioritize the threats to his life, "then the crowd outside is likely to come in here and tear everything and everyone apart till they get him."

"I really have been meaning to preach to them about that," said Firkin. He wasn't above lying utterly.

The third priest hesitated, blade quivering against Firkin's Adam's apple. Then he sagged, let the knife drop. "Barph shit on it," he said.

Firkin's sphincters all relaxed in simultaneous relief. He quickly cinched them again to stop this moment of victory from transforming rapidly into one of disaster.

"Be seeing you then," he managed as he stepped past the High Priest and toward the room's door. Then the blade was back against his gut, bringing him up short.

"This isn't finished," hissed the third priest. "We don't just forget about this. You live now, but I want you to understand..."

You don't need your balls to preach. You don't need your toes. You don't need your eyes. You can do without your fingers. We can take pieces of you. And if you don't get back in line, we will. We are bigger, and stronger, and more resourceful than you. So shape the fuck up, if you ever want to piss standing up again."

Then the knife was gone. A moment later so were the High Priests.

But as Firkin made his stumbling way out to the crowd, the whisper remained.

25

The Burdened Beast

"No, Balur," Quirk said for what had to be about the fifteenth time today.

"But they are retreating!" Balur pointed out.

"No."

Sixteenth time.

"But now is being the perfect time to be using the bowels of their fallen companions to lasso them."

"No." Seventeenth. Quirk's mouth was a thin line.

When he had been with Quirk in Kondorra, Balur had always been of the opinion that if she only extracted her head from her own arsehole, and set fire to a lot more people, she would be a lot more fun. Sexy fun at that. To be frank, Quirk setting fire to people was one of the hotter things Balur had ever seen.

Sadly, the reality of the situation turned out to be total bullshit.

It was now approximately three weeks since he had arrived in Birchester, at the foot of King Todger's throne. It was three weeks since Quirk had interceded on their part. It seemed she had quite a lot of sway with King Todger. Mostly because of her ability to set fire to a lot of people.

Once Quirk had managed to extricate them from the elven throne room with their bowels intact, Balur had had his own suspicions about Quirk's authority, though.

"You were sleeping with him, weren't you?" he'd said.

"With who?" Quirk had looked comically puzzled.

"A man who is calling himself Todger." Balur had shaken his head. "And I was always thinking you had standards. Now I am finding out it's just a really weird kink."

"I did not sleep with Todger!" Quirk had seemed genuinely offended.

"Blow him? Hand job?" Lette had joined in. "It's all the same thing to them."

"I did not give the king of the elves a hand job!" Which had been when a lot of other elves had started to stare. Quirk had lowered her voice. "I'm not..." she'd muttered. "I don't do that sort of thing. Not with anybody."

Lette's brow had furrowed. "Really?" she'd said. "You should. It's more fun than you might think."

"Why are you here?" Will had broken in, which had rather disappointed Balur, who had enjoyed the track they were on.

Quirk had looked momentarily relieved at the abrupt change in topic, then narrowed her eyes. "Why are *you* here?"

Will had put on his earnest face. "It's our plan," he'd said. "We want to help."

Quirk's eyes had remained narrow. "Help with *what*?"

"With killing the dragons." Will had looked confused by the question.

"Why?"

Balur had not been convinced that with her eyes narrowed that much, Quirk would actually be able to see anything, let alone signs of subterfuge.

Will had persisted with his puzzled expression.

"Really?" Quirk had finally widened her eyes just so she could roll them. "Because I've never seen any of you do any-thing out of self-interest, right?"

"Hey," Lette had broken in. "We're not total arseholes. We're not going to let the whole world burn just because no one's pay-ing us. We live here too."

And that, Quirk had actually accepted. And Balur supposed

he did too. He had occasionally wondered why they were bothering.

"But why did you come here?" Quirk had asked finally.

Lette's face had fallen. "There's nowhere else, Quirk. It's all gone. The dragons have taken over. They've fought a different war this time. Not blood and tears, but hearts and minds. They've lied their way into power. And apparently every legitimate ruler in Avarra has been such a colossal dick that the people of this world have been happy to let them do it."

Quirk had thought about that too, then nodded, and then grimaced. "You won't be able to organize an army here," she'd said. "That's not how the elves work. They're more of a loose collective than any sort of traditional nation. A lot of individual tribes retreated here after the Century War. And yes, Todger is the chief of the biggest tribe, but he's also mostly a figurehead that the other tribes can shake at the outside world when they need to appear like they have a traditional king. Plus none of them care if the rest of the world goes to shit. As long as the dragons stay out of the Vale, they're fine. I've been able to operate here, because Tamar borders the Vale. I make guerrilla raids, and keep their border clear of trouble. But that's all I've been able to manage."

Which was when Balur had started to get excited about the possibilities of Quirk as a guerrilla fighter. This, though, was his eighth raid into Tamar, and it was also the eighth raid where Quirk had not allowed him to have any fun.

Balur picked up a rope of intestine from the floor and swung it experimentally. "I am thinking it would be perfect for the lassooing," he said, looking around for support.

A couple of the elves shrugged. They, for the most part, seemed to like him. They respected what they referred to as his "murder boner." There had been a few dustups over his tendency to buy up all the best women at brothels, but given that he outweighed most elves by a factor of three or so, those had all been resolved relatively quickly.

Quirk hadn't been any fun about those incidents either.

"We are giving chase," he said, trying to lay it out for her in a way she might understand. "We are capturing them. We are tearing the arms and legs off all but one of them, and then putting that one in a cage made of his friends' body parts. There is being a lot of weeping and self-defecating. Then after a day or two he will be telling us everything we are wanting to know. I have been doing it before. It is being very effective."

He looked around hoping to have swung popular opinion a little further.

"Shut up, Balur," said Lette.

"Shut up, round-ear," he barked back. There were a couple of laughs at that. And a few of the elves did look like they thought making a cage of human limbs could be a fun way to pass the time.

"We don't need to know anything," Quirk hissed. "We know where Diffinax is. We know where the Diffinites have set up camps. They aren't the ones hiding. *We are.* If they find us, we are utterly screwed. So when they run, we slink back in the shadows, so that they can't hit us back. Fear and doubt. Those are our weapons. Diffinax wants everyone to believe in his omnipotence. We undermine that belief. We kick out the supports. And slowly we wear down his power base. And when he's teetering, that's when we push him over. Tactics, Balur." She looked at the whole group. "Tactics."

There was silence for a moment.

"Come on." A dark-skinned Tamathian called Afrit, who seemed to have been fulfilling the role of second in command until Lette's arrival, circled a finger in the air. "Let's wrap this up and head home."

Balur sighed, then headed after the rest of the raiding party, all loping back toward the Vale.

He caught up with Lette, who was forming a rear guard. "This is being pussy bullshit," he said to her.

Lette shook her head. "Quirk is being cautious in the face of overwhelming forces, Balur. It's the sensible play."

Lette, Balur knew, had some strange aspirations toward living a less vigorous and rewarding lifestyle. One that involved things like kindness, and softness, and being stabbed when your guard was inexplicably lowered. But surely despite even that she could see the folly here. "When has caution been winning a war?"

"Recklessness has lost more."

"Reckless!" Balur threw up his hands. "We are being three miles from the nearest Diffinite camp. She is wanting to erode Diffinax's power base but where are being the witnesses to this victory that might be helping with that? Diffinax's power base is solidifying faster than we are eroding it. We are needing a grand gesture, and we are needing to be making it fast."

In front of them, a pair of elves were running, heads down. One raised a fist at Balur's words.

"Don't encourage him," Lette said.

The elf glanced over his shoulder. His name was Ethen. Balur had seen Lette sparring with him several times. He was fast and aggressive—a good man to have beside you in a fight. He had taken several lives today and their blood was painted across his cheeks in a thin spray.

"The Analesian is speaking the truth," said Ethen.

The elf beside him, Sallell—a fine shot with a bow, in Balur's opinion—turned to look too. "Quirk has given us victories. She knows what she's doing."

"She's a round-ear," Ethen said.

"And that's blind prejudice," said Sallell. "She's proved herself. And she's proven she won't spend us like someone else's coin."

It was Lette's turn to raise her fist this time.

Balur decided that it was being his opinion that people who used bows were cowards who were afraid of getting someone else's liver on their hands.

"We should let Diffinax know who opposes him," said Ethen, unrelenting. "We should make him howl our name in rage."

"And then," Lette pointed out, "he can chase you home, burn your forest to the ground, and ensure that Vinland is the only place holding out against the dragons. Well done."

Sallell flashed a smile at Lette.

Balur grunted. But he decided to remember for later the flash of defiance he saw in Ethen's eyes.

They regrouped in Elmington. It was a small village, a few miles across the border of the Vale, serving as this week's staging ground for Quirk's raids. Their band of a hundred or so warriors was standing around and engaging in their two favorite pastimes: whittling wood and talking shit. Balur had tried to get a few games of dice going, but the elves had laughed it off as an odd human custom he had picked up. He'd needed to bite off the faces of several Diffinites before they forgave him for that one.

And then the face-biting had gone and made it impossible for him to talk people into setting up a fighting ring.

So, despite his monumental lack of interest, Balur traipsed after Lette, Quirk, and Afrit to the debrief they were having in a large room, suspended between several oak trees. Its floor creaked ominously beneath Balur's weight. Will looked up from a table full of charts as they came in.

"How did it go?" he asked.

The elves, for their part, ignored him. Will did a poor job of hiding his disappointment. Personally, Balur didn't understand why some of the elves hung on to their hatred of humans so hard. They had been able to retreat to a forest at least. The Analesians had been stuck with a gods-hexed desert.

"Fine," Lette said eventually.

"You won?" Will was a clucking mother hen.

"Of course we were winning," said Balur, mildly insulted by the question.

"Stop fretting." The elf Ethen had accompanied them, and was looking at Will as one would a child who had just shat upon the kitchen floor.

"Everything went well, Will." Quirk at least smiled at the farmer. It was she who had invited him to come along with them, who had asked him to sit in and help plan with them. And no one questioned Quirk, no matter what the shape of her ears was. She had proven herself a warrior, even if she was part of a group that had historically been titanic dicks to the elves. Will, on the other hand, had not.

Will returned Quirk's smile. And Balur could not, at least, question his enthusiasm for the fight. Even if he let others actually fight it.

"I was looking at this map of the plains to the southwest." Will grabbed a map off the table and thrust it toward Quirk. "I'm thinking a series of coordinated attacks. All at the same time. We have the timing of a lot of their patrols now. We could prepare the area overnight. Use tar and pitch to draw symbols of the gods on the ground. Barph's flagon. Lawl's scepter. Klink's open palm. Then we could strike, kill the patrol, and torch the designs. We would have to get close to some of the encampments, but imagine…all across the country the seven symbols of the seven gods flaming to life at the same moment. Imagine the way people would talk."

Quirk smiled. "I like it. I like it a lot. But it will have to wait until after we go back to Birchester and resupply."

Will leaned forward. "The iron is hot now. The sooner we strike—"

Quirk shook her head. "We cannot impose on the people of Elmington any longer. We're taxing these villages beyond what they can support."

"We don't need that many to remain—" Will started.

"I said—"

And at that point, Balur couldn't take it anymore.

He slammed his fists down on the map table. Its legs punched through the wooden floor and dangled above the ground thirty feet below. In Balur's estimation, the craftsmanship of the elves was highly overrated.

"What," he said, "in the actual fuck?"

There was quite a long silence. To Balur's mind this just condemned them all further.

"Emblems of the gods? Out in fields? Waylaying patrols?" He stared at them. "This is being how you are planning to topple an empire? Do you also bed whores by staring at their thighs from across the room? This is being so very fucking pointless." He turned and pointed at Quirk, the epicenter of this whirlwind of bullshit that had somehow caught Lette and Will in its grip. "You," he said. "You are being a literal fucking torch we could be using to burn a path straight to Diffinax's doorstep."

"Where we'll lose." Quirk didn't back down an inch. "We need an army. And for that we need the Tamarian people."

Balur batted the objection aside. "I have been killing a dragon before. I can be doing it again."

He remembered blood and heat. He remembered balancing on the knife edge of death. And yes, he remembered fear. But he also remembered surviving. Could he guarantee victory? Of course not. No one could. But he could guarantee that if they lost they would die standing on their feet.

"That," said Quirk, looking him directly in the eye, "was luck."

Balur lost a few seconds. The next thing he knew he had Quirk by the neck and a lot of people were pointing swords at him.

"Put me down, Balur." Quirk's voice, while constricted, was calm.

"Say that again," said Balur. He was breathing hard. His vision seemed narrow. "I am fucking daring you."

Flame burst to life in Quirks hands.

"Put me down before I melt your eyes."

And there she was. She was hidden deep, beneath books and bullshit. But there was a savage inside Quirk. Balur smiled long enough that she would know what he saw, know why he was letting her go.

He put her down. Around him elves put their swords and bows away. Ethen, he noticed, had never drawn his blades. He filed that away too.

"Be melting Diffinax's eyes," he whispered. "Fight him like you fight me."

"We operate," Quirk said, her voice strident and harsh, "from a position of weakness. We do not challenge him until we operate from a position of strength. I will not risk one of the two remaining nations that stand against these dragons on the strength of your fucking murder boner."

Balur stroked self-consciously at his neck where small purple frills sometimes gave away his arousal. In his defense it had been really, really hot when Quirk had threatened to melt his eyes.

"To be in a position of strength," he said, trying to mask his embarrassment, "you have to be strong. We are being weak. We are being cowards."

"That's not fair," Will cut in.

"Shut up, round-ear." Enough voices said it, it was almost a chant.

Will stared around, wounded. "But…I…I'm defending you."

"We are fighting back with what we have," Quirk said, ignoring Will. "And we are building momentum. That takes the time it takes. It takes the focus and discipline it takes. And if you don't have those qualities then I cannot use you in this fight."

For a moment Balur was actually speechless. "You—" he started. "You are…?" He shook his head. "If this is being how elves are fighting," he said finally, "then there is being a reason they were chased back to the forests."

With that, he left the stupid fucking room.

*   *   *

He was waiting impatiently for the tavern to open when the group of fifteen or so elves found him. It was a mixture of hard-looking men and women.

"You," said a women. "You pinned the firestarter by the neck?"

Balur rolled his shoulders. He had half-expected this, had been looking forward for a chance to work out some of his pent-up aggression. He decided he wouldn't use his swords. He wanted blood on his knuckles.

He leaned toward the woman. "I was calling her on her horse dung. And I was calling everyone who follows her without questioning on their horse dung as well. She will lose this fight for you." He curled his lips, showed his teeth.

Let us be seeing what fangs you are having, little one.

And then, from the back of the group, Ethen stepped forward. "I told you," he said.

The woman held Balur's yellow eyes steadily. Then she nodded. "Good," she said. "We agree. So let's talk about how we're actually going to win."

26

Mistakes Were Made

Will woke, and found that despite everything, he had a smile on his face. Dragons still controlled Avarra. Lette still showed little inclination to allow him into her heart, or even ride his body around the bedroom like a hobby horse. Most of the elves treated him with barely concealed disdain. And yet still he was happy.

There was a satisfaction to the work they were doing here. The raids he was helping to organize—they were making a difference in Tamar. They were part of a slow but steady change in the tenor of the country's rulership. The people would not put up with Diffinax's oppression forever. The people of Kondorra hadn't. And this time, it wasn't some slapdash accident that would push the populace over the edge, but a carefully coordinated effort. This time, things would go smoothly.

And on top of all that—he was doing everything from within the safety of a heavily defended, barely penetrable forest. All the people interested in introducing sharp bits of metal to his spleen were in an entirely different country. It was fantastic.

He washed and dressed quickly, then headed out into Elmington. The day was fresh and young, branches rattling and a slight breeze whispering about him. The early morning bustle of elves made the wooden walkways thrum beneath his feet. Below, carts were spread out in preparation for today's return to Birchester.

He headed down a spiraling set of stairs—little more than notches circling the trunk of a tree. There weren't many tasks left to be done, but he just liked being in the thick of things. He prowled between the carts, plucking at ropes, checking the wheels for rotten spokes.

"Restless?"

Will looked up. It was Afrit, Quirk's friend from Tamathia. She held a bundle of sticks in one hand. She saw him looking at them.

"Pine," she said. "I mean…they're pinewood. It's light. Celter… one of the elves. She told me that pine is good for arrows. I'm trying to work out how to make them." She smiled apologetically. "I'm not very good still."

Will smiled sympathetically. "You were a professor, weren't you?" he said. "Before all this."

"Practical politics," she said.

Will guessed that must be a subject of study.

"I am, by the way," he said. And then off her look, "Restless, I mean."

"Me too." She nodded.

They hadn't really gotten to know each other well in the weeks they had been raiding into Tamar. Afrit had tended to steer clear of him and Lette and Balur. He had seen her several times, standing apart, waiting until Quirk walked away from them.

"So," she said after an awkward pause, "you were the prophet of Kondorra?"

"Erm…" Will said, because that wasn't strictly true. "For a while some people thought I was."

"I read what Quirk wrote about you." Afrit studied her arrows.

"Quirk wrote about us?" She had, Will thought, stayed very quiet on that subject.

"Oh." Afrit studied the arrows harder. "I didn't realize…

She wrote about everything. The dragons mostly, of course. But everyone was interested in…well, everything. The whole social history of the uprising. So she wrote about that too. You were obviously important."

Will tried to absorb that. People in a country he had never personally visited had read all about him.

"Gods," he said. "No wonder you normally avoid us."

"What…I…oh…" Afrit looked about, apparently for any patch of earth that seemed like it might conveniently swallow her. "No. It's just…" She seemed to reassess her exit strategy, and then collapsed inward, sighing. "I'm sorry. I…Okay, this is just embarrassing. I was what can best be described as a fan of Quirk's. Academically she is my…was…I idolized her. It was pretty awkward. We've got past that, obviously. But it's still…" If Afrit twisted her pine sticks any harder she was going to be left making some very short arrows. "Anyway, she doesn't really talk about Kondorra. And I mean, obviously I've read everything she wrote about it all. And attended all her lectures."

"Obviously," Will said.

"But that's all from her perspective. And I was just sort of wondering…" Afrit hesitated. "What was she like? Quirk, I mean. When she was there?"

Will thought about that. About everything that had been said and done there. Finally he said, "Increasingly angry."

Afrit waited for more. Will waited to see if he had more. Then a question occurred to him.

"Wait," he said. "Are you and she…?"

Afrit's blush was readily apparent, despite the darkness of her skin. "No," she said quickly. "No, no, no. I'm not. We're not." She looked up at Will, a look of slight desperation in her eyes. "I don't think she's interested in that sort of thing at all." Another desperate glance. "Is she?"

It was Will's turn to consider if legging it for the trees was socially acceptable.

"I don't...I wouldn't..." He spluttered. Then, because Afrit's desperation seemed to demand it, he gave it two seconds of thought. "No," he said. And then, because it seemed like the right thing to say, "Sorry."

"It's okay," she said. She seemed a little more at ease now that that was out of the way. "Friends is good. I can live with friends."

Will considered. Were he and Quirk friends? He wasn't sure. He thought she found him familiar in this sort of situation, but...friendship?

What about him and Lette?

"I hope so," he said finally. It seemed the best resolution to what was essentially a bit of a mess. He sought desperately for a new topic to take them far, far away from this one.

"If you are friends with Quirk," he said, forcing cheer into his voice at knife point, "would you mind having a word with her about this idea of joining forces with Vinland? I keep bringing it up, but I think she's stopped listening to me."

"Vinland?" Afrit looked at him askance. "You want to align with the Vinlanders?"

Why? Will wondered. *Why does everyone look at me like I've started lactating when I say that?*

But rather than say that, he said, "Yes. They've held the dragons off. They're so enamored with Barph that they're basically impervious to the dragons' criticisms of the gods. They're an obvious ally. And our forces stand a greater chance united."

"The Vinlanders," Afrit repeated, in a more contemplative tone. "A nation of people who have dedicated themselves to the worship of Barph, the god of, basically, drunken anarchy. A god whose entire corpus of mythology consists of him consuming vast amounts of wine, and then talking people into doing incredibly unwise things. In fact"—she held a finger up in the air—"from what Quirk has written, he's basically a godlike version of your friend Firkin. That's who the people of Vinland worship. A giant, almost omnipotent version of your village drunk."

"But—" Will started, then found he knew exactly why everyone had looked at him like that.

"And," said a familiar voice, "he's an absent god, who never manifests, or does anything whatsoever, so worshipping him is a particularly stupid thing to do."

Will found himself wishing that Lette had not arrived at this exact juncture.

"Is Will talking about Vinland again?" Quirk's voice also wended its way between the wagons, quickly followed by its owner. She was rolling her eyes as she approached. It was not, Will thought, half as appealing a habit on her as it was on Lette.

"I wasn't—" Will started.

"Yes you were!" Afrit stared at him outraged. "You were literally just asking me to make your case to Quirk on your behalf." She seemed simultaneously more relaxed and more on edge as Quirk approached. She pushed one braid behind her ear.

"I think you're misunderstanding the point I was trying to make." Will lied straight through his teeth.

"I think you misunderstood the bit where you're not meant to make a jackass of yourself." Lette wrapped a companionable arm around his shoulder.

Will was momentarily struck dumb by the fact that this was the sweetest thing Lette had said to him since they met in a Batarran brothel.

Carefully Lette removed her arm.

"I should probably..." said Afrit, stepping away, looking down at her feet, and clearly with no intention of actually finishing that sentence.

"Actually." Quirk caught Afrit by her sleeve. "I was wondering, have you seen Ethen this morning?"

Afrit furrowed her brow. "Ethen? No."

Quirk wrinkled her nose. "Gods piss on it. It's already after I wanted to leave. I said to him..." She shook her head. "Him and a bunch of his cronies. They're all..." She waved a hand vaguely at the forest.

"Have you tried the tavern?" Lette asked.

Quirk nodded. "First place I looked. I thought I might find Balur there as well." She looked at Lette. "You don't know where he is, do you? This time I picked a staging ground without a brothel to try and avoid exactly this sort of problem."

Afrit cocked her head. "So Ethen and Balur are missing?"

"Well." Quirk shrugged. "The word *missing* seems excessive. 'Temporarily misplaced.'"

"Is Ethen the superaggressive one that weighs about eighty pounds?" Will asked. There were a lot of elves, and he still had trouble remembering everyone's names.

"How many cronies?" asked Lette. Her eyes had narrowed again. "And are we sure we want to be seen in public using the word *cronies*?"

Quirk looked at Lette. "You're suggesting something, aren't you? What are you suggesting?"

"That using archaic words like *cronies* makes us sound like the sort of people who shouldn't be allowed to organize large military raids into neighboring countries."

"Not that," Quirk snapped. "The other thing."

Lette opened her mouth.

Which was when they heard the running feet. They all turned to look, trying to peer between the thicket of parked wagons. Will grabbed the side of one, hoisted himself up for an unobstructed view. So he was the first one to see Balur come tearing into the clearing.

The lizard man was bleeding heavily from a broad gash to the skull and another to his arm. His armor was blackened, and a savage burn crept up over his right shoulder. Ethen was close behind him. Half the elf's hair was gone, and the left-hand side of his face was lost in blood. There were a few others, ragged, half-broken, stumbling in their wake.

Balur looked up, saw Will, adjusted his course. He came around the corner, saw all of them gathered together.

"Oh fuck." Lette hung her head, started to shake it.

"What?" Quirk looked from Balur to Lette, back to Balur. Her eyes were wide, her breath coming quickly. "What have you done?"

Balur held up a finger, sucked down a few lungfuls of air, met Quirk's eye, looked away, breathed heavily a few more times, and then finally said, "Okay, I am admitting it. Raiding their encampment was not being a fantastic idea."

27

Monstrous Truths

Lette had been tortured before. It was an occupational hazard. And so she knew that everyone broke. It didn't matter how tough you were: Everyone had a limit. And knowing that meant that she normally gave up information pretty quickly. Being certain of the inevitable endpoint, she was generally inclined to avoid the messy middle. Occasionally she had toughed it out, either waiting for Balur to arrive, or simply because the prick torturing her was just so very annoying. And she had found that she had a pretty high tolerance for a lot of your average torturer's bullshit. But just like everyone else, in the end, she always broke.

Still, she was fairly sure that the one secret she might actually take to her grave was that she loved Balur.

It was not a romantic love. That was one reason she would never admit it. Because Balur would never be able to understand that. But it was not exactly like the tiny ember of love she still kept alight for her parents and her siblings either. Which would only complicate matters should she need to describe it. It was simply this: that she would defend him to the death. And she had no doubt he would do the same.

He called them a tribe from time to time, but it was not that. Tribe could betray tribe. Tribe could kick out the weak. Tribe could be ruthless, in a way she found herself powerless to be. No, she would defend Balur no matter what incredibly stupid or dangerous thing he did.

Like bring a fucking dragon down on their heads, for one very specific example.

28

Monstrous Consequences

Lette saw the look in Quirk's eyes and before she quite realized what she was doing, she put a knife to the woman's throat.

"There's no time for that," she whispered into Quirk's ear.

Afrit saw the reflection of light on the blade, let out a yell, and lunged, but Lette was already pulling the knife away. She stepped, stiff-armed the professor in the solar plexus, and brought the woman to a sharp halt.

Then she took a breath.

She could hear shouting. Stamping feet. She could hear branches breaking. The feet of the elves tapping on the walkways above. She could hear the horses for the wagons shuffling about. Smell the tang of their shit and piss. She could smell the sap where branches had been sawed from trees to make fresh arrows and bows. Last night's rabbit being heated up over breakfast fires. She could feel a slight thrum in the ground beneath the leaves at her feet.

And she could hear the beating of wings.

"Abandon the wagons. Abandon everything." She spoke low and fast. "And run."

Then she turned and did just that.

Lette had come to like these elves. They were insular, and rude, and were so accustomed to poverty that they didn't even realize they should complain about it, but they were also tough as old leather, and didn't give a shit about what you thought.

They did not play half as many harps as bards suggested. In fact she suspected bards mostly just wanted to believe that somewhere out there was someone who believed all the harp practice they did was sexy and worthwhile. Most of the elves she had met, though, would rather use a harp to make a fire that they could roast a bard's balls over.

But despite liking them, there was no way she was going to hang around and get killed by a dragon on their behalf. Gods, she was helping them all by setting a good example. If they all just turned and hoofed it, then they'd all be fine and dandy. Or at least they would be for about thirty seconds longer than if they stood still.

She covered ten yards, heard Balur's heavy footsteps fall in behind hers.

Fifteen yards. Quirk started screaming at people that they needed to run.

Thirty yards. Quirk began to run as she shouted.

Forty yards. Elves were asking what was going on. A few were starting to move. More people were yelling from between the wagons.

Fifty yards. Had she imagined it? Had she made a fool of herself? Was there no dragon coming?

Fifty-six yards. The whole world detonated. A series of short, sharp blows to her skin and her sanity. Heat roiled over her. And no, she had not made a fool of herself. The screams confirmed it. The cracking wood and sound of parting flesh confirmed it. The sense of horror in her gut confirmed it. Splinters and shrapnel peppered the ground around her. Branches slapped at her. The ground churned beneath her feet. Fear rode her as if she wore a saddle and bridle.

Seventy yards. Chaos. A churning, roaring tidal wave of madness racing after her. A deer burst past her, its antlers on fire. Screams and running feet swallowed the world behind her. Waves of heat rose and fell at her back. She could hear the forest burning. Living wood cracked and shrieked in protest at the impossible heat. She couldn't make out the individual screams anymore. She did not dare look back.

A hundred yards. Balur pulled up alongside her, head down, eating up the ground with long, loping strides. When she glanced over at him, he did not meet her eye. Blood ran freely from the wounds in his head and arm, leaving a trail of glistening beads behind him.

A hundred and twenty yards. Trees were falling, crashing to the ground. Something vast was in the forest behind them. It roared. A massive sound. The ground trembled as if in fear. Heat battered her, the fire racing her, pace for pace. Drops of sweat poured off her like rats fleeing a sinking ship.

A hundred and fifty yards. Starting to get a sense for the size of the group fleeing with her. More than she had suspected at first. There were more figures in the corners of her eyes. She glanced, caught sight of elves. And then Will. Head down, legs pumping. Her heart skipped a beat it couldn't afford to miss.

Two hundred yards. Out of the clearing, in the forest proper. Hurdling branches. Dodging tree trunks. The sound of crashing trees, of massive footsteps no longer advancing. Falling back slightly. Could she still make out the screams?

Two hundred and twenty yards. Wings again. Her legs weak. She realized she was praying.

Two hundred and fifty yards. Fire fell like rain. Screams rose. A few people stumbled to a halt, pulled arrows from quivers. Too little. Too late. The dragon swept past. A shadow in the heavens. A vast column of flesh and scale. It blotted out the sky. And then gone. Its wings crashed through treetops, sent flaming branches hurtling down like ballista bolts. She darted left, right, sprinted down the very cliff's edge of her own mortality.

Two hundred and seventy yards. All of them stumbling now. Another lance of flame, crisscrossing the forest ahead of them. People looking for a path forward as the dragon boxed them in. Fear clawing at the back of Lette's throat. Desperately shoving it back down. Begging that little quiet voice to come back and help her.

Oh no. You're fucked now.

Two hundred and eighty yards. Fighting through branches. Trying to keep track of the others. A beast's instinct for the safety of the herd. Fighting to keep control of herself, to think straight. Heat on all sides. Smoke clotting the world. Women and men on fire. Quirk howling something inaudible.

Three hundred yards and through the worst of it for a moment. The stitch building in her side. Looking around. Balur was still there, still bleeding, still running. She glanced for Will despite herself, couldn't see him. Afrit was dragging Quirk along. Lette didn't have time to figure out if she was injured or not.

Four hundred yards. Waiting. Waiting for *it* to come again.

Five hundred yards and she dared to hope.

Five hundred and fifty yards. It had known. It had known they would be thinking that maybe, just maybe they were in the clear. That they would be thinking that perhaps they could survive this. And then fire to the left. A quick blast. The sound of sap boiling, trunks cracking.

Five hundred and seventy yards. Fire to the right.

Six hundred yards. They were being herded. This was fun for that sick fucker in the air. This was sport. Lette didn't have the breath for it, but she bellowed out her rage anyway, her sense of desperation, of futility. Fuck this monster. Fuck him to the Hallows.

Six hundred and thirty yards. The fire came again. The world clenching down, becoming only the space in front of her. All futures shortening to the next few seconds. Leap that way. Hurdle that branch. Duck back here. Drop low. Skid through that puddle. Am I still alive? How about now? How about now?

Six hundred and fifty yards. Through the smoke. Through

the confusion, staring at trees. Endless trees. The whole world a maze. The whole world the same repeating pattern, over and over. And she could not run anymore. She stopped, stared. Balur emerged from the black clouds of ash, skidded to a halt.

"What are we doing?" he asked.

"There's no escaping this." She stared at the tangled web of forest in front of them.

Balur grinned. "We fight."

"We'll die." It was Quirk, emerging, choking. She was supporting Afrit now. There was a gang of elves around them. "We have to run. But not back to Birchester. We can't lead them that way."

"How is us dying while we lead a fucking dragon away from Birchester any different from us dying making a stand here?" Lette was in Quirk's face, flecking her with spittle.

Afrit was trying to get between them, saying, "No. Don't." Quirk was crying.

"We make a stand," Balur bellowed.

And then the dragon roared.

Seven hundred yards. Wishing she had not run. Wishing she had stood her ground. And so very glad she had not. Fire chasing after her.

Eight hundred yards. *Where was Will?* Trying to push that thought away. But it pursued her as relentlessly as Diffinax.

A thousand yards. They were a tight knot now. Perhaps sixty survivors. She glanced left, right. Balur was easy to make out, two and a half feet taller than any of the elves. Quirk made herself obvious, screaming directions no one was listening to. But where was—

And then she saw him. Near the back of the group. And the sense of relief was so large it almost overwhelmed her. She stumbled. An elf grabbed her elbow, pulled her upright. She looked back again. And yes, it was Will. She tripped over a branch, staggered, managed to catch herself. She couldn't afford to keep looking back. She looked back again. It was him. Smeared with smoke and blood. But him. Him alive.

Fifteen hundred yards. They could hear roaring. They could hear the rush of flame. They could hear screams. But it was moving away from them. Diffinax was attacking but…not them. The pace of the group faltered.

"No," Quirk was saying over and over. "No. No."

"What?" Lette asked. "What is it?"

"Other survivors," said Afrit.

"No. No. No." Quirk's litany continued.

"Better them than us." It was not a kind thing to say, Lette knew, but it was the truth.

Afrit shook her head. "It's not that. It's…They didn't hear Quirk. They're running back home. They're leading Diffinax straight to Birchester. Straight to the capital of the Vale."

29

In the Land of the Drunk . . .

Quirk knew that she shouldn't. She knew that it was self-indulgent, and foolish, and worst of all dangerous, a threat to the lives of all who followed them. But she still dropped to her knees and screamed.

Birchester was a smoking ruin of ash and rubble.

She wanted to set fire to something. To someone. To Balur.

That so many should die and he should live . . .

"Hush. Hush." Afrit rushed to her, wrapped an arm around her.

Lette was less subtle. "Shut the fuck up," she snapped.

Quirk was still not talking to Lette. Lette wouldn't let her kill Balur.

It was five days since they had left Elmington. Five days of praying that Balur's rashness might not have led to total disaster. And now she stood in the ruin of a nation's capital, with the smell of blood and charred meat still thick on the air. With the vast path that Diffinax himself had bulldozed through the forest and the city still clearly visible. Now she stood in the ruin of all her hopes. In the ruin of lives. In the ruin of a civilization.

And Lette told her to shut up.

She stood, and she wore a crown of flames. Afrit backed away fast.

"Don't you dare," Quirk said to Lette. And even her words were fire—tongues of flame darting out from her mouth. "Don't you dare tell me what to do while you still defend him."

Lette had the good sense to keep quiet. And part of Quirk was glad. Part of her recognized that she would have had a hard time living with Lette's life on her conscience.

Part of her.

Will found her, half an hour later, leaning up against one of the few oak trees that were still standing. The tattered remains of a walkway hung halfway down its trunk like some severed limb.

"What?" she snapped when it became apparent Will wasn't about to take her turned back as the hint it was, and leave her alone.

"They haven't headed back to Tamar," he said.

At first she couldn't parse the words. They were just sounds. "What?" she snapped again, channeling her frustration into this confusion.

"Diffinax. The Diffinites." Will looked nervous. "They haven't turned back. They're still pushing on through the forest."

And that...that didn't make sense. Because Diffinax had already won. There was no bigger prize in the Vale than Birchester. The dragon had already torn the heart out of the nation.

And so...So he was after something...Could he and his followers be chasing after survivors? Her heart leapt in her breast. That would mean there *were* survivors. She could rescue them.

"Which direction did they go in?" she asked. She tried not to voice her hope yet.

Will looked anywhere but at her. "Before I tell you," he said, "I want you to know I'm not making this up, and I'm not happy about it."

Will, Quirk thought, had a shitty way of not getting to the point. She arched an eyebrow and grit her teeth.

"Toward Vinland," Will said quickly. "They headed toward Vinland."

For a moment the words meant nothing. She was still too mired in *now*, in *this*. The future was still obscured by ash, and smoke, and piles of dead bodies.

And then she saw it. Saw why Will looked almost embarrassed. "You think we should go there," she said.

"They deserve to be warned." Will finally met her eyes.

Fuck you! she wanted to scream. *You and your obstinate insistence on this.* And part of her wanted to laugh in his face. *Warn them? Save them? Like you saved these people?*

And part of her...part of her had Hethren whispering in her ears.

But instead she took a breath, and was for a moment just a professor from Tamathia, alone and lost in the woods.

"Yes," she said. "You're right."

Will let out a long breath, turned away, then hesitated. "There aren't enough bodies," he said at last.

"What?"

"Erm..." Will shifted his weight. "I don't mean it's like we're trying to fill a quota or anything. But the dead bodies here. It's a lot, but it's only about a quarter of the people who lived here. A lot got away."

Quirk took that in silently. Because Will didn't deserve her relief, or her tears. She would wait for him to leave, which he did, slowly. Still, just before he left her, she decided she deserved the last word.

"You should have led with that, you moron."

Then he was gone.

It turned out that Will was right. In the ensuing days they came across more and more groups of bedraggled, exhausted, and terrified survivors. As the days went on, they encountered groups who weren't even from Birchester, but rather were from other villages in the Vale, had heard the news, and were already fleeing.

No matter how much their numbers bloated, Quirk kept pushing them harder. She could feel history chasing them, and she began a desperate sprint for the Vinland border.

On the second day out of Birchester, they got past Diffinax.

His army had, in fact, been camped barely a mile outside the ravaged city. And the dragon's army seemed to have lost a considerable amount of its momentum in the aftermath of their victory. They no longer charged through the forest, but slowly marched—implacable, and irresistible to be sure, but no longer with such awful speed.

And then Will came to her and said, "I don't think we should go to Vinland."

After cycling through a couple of possible responses, Quirk decided to laugh in his face.

"Well, where in the Hallows should we go, Will?" Quirk put her hands on her hips and cocked her head to one side. "What would finally make you happy?" She wished she could be sure he caught the sarcasm.

"They're all people who actively chose to worship Barph," Will said, which wasn't exactly answering the question.

"How is this news to you?"

"I've been thinking," he pressed. "What about the Fanlorn Empire? They're hidden behind mountains. We could head to the coast right now. Get a boat and take it there. The Fanlornians might not have dragons."

"And if they do?"

"Fine." Will wasn't done. "Thresnia," he said. "In the Arid Bay. Nobody is going to bother conquering there."

"Because we'd die after about three days from lack of water. It's a city of the undead, you dullard." Quirk shook her head. "And I have been accused of having trouble being happy." She looked over at Lette. The mercenary was extravagantly drunk. "Getting in the Vinland spirit," she called it. "How long did you and Lette last again?"

It was a low, low blow, but she really wanted Will to regret this conversation.

"Listen," she said to him, leaning in. "There is, as you already know, as you have even said to me, nowhere else to go but

Vinland. And now Diffinax is marching on it. And thanks to new refugees near the Batarran border, we know that Theerax is mobilizing his troops, marching an army south."

Will reeled. "Another army? Theerax?"

"Yes." Quirk wanted to hit him with the words. "And apparently he has Gorrax from Salera coming down to help him as well. It's going to be a big push into Vinland. So all we have now is the time it takes them to marshal all their forces. That's all the time we have to warn Vinland and get them in a state to defend themselves from three invading armies at once."

"Oh," said Will. He chewed his lip. "I mean..." He looked away. "Now part of me really thinks we shouldn't go to Vinland."

Suddenly Quirk wished she was as drunk as Lette.

It felt strange to leave the trees behind. Quirk stood at the Vinland border, watching the elves hesitate, stare about themselves, blink in the abrupt brightness of the sun. She sympathized. After only two months of forest living, she felt curiously exposed without a tree at her back. And for some of these people, it was their first time out without a canopy above their heads.

Their numbers had swelled to just over five hundred now. Of King Todger, though, there had been no sign. Quirk suspected that his corpse was far behind them now. And in his absence people again seemed to be looking to her for leadership. She tried not to resent it. Not to worry that she was fulfilling a culturally insensitive and stereotypical "savior" role. Sometimes when she got to brooding she would catch Afrit looking at her. That helped.

Vinland seemed a simple and pleasant land from this vantage. Sun splashed over gently rolling hills that alternated between meadows, vineyards, and orchards. A few copses of trees stood out sharp against the horizon. A handful of farmsteads were scattered about.

But what defense did it offer? What natural choke points?

What strategic strongholds? In the end, this landscape could hold no reassurance for her.

It did, however—she discovered after two leagues—hold a surprisingly large number of soldiers.

There were perhaps sixty of them, heavily armed, with a contingent of twenty aiming crossbows. They appeared from between the rows of a vineyard, rushing forward at a controlled march, surrounding them. It was, Quirk was forced to concede, fairly terrifying, despite the fact that half of them were cross-eyed and slurring.

The elves, exhausted as they were, reacted as quickly as they could. Bows were pulled from shoulders, strings stretched. But before they could fumble for their arrows from their quills, both she and Will were shouting at them to stop. This was why they were here.

One of the Vinlanders, possibly a captain, weaved a path toward Will and Lette.

"Who in the Hallows are you?" he slurred.

"Political refugees," Quirk said, trying not to glance at Afrit to make sure she was getting her terms right.

"What's that when it's at home?" asked the Vinlander captain, which did make her glance at Afrit. Which in turn, didn't help at all.

"We're being pursued by the dragon Diffinax," Will cut in. "We need help or we'll die."

"How's that my problem?" The guard hiccupped into his clenched fist, but didn't offer up an apology.

Which was when Quirk started to lose her patience. "Because he's coming here." She tried not to grit her teeth while she spoke.

"Wait," said the captain. "You're running away from him, right?"

"Yes," said Quirk.

"And you know he's coming here, right?" said the captain.

"Yes," said Quirk again. Her fists were clenched.

"You're shit at running away."

"The dragons are everywhere." Quirk wanted to beat the words into the guard's skull.

"The dragons have taken over all the rest of Avarra," Will cut in again. Quirk actually felt grateful. She wasn't sure she could maintain a diplomatic tone. "This is the only place they haven't conquered yet." He paused. "You do know all this, right?"

The captain blinked at him. Then he said, "So you're political prisoners, is it?"

"I said *refugees*," Quirk said firmly. She wanted that distinction to be very clear.

"Who's pointing a crossbow at who here?" asked the captain.

Quirk could resolve this quickly, she knew. She estimated she could put an end to all of these soldiers before they got many shots off.

That didn't feel particularly diplomatic.

"Look," she said, trying to force herself to relax, to think about who she was talking to. A Vinland soldier. "We are running for our lives here. Utter terror and devastation are behind us. And these dragons are coming looking for a fight. And we just want to sleep it off for a night or two, so we can get up, fresh and invigorated, and kick some dragon arse with you. Now how does that sound?"

"Like you're trying to pander to me based on my religious affiliation," said the captain, which was a lot closer to the mark than Quirk had hoped.

"Look," Quirk felt diplomacy slipping away from her again, "we're not here to pick a fight. We're here to join with you if you'll have us. And if you won't, it's pointless to keep us here. We're not a threat to anyone. Either help us get to shelter or don't."

"Strange times it is," said the captain, rubbing his chin. "Talk of dragons taking over beyond the borders. War in the capital." He took a swig from his flask, smacked his lips. "And I don't know where you land in all of this, or where you tip the scales."

"War in the *where*?" Quirk almost squeaked. That was new, and about as reassuring as a rash in her britches.

"You know what?" said the captain, who smiled. "I know where my loyalties lie, don't I?" He draped an arm over Quirk's shoulders.

"Probably." Quirk tried to make her response sound more conversational than acerbic as the captain steered her along the road.

"So I know what to do with you then, don't I?" said the captain.

"Give us shelter, recruit us in your highly coordinated and efficient efforts to fight the dragons, and explain what you meant about the war in the capital?" Which probably didn't help her sound any more conversational.

"I was thinking," said the captain, wrapping his arm more tightly around Quirk's shoulders, "that I'd drag your arses to Vinter and then pass the buck. How does that sound?"

Considering how inebriated they were, the Vinlanders set a harsh pace to Vinter. It was the evening of the third day when they stumbled through the thick, tumbledown walls of the capital and into the sweating, stinking heart of the country. They'd been able to smell it coming for miles, the reek of stale alcohol, urine, and vomit, mixed with hops and sour grapes.

As they progressed through the city, the roads changed from dirt to straw-strewn cobbles. Buildings were made of clay bricks. A pall of smoke lay across the sky like a blanket. The sun winked redly through. Ramshackle houses gave way to ramshackle warehouses and workshops. Armed gangs crowded inside warehouse doorways, watching them while fingering cudgels and short swords. Their guards kept their heads down and gripped their swords tighter.

If Vinter was a drunken city, it did not feel to Quirk like it was one of those happy, relaxed drunks. Instead there was a sense of building, belligerent violence to the place, as if at some point the whole city would unfurl and start yelling incoherently about that one time you borrowed its mother's best china and never gave it back, despite the fact that you'd never borrowed any china, and their mother had never owned any in the first place.

Quirk leaned over to Lette, who was walking alongside her, behind their captain of the Vinland guard. "Something very bad is going on in this city."

Lette nodded. "In other news, the sky is blue."

Which, considering Quirk had chosen not to roast Lette alive after her defense of Balur, seemed a little uncalled for.

Lette rolled her eyes. "Look," she said. "I was a mercenary for ten years before you knew me. If you can sense trouble in a place, then rest assured that not only do I know about it, but I have met it, gotten on a first-name basis with it, and been introduced to its mother."

Quirk decided to ignore that and push ahead with what she actually wanted to talk about for once. "We'll need a plan."

Lette shrugged. "We're where we want to be. So if there's trouble here, we try to dodge it as soon as we see it coming. And if we're not fast enough, we hope we're strong enough to take the punch. Then, assuming we're still alive, we kill the trouble, piss on it to let it know who's boss, and get what the fuck we came here for." She smiled sweetly. "That's my plan anyway."

Quirk sighed. "I always thought you were more nuanced than Balur."

Lette kept right on smiling. "There is a time for nuance, Quirk. The moment before a fistfight is not it. And Balur is like a stopped clock. He's still always right when it's time to punch someone in the face."

Abruptly the Vinlander captain raised a hand, and their troupe came to a halt. Caught off guard, elves stumbled into each other, then looked around blinking. The house they were standing beside was perhaps a little larger and more ostentatious than the others about, but that was a little like saying one cow's pile of dung was larger than another's.

"All right," said the captain, who then hiccupped into his fist one more. He looked the street up and down, then seemed to sigh in relief. "Whoever's in charge of you tossers, let's go have a natter with the boss man, shall we?"

"The boss man?" It was Afrit who spoke up. She pointed back up the slope. "Why didn't you take us to the High Priest-hood?"

In response, the captain rolled his rather bleary eyes. "What part of civil war was confusing to you?" he said, sounding tired.

"You *never* mentioned a civil war!" Will couldn't quite keep the volume of his voice within normal limits.

The captain looked at him cross-eyed. "Really?" He shrugged. "Well, we're here now, aren't we?"

Quirk took a breath. *If there's trouble we hope we're strong enough to take the punch.* She looked to the elves. They were looking at her. That still felt wrong.

"Let's just get this over with," she said. "Lorell, Forette, Nottram, Collabell, Rickert, come with me." She pointed at the elves one by one. Will forced his way into her field of vision, making puppy-dog eyes at her. She sighed inwardly. "Afrit, Will, Lette, you too."

"What about me?" said Balur, looking hurt.

But there was no way Quirk was letting Balur near anyone referred to as a "boss man."

The lizard man was still grumbling as she followed the Vinter captain through the house's doors and into its hot, humid interior. About ten guards came too, crowding around them.

Inside, the house opened up in large, well-appointed spaces. Books lay scattered everywhere, and delicate paintings in gilt frames hung from the walls. If it hadn't been for the empty bottles and stench of stale alcohol, Quirk might even have called the place nice.

This was, she thought, the abode of someone important in whatever civil war was going on. And that war was more than a small hiccup in their plans. Hopefully this leader, whoever he was, would prove themselves intelligent and strong-willed enough to look past factionalism in the face of the larger Dragon enemy. Or, she supposed, someone drunk and weak-willed enough that they could manipulate and bully him easily.

Ahead of them, in a doorway, a small boy appeared. He wore a loincloth, and a halo of yellow curls surrounded his dirt-smeared face. He peered at them from behind an enormous wine pitcher that he carried.

"What you want?" he asked with a level of imperiousness that his loincloth did not seem to support.

"We are here to see your master," said the captain with a dutiful nod of his head.

Would the boy be drunk? Quirk wondered. *How young did they start them here?*

"Oi!" yelled the boy over his shoulder.

"Wotsit?" came back the slurred reply from deeper in the bowels of the house.

"Folk," yelled the boy.

"What they want?" The voice of the boy's presumable master was high, reedy, and so thick with drink a spoon would stand up in a tankard of it.

"You!" the boy yelled back.

There was a sound of exasperation. "I fucking...I know me, you daft bugger. Not here to see you, are they? Why are they here to see me?"

"Didn't say that," said the boy, sounding sullen.

"I just...literally just...just now. I said it to you just now." The boy's master didn't sound like his mood was improving.

"Before that," said the boy.

"It was implied!" roared his master. There was the sound of someone stumbling into something.

Quirk's hopes, which had not been high, pulled out a shovel and started digging for rock bottom.

Next came a long sequence of grunting, and then finally silence. The boy rolled his eyes. Then his master's high, screeching voice came once more. "Well, come and get me out of this gods-hexed chair then!" he yelled.

The boy sighed, rested his pitcher against the door frame, and scampered away.

The guard captain glanced back at them, looking vaguely apologetic. "He's a very great man," he said, sounding more than a little defensive. He tapped the side of his head. "Up here."

Which, considering the captain had been drunk most of his life, was probably not the endorsement he meant it to be. Still, someone who could unite such a drunken and disparate populace as the Vinlanders surely had something going for him.

Then the boy's master appeared in the doorway, and all of Quirk's hopes abruptly came crashing to a halt, fell to the floor in pieces, and drowned in spilled wine.

30

... The Utterly Obliterated Man Is King

Firkin stood in his mansion and tried to work out how two Wills had gotten in there. Then he blinked, focused, and tried to work out how one Will had gotten in there, and where the other might have gotten to.

He was vaguely aware that being this drunk was probably not completely advisable. There was a civil war on, and he was fairly sure that most days he played a pretty important role in it. On the other hand, staying this drunk made it easier to explain the blackouts and the moments of dissociative thought.

He stumbled, managed to find a seat, collapsed into it.

"You," he managed, pointing at Will. "You." He nodded. "Yes."

That seemed a sufficient greeting for now.

"Gods," said Will from what sounded like a very great distance. "What's wrong with him?"

Firkin really hoped someone answered before he did. Unless it was the whisper. He tried to distract it by pouring wine down his throat.

"He's holy," said his houseboy, displaying unexpected loyalty.

"He looks half-dead," said a woman behind Will. She had red hair, and Firkin was pretty sure they had shared a major life event together.

"We never...?" he said to her and made vague, suggestive motions with his fingers.

"Gods no!" The woman recoiled. "I have things like self-respect, and a memory that is hard to scrub clean."

"Don't fancy...?" he hazarded.

"Fuck off, Firkin!" the woman snapped.

"Someone sober him up so we can end this absurd civil war already," said another familiar-looking woman. She had dark skin and close-cropped, tightly curled hair. Her name started with *Q* or *Kw* or something of that sort.

"Shh!" he hissed, pressing his fingers to somewhere vaguely proximal to his mouth. "He doesn't like that talk."

"Who doesn't?" Will asked, looking around the room like the idiot he was.

"*Him,*" Firkin said with the degree of urgency everyone seemed to be failing to realize the situation demanded. He tapped the side of his head.

"He hears voices," said the houseboy. "Barph speaks through him."

"He speaks through his arse," snapped the redhead. Firkin was beginning to understand why he hadn't slept with her.

"Don't wake it up," he hissed at Will. Will was a sympathetic ear. "Let it sleep."

"This is bad." Will wasn't talking to him anymore. "Even for Firkin, this is bad."

"Knole's knockers, it's bad." Quirk had apparently learned to curse properly since Firkin had seen her last. *Quirk, that was her name.* "He's managed to incite a civil war in the one country that could actually help us."

Inside his head, the whisper twitched in its slumber.

"Shh," he said again, almost a crooning this time.

"The only way to end the civil war is to kill the High Priests and take this city." Another fervent voice. He thought he recognized it as one of his captains. He'd glimpsed the man along with Will and the others. They must have become friends. It was a terribly small world after all.

"Is that even viable?" asked Quirk.

The captain's response took so long to come that even Firkin was a little disappointed in the man.

"Right, then," said Quirk. "We sue for peace."

"They'll kill Firkin," said the houseboy.

"Not necessarily a bad thing," said ... said ... Lette! That was the redhead's name. Lette. He knew that. Nobody could say he didn't know that. Shut up.

"Can the High Priests win the civil war?" Will asked the question Firkin had rather been hoping no one would ask.

"Well ..." said his captain.

But it was too late, the whisper was awake.

"We will paint the streets with their blood!" it said, snapping Firkin's eyes open. It stood him up and filled him with thunder that crashed out of his mouth and boomed around the room. "And we will drink it! And we will feel its fire in our balls! And we will spill our potency on the world and seed it in grapes and ruin!"

The long silence that followed this was only punctured by his houseboy saying, "I bloody told you he was holy."

31

With Friends Like These

Will stared at...Firkin? At the thing talking through Firkin? At whatever trick Firkin had figured out to convince the world to give him an obscene amount of alcohol this time?

And yet there was an unfamiliar power to his old friend's voice as it boomed through the cluttered room. And Will did feel some rebellious urge stir in his gut, because screw these High Priests. It *would* be good to drink their blood...

"Shut up, Firkin," said Lette, "you're drunk."

Will shook his head. And he was standing in the same stagnant room, and Firkin was staring at him, and the old man looked...He looked genuine. And that was not a tool he expected to find in Firkin's armament. Will examined his old friend. And there was something else in Firkin's manner he saw now. He had seemed...nervous. Uncertain. The veneer of slick bullshit was gone from him, and up until a moment ago he had looked exposed. "I really think there's something wrong with him." Will was more convinced of it than ever.

"Look," Quirk snapped, "I genuinely do not care what is wrong with Firkin. He's embroiled this city in a war neither side can win, and we need unity. All of Avarra does. We need him sober, and sitting in front of the High Priests suing for peace."

"You don't care?" That had genuinely caught Will off guard. He knew Quirk had hardened since Kondorra, but part of what had made it feel good to follow her was that there was a moral compass still intact somewhere inside her.

Quirk closed her eyes, and Will honestly wasn't sure what he'd see when she opened them. Then her face softened. She looked at him. "I do care, Will. I'm sorry. There's just…" She shook her head. "We're losing. You get that, right? And all we have is this place. These people. And Firkin's ruined it. Because that's what he does. And I'm very stressed right now. And I want to make sure he's okay, but partly it's so I can yell at him for an hour and be sure he understands me."

"The question is," Lette said as if none of this had taken place, "how do we get him in front of the High Priests?"

"You—" started the captain, but whatever wisdom he had was never shared, because at that moment an unfamiliar voice from behind them said, "Like this."

They all turned, and it turned out the unfamiliar voice had an unfamiliar owner, and she was dressed in black, and held two swords, and she had lots of friends, and they were all charging into the room.

And then Will watched as Lette killed.

She wasn't the only one, of course. There were others. The elves reached for knives and short blades. And the Vinter guards who weren't abruptly bleeding from the neck got their swords up as well. But Will watched Lette.

She whipped her short sword from its blade, hacked upward, and cut one of their swarming attackers from crotch to breast. Her blade lodged into the sternum. She kicked the lifeless legs out from the corpse, wrenched. The blade came free just in time for her to catch the blows of a woman swinging two blades at her skull.

And part of Will had realized by then how counterproductive this was. How actually they wanted to go with these people, that this was the perfect way to get in front of the priests, but… he watched.

Lette grunted, kicked out, aimed for her opponent's midriff. The woman fighting her grunted, staggered back. Lette closed, thrust her blade after the kick. Flesh gave way.

"Hold! Hold!" Quirk started shouting. She'd got there too. She knew that this was a mistake.

Blows were still coming at Lette, though, and she ducked low, and threw her body into the thighs of another of the black-clad figures, tossed him over her shoulder. He landed on the ground with a crack and an expulsion of air. She thrust down, skewered his throat, straightened, looked for another victim.

"Hold!" Will finally found his tongue. He was breathing as hard as if he had been fighting at Lette's side, but…

Something Firkin had been shouting about blood was in the back of his heads, and gods…gods…

Lette finally held. Will raised his hands, kneeled. Quirk and three of the Tamathian guards did the same. The guard captain who had accompanied them from the Vinter border was on the floor, bleeding out, gasping feebly. One of the elves, Nottram, was already dead. Five of the black-clad attackers were dead, to their two, but twenty more were still standing.

"We surrender," Will said.

Just one of Lette's eyebrows rose.

"We *want* to meet their masters," Quirk said slowly. "We were literally just saying that. We *want* them to take us."

"Remember," said Will, "when you said you wanted to lead a better life? One where you chose the path less bloody just a little more often?" And maybe, just maybe she had shared the moment of connection he had felt.

"I did choose those paths," said Lette. "They led here." Then she threw her sword down on the ground.

Much to Will's shock, it turned out that not all of Vinland was a decrepit shithole. Some of it was a quite well-constructed shithole. The High Temple, which held the High Priests, for example, had clearly been a fairly significant edifice before nobody had bothered caring for it for the best part of a millennia.

He did worry about where the several hundred elves they'd left cluttering the streets had gone, but he was sure he would have noticed if they'd been slaughtered and left on Firkin's doorstep. Plus Balur was with them, though Will wasn't wholly sure if that was a source of reassurance or not.

He glanced at the others as they were dragged into the High Temple's stone confines. Lette looked almost bored, but her professional nonchalance was a point of pride. Afrit was surely at the opposite end of the spectrum. Will had expected her to be in free-fall freak-out but instead her fear seemed muted. She had her eyes on Quirk. And she assumed Quirk had a way out. A plan. Will looked to Quirk too, hopeful. But all he saw was the same fear he felt. Because she didn't have a plan either, and she was having as much trouble coming up with one as he was.

Gods, please, please, help them all. They were trying to help the gods after all. It only seemed fair.

And then the main chamber of this temple—dedicated to one of those distant deities—opened up around him. It was vast and cavernous and replete with a sense of decaying grandeur. Pillars trimmed in gold and draped in red velvet towered all around her. Moth-eaten tapestries hung on the walls. The three High Priests sat on imposing thrones, shrouded in red and cream. Ceremonial guards stood in crumbling archways. Children grasped massive, dented pitchers of wine.

"The fuck is this?" asked one of the priests, a crinkly old man who had the bloated appearance of a drowned corpse, and much of the same charisma.

"We bring you the rogue preacher, Firkin," said one of the black-robed women, and kicked Firkin a full yard forward. He sprawled on the floor and promptly vomited all over it.

As one, the High Priests curled their lips.

"What about the rest of them?" The priest in the middle was a woman in her mid-fifties. Will had the impression she had been good-looking about five million glasses of wine back.

"His associates," said the guard.

"Well actually," Quirk cut in, trying to get things back on track, "we are political refugees seeking—"

A spear butt to the back of the skull cut her off. She sprawled forward as well, but managed to twist so that her cheek took the brunt of the impact against the floor instead of her nose.

"Gods!" she came up spitting. "What part of political refugee do you not understand?"

The High Priests all exchanged glances.

"Well, don't look at me," said drowned-corpse priest with a shrug.

And it was the same thing again. The same corruption. The same detachment. The same useless, stupid bastards in charge of everything.

"Dragons!" Will shouted. "There's fucking dragons! They've conquered the entire world around you. Avarra has fallen to them. You're the last holdout. Does any of this ring the slightest sort of bell? They're coming here, you dullards!"

Afrit actually gasped at that. Will suspected he might not have earned a passing grade in Introductory Practical Politics.

A shocked silence permeated the moldering atmosphere of the great hall.

"We come to negotiate peace," Quirk said into the pause. There was an element of desperation in her words now. "Our friend, Firkin"—she glanced at the old man who was writhing in his bonds and muttering some spectacularly vile curses—"has gotten himself embroiled in local politics he is not capable of handling, and we wish to extricate him from any misunder-standings to aid Vinland in meeting the dragon threat with a united face." She smiled at the priests with hope she did not feel.

And that, Will supposed, was probably what he ought to have said.

The priests looked at each other. "She talks funny," said the drowned-looking one. Quirk's smile wilted.

Will glanced over at Lette to see how she was taking all this. The mercenary just rolled her eyes. "Don't look at me," she said. "You asked me to let them bind my hands. You have to live with that now."

Will thought maybe there was a chance that shouting at the priests was a viable option after all. "If you don't meet the dragons head-on, with everything you have, they will rip you and this kingdom apart." He took a step toward the priests and was struck in the back of the knees for his trouble. He collapsed with a grunt, but he didn't let it break his flow. This was too important. These idiots had to listen.

"Your only hope is unity," he said. "Your only hope is desperate, thorough preparation. You have to take this threat seriously. Nowhere else did, and everywhere else has fallen. Now the dragons have united, and so—"

One of the priests nodded, and Will momentarily felt hope leap in his heart. He had—

Then he was struck in the side of the head with a spear butt.

Lette looked over at where Will found himself on the floor. "You did have a plan, right?"

"Can we execute all of them yet?" asked the wasp eater.

Will was saved from having to work out if he did still have a plan by a deep, gravelly voice from the other side of the chamber. It said, quite distinctly, "Be getting off me, you fucker of whores."

Protecting the elves, thought Will, discovering that the sinking feeling in his chest hadn't quite reached rock bottom yet. *Yes of course that's what Balur would be doing.*

The lizard man had been chained hand and foot—not proper shackles, simply link after link of heavy steel wrapped around his wrists, and then inexpertly looped around his ankles. About fifteen more guards were surrounding him, hemming him in with spear points. One had evidently just pricked the lizard man, and the spear's owner had gained his ire. He perked up, though, upon seeing Will and the others.

"Hello!" he called. "It is being good to be seeing you again."

"Balur, you..." Quirk seemed to froth with expletives she didn't quite have the ability to deliver.

"Drunks, Balur?" asked Lette. She shook her head. "You were captured by drunks. How in the Hallows are you meant to live this down?"

"In fairness, I was being unconscious, at the time," Balur called across the hall.

The High Priests seemed more than a little annoyed by all this conviviality among their prisoners. "Shut him up!" screamed the wasp eater. "This is a hall of motherfucking worship!"

An eager-looking guard cracked his spear butt across Balur's back. Balur turned and looked at him. "I am warning you," he said. After consideration, the guard took a significant step back.

"What is the meaning of this interruption?" asked the female priest. Even she seemed bored by the roteness of the question.

"We bring before you the mercenary known as Balur, also as Balur the lizard man, Balur the Analesian, Balur the Whore-slayer, Balur the Tribeless, Balur the Fuck-monger, Throat-gargler, and That Big Lizardy Bugger," intoned the guard, in a strident voice. Balur nodded, seemingly pleased by this list of titles. Quirk filed *Throat-gargler* away for later investigation.

"Who?" asked the bloated priest, and Balur seemed to sag a bit.

"One of the two mercenaries," said the guard, also seeming a little deflated, "who attempted to steal Barph's Strength last year. The ones you ordered hunted down to the ends of the earth and killed in as vile and painful a way as possible."

"They remember us, Lette," said Balur with a happy smile. "They are knowing our names."

"Oh you stupid, silly..." Lette groaned.

The lead guard's eyes bulged and he lunged toward Lette, but the black-clad women shook their spears at him and he retreated back.

"She's the other!" the guard hissed. "I knew she had to be close. I knew it!"

And Will knew he should have been using this time to come up with a plan, but...seriously. He looked at the expressions on the priests' faces. Indignation, perhaps, but not interest. Because they just didn't care. Everything being performed before them was something that happened outside their holy walls. And that just didn't interest them. Which meant they weren't fit to rule.

Which meant perhaps he did have a plan after all.

But still, before he resorted to that...

"Dragons," he tried one last, desperate time. "Dragons are coming, and they are coming to kill you all. You have to be united. If you kill Firkin then you'll just be making a martyr of him. You'll be dividing yourselves even more deeply, and making the dragons' job even easier. You have to be united to face them."

Nearby, Firkin rolled around on the floor muttering, "My head ain't no shithouse."

The female priest looked from Firkin to Will with nothing but contempt written on her face. "You come here," she said, "in the company of a known agitator, and a mercenary who has tried to defile one of our most sacred treasures, and you have the gall to tell us what to do? To believe that we give a shit about your advice? I commune with Barph himself. Your advice is so much piss in my wine."

At this, Firkin suddenly came alive. "You commune with my arsehole!" he screamed. "Barph shits on you and your lies! Barph wouldn't talk to you if you fermented your own corpse in a goblet made of virgin's bones!" Which was about all he managed to get out before the guards kicked him into unconsciousness.

The female priest attempted to lift herself out of her throne, and on the third attempt actually made it. "All these arseholes. They're all condemned to die."

The third priest clapped his hands. "Yay!" he said, and upended his goblet into his face. "Executions!" Wine dribbled down his chin.

"No!" snapped the female priest. "Executions are too good for them. This will be messy, and painful, and very, very public. This will be a spectacle." She drank very deeply from her goblet. "This will be holy rage."

"Oooh," said the third priest. "I like the sound of that."

Well, Will couldn't say he hadn't tried.

Lette looked at him. "So," she said, "now do we get to do things my way?"

Balur brightened. "I am typically liking Lette's way."

"No," said Will. "That's not the plan."

Lette's brow furrowed. "Really? Because this is typically the point where you lose patience."

And Will had, but making the High Priests into martyrs wouldn't help them any more than turning Firkin into a martyr would help the High Priests.

"Silence!" the female priest shouted in their general direction. Then she turned back to the guards. "To the dungeons with them," she said. "Then prepare everything so we can defile them with goats tomorrow."

The guards closed. Spears tickled Will's skin, and together they were all dragged away down to the dungeons.

All in all, Will found he was quite relieved. He had really been hoping they wouldn't have to kill the High Priesthood of a nation that day and he'd finally figured out a way to avoid it.

32

Temporary Accommodations

In Lette's experience, most people tended to assume that there was a strong correlation between the state of a kingdom and the state of its dungeons. If a kingdom was well tended, then surely its dungeons would have fresh straw and few rats. As a woman who had spent slightly more than her fair share of time in a variety of dungeons, jails, penitentiaries, and prisons, Lette also knew that most people were ignorant asses. The state of a cell was actually directly proportionate to the wealth disparity between the jailer and his master. The greater the gulf, the greater the squalor that prisoners would endure.

Thus, as she was shoved into a cell ankle-deep in rotten straw and other, far less pleasant things, Lette's suspicion that the High Priests of Vinland were a bunch of stingy bastards was confirmed.

The cell door swung shut behind the six of them, and a heavy key turned in a heavy lock. A bar fell into place. Several bolts were slid home. Any hope Lette had of the Vinlanders being sloppy guards slipped away.

Lette looked around. Balur was busy assessing the cell, but looking far from hopeful. Firkin was sitting in the unspeakable mess on the floor, looking vaguely dazed. Will stood next to him. Quirk and Afrit were standing close together near the door of the cell, and in Lette's opinion they did not look half scared enough.

And that swung the decision in her head about whether she would ream out Will or Quirk for this one.

"This is your fault, you realize?" she said to Quirk. "This whole captured-and-going-to-be-put-to-death thing. I try to be nice. I try to be a better person. I think twice, and I put my blade away. I really fucking try. And now I've got to come up with a way to kill everybody between us and the exit. And it's all because you want to be the pacifist fucking war general. Every life we take in here is on your head. I want you to know that. I want it to haunt your gods-hexed dreams. That—"

Abruptly flame flared behind Quirk's back. Ash and tattered rope fell to the floor. Quirk worked at the sore wrists of her freed hands, then seemed to notice Lette had stopped talking.

"You were saying?" she said innocently.

Lette took a moment to just fume.

"Not our first jailbreak," said Afrit, who had decided to pause from staring lovingly at Quirk in order to feign an unconvincing apologetic tone. Quirk was going to have to put that poor girl out of her misery one way or another.

Will stepped in between her and the Tamathians. "Sorry," he said, which was actually the first time in a while someone had said the right thing to Lette. Still, she wasn't sure she forgave him. "I figured the High Priests didn't know Quirk is a mage."

"And if they had tried to kill us in the chamber upstairs instead of throwing us down here?" asked Lette, because she was pretty sure that couldn't have been part of anyone's plan.

"Then I would have tried to spare as many lives as possible." Quirk was quite calm as she moved to set Will's hands free. Lette tried reassessing the woman.

Quirk turned to look Lette directly in the eye. "I spent my whole childhood killing people, Lette. I spent most of my adult life trying to forget that. But you all took that hope away from me in Kondorra. Now the dragons have reminded me that I am actually very good at it. And I hate that, but in this world, in this time, that is the skill I have. And I will use it if necessary. Not wantonly like Balur, and not savagely, like you. But I will."

Lette considered. "I'm not a fucking savage."

Quirk didn't even bother with an apologetic expression. "We had to try to talk everything through. If this could have been resolved peacefully then it would have been far, far better."

"This is a nation run and populated entirely by drunk people," Lette pointed out. "Balur has led a life of relative sobriety in comparison with them. And you were expecting rational conversation?"

"I was hoping," said Quirk, reaching out and burning Afrit's bonds. "Not expecting. Now, do you want me to free your hands or not?"

Reluctantly Lette held out her hands.

"Me too, please," said Balur, holding out his chained fists.

Quirk cracked her knuckles. "This will take a moment longer."

"Did one of you bastards shit in my head?" asked Firkin from the floor. "It feels like one of you shit in my head." He tipped one ear toward the floor and tapped the other experimentally.

While Quirk grasped Balur's chains and the links slowly started to glow, Will went over and knelt beside the filthy old man. "Are you okay?" he asked. "What's going on with you?"

Lette understood loyalty. She knew its importance, its strategic value. And she knew her own loyalty to Balur could pass the boundary into unreasonableness. But still, she did not get Will's dedication to the old man. She could smell his funk even above the fetid air of this dungeon. Why would you be loyal to someone it was difficult to approach too closely?

Firkin looked up at Will. And for a moment, Lette glimpsed something unexpectedly genuine in the old man's eyes. Something that looked like desperation. Then he shook his head. "Just the drink," he said.

Abruptly, Balur cursed and shook his hands. The chains fell away, spattering molten metal around the room.

"Okay," said Quirk, "the lock's next."

"Can I be doing that, please?" asked Balur.

Afrit looked confused. "But…"

"He likes to punch locks," Lette said, as Balur smiled smugly. "It makes him feel better about his tiny, useless genitals."

"This is an escape," Quirk said, ignoring any and all references to Balur's genitals. "We are trying to sneak out. Punching a lock repeatedly does not seem entirely compatible with that plan."

"There is one thing I'd like to cover," said Will, still standing at Firkin's side. "What in the Hallows are we going to do when we actually leave this cell? Our best shot was convincing the High Priests to make some sort of peace with Firkin. That's clearly not going to happen."

Quirk looked at him as if he were standing in the room speaking tongues. "We fight," she said, as if it were the most obvious thing in the world. "We tried peace. We failed. Now we fight, and we win. And then we muster the Vinland forces and march to meet the dragons."

There had always been a streak of arrogance in Quirk, but Lette found it interesting to see it so close to the surface now. There would come a time when she would have to beat it out of the woman.

"And say we win," said Will. "Say we pitch half of Vinter against the other, and our side comes out on top. What are we left with? An exhausted, depleted, demoralized excuse for an army?"

Quirk spread her arms. "What else would you have me do? What other options do we have?" She looked around the cramped cell. It appeared that other options were not leaping out of the shadows to embrace her.

"We'll lose," said Will plainly. And Lette had to agree.

"We *might*," said Quirk. "We have to take that chance."

Afrit nodded vigorously.

"So if we are fighting," said Balur, "why are we not punching the lock already? I am thinking that was being the core of Will's point."

"Just be quiet for a while," Lette told him. "The grown-ups are talking."

Balur stopped pacing and turned to look down at her. "Just because I am preferring a straightforward approach to life does not mean I am appreciating being condescended to."

"Then don't make it so easy."

"We need a better plan," said Will, ignoring them both.

"Well, I am all ears." Somehow, from the way Quirk said it, Lette doubted that she was.

"Barph's Strength," said Firkin from the floor.

Lette froze.

"What if we can get leverage on the priests?" Will said. "Something to force them to concede to Firkin's will."

"You mean like defeating their army?" Quirk wielded sarcasm like she wielded fire.

"Barph's Strength," Firkin repeated, his voice stronger.

"I mean like blackmail," said Will, who apparently couldn't take sarcasm the way he sometimes liked to dish it out.

"Was Firkin saying . . . ?" Balur pointed down at Firkin.

"They're Barphists," said Quirk. "It's in their job description to be corrupt. And all the people pissed off about that are already at war with them. And all the people who don't care are fighting to defend them."

"Barph's—" Firkin started a third time.

"Shut up," Lette snapped. And of course that was when everyone chose to look at her and Firkin.

"He was saying—" Balur started.

"Shut up!" Lette snapped. "We're not talking about it."

"There's a way." Firkin was nodding to himself. He rubbed at his forehead. "I know a way. I do. It's in my head being known. By me." He pointed to himself and looked surprised. "I know the trick. I know the answer. I have the plan." He clapped his hands. "Me! Not you!" He stood up, one hand still pressed to the side of his head. "I'm the big man with the big plan swinging between my legs. All of you have to listen to me now."

But that was not an eventuality Lette was willing to let happen. And while she did not have time to extract the knives that the High Priests' guards had missed on her, she did not need them to shut Firkin up. She stepped across the room and delivered a hammer blow to his jaw. Firkin flew, spindly limbs flying, and crashed to the floor.

Lette pointed at him. "Did I, or did I not, tell you to shut the fuck up?"

"Gods, Lette." Will was at Firkin's side again. "He's not well."

"I think," Lette said through gritted teeth, "that there's room for him to get worse."

"What's he talking about?" Afrit, it seemed, had still to learn exactly how willing Lette was to throw her weight around.

"You're next," she said, pointing at the Tamathian.

Quirk bristled.

"Barph's Strength," Balur rumbled from behind her, letting her down for yet another innumerable time. "He was saying it about three times already."

Lette turned to him. "Why?" she asked. "Why haven't I slit your throat in your sleep?"

Balur shrugged. "Because you are being a pussy."

That was it. Lette decided to get a knife out. It would take a minute, but it would be worth it.

"I'm not completely sure," Will said, still at Firkin's side, "but I think we've discussed how repeating something is not the same as explaining it."

Firkin was unfortunately still conscious. "I explain it!" he shouted from the cell's floor.

"Barph's Strength," started Balur blithely, "is being—"

"I explain it!" Firkin roared. Lette almost reeled. His voice suddenly felt like being hit by a thunderclap. The walls seemed to quake. What in the name of Barph's ball sack was going on with the man?

Firkin was massaging his head again. He sat down on the floor. Will knelt beside him. Lette felt a sudden unexpected stab of jealousy.

"Barph's Strength," Firkin said, and now his voice was barely above whisper, "is a drink—"

"It's a cup," Balur interjected. He had always been slow to learn anything that didn't involve his fists. "A big shiny gold cup studded with—"

"It's a fucking beverage," Firkin snapped, some energy returning to his voice. "I know my drinks and I know my cups, and Barph's Strength is a gods-hexed drink. Delicious, and sweet, and rich as honey."

Will stood up. "A drink. You need a drink. That's your big plan? You get to have drink?" He sounded disgusted, but more at himself for having believed Firkin's latest stream of bullshit.

"No," Firkin snapped. "No, no. Totally different plan. There's a story. Just need to remember the story."

Lette went back to trying to extract the needlelike stiletto she had stitched into the seam of her jerkin.

"Barph. And Lawl," Firkin mumbled. "Barph did something." He grimaced. "Something very naughty. Spank him and call him Tuesday. Shouldn't have tricked Lawl into doing it. Because Lawl always did get so precious pretending to give a shit about human life. He doesn't mind smiting a city because it defies him, but if someone tricks him into smiting somewhere… suddenly that's a travesty. That's trickery and bullshit."

Lette caught Quirk's eye. The professor shook her head. This was not a story either recognized from any temple or street preacher.

"So Barph tricks Lawl, and a city gets smote. And Lawl gets his rage on," Firkin went on. "Mounts up on his hobby horse and rides it all about the room. A punishment. A mighty punishment. And not one with whips, and chains, and women in leather outfits. Something serious. Something so Barph learns. So Barph grovels. And so Lawl cuts Barph. Slices his divine skin. And Barph's blood bursts out like crimson jewels. Blood and wine streaming out of him. And he..." Firkin closed his eyes hard, held on to his temples. "He screams. Barph screams. But Lawl doesn't care. He is the god of the law, and this is his new law. Because laws don't apply to him. Oh no. He just takes the goblet out of Barph's hand. And it's beautiful, shining and studded with jewels."

"I was knowing there was a cup," said Balur loudly. Lette slapped at him.

"And Barph's blood..." Firkin nodded to himself. "It fell into the goblet. Blood and wine mixing. But more than blood and wine. Blood, and wine, and power. And Barph became the absent god. And Lawl put the cup down on earth where Barph couldn't get at it. Put it right in the city dedicated to him, taunting him. And he set a guardian over it so no man could rescue it for poor, bleeding Barph. And that was his lesson. That Lawl was the big man. That he did whatever he wanted and no one fucked with him."

And suddenly Firkin was weeping, great tears rolling down his face. He held his head and whispered, "It hurts, it hurts," over and over.

"A cup with...Barph's power?" Will looked confused. "What do we do with it? How do we even get it to Barph?"

But Lette saw. "No," she said. "That's not it. Barph doesn't drink it. We do." She pointed at them each in turn. "We drink the power of a god."

"No," Quirk cut in. "Not just us." She swept an arm expansively. "*All* of us. Everyone here. The whole army."

Firkin nodded. "She understands. She sees."

"Oh," Balur groused. "She is being allowed to explain, but I am getting shouted down. That is being totally fair."

"But it's just one cup," Will pointed out. "We can't have a whole army drink from one cup."

"Never runs dry, does it?" said Firkin from the floor. Tears had run tracks in the dirt on his face. "A god's power is infinite, so the cup never runs dry. Can drink, and drink, and drink and there will always be more. It's a good cup it is." He nodded. "And it's good wine. Power for the drinker. A god's power. Strength. Stamina. Farts that could cause a room full of grown men to all pass out." He smiled beatifically.

"We feed it to the army," Quirk said again. "All of them. And so the dragons don't face a nation that's exhausted from fighting itself. They fight a group of divinely powered warriors." She smiled. "And we win. And they lose."

"My plan," said Firkin proudly from the floor. "Mine. So all of you can suck it."

33

Asking Awkward Questions

Lette knew that she should be glad. Because they actually had a plan that could work. They actually had a way forward. But all she could do was stand there waiting for the past's bloody corpse to pick itself up off the floor and shamble toward her with its arms outstretched.

That it came from Will somehow made it worse.

"Wait," he said. "Back with the priests. They said...Barph's Strength was the thing you tried to steal. That's what they want to kill you over." He smiled. The bastard smiled. "You must know all about it. What happened?"

"It did not go well," Lette answered in a rush, cutting off Balur before he could be an enormous ass about the whole thing. "Our plan didn't work. We didn't even get into the temple where the thing is held. We were caught. We escaped. We ran. We were pursued. We wound up in Kondorra and you pretty much know the rest."

Will blinked. "Well, erm, okay, but..."

He was interrupted by Balur clearing his throat. Lette saw Will's eyes sliding over to the lizard man and she began desperately to twirl her finger in her hair and make Afrit-eyes in his direction.

Will's eyes flashed back to hers. She saw them widen slightly.

"Yes?" Lette asked Will, trying to sound as interested as possible.

"Erm..." said Will, who stared around the shitty little cell as if divine inspiration hid in one of its vile little corners. "I mean...what I was going to ask was...erm..."

Balur cleared his throat for a second time. If Lette could have torn it out without prompting any additional questions, then she happily would have done so.

"There's a temple," said Lette, still desperately trying to control the story, "in the city's Eighth District, to the north of here. It's small, shitty, and heavily guarded. And inside—"

Balur cleared his throat again.

"Are you all right, Balur?" It was Afrit who said it. It was Afrit whom Lette would have to kill once she was done flaying Balur's corpse.

"I am being okay," said Balur, massaging his throat like some third-rate actor upon a fifth-rate stage. "It is just I am seeming to have some total bullshit stuck in my throat."

His eyes flashed and he fixed an accusatory stare on Lette.

"What?" She threw up her hands. "What have I said that is untrue? What lie have I told?"

"The lie of omission," Balur said loudly, just in case there were any prisoners in nearby cells who wanted to hear the whole shitty story.

"Fuck you, Balur." And this time she said it with considerable rancor.

And she could see, she could just see the question forming on Will's lips. He couldn't help himself, the curious little bastard. He hung around her like the stink on shit, but he just could not spare her this last humiliation.

Then he caught her look, and she saw him bite his bottom lip, and hold his tongue.

Which all added up to it being Quirk who asked, "What did she omit?"

Which meant that Quirk was going to have to die too. Really she should just slash all their throats and be done with it.

Except, of course, this whole story was rather about why she was trying to not do that anymore.

"For starters," said Balur, "she has been omitting that our plan to infiltrate the temple involved her being dressed up as a holy whore."

And Will's treacherous little eyes did go wide at that. And while he tried very hard not to glance at her, she caught it when he did.

"There was being a bikini of fine copper involved, and a whole weird hairdo that she was taking a lot of time to get right."

"The hair was an important part of the disguise, you ass," Lette spat. "It's ceremonial."

"Was it being ceremonial to be stabbing a guard in the throat fifty paces from the temple?" Balur asked her. "Just because he was saying something disparaging about your pancake arse?"

Lette chewed her tongue. "He shouldn't have said that."

"You have been saying worse," said Balur mildly.

"Not to incredibly dangerous people," Lette pointed out.

Balur looked scandalized. "Yes you have been doing!"

Lette took a breath. She had to control this story, not get caught up in Balur's nonsense. "It did not go well," she repeated. "I was very up front about that."

"She was killing this guard," Balur went on, unabated. "And other temple guards were seeing. And we were getting into a fight. But more and more reinforcements were coming. And—"

"And we failed!" Lette shouted. "What else is there to say, gods piss on it?"

Silence.

Silence filled with a lot of people staring at her. And maybe she had gone in just a little strong there...

Balur looked at her. "Erm..." he said. "I...I am not knowing." He shrugged. "That's about it."

Lette glanced at him. He appeared genuinely clueless. "Oh," she said.

He looked about the cell. "What else is there to tell? We ran away. We fired the convents to distract our pursuers. We arrived in Kondorra."

Slowly Lette closed her eyes. So close. So very close.

Afrit got there first. "Wait...you fired what?"

Even with her own eyes closed, Lette could feel Will staring at her.

What did she care that he was looking at her? What did she owe him? He had no ownership or hold over her.

Except...Gods piss on it.

"Convents," said Balur, matter-of-factly. "The Vinlanders were getting very touchy about their sacred cup and were sending a fairly significant number of people after us. And so Lette was suggesting—and I was thinking it was a very good suggestion— that as they were being so uptight about religion nonsense, we should be burning down some convents to distract them. And so we were doing it, and it wasn't working the first time round, but by the fifth time they were deciding they better be backing off, and we were escaping. It was being a good plan."

"You fired *five* convents?" Afrit said, and the pretentious judgment in her voice almost lifted Lette's spirits.

"Yes," said Balur. "Was that being confusing to anyone else? Is it being the syntax thing?"

"Full of..." Afrit persisted.

"Idiots who had been dedicating their lives to Barph?" asked Balur. "Yes. So we were doing them a favor, I am believing."

And then Will asked, "It was Lette's idea?" He even had the audacity to sound just a little bit heartbroken. It was all he said. But it was enough.

"Yes," she spat. "Fucking convents. Fucking nuns. What about me makes you think I give a shit for nuns? Fools who dedicated their lives to those callous bastards we call gods. Respect the gods? Surely. Bow your head, and scrape? I am with you. They are powerful beyond our imagining; it only makes sense to watch where you step around them. But worship them? Screw you, and your stupid life choices. You should expect your home burned down around your ears."

She stood there, staring them down, one by one.

Will chewed his lip. Afrit studied the floor. Quirk just looked back, weighing, assessing, being a judgy bastard.

"But if you..." Will's face twisted in sympathy that she would have loved to carve from his skull. "If you don't care, then why are you crying?"

Lette blinked. What was he...? Then she reached up and felt the dampness on her face. Gods piss on it.

She stared at him. And the bastard really did want to understand. He was trying so hard. And she wanted right then to cross the room and punch his nose so hard it came out the back of his stupid fucking head.

"You want to know?" she asked. "You really want to know?"

And he even went and opened his gods-hexed mouth to reply, to say yes, and so she had to keep talking just to shut his gods-hexed face up.

"You know where the Vinlanders send their orphans, Will? Do you know that?"

And he hadn't but then he did. "Oh," said Will. "Oh, Lette."

"Yeah," she said, and she really could feel the tears now, though they felt like something that someone else controlled. There was almost a calmness in her now. "Neither did I." She shook her head. "Not till the fourth one."

And that was close, but she knew they would make her spell it out.

"Balur said you torched five," said Quirk quietly.

"Yeah," Lette spat. "Yeah, we torched five."

Will closed his eyes.

"You are being judgmental arseholes." Balur's passion surprised Lette. "It was being us or them."

"You or them?" Afrit almost screamed the words. "They were

children! You were using them as a distraction! You couldn't think of a better fucking distraction than burning fucking children?"

"Their homes," Balur rumbled. "No one was taking hold of a child and holding her over an open flame. That is being impractical on a whole number of levels."

"Impractical?" For a moment Lette thought Afrit really was going to fling herself at Balur.

"Of course," said Balur. "You need good kindling to burn people. They are very wet. All the blood."

"You fucking..." Afrit growled. Quirk put a restraining hand on her arm.

"Your idea?" Will asked her quietly. As if all the rest of the room weren't there.

She didn't owe him an answer. She didn't owe anybody an answer.

Except herself.

"You kill," she said to him. "And you kill. And you kill. And you make money. So you kill more. And that is how you live. So you kill more. And you are so good at killing. And so many people deserve to die. This world is so full of terrible people who deserve to have a blade slipped between their ribs. So you kill. And you kill. And you kill. And lives become...they are just the irons in the smith's forge. They are just the flour in the chef's kitchen. They are just part of the trade. Part of what you do. You are not a killer. You are a merchant, trading lives for coins. Nothing more than that. A life is as meaningless as a bolt of cloth. And the only life that truly has any value is your own. And so when someone threatens that life, that one precious life...why hesitate to take others' if it will save yours?"

She looked at them. And it was Afrit's face that twisted in horror.

"Because it's a convent full of *children*."

Lette nodded. "Yes," she said. "A thousand times yes. That is *exactly* why you hesitate. I just got there a little too slow. I was so inured to... to killing... I couldn't figure out what was wrong, why I was throwing up." She shook her head. "I thought I was sick. That maybe I had a fever. That was where my mind went first. That's how fucked up I was."

She closed her eyes, saw it all in front of her again. "I figured it out when I heard them screaming in that fifth convent. That's when it hit me. And I turned around, and gods, I prayed for them to get out before the flames took them. I got down on my knees and I implored Barph. Because they were his people. He should have cared, shouldn't he?"

She pawed at her eyes. Gods-hexed tears were making it hard to see.

"So I said no more. I said I'd be a better person. I was going to make a better life for myself in Kondorra. And then some shitting goblin stole my gold and I got mixed up with you people." She shook her head. "But I tried. I really did try. I'm still trying. And I don't think I succeed very often, but I am trying."

She sniffed. She felt stupid. Gods piss on them all for making her say it. She looked around the cell. Fucking typical. Here she was in Vinland and there wasn't a drink in sight.

Of all of them, it was Balur who spoke. "The convents?" he said. "That was what was bringing all this better-person shit on? Those stupid convents?"

Gods curse her, she almost laughed. "Yes, Balur," she said. "Burning several convents full of children did make me reevaluate my life choices. It really did."

Balur cocked his head. "I was always thinking you just took that comment about your arse really badly."

"If you say arse again, I will chop off your balls, gouge out your eyes, and shove your nuts into the sockets."

"You... you..." Afrit seemed to be having a great deal of difficulty with this conversation. She looked at Quirk. "They're killers of children. We can't...They have to..." She looked around her.

"Be locking us in a jail cell and sentencing to death?" asked Balur. And gods she was smiling again. The big bastard was trying to cheer her up. Arsehole.

"I am so filled with fucking disgust at—" Afrit started, stalking toward Balur, stabbing a finger at him. Quirk caught her by the arm.

"Hush," Quirk said. "It's done."

And there really was no judgment. Quirk just stared calmly into Afrit's horrified eyes.

"Done?" asked Afrit. "This remorseless—"

"It's done," Quirk said with a sharp jerk of her head.

"We have to—"

"No," said Quirk. "No we don't. It's done. It's over. It has absolutely no bearing on this situation here and now."

"No bearing?" Afrit stared around at them as if seeing them all for the first time.

Quirk licked her lips, but that was the only hesitation she allowed herself. "You know my past," she said quietly. "We all have our convents."

"I never burnt no gods-pissing convent," said Firkin from the floor. "Don't loop me in with you animals."

Afrit was backing away from Quirk. And there went puppy love, kicked across the floor, whimpering all the way.

"The dragons," Quirk said, speaking to the room at large. "That is honestly all that matters. Them and our ability to fight them. I cannot afford to give a thrice-cursed pig's shit about anything else, right now. None of us can. So we must win this civil war, and we must retrieve Barph's Strength. Everything else is negligible." She looked around the room. "Would anyone care to disagree with me?"

And despite herself, despite the fact that her eyes stung and her nose still ran, Lette found she was impressed by Quirk. This was leadership. Cold and brutal, and everything it needed to be.

"No," she said into the silence. "No, that sounds good."

"Good." Quirk nodded, and reached out a hand to the lock of the door. The metal glowed red and then fell to the floor. Quirk pushed it open. "Then let's get out of here and do this."

34

As Simple as Stealing Beers from a Drunkard

It was difficult, Will found as they left the High Temple behind, to figure out exactly what to say. The actual escaping part had been fine. That had all been creeping around and watching Balur punch people halfway across rooms. Not talking was kind of critical at that point. But then once they had hustled down the last corridor, and out of the final door, and stood blinking in the last rays of day's light, words seemed inevitable.

They managed to put it off until they were several streets away, but then Quirk turned around. Everyone failed to meet everyone else's eye.

"All right," Quirk said, grabbing the verbal bull by the horns. "Given the brutally short timeline we have before us, I think we have to divide and conquer. Balur and Lette, you know about this wine and this goblet. You, I think, should try to retrieve it again. In the meantime we also need Firkin to stay up here as a figurehead of this war. So that's three of you accounted for. Given everyone else's emotional state, why doesn't Will go with you two"—Quirk pointed at Lette and Balur—"while Afrit and I remain here to help guide Firkin and stop him from making this any more of a screwup than it already is?"

Still nobody seemed up to conversation. Balur shrugged. Will said, "Sure," and then Quirk and Afrit pulled Firkin away. They seemed eager to get clear. Which was probably a good idea, Will thought, especially considering his suspicion that Afrit had been tempted more than once to scream at a guard to be rescued from them all.

In a way Will couldn't blame her.

Convents. Convents full of kids.

Gods...

He had...with someone who had...And yet, as he looked at Lette, so broken and yet so defiant, he still loved her. He still wanted her. He was still desperately searching for a way to bring a smile back to her face. And he was trying to find ways to sanitize what she had done somehow. She had not known. She—

He stopped himself. Was that worse than what Lette had actually done? Just being okay with it?

Well...probably not. No kids got harmed in his mental processes.

And so...what to say?

The three of them stood staring at each other.

And then from somewhere, perhaps even due to the kindly intervention of some god, he found the right words.

"Well," he said, "this is Vinter. We should be able to find a drink somewhere."

Will watched as Lette slowly slipped off the bench and slid into an unconscious pile on the floor. The bartender, watching them carefully from behind the shelter of his bar, took half a step forward, then thought better of it and went back to polishing the pewter goblet in his hand.

Vinter seemed surprisingly functional considering the civil war. On their way from the temple to the tavern they had seen little evidence of the conflict, outside of the grim looks on the people in the streets. There had been a few shouting preachers on the street corners, but in this part of the city the soapbox speeches had all been in favor of the High Priests. At one point, they had heard shouts of panic from ahead, but when they had arrived, there had been no signs of anything amiss. Wherever the fight was truly being fought, the battle lines were stable for now.

Balur leaned down, picked Lette up by the back of her jacket, and dumped her sprawled across the table. He looked at Will, looking at Lette, and he smiled. Balur's smile always struck Will as involving far too many teeth.

"You should just be saying it," he said, breaking a silence that had lasted almost three hours now.

Will blinked. "Say what?"

Balur shrugged. "Whatever it is being. That you are loving her. That you are being horrified by her. That you have always been harboring secret fantasies of infanticide yourself and are wanting to go on a murder spree with her. I am not caring. What is being important is that it is said."

Will thought about that. "It's not that easy," he said.

Balur thumped his goblet down on the table. Beer flew, and all the other goblets jumped. "Yes it is being simple," he said with force. "You are opening your mouth and flapping your tongue. You are doing it all the time. You are just never saying whatever it is you actually need to be saying."

Will sagged heavily on the table, planting his elbows and putting his head in his hands. "It's not. I don't...I mean..." He stumbled for a phrase Balur might sympathize with. "She could do me serious physical harm" seemed safe.

"I am not giving a shit what she is doing to you," said Balur, with so much scorn, Will thought he could almost taste it in the back of his throat. "I am caring about Lette. She is waiting for you to be saying whatever in the name of Lawl's black eye it is that you are needing to say. She may not be knowing it, and she may be denying it if you are asking her, but she is waiting. She is as stuck as you are. So say it. Let her be sad, or happy, or enraged, or relieved, or murderous. I am not caring what it is, but let her be it." He slammed his goblet down on the table again, then seemed to realize that he had said all he had to say. He settled for glaring at Will.

"What...What if I don't know what to say?" Will ventured.

Balur threw his arms up in the air. His goblet went flying, landed with a crash ten yards away. The bartender flinched.

"What is that even meaning?" roared Balur. "You are not know what to say? You are not knowing what it is you are thinking?"

"I'm conflicted, okay?" Will felt like he deserved a little understanding here. "I love her. I don't think she loves me. She's apparently done some pretty monstrous things, but she's striving for redemption. I don't know what to think."

"So be telling her that!" Balur looked exasperated.

"But—" Will said. And then he looked at the big, copper-colored Analesian sitting in front of him. And what did Balur know of love?

"Ale already!" Balur yelled at the barman, cutting Will off. He looked at Will and shook his head. "Was he not seeing me flinging my drink around the room?"

"I want her to love me again, Balur," said Will, unable to contain the words any longer. "I don't want to say something that'll take that off the table. I want to say the thing that makes it more likely."

Balur cocked his head to one side and waited until the visibly quaking barman slapped another beer down in front of him. He took a long sip, smacked his lips, and set the fresh goblet down. "So," he said, "you are thinking that the best way to win back the affections of Lette is to be hiding your emotions away so that she cannot be seeing the true picture of you."

"Erm..." said Will, because that didn't sound like a tremendously good idea now that Balur put it that way. "I just want to present myself in the best light."

"To be tricking her, in other words," Balur went on.

"Well…" said Will. He felt decidedly uncomfortable now. "That's not…"

Balur nodded. "Yes," he said. "That would probably be working."

"Wait. What?"

"Trickery," said Balur. "It is being a thing you are good at. Which is being a pretty short list if you are not minding me saying. So really you are needing any advantage you have got."

Will was beginning to think asking Balur's advice on this was not a tremendously good idea.

"But you just said I should tell her what I'm thinking."

"Yes," Balur agreed, "but that was before I was knowing what horseshit you were thinking. Now I am thinking you should make up something better to be thinking and be telling her that."

Will hesitated. Balur was much bigger than him. And maybe this particular situation was a good example of where the truth wouldn't help. "Sure," he said. "Thanks." He slapped the lizard man on the arm in as companionly a way as he could manage.

Balur stared at Will's hand on his arm. Will removed it. He looked around the room. He leaned in closer. "So," he said, lowering his voice, "now that's sorted, maybe we should figure out how to raid this temple too. What do you know about it?"

Balur shrugged. "The entrance is being a temple in the Eighth District, which is mostly being abandoned ruins. Not much is going on there. It is being an unpopular relic. But it is being an important one. So mostly you are having a lot of bored guards. And lots of other bored guards nearby, guarding other artifacts. The Eighth District is big on artifacts. And Vinter is taking training its soldiers very seriously for a bunch of drunkards."

"Which is why you tried to trick your way in," said Will.

"Until pancake arse," said Balur heavily.

Will thought about that. "That was the only reason your plan failed?"

Balur thought about that as he finished off his pint. "Maybe," he said.

"So we could try it again," Will said. "And we could talk to Lette beforehand so she takes any insults less personally."

Balur nodded. "I could be seeing that. Then we get in the barracks, killing everyone quietly, and descending."

"Descending?"

"The temple is being an entrance to catacombs," said Balur. "Great, winding dungeons full of monsters and rage." He grinned savagely. "And then at the base, the great guardian Lawl was setting to watch over Barph's Strength for all eternity. His champion which any intruder must be defeating if he is wishing to return to the surface victorious."

Will wasn't entirely sure, but he thought Balur was flexing. He decided to move on.

"So," he said, "you don't happen to have a map of these catacombs, or a route to get to this champion?"

"Was I or was I not saying, 'descend'?"

Will felt his eyebrows climb up his forehead. "Okay then. And are there any legends that tell of some special weakness that this champion of Lawl has?" In the tales his mother had told him as a child, the enemy and the hero always owned fatal flaws. Some weak point that you were always waiting to see exploited.

"I am knowing its weakness," said Balur. "I am stabbing it in the crotch repeatedly until it falls over."

Will tried to suppress his sigh. "You don't know anything about it, do you?"

"There is not being one creature that does not fall down when you stab it repeatedly in the crotch," said Balur obstinately. "That is being science. Ask Quirk."

And that, Will realized with a small, sad sigh, was the plan.

35

Inaction Plan

Once, Balur had aspired to understand humans. When he had first met Lette she had seemed such a fascinating creature. The Analesian brood mothers had told him about humans, of course, but they had always spoken of weakness and frailty. But Lette—she had been fast, aggressive, almost as deadly as an Analesian. She had not been anything he had heard about before.

And then he had followed her out of the desert, and he had met other humans. He had met other human women, and discovered that not all were as flat and sharp as Lette. Some were curvaceous and bountiful. And they would do some quite frankly incredible things in return for coin.

To be sure, he also found the weak, fleshy humans, and they fell like so much wheat before his war hammer. But not all had been like that. There had been others like Lette. And others still not like the weak ones or the sharp ones. There had been clever ones, and funny ones, and conniving ones, and sneaky ones.

But still in the face of all this variety, Balur had thought that the sum of humanity would reveal itself to him. He got paid to kill all sorts of humans, after all, and noticed some clear common anatomical denominators.

And yet now, as he walked the streets of Vinland alongside two representatives of the human species, he decided he still knew almost nothing.

"You know," said Will, "this plan seemed a lot better when I was drunk."

Balur found this statement highly objectionable. "You are calling what you were drunk?" he said. "That is like telling me you were drowning in a piss puddle."

Lette scowled at them both. Her hangover was clearly a thunderous one. "You're telling me that there was a time when this seemed like a good plan?"

To be fair, Lette had changed the plan. There had been her flat refusal to dress as a ceremonial whore, for example. And her insistence that she would kill Balur and pimp out his corpse until it garnered such a reputation that she could pass it off as the most popular whore in Vinter if he mentioned it again. Then she had made herself the master, and them her slaves, and stolen a barrel of beer. Still, given the corpse-pimping mood she was in, Balur decided to not point any of that out.

Will grimaced. "I just wish we'd thought of a plan that allowed us to wear swords and armor."

Balur nodded. "You are meaning the sort of plan where we are posing as relief guards?"

Will ground to a stop. "Well," he said after a long pause, "why in the Hallows didn't you suggest that last night?"

"Because," Lette cut in before Balur could fully express his disinterest in plans, "Balur didn't want to pose as a relief guard. Did you, Balur?"

Balur shrugged. He knew she knew.

"Tell him the plan that you would have suggested, Balur," she said.

Balur wondered if this conversation was worth it. On balance he decided it might get him out of future conversations about planning.

"My preferred plan," he said, "is to be running in there and stabbing everyone repeatedly in the face until they stop breathing."

"But…" Will cocked his head one way then the other. "That's a terrible…You said…All the other guards…They'd…outnumbered by a factor of…"

The thought brought a smile to Balur's face. "Yes," he said. "But I cannot be dealing with all the stupid conversation, so I am letting you come up with silly bullshit like this."

He started walking again. What a stupid conversation to have had. Personally, of course, he would rather eschew conversations in favor of working issues out through fucking or fighting, but it had always seemed to him that Will was ill-equipped to compete with Lette in either of those arenas. So, in this particular case, he was willing to concede the need for a discussion before Lette slew Will either with her blade or her loins. But this extended dialogic foreplay before they got to the conversational climax was not his style at all.

The land Vinter perched upon was steep and craggy on its northern edge. Here in District Eight, streets were hacked into the rock, creating a series of steps. Overhangs cast everything in shadow. Most buildings were abandoned, half-collapsed affairs. A few were still populated by destitute-looking families.

A woman scrubbing a child clean in what looked like a tub of beer stared at them with a blank expression as they walked past. A dirty fire just inside the entrance of her house made it appear to be little more than a cave. Guards wearing the High Priests' colors marched back and forth down a few streets and clustered about run-down temples.

The street leading to the temple they were aiming themselves at largely consisted of a narrow gully running back into a steep-walled cliff. A few façades had been chiseled into the slowly narrowing walls but all of the houses appeared deserted. A few desultory strands of ivy were stretched across the stone, reaching desperately for the narrow slice of daylight that lay far above. At the street's far end, the walls abruptly opened up to form a broader opening. On the far side of this opening lay the temple.

It was, even to Balur's uneducated eye, impressive. Care and love had gone into the carving. Elegant columns, delicate relief sculptures, and windows laced with spidery strands of stone mounted toward the heavens. There was an air of divinity clinging to the place, as if human hands had perhaps not been wholly responsible for the work done.

There were also eight of the dozen soldiers who guarded the place, lazing in front of it. Five sat on the ground, casting dice, while another three leaned on halberds, watching from the small splash of light that fell from the gap in the rocks above. One stretched lazily, bronze armor clanking as he did so.

Balur waved as they approached. Will looked at him. "Is that…"

"Important subterfuge?" asked Balur. "I am thinking so, yes. Or were you thinking going in as a knock-kneed quivering mess would be being more convincing?"

He didn't wait for an answer. Instead he pushed into the opening and dumped his barrels on the floor. Beside him, Will sighed. "Okay," he said, "who wants a fresh tipple?"

Which is not how Balur would have phrased it, because he had things like pride and self-respect, but he supposed it was good enough. And the guards seemed happy with it. And the four other guards even came out of their quarters to join in. When everyone's hands were full. And so, all in all, for all Will's unnecessary whining, it was a good plan.

He looked at Lette and smiled. "Now?" he said.

"Now what?" asked one of the guards, as guileless as a fucking lamb.

"Now," said Lette.

So Balur reached out and, with a short, sharp wrench, snapped the guard's neck.

It was all over in a few seconds. The guards hadn't really even been ready to shout. And they'd all been so raucous before, it would have been hard to notice the change in pitch. On the whole, Balur thought as he wiped a man's intestines off his claws, and Lette wiped her knives clean of blood on her britches, it had gone well. And yet, of them all, Will, without a life on his conscience, was standing there with a look of mild horror and revulsion on his face. And Balur's conviction that he would never understand humans at all was strengthened.

Balur ignored the bodies and strode into the temple, only mildly concerned that his bloody footprints were sacrilegious. The gods tended to be keen on blood, so, he thought, it was probably okay.

The temple's interior was less impressive than its exterior. A narrow oval of space had been hollowed out of the cliff face, the ceiling arching up so high that Balur had to crane his neck back to see all the way to its peak. The place was thick with shadows, barely half a dozen flickering torches lighting the way, each one tactically placed to ensure visitors were fully aware of exactly how many screaming faces had been carved into every available surface. Columns of screaming faces supported ceilings carved with screaming faces. Instead of windows, the walls held large rectangular plates of stone carved with... well, to be fair, some of the faces appeared to be weeping, and some had more of a grimace, and one or two just looked to be deeply constipated, but overall most of them were definitely screaming.

"So I guess Lawl really didn't want people to go down and get this beverage then," Will said, pushing in behind Balur.

Lette nodded. "He's not subtle, is he?"

"Well," said Balur, "he was not actually writing the words 'fuck off' across the back of the temple, so for Lawl that is being pretty restrained."

But then, at the back of the temple, they found a small circular opening, black as a dragon's maw, ringed with stone thorns, leading down into a roughly hewn opening. And in ornate script, carved into the stone above that opening, were the words...

"Well," said Will, "it's not literally 'fuck off.'"

" 'Abandon hope all ye who enter here'?" Lette arched an eyebrow. "That's like the definitive divine code for 'Fuck off.' "

Will sighed. "Well, I didn't bring any hope," he said tiredly. "I gave up on that a long time ago. Now I just bring my own shitty expectations."

And perhaps, Balur thought, that was Will's problem. That he thought reality was shitty. That someone had been giving him unrealistic hopes of something better. In the desert, every Analesian grew up with a comprehensive grasp of exactly what reality was. And thanks to that, through all the beatings, liver stabbings, and ego scourings it had delivered, Balur had found himself pleasantly surprised by life outside the desert's sandy confines.

Then Will went and ducked straight through the hole.

Lette looked at Balur, then at the hole, and then back at Balur. "You okay with that?"

"Yes," Balur. He did not like the insinuating tone in her voice. "Why would I not be?"

"No reason," she said.

Balur examined the hole. "It is looking like a very tight squeeze for an Analesian," he said, by way of interesting commentary.

And then Will popped his head back out. "It really opens up once you're through," he said with what he probably imagined was a reassuring grin, and not the rictus smile his corpse would be wearing.

Balur considered the hole. "I am being very broad in the shoulder," he pointed out. "Maybe I should be guarding the exit in case more guards are coming to investigate."

Will pulled himself out of the hole, looked back at it, and then looked at Balur. "Are you…"

Balur's eyes narrowed and he gripped his sword tighter.

"Are you sc—"

"Don't say it!" Lette shouted just as Balur prepared to pull his blade and answer Will's impudent question.

Was he... Was he... As if he was... that of anything. He had killed a dragon. He was a fucking warrior. He was offering to put himself in danger. He wasn't... that of anything. Certainly not of a hole.

Stupid hole.

Will was frozen like a cornered rabbit. His eyes flicked to Lette.

"Be finishing your sentence, Will," said Balur. "I am being interested in what you had to say." They would see who was... *that.*

"Are you..." Will pursed his lips.

Balur's growl lacked words.

"Are you scontemplating taking off your robe so none of the fabric gets caught?" Will said in a rush.

"Scontemplating?" Balur had not been expecting that.

"Yeah," said Will. "Scontemplating. It's how we say it sometimes in Kondorra. It's a dialect thing."

Balur wondered if he was willing to believe this. "I have never been hearing you use it before."

"Well," said Will with a not particularly nonchalant shrug, "I don't have a very strong accent."

Balur decided that this time he would let that pass.

Of course Balur went through the hole. He did not even take off his cloak. It didn't get caught. And it wasn't at all harrowing. And anyone who said that he thought it was would die while watching him use their intestines as a skipping rope. And he was glad to see that Will quickly agreed that the loud, high-pitched whimpering sound that was heard as he went through the hole was definitely due to the rock walls squeaking against his scales.

And then Will grinned at Lette, and both of them seemed to suddenly be a lot happier, despite the continued absence of conversational climax.

Balur licked the air experimentally, but they definitely hadn't been fucking while he was going through the hole.

Stupid humans.

They lit a torch and went on down the tunnel that opened before them. After the grandeur of the temple, the space beyond felt oddly anticlimactic. It was a featureless tube of dry rock that they walked through for almost ten minutes before Lette came to an abrupt halt.

"Oh," she said, holding the torch higher still. "Oh my."

"What?" asked Balur from the back. He couldn't see much past the glare of the torch.

"Oh," said Lette from the front, "just Lawl dropping the architectural boom, that's all."

And then she lowered the torch, and Balur saw.

The walls of the tunnel ended and space began. Simply space. Whatever walls existed, they were lost to it all. The only floor was shadowed depths.

It was not empty space, though. "Are those—" Balur checked himself.

"Yes," said Lette.

Staircases. A labyrinth of staircases. They crisscrossed back and forth through the gigantic space. They split apart. They merged. They wove in and out of each other. Massive, impossible staircases, balanced on pillars that seemed to stretch down for eternity. In one or two places they appeared to pause at platforms, large enough to camp on, perhaps, but always these platforms led to simply more staircases. All of them leading down, and down, and down.

"Now that," breathed Balur, "is being a fucking catacomb."

Lette shook her head. "You and bloody catacombs."

As if they weren't the most exciting thing in the world.

Stupid humans.

36

To Forgive Is Profane

Quirk refused to apologize. It didn't matter how long Afrit kept that sour expression on her face, she wasn't going to apologize.

Instead, she looked away from her friend and looked out at the small, stinking temple that was currently trying to contain what appeared to be a riot. The decrepit old pews had been stomped to splinters and cast out onto the streets, and that had just been to make way for more people to enter. It was standing room only, the sweating, seething mass of people crushing into the room so thickly that they could barely move, only pulse backward and forward chanting Firkin's name.

How did he do it? She knew Firkin would stand up there and tell them what they wanted to hear, and he would do it with a surprising amount of passion, but that was hardly a unique skill. Anybody lacking enough moral fiber could do that. What, aside from his unusually overpowering body odor, made Firkin so special?

Firkin himself stood in the wings, peering out at the crowd from behind a tattered curtain. He had stripped down to his dirty loincloth once more. She was trying to be grateful for the loincloth at least. She also wished his back weren't turned, so she could tell if his expression was one of horror, or greed, or something in between.

She stared at his back as if trying to tell. Mostly because she knew exactly what look Afrit was currently giving her back. A judgmental one.

Which was, quite frankly, unfair. And wrong. Yes, Lette and Balur had done terrible things, but in this moment those things were simply no longer relevant. Perhaps in a time of peace they could be addressed, but perhaps in this time of war the two mercenaries would redeem themselves. Had Afrit considered that possibility? That resisting the urge to punish laid open the doors for potential good?

So piss on Afrit's accusing stare. She would not apologize.

Instead she would go and make sure Firkin stayed on gods-hexed message. It wasn't a difficult message, but that had never stopped Firkin from screwing things up in the past.

She took a step toward the old drunkard.

"We have to be better than the dragons," Afrit said behind her.

Quirk hesitated.

"It doesn't matter if we beat them," Afrit said, "if we're no better than them."

Quirk shook her head. "I'm not having this, quite frankly, stupid conversation right now," she said, and walked away.

"Shouldn't you get out there?" she said to Firkin.

Firkin licked a dirty finger and held it up as if testing the wind. "Just a little longer." He smiled at her, showing all of his browning teeth.

Then he rubbed his temples and said to himself, "Just a little longer."

She put a hand on his shoulder. "Are you all right, Firkin?" And she knew that she already knew the answer to that. She had been in the cell, and in his chambers; she had seen what was happening to him. But she would feel a lot better about everything if she could say that he'd lied and said he was fine.

But Firkin didn't say that. Instead he looked deep into her eyes and asked, "How do they know blood tastes coppery?"

Quirk fought to keep her groan inaudible.

"Who's eating all the copper?" he asked her. "How is it different from iron? Who is this culinary metalsmith that has educated everyone's palates?"

"If you're not up to this…" she started, but she didn't really mean it.

"How do I know what blood tastes like?" His face was as open as a child's. "When did I drink all that?"

Quirk wasn't sure if answering the question would make things better or worse. "I think most of us suck a cut at some point in our childhood, or put a shek in our mouths to see how it tastes."

Firkin shook his head. "Don't trust children. Always sneaking sips of your wine when you aren't looking. I never wanted children. Look what I did to my father."

Which was the first time Quirk had ever heard Firkin talk about his family. And she was curious enough to follow this strand of madness just a little further. "What did you do to your father?"

Firkin stared at her in utter bewilderment. "What?"

"You just said…" But she trailed off. Firkin was shaking his head vigorously, as if trying to dislodge something.

Then something in Firkin changed abruptly. He almost snarled and he twisted away from her, shaking off her hand. "You need me, woman," he barked. "Not the other way."

Quirk closed her eyes. May Knole grace her with patience. She was trying to organize a rebellion with a quixotic, mentally unhinged alcoholic as its figurehead. This was not anything that an upbringing under a brutal half-divine warlord, or a subsequent rehabilitation in academia, had prepared her for.

"You're right," she said, trying to hide the fact that she was gritting her teeth. "I need you. We need you. All of us. We need you to say just a few things. Just tell them you were captured by the High Priests. Tell them we're going to fight those bastards. Tell them we're going to fight to win. That it's open warfare in the streets now. And then tell them who I am. Make them trust me. That's all I need. All *we* need." She almost touched his shoulder again. "Please."

Firkin scrunched up his nose. "Maybe," he said finally.

"Firkin, plea—"

But he had already pushed past her, and out onto the stage. "Yes!" he bellowed at the crowd.

"Yes!" they roared back. What in the Hallows they were all agreeing about, Quirk had no idea.

"I am returned to you!" Firkin roared to the crowd. They cheered back. "The High Priests thought they could shut me up. So they did. Wanted to take me off the streets. So they did." The crowd howled and booed. Their hatred was a palpable thing. Quirk took an involuntary step back from where she waited in the wings.

"They thought they could shut me up forever. But they can't hold me." Firkin grinned a manic grin. "Can't hold me forever." As he spoke, his voice dropped almost an octave, its timbre changing, turning from shrill and piercing to loud and booming.

"Returned!" he bellowed, and the whole crowd seemed to rock back, candle flames in the face of a great wind.

Then suddenly Firkin dropped to one knee, grabbing at his head.

Oh piss, Quirk thought, *Afrit is going to hang me on this one.*

Then she recognized the thought for the self-centered idiocy that it was, and rushed out onto the stage. The crowd, already gasping from Firkin's rapid series of transformations from rabid preacher, to voice of god, to collapsed invalid, gasped once more at this new arrival on their stage.

"Firkin?" Quirk shook the man by his shoulder. "Firkin, are you okay?"

"Sleep," Firkin moaned. "Shut up and sleep."

"I can't sleep right now," Quirk said, trying to keep the panic at bay. "I'm trying to organize a revolution."

There was a rumbling coming from the crowd that did not sound entirely compassionate. They had come here for a show, she knew.

"Can you get up?" she whispered to Firkin. "Can you...shout and wave your arms more? You know, do your thing?"

"Get off me!" Firkin shouted, standing up suddenly. He was still clutching at the side of his head with one hand. The crowd cheered, even as Quirk staggered, trying to avoid being sent sprawling by the pinwheeling old man. This was some proper theater.

"Want to lock me up!" Firkin howled. "Well fuck them. How would they like it?" He stared balefully at the crowd.

Quirk stood feeling exposed on the stage. Was it more awkward to stay or to leave? And she didn't want to disrupt whatever spell Firkin was weaving.

"What if we locked *them* up?" Firkin asked. And, yes, the crowd liked that. "What if," Firkin asked, his smile almost lascivious, "we locked up *pieces* of them?"

The crowd howled with joy. The volume of their exhortations battered at Quirk. The physicality of their exuberance made the experience onstage feel almost like a physical assault.

"What if—" Firkin threw both his hands up in the air and the crowd rose to the tips of their toes. Then Firkin hesitated. And then he keeled over backward.

The crowd gasped.

"Oh for fuck's..." said Quirk, which was uncharitable, and which she would almost certainly regret later. She ran to Firkin's side once more. He was covered in a sheen of sweat, muttering something under his breath.

"Are you okay?" she asked yet again, but he didn't seem to be listening to her. "Come on," she said, shaking him lightly. He stared at her wild-eyed, then focused on some spot a mile above her head.

Hold it together. Just hold it together a little longer. "A drink!" she said out loud. "He needs a drink!"

She was almost immediately drenched in wine. Skins exploded on the ground all about her.

"Water, you ignorant arseholes," she muttered to herself. But she knew she was unlikely to find that here. She picked up one of the skins and upended it over Firkin's mouth. He gasped and gulped and then flopped back panting.

"Can you hear me?" she asked him. "Can you understand me?"

"Floor hit me in the face." Firkin sounded confused.

"Can you get up?"

"Done it a thousand times," said Firkin, without any sign of moving.

"Can you do it now?" Quirk could feel the crowd's mounting frustration at the delay. They were like toddlers in need of constant distraction.

"Think I'm going to go to sleep right now," said Firkin, rolling over onto his side.

One other sober person, thought Quirk. *That's all I ask.* Then an image of Afrit floated into her head. *One sober, nonjudgmental person.*

She shook Firkin once more. He snored theatrically. The crowd booed. Gods piss on them.

She didn't see that she had much of a choice. She stood, whirled on the crowed. "The priests have struck against Firkin!" she said as thunderously as she could. "Now we must strike against them!"

Silence fell upon the temple. A thousand pairs of eyes settled upon Quirk, judged her, and found her wanting.

"Who the fuck are you?" A voice floated out of the crowd.

Quirk took a breath. "I am Quirkelle Bal Tehrin of Tamathia. I was Firkin's companion in the liberation of Kondorra. I am Avarra's foremost dragon expert. I am a defender of the Vale. And I am here to organize you into the fighting force that will wrench control away from the High Priests and deliver it into your waiting hands."

The silence continued.

"Well fuck me then," said another conversationally.

"Is there going to be a buffet?" said someone else, quite clearly. "I could have sworn they said there was going to be a buffet."

Quirk licked dry lips. She'd known organizing the religiously drunk was going to be difficult. She'd hoped for Firkin's and Afrit's help, but clearly she didn't have to time to deal with either of them.

She blew out a breath, touched the fire inside her.

"We will take this city," she said, letting her voice ring out through the silent hall. "In Firkin's name. In Barph's name. And we will start tomorrow, with day's break. We will mass in Mead Square." She had spent a lot of the time since their escape examining a series of haphazard, half-scribbled maps of the city, which was the best any of the Vinlanders could provide, and she thought she had a rough idea of how things were laid out. "From there we shall push forward in three divisions. One group will go to the east, toward the Second District. They shall take and occupy the Barcian Cathedral. The next group shall go southeast to the Twelfth District." As far as Quirk could tell, the districts of Vinter had been named by rolling a dice. She was pretty sure at this point that there were at least two separate Ninth Districts. "There they will take and hold Municipal Hall. Finally the third group will proceed south to the Fifth District. There they shall hold and take the Trinity Chapels."

Silence. A belch. Someone muttering, sotto voce, "Bossy bitch, ain't she?"

"Is that clear?" Quirk barked. "Mead Square. Daybreak."

"If she thinks I'm getting out of bed before my head clears…" said someone in the front row. There were giggles.

Knole piss on these people and their idiot religion. She didn't want to lead them. She didn't want to order them about. She only wanted to help them achieve what they themselves said they wanted to achieve.

She held out her hands, palms up, facing the moldering ceiling, and with a twist of her will and the utterance of two inhuman words, sent two frothing pillars of fire three feet into the air. She held them there for two seconds, bathing in the blast of heat. Then she let them fade, leaving behind a lingering flare in their eyeballs, and the smell of scorched hair from the front row.

Now she had their gods-hexed attention.

"Is that clear?" she thundered.

The response was not coordinated. It was not organized. But it was definitely an affirmative as the crowd backed for the exits as fast as their feet and volume would take them.

"Tomorrow we take the city!" Quirk yelled after them. She didn't need them too chastened. "Tomorrow we rip it out of the High Priests' hands." There were a few cheers. Enough, she hoped.

And if it wasn't enough? Well then, gods forgive her, she would burn this whole city down herself if that was what it took.

She waited until the place was empty before she started to peel Firkin up off the floor. He was dead weight, betraying no signs of consciousness. As she struggled, several altar attendants ran forward and took him from her. She chewed her lip as they bore him away. Then, when she turned to leave herself, Afrit was there. She was still giving Quirk the same disapproving look.

"Really?" Quirk asked. "Really?"

"One of the first things I teach," Afrit said, "is that even in the brutal practicality of real-world politics, you have to draw a line. You have to say what wrongs you will not do, no matter the benefits. You have to say that some goods are not worth it."

This was followed by a condescending stare.

Quirk sighed. Apparently she was going to have to do this. "Yes," she said. "Lette and Balur have done terrible, terrible things. They are low, base, awful people. But they are effective. And I hate that that is all that counts right now. But that is all that counts right now. If we had access to a pair of people who were just as likely to return with Barph's Strength and whose ideas of morality didn't make me want to vomit, I would suggest we use them. But we don't. So if saving Vinter, saving Avarra takes us using them, then we use them."

That wasn't an apology, Quirk told herself. It was an explanation. Not an apology.

"This isn't about Lette and Balur," said Afrit, with what Quirk suspected was an absence of patience that matched her own.

Quirk was now confused as well as impatient. "It's not?"

"Firkin is sick, Quirk." Afrit's anger was a hot flame in her eyes. "He's really, really sick. And this is far too much to ask of him. This is taking advantage."

Quirk closed her eyes. And she tried to hear Afrit. She really did. But did the woman not understand?

"You're right," she said. "He's sick. And this may break him. But that thing I just mentioned? That thing where we save all of Vinter? Where we don't oppress them? Where we don't eat them? Because dragons really do actually eat their subjects, Afrit. That bit where we save a whole country from all of that? That makes us different from the dragons. And so if breaking Firkin will save all the other lives in Vinter? In Avarra? Yeah, then I'm okay with that."

"So we're only like the dragons for Firkin?" There was

no bend in Afrit. And Quirk could almost admire her in that moment. Almost.

"I'm not going to apologize." Quirk thought perhaps it would be easier just to say it out loud.

"You don't have to," said Afrit, her face cold. "Not to me. But before all this is over, I think you might need to ask Firkin for his forgiveness."

37

Punch Drunk

Quirk watched as the sun slowly inched above the rooftops surrounding Mead Square. Its warm glow splashed onto the haphazardly cast flagstones and spread with slow majesty to fill the space, like well-aged whiskey suffusing a man's soul.

For her part, if Quirk could have ripped the sun from the heavens and shoved it up the collective arseholes of all the Vinlanders clustered in this city, she would have happily done so. *Daybreak*. She had said daybreak.

It was half past nine in the morning. Daybreak had come to Vinland three and a half hours ago. And how many Vinlanders were here? How many were ready and willing to throw themselves against the High Priests and free their city from tyranny?

Twelve.

"Where are they?" She wheeled on Afrit and Firkin, who were huddled in one of the remaining shadows.

"Sleep, I think," said one of the Vinlanders. He had showed up early and stood with them, taking turns sucking on the neck of a wineskin that he was passing back and forth with Firkin. Quirk thought his name was Durmitt.

"Never liked mornings," slurred Firkin. "Bet Lawl came up with mornings. Seem like the sort of think he'd do." He spat a wad of phlegm the color of Quirk's nightmares.

"Barph never shows up on time," said Durmitt, holding up the wineskin like a talisman. "Been waiting for him to show up for eight hundred years now, and he's still late. Fine divine example that is."

"Didn't Lawl banish Barph?" said Afrit. "Where I grew up that was the story I always heard."

"Fucking Lawl," Firkin spat again.

Quirk wheeled on him. He was as good a target for her frustration as anyone else. "Where did all this hatred of Lawl come from anyway? Weren't you happily telling everyone that Will was his prophet back in Kondorra?"

Firkin shied away as if she'd struck him, wrapping his hands protectively around his head. "Shh!" he hissed. "It sleeps."

Quirk could have lived without Afrit's accusatory stare.

Durmitt, it turned out, was right though. By midday Mead Square was full. People were starting to throng in the streets beyond its edges. Quirk clambered astride the fountain at the square's heart to get a better look. Once the fountain had run with mead for all to sup from. Now it was dry and dusty. The gathering around it still resembled a party far more than the warband she wanted—there was far too much drinking, barbecuing, and singing about bawdy tavern girls and boys in her opinion—but it was a start.

"Okay," she shouted down to Firkin, "now you speak to them!"

Firkin blinked at her. "Oh," he said, "you're doing a fine job with all that." He flapped a hand at her. "You run along and do it. I'm fine down here."

Quirk felt the lid she had been clamping down on her anger all morning quake. She knelt down and hissed in his face. "Listen to me, you disgusting old drunk. You are, for better or worse, the leader of this ragtag bunch of idiots. And quite frankly, you are welcome to the job. I don't want it. I am not a leader. I am not a general. I am, at best, the secretary for this war. I am behind the scenes, organizing people, and keeping others on schedule and on task. That's all. Now someone needs to stand up and lead. Someone needs to put passion in these people. Because they have to fight, and they have to win. And I will fight today. I will do that for you. Because I know, as much as I hate it, that I can do it, and I can do it well. But that's all. So get your filthy, sour-smelling arse up there and tell everyone to fight, before I set fire to your feet to make you dance for them."

Firkin belched, apparently opening up a portal to the sulfur pits of the Hallows somewhere in the back of his throat. But then he shrugged and said, "Fine then. If you're going to be pushy about it."

She had to help him to his feet, but he got up.

"Get up where they can see you," she said, helping him over the ledge and into the bowl of the fountain. He seemed more frail than his ropey muscles would suggest. "Tell them the plan." Then she decided she should check. "You remember the plan? Three prongs…"

He pulled away from her with a grumble, grabbed the fountain's stone spire, and hauled himself up into view. It took perhaps half a minute for those closest to the fountain to see him. Then a hush fell, slowly rippling out through the crowd until everyone was staring up at him.

Firkin swallowed and then grimaced as if he'd tasted something foul. "All right," he said, and even Quirk could barely hear him. "So we've got here, and…" He shook his head. "So you're meant to be splitting up, and…" He sighed. "Three prongs…"

There was silence in the square. The crowd stared up at Firkin in confusion. And Quirk was going to kill him. She was actually going to kill him. Not in self-defense. Not to achieve the liberation of the masses. Simply because he had dragged her down to the level of Lette and Balur. She was going to kill him purely out of frustration.

"What?" yelled someone out in the crowd. "We can't hear you."

Firkin sighed again heavily. He looked all about him. He

looked down at Quirk. And just for a moment, she thought she saw something glimmering in his eyes. And then he looked away. He grimaced at the crowd once more. And was there some theatricality to it? Some exaggeration?

"You know what?" asked Firkin. And suddenly his voice was clear and loud, shrill as it was. Quirk felt the energy of it go through the crowd like the crackle of magic running down her spine.

Firkin grinned, showing all his rotten teeth. "Just get out there," he bellowed, "and rip this city a new arsehole!"

The roar that rose up seemed to shake the world. And then, with an enormous heave, Mead Square vomited the drunk, madcap devotees of Barph and Firkin out onto the streets of Vinter.

Quirk burned. She truly burned. She could feel the fire inside her, desperate to leak out, desperate to spark and jump and ignite. It wanted to be alive, writhing out of her and gathering up this stupid little man and whisking him away to a place of ash and obliteration so that she would be free, free and dancing in the ruins of this city.

"You," she hissed. "You..."

Someone put a hand on her shoulder. Afrit, she suspected. Afrit was a big one for putting her hands on people's shoulders. Quirk shook it off.

Firkin shrugged. "Seemed the simpler message," he slurred. "And who likes prongs. Stabby things. Mostly associated with pitchforks. And pitchforks are mostly associated with shit. Don't want folk thinking of shit when they're ripping up a city." He looked off to the heavens. "Well, perhaps you do?" He looked back at Quirk. "Are you kinky? I never could figure you out. Got to be something really messed up the way you keep your gusset closeted away."

Quirk breathed slowly. There was smoke on her breath.

From all around she could hear the sound of chaos on the

streets. Wood splintering and glass shattering. Tendrils of smoke were already reaching up into the sky.

Firkin nodded. "Seems like they've got the general idea."

Quirk let the flame fill her. Calm came with the flame. "This is *our* territory," she said quietly. "They're destroying what *we* control. There are tactical objectives we need to achieve. *You* need to achieve. There—"

Firkin was looking at her with such contempt it actually brought her to a stop. It was such an unusual look to find on the old man's face. As if he actually cared about something.

"Barph is an anarchist," the old man said. "He doesn't care for your tactics. He doesn't care for objectives. He wants to tear, and rip, and laugh, and fuck. That's all." He pointed a dirty finger at her. "You should understand, little firefly. Little spark in the night. Barph wants it to burn. Barph loves you."

And his words cut, because they were unfair, because they were everything she was striving to not be, and because they were everything jackasses like him were forcing her to be through their stupidity and their inaction. And Quirk wanted to cut him back, wanted to use her own words to hurt and wound.

"You're not Barph," she told him. "You speak for no one except a bottle."

And Firkin started to laugh at her, and Quirk reached for more words, but then she saw he was crying too.

She did not understand Firkin. She truly did not. Was there a plan? Was it all madness and unlikely events? She didn't know, and she didn't have time to figure it out. A city was burning, and now she was the only one who could even try to control the flame.

The streets were a swarming mass of people cheering and smashing, drinking and laughing. Some held blades, others had heavy clubs; yet more wielded burning torches. Some held no weapons at all. They pushed forward in loose waves, breaking upon street corners, spilling and flowing, slowly losing coherence, spreading thinner and thinner.

"This way!" Quirk called at the top of her lungs. "This way!" Desperately she tried to steer the crowd in the direction of the Twelfth District and the Municipal Hall. Of all her targets, the hall was the one she valued the most. As little bureaucracy as there was in Vinter, what did exist all passed through the Municipal Hall. If she crippled the High Priests' ability to communicate, while she relied on Firkin's more informal but significantly more robust network, they should be at an advantage. Unfortunately, it was a lot like trying to steer a Placid Ocean galleon by standing on the deck and blowing at the mainsail.

Someone was pulling on her arm. She ripped it away. She had to get to the head of this crowd, lead from the front.

"Quirk!" She spun around at her name. It was Afrit reaching out for her sleeve again.

"What?" she snapped.

Afrit was shaking her head, bellowing to be heard over the sound of the crowd. "We have to abandon this. We have to just let them tire themselves out. Figure out a new way to come at this."

Quirk furrowed her brow. "Are you *insane*?" Was she the only one who understood the urgency of what was going on?

"The day is already lost!" Afrit shouted.

Quirk's eyes flew wide. Truly? Truly in the middle of this crowd? She grabbed Afrit by the lapels and pushed her out toward the edge of the crowd. "Be quiet!" she hissed. "Everything hangs by threads, and you try to demoralize everyone? That will not stand. Help me or get back to Mead Square to wait until we've taken some gods-hexed buildings."

"You will take nothing," said Afrit. "I am a student of politics, Quirk. Of history. This is not how change happens."

Quirk didn't have time for this, but the academic inside couldn't resist the siren call of barbed debate. "The will of the people?" she said. "That's not how change happens?"

"This isn't the will of the people, Quirk." There was sadness in Afrit's eyes. "It could be, if you did this right, if you made them see this world clearly. But right now, this is just your will. Right now, you're just another dictator."

Quirk just stared at the woman she had thought of as her friend. And she did not understand. What had happened? Was it in the Vale when the dragons had come? Was it below the High Priests' castle? When had Afrit lost her nerve, her stomach, her sense of pissing urgency?

"Don't bother meeting me back at Mead Square," Quirk said, and she pushed Afrit away.

She fought to the front of the crowd, not bothering to look back. She doubted Afrit was following anyway. At the leading edge of the crowd she stretched a pillar of fire up toward the sky.

"This way!" she bellowed, pushing forward. "This way!" She loosed a second pillar of fire.

And praise be to Knole, to Lawl, to Betra, and Klink, and Toil, and Cois, and even Barph. They came. Stumbling, and yelling, bumping into each other, yes, but they came. And as they picked up steam, they found their voices once more. Yelling and howling, they plunged down the streets, toward the Twelfth District.

Quirk, was in fact, finally feeling confident, right up until the moment when they ran into a small army.

They rounded the corner onto the broad thoroughfare that led directly to the steps of the Municipal Hall and saw that fifty yards down, the street was completely blocked by a wall of guards, perhaps thirty across and five men deep.

She skidded to a halt, tried to think quickly. A hundred and fifty men. She had them outnumbered at least three to one. But these guards were heavily armored, holding tall shields in a tight wall, armed with short stabbing spears.

Quirk knew what had to be done. "Knole forgive me and know I do not enjoy this." She planted her feet, stretched out a palm.

And then the crowd at her back broke around her, plunging toward a sharp, pointy death with drunken howls, and blocked her shot completely.

"Wait!" she yelled, but it was about as effective as telling Balur about the risks of venereal disease.

Then bellows turned to screams.

"Shit!" She fought forward, riding the crest of the crowd's pressure from behind. Ahead of her she could see people faltering, trying to turn away from the soldiers' spears. But the rear of the crowd smashed into them, hurled them forward.

She screamed. Because gods piss on it. It should not be this way. And she had tried. Over and *over*.

Then she turned her scream into fire. She thrust both hands at the guards, leaned all her weight into thrusting a pillar of flame into their ranks. It smashed into the shield at the center of the wall. She watched the wall buckle, the shock wave rippling up and down its length. She roared, poured more of herself into the effort.

The shield wall broke. Her flame ripped through the shield, through the man behind it. It ripped through the men behind him. It hurtled down the thoroughfare, tearing the High Priests' army in two.

Then the two halves of the shield wall split, spilling out to the left and right, falling away from the wound she had scorched in their heart. She bellowed a rallying cry, pushed forward into that space, lashing out to the left and right with twisting ropes of fire.

But the High Priests' guards did not break, did not turn screaming. They kept falling away to the sides, opening up the path forward, but continuing to hack and slash at the rioters' flanks as they pressed into it. And she felt the cresting force that had been pushing her forward waver behind her.

"Forward!" she yelled. "Forward!"

But no one was listening to her. She honestly wasn't sure if anyone had ever been listening to her.

Fear clawed at her. She didn't want to call it fear. She wanted to call it frustration, or anger, or even arrogance if she had to, but it wasn't that. It was fear. Fear that they would lose. Fear that this city would be crippled. Fear that the dragons would win. Fear that she would be responsible for all these pointless, stupid deaths and fear that she would be responsible for all the ones to come in their wake. Fear that her fear made her culpable for this unmitigated disaster.

She had known fear before. Fear had been Hethren's weapon. He had made fear her master. And then, after that...then fear had been her excuse. Fear had been how she had justified the things she had done in Hethren's name. Fear had been the shield she had held up when the truth was, she had started to enjoy it.

So Quirk knew fear, and Quirk knew she felt fear now. And she knew that she needed to be careful. That she could not let fear drive her. But in the cut and thrust, and push and shove, there was just not time.

She pivoted, chasing after the guards' retreating right flank, flinging fireballs at them. And she tried to be tactical, to aim only where she had to, to take only the lives that were absolutely necessary, but gods it was so hard. People were moving, and shouting. The stench of sweat and blood were thick in the air. Fists and bodies hammered at her. She threw another fireball. She watched guards fly into the air, smoke and flames making bright trails.

"Forward!" she shouted, even as she fought at standstill. Everything was a balancing act. Some of Firkin's followers were hacking and kicking at guards. Others were fighting to get free. Others were just bleeding and dying.

A guard, thrown out of the enemy's flank, darted toward her, lunging with his spear. He hit a wall of fire, which washed over him, left him screaming. She spun around, trying to assess, trying to think where to strike next. The noise was incredible, a battering wave smashing at her. Screams and the sound of metal against meat.

And then pain. Pain like fire. Pain that made her scream. A vast, ugly violation in her shoulder. Something striking her from behind. She staggered, and there was an ugly ripping feeling.

She fell, spinning as she did so, landing on her back. She stared up, saw the guard above her, preparing to thrust down. And the crowd didn't care. The crowd kept pushing and stamping and raging. Feet stepped on her hands, her chest.

She screamed again. She could feel the blood pouring out of a ragged hole in her shoulder. He'd stabbed her. The whoreson had actually stabbed her.

The guard above lunged down, aiming the spear straight at her face. Her fucking face.

Quirkelle Bal Tehrin dreamt of fire.

She felt power burn through her, pleasure and pain so close to each other. The thrill of it. The release. As if iron bands were bursting from her soul. And for a moment she was nothing but a conduit, nothing but a faucet through which fire flowed. Self-awareness flickered, threatened to be burned away. She wrestled for self-control. *This is weakness,* she told herself. *This is fear. Let it go. Just let it go.*

It was harder than it should be. But then she did, the flame shutting off, leaving her feeling hollowed out and useless. She was panting, lying on her back, sweating. The world was silent, just a faint ringing in her ears, like the echo of a memory.

She blinked, and breathed, trying to bring herself back to the world entirely, away from the sense of aching loss. She couldn't hear anything. Why couldn't she hear anything?

She picked herself up. They were gone. All of them were gone. Firkin's followers. The soldiers. And for a single, heart-stopping moment she was sure it was all her fault. She was sure that she had burned them all. It was always there, that thought. Quiet, ignored, but there, waiting to slip like a stiletto into her mind.

But though the street was full of bodies, only a handful were blackened and twisted. She had not wrought most of the carnage here. Instead, the fact that only a dozen or so of the hundred or more bodies wore the High Priests' armor told the real story. This had not been a victory. This had been a rout. Her army had fallen. So had her cause. So had she.

38

What's Small, Red, Furry, and Smells of Dried Blood?

Lawl, Lette reflected, clearly had no respect for anyone's thighs. Eight hours, they had been descending these stairs. Eight hours of step after step without break. She collapsed onto a broad stone platform suspended somewhere in the middle of nowhere and clutched her aching legs.

"Remind me again," she said, "why we're struggling to save these cursed gods anyway?"

"Arsehole gods who exist on some distant plane and mostly ignore us," said Will, "are better than arsehole dragons on Avarra directly interfering with our lives."

"Couldn't we just let the dragons kill the gods"—Lette managed to summon the energy to start massaging her throbbing legs—"and *then* kill the dragons after that?"

"Don't they somehow become gods when they kill the existing ones?" Will asked. "I mean I thought that was the point of it all."

Lette didn't have the energy to shrug. "I honestly don't know. That part of their plan has seemed stupid to me since day one. It's just their frightening efficiency at the bit where they conquer all Avarra that has me worried."

"Well, we can't kill gods," said Will, managing to rub his own calves now. "So I think we should kill the dragons now just on the off chance they become them."

Lette thought about that. Normally she might have enjoyed debating the point. Despite his flaws, Will could be an entertaining conversational sparring partner. She would concede that. And in this light, even bedraggled as he was, he was still a good-looking man. In fact, bedraggled was quite a good look on him. Which was, of course, neither here nor there. Just an observation. Anyway, she didn't have the energy to argue. So she might as well just enjoy his biceps while he rubbed his legs. There was no harm in that.

What had she been thinking about, again?

"Why have we been stopping?"

The platform they were on marked the junction of three separate staircases. Balur stood at the top of one, looking back at them.

Lette grunted. "For all the obvious bloody reasons. But," she said, "if you're feeling so chipper, I've seen dead ivy all over this place. Go grab some and let's make a fire."

Balur stood, staring at her with distaste, but unable to say no without conceding that he felt tired. "Fine," he said eventually, and stomped off.

Lette lay on her back. Their entrance into the labyrinth of stairs was invisible now. Only interlacing stairways were visible above them.

"It's actually kind of beautiful," she said, looking up at the interlocking architecture, at the towering columns of rock, all of it madly suspended in the air.

"What?" Will had been concentrating on his aching legs.

"All of this." Lette swept a hand at the world around them. "This, well, let's face it. It's obviously a divine creation. People couldn't have made this. Those pillars are just too tall and too thin. Rock doesn't work that way. And the light. I shouldn't be able to see my own hands, but I can see almost a quarter mile up before the shadows obscure things. It's all divine. But it's..." She struggled for a word. "It's sort of magnificent," she finished. It wasn't, she thought, a word or even a thought she'd be comfortable sharing with many people other than Will.

Will took a pause from kneading his calf like it was yesterday's leftover dough and considered the space. "Yes," he said eventually. "Yes, I suppose it is. But it's all built in the service of self. Lawl didn't build this to impress anyone, or to help anyone except himself. He did this to punish Barph, to show his dominance over him. This is buried. It's not for anyone to see."

Lette nodded. "Well," she said, "I didn't say that Lawl wasn't an enormous arsehole. Just that he was also capable of beauty."

Will lay back on the rock next to her. Not too close. He seemed well acquainted with the politics of their personal space. He sighed. "When I look at this," he said, "I can't help but feel... disappointed."

Lette arched an eyebrow even though she knew he couldn't see it. "You were expecting a more impressive underground labyrinth of impossible staircases?"

Will huffed a small laugh. "No, I... Just imagine if all this had been built in the service of making things better for humanity. For people like you and me. For the elves too. And dwarves, and centaurs, and giants, and Analesians, and everybody. What if someone wanted to rule not because it was a way to increase their personal power and wealth, but because they actually cared. Because they wanted to make things better."

Lette thought about that. "Well," she said, "there were preacher men who used to wander through Salera when I was a child and tell saint stories about people like that. About kingdoms where justice reigned. But I never met a saint. And I've never seen a kingdom like that. And I've been to more than a few places. I don't know if real people work like that. Taking power usually requires force and compromise. And once someone's got power...it's not good for them."

Silence from Will. She didn't look over at him for a response.

"I'm thinking about my parents' farm," Will started again. "I think they were like the people in your preacher men's stories. There was only me and the three farmhands, but I think they were genuinely interested in making it the best place it could be for all of us. Maybe it's just when it gets big, it gets out of hand."

Lette chewed on that for a while too. "Wasn't Firkin one of your father's farmhands?" she said eventually.

"Yes," said Will. "Before he went drunk and crazy. Or when he was drunk and crazy less often."

"But he went drunk and crazy, right?" Lette went on. She wasn't sure she could buy into Will's paradise, but for once she didn't just want to kick it out from under him either. "And your father and he quarreled and he left. That's what you told me back in Kondorra."

Will grunted his assent.

"So even that small paradise," she said, "and I'm sure that's what it was for you, for your parents' only child...it wasn't paradise for everybody. Somebody had to leave. Your father had to exercise his power, and he did it in a way that didn't benefit everybody. It certainly didn't benefit Firkin."

She heard Will twisting beside her, could feel the companionableness of the silence fleeing. Gods piss on it.

"I'm not saying this to criticize your father," she said. "I think he made a fine call. He was looking out for his wife and son. That was the right thing to do. I'm just making a point. There are no perfect systems. Someone always gets fucked."

Will settled down beside her. "So what should we do then?" he asked. "Just accept it? Just say 'okay' to the dragons and accept that it's our turn in life to be oppressed? There's got to be a better system. A way where the fewest people possible get screwed over. There's got to be something...maybe not fair, but *more* fair."

He sounded so utterly desperate, so exposed then. And she didn't know how he did it. She could not. Never. It would be like walking into battle naked. She was simply not that brave.

"Hey," she said, making her voice intentionally rough to crush the sound of any rogue emotion out of it, "I'm here, fighting with you, aren't I?"

And she looked over at him. She knew she shouldn't, but she did. And there he was looking at her, his face all open, and everything on display, all the hope and the hurt writ so very large in his big, deep eyes.

Oh gods, piss on it.

He rolled onto his side to face her. And she was rolling to face him too.

It's a mistake, said a voice that was entirely correct and about to be completely ignored.

"There," Balur boomed. "Pissing ivy." He crashed down onto the platform in a clatter of clanking armor and thundering feet. He threw a bundle of scraggly brown leaves and creepers onto the floor.

Lette rolled onto her back and heaved out a long, frustrated breath. It had been far, far too long since she had had a tumble in the sheets.

"Food, sleep," she mumbled as she fumbled in her pack for a steel and flint, "and no more pissing talking."

"I am thinking we are approaching a wall," said Balur.

It was the next...day? Perhaps. Lette wasn't sure in the constant twilight of the labyrinth. She had slept. She had walked. She had tried to forget about Will's big eyes.

The staircase they were on was a broad and unusually ornate thing with low, fluted banisters. It ended as all the staircases did, in shadow. She peered into the gloom. Could she make out slight subtleties in the darkness ahead of them? Perhaps. Some lines and shapes of a minimally lighter gray. But nothing regular enough to be pillars or steps.

"Is it a dead end?" Will asked Lette, peering ahead of them. "Have we come the wrong way?"

"Well," said Balur, "having been here several times before, I am totally knowing my way through this impossible labyrinth."

They kept pushing forward. Lette's eyes strained. Then she realized the problem wasn't her vision, but her sense of scale. The wall wasn't hidden in shadow. It was the shadow.

The wall was as impossibly vast as the rest of the whole impossible space. It stretched up like the end of the world itself. The stairs met it and took a sharp right angle, leveling out somewhat into a wide, sloping platform.

As they got closer, Lette sniffed the air.

"Do you smell something?" Will asked.

She shook her head. "No, I just like to sniff at the air curiously for no good reason from time to time. I'm surprised you hadn't picked up on that."

Will looked at her. "That's sarcasm, isn't it?"

She didn't bother acknowledging that. He was lucky he had those eyes. She turned to Balur. "Dried blood?" she asked.

"Of course." Balur's narrow tongue whisked out of his mouth. "I have been tasting it on the air for the past two hundred yards."

"Dried blood?" asked Will, sounding alarmed.

"And you didn't think to mention it?" asked Lette, who was generally of the impression that regardless of whether you liked someone or not, if they were on your side in a fight, nine times out of ten you tried to keep them alive.

"I knew you would be noticing eventually," said Balur with a shrug.

"So," said Lette, "I'm assuming that at this point you're actually actively encouraging me to remove your balls?"

"Could you perhaps be waiting," asked Balur, "until after we get to the kobolds."

"Kobolds?" asked Will in the same alarmed tone.

Balur nodded. "Having a very distinctive flavor, kobolds are. Once you are tasting it you are not easily forgetting it."

Kobolds. Lette tried to think about them academically. They were barely sentient pack rodents. Big teeth and big claws. They tended to like dark, quiet places with plentiful food sources. Like nearby villages. Clearing ruins of kobolds had been the backbone of her income back in the days when she and Balur were just starting out as mercenaries.

"So where's the nest?" asked Lette.

"Nest?" said Will. He seemed to have become stuck in panicked mode.

Balur shrugged. "Must be close. Give me a minute and I'll find it."

"Or," said Will, finally finding his normal register, "we turn around and go back to one of the other staircases?"

"This is being a catacomb!" Balur sounded offended. "You are going into catacombs to be murdering monsters, not to pussy out of the fight when you finally come across it after two whole gods-hexed days of waiting."

"I just don't see why we would purposely wander into a fight we could actually avoid," said Will as if purposely taunting the lizard man with arguments he was incapable of understanding.

"It is being times like these," said Balur, "that I am wondering why we keep you around."

"You're sure they're close?" Lette wanted to be sure a fight was actually going to happen, before they got into the specifics of whether it was a good idea or not.

"They are being close," Balur said, turning around. "I can veritably be tasting their shit upon the air."

He walked away from them, tapping the rock wall. Glancing up and down. Lette didn't wait to see if Will wanted her to respond to some sort of bewildered look. She just followed her longtime partner and drew her sword.

"I am not understanding," Balur said after a minute's slow progress. "Where is this gods-hexed nest being?" He swept his sword at the air, which, as usual, failed to bleed. "We should be seeing signs of their devoured prey."

"What are kobolds even eating down here?" asked Will.

"Do I look like a biologist?" Lette was pretty sure she knew the answer to that one.

"We're more than a day below the surface of Avarra," Will pointed out. "I can't imagine that there are many fields of live-stock around here to keep them satisfied."

"Why are we making this complicated?" asked Balur. "All we are needing to do is to be finding an opening, to be finding a nest, and to be hitting things in the face until they are stopping breathing."

"Well, to find the nest," said Lette, "it would be helpful to see some evidence."

"Which is *why*," Will put in, "it would be good to know what they were eating so we would know what to look for."

"Okay," said Balur, "if I am not getting to kill kobolds in a minute, I am going to be killing Will."

"That," Will informed Balur, "is uncalled-for hostility."

Balur was on the verge of responding, quite possibly using the universal language of pummeling sense into someone with one's fists, when the first of the kobolds fell onto the ledge around them.

At first, Lette didn't know where they had come from. One moment there were no kobolds, the next three stood among them, snarling and spitting. Then there were five, then eight, then ten. One leapt at Balur and he swept his sword in a short, savage arc, splitting the thing almost in two, sending the bisected corpse flying out into space. Then there were briefly nine kobolds. Then thirteen. Fourteen.

Then Lette looked up. Then she understood. Kobolds were scrambling down the wall above them. Sharp yellow claws dug into crevices in the rock. Black eyes glittered like spurs of polished jet. She could just make out the darker shadows of cave entrances above. A score more kobolds emerged, flung themselves down, claws spread. Then she didn't have much more time for assessing the immediate situation, only to cut, and slice, and stab, and parry, and curse, and spit, and stab, and slash, and sidestep, and whirl, and curse, and stab, and twist, and stab, and stab, and stab.

Balur was whirling his swords around in great scything arcs, knocking bodies left and right, up and down, hurling them off the edge of the pathway in pieces. Kobolds fell screaming, claws slashing at the air. Balur was yelling, almost singing, emitting a sound of near-perfect joy even as kobolds clambered onto his back. He was bleeding liberally from gashes to his arms and forehead.

Will was stabbing and thrusting desperately, letting out short, barking yelps as he did so. He too bore wounds on his arms and legs, and he was already panting heavily.

Lette whirled, thrust her sword into the face of an oncoming monstrosity, yanked the blade back, and jammed it into the neck of another creature closing on her right. But even as she did so, she felt two heavy impacts against her left side and was sent staggering.

More kobolds were falling, their numbers pressing in tighter and tighter. Bodies were packed in a heaving mass along the path carved into the wall of the labyrinth. As the crowd shifted, so did she, and it was only a matter of time before she was pushed to the blind precipice, sent chasing down after so many of Balur's victims.

"There's too many!" she shouted. "We have to get out of here!"

"Pussy!" yelled Balur, using another sweep of a sword to

open up a momentary space in front of him, which was almost immediately refilled by thrashing red bodies, gnawing and clawing at him.

Lette was long past having her bravery challenged by a homicidal lizard man, though. She pushed toward Balur, hacking and slashing a path, picking up several more gashes as she went. They could not sustain this.

"To Balur!" she yelled at Will, but Will was as incapable of getting out of his current situation as Balur was of getting out of a whorehouse offering free beds for the night.

"Balur! To Will!" she shouted instead, changing the angle of the bloody path she was cutting through the kobolds.

Balur looked at her. "But this is being—"

Then a kobold jumped on his face. Balur ripped it away— taking off chunks of his cheeks as he did—and flung it out into space. It screamed as it plunged down and away. "Fine then," Balur grumbled, and began smashing a path through the kobolds toward Will.

Lette stood with her back to Balur, sandwiching Will between her body and the Analesians.

"Okay," said Lette after a few panting moments of respite. "Now we move."

Slowly they inched down the pathway, beating back the kobolds as they went. Lette felt dirt and dust and gravel grind beneath her feet. The musky, wet smell of sweating kobolds pressed in on all sides. Their heaving breath, Will panting, Balur shouting, "Come on, you fuckers! Test me! Test me!"

The kobolds shifted with them, keeping a safe distance but only just. Occasionally an adventurous creature would dart in, snapping at Balur, and he would whip his blade around to smash into the creature's neck. Then as he wrenched the weapon free, two or three would dart in on the opposite side, trying to take his legs. Each time, Balur got the blade back in time, but the window was closing. Lette herself nicked the gut of one the struggling kobolds. It screamed, an almost human sound emerging from around its massive protruding teeth, and then its intestines were tangling her feet. She almost tripped and it was a few harrowing seconds of smashing skulls and stabbing eyes before she established the safe zone again.

Her arms throbbed. Her breathing grew ragged. She could not keep this up indefinitely.

"We've got to get free of these things," she snapped over her shoulder to Balur.

"They are being kobolds." Balur sounded disgusted.

"They are being, Balur," Lette said acidly, "an absolute crap ton of kobolds. It would be embarrassing to tactically withdraw from one kobold. A crap ton is an acceptable number to tactically withdraw from and reassess one's life choices."

"Is there a nunnery around here I haven't seen?" asked Balur, kicking an adventurous kobold out into the void. There was an ugly snapping sound as its spine hit something on the way down.

"That is not okay to joke about!" Lette almost turned around to slash him across the back. A scar might get him to remember her point.

The kobolds surged then, some mass frenzy grasping them, and for a moment Lette had to forgo the pleasures of conversation. Hack, and thrust, and parry, and thrust, and hack, hack, hack away.

When they were done, the precipice was dangerously close.

"Fuck," she said, as her heel swiveled out over empty space. She pressed away from it, cutting for every shuffled inch. "They're trying to push us over."

"Maybe," said Will, "we're not that far from the bottom. Maybe that's where their food source is. If they push us down, then we're easy pickings."

"Wow," said Lette, only wowed by the vast inappropriateness

of his timing. "That seems like a really relevant insight to discuss at this juncture."

"Well." Will shoved past her, and for a moment she teetered dangerously. "Maybe we don't have far to go before we can safely jump down."

"Jump?" Lette grabbed on to the back of Will's shirt for support. He tottered backward with a short yell, and she had to hack the claws off some grabbing kobold before it could reach him.

"You want to get away from these fucking monsters, don't you?" said Will, ducking lunges from one of the larger kobolds.

"This is definitely being a tactical withdrawal we are talking about is it not?" asked Balur.

Lette ignored the lizard man. "Jump?" she said again.

"There." Will pointed while she fought desperately to save his oblivious life. "Twenty yards downhill, look. There's another staircase passing directly below us, maybe only ten feet down. Then there's another bisecting it. And…maybe…maybe that's a third, there." He pointed into blurry shadows. "That's three jumps and we put significant distance between us and these things. Enough distance to find some shadowed corner where we can hid—" He looked up from the ledge, and at Balur's back. "Where we can tactically withdraw until we're better positioned for our counterstrike," he said instead.

"Jump," Lette said, "ten feet down onto a staircase that is probably almost a millennia old, pray we don't fall off its unprotected edge or shatter its shoddy workmanship, and then repeat the experience one or two more times?"

"Or," said Will, "you know, eventually get overwhelmed."

"Be speaking for yourself," said Balur, trying to shake a hissing, snarling kobold off his free arm.

"Fine then." Gods, she had wanted Will to grow a pair, but now? Here? Will had always been a master of shitty timing.

"On the count of three," she told Balur. "Charge?"

"Charge?" asked Balur, finally flinging the kobold free from his arm. "Wheee!" And with that questionable battle cry, he lowered his shoulder and plunged into the ranks of kobolds.

Lette—just for a fraction of second—closed her eyes. *If he just waited for the count just one single gods-hexed time.*

Then she was off, running in the bastard's wake, dragging Will by the sleeve, waving her sword with the other arm in a desperate attempt to discourage any other kobolds from jumping.

They were just about to launch themselves when one kobold charged in below her guard, grabbed her by the ankles, and brought her crashing to the ground. She felt her jaw slam closed, the skin on her chin open in a hot gush, her teeth smash together, her brain rattle. She fought on instinct, trying to turn, but the thing was on her back. She could feel its sharp claws scrabbling at her, tearing her clothes, scoring her back. Its hot breath was on her neck. Drool trickled down onto her ear. Her swords were trapped awkwardly beneath her. She heaved, couldn't shove it. She felt its whole body tense.

Then it fell away. The weight gone. She scrambled to her feet. Will was standing there, holding his sword in both hands. Its blade was drenched in blood and gore.

He also seemed oblivious to the three kobolds about to gut him.

There would be time, Lette decided, to thank him later. For now she just pushed him out into space and followed him down.

He screamed. She jumped into the sound. Hard stone slapped the breath out of her. She felt herself roll, somersaulting backward, her head clattering against steps, dirt grinding beneath him.

"Fwah!" She tried to curse but couldn't quite get the word out.

A massive hand seized her arm, hoisted her aloft. Balur held her clear off the ground. The lizard man was grinning.

"For being a tactical withdrawal," he said, "this is not being so bad." And then, using her arm like a pendulum, Balur flung her off the edge of the stairs.

She landed better this time, kept her feet and her breath. Balur landed next to her. "Try that shit again," she said, "and you'll lose the hand."

Balur fluttered nictitating membranes at her. "You are always being such a romantic."

Will was scrabbling to his feet beside them. He glanced back. "One more jump," he said.

Lette looked back. The kobolds were flooding over the first lip, scrambling down the rock wall. As she watched, some leapt for the stairs they had made. A few fell short, falling screaming; others made it.

She jumped, landed, turned. Balur was crashing through the air. And Will, sprawling, arms spread. And gods, he was not going to make it. His desperate fingers clawed at stone just one unforgiving inch below the lip of the step. But almost instantly it was three inches, six…

And then she had him.

She was lying flat on her stomach, feeling the shouting strain in her shoulder. Will screamed. Then he realized he wasn't falling to his death. He looked up at her.

And gods…such good fucking eyes, gods hex him.

But she was smiling despite herself. "No you don't," she told him. "If anyone gets to kill you, it's me."

Then she heaved him up onto the stairs, and they were running again.

An hour later, they reached the bottom.

Lette looked around. It was, she supposed, pretty much what she would have expected. The world's largest stairwell. The ground was sandy in places, rocks studding it here and there, but mostly occupied by pillars of stone supporting the stairs above, and other staircases making landfall.

Will stared around, his brow creased. "Is this place really a labyrinth, or just really overdesigned?"

"Yes," sighed Balur, "that is totally being the relevant question."

Lette was a little more focused. "There has to be a champion around here somewhere." She peered down corridors of stone. "Avatars of the gods are hardly known for their subtlety."

"Wait," said Will, "have you fought a champion of the gods before? Because that sounds as impressive as... well, as a divine labyrinth of stairs, and, well..." He hesitated. "Well, I'm sort of shocked neither of you have bragged about it before."

Lette licked her lips. And she would like to have been offended, but actually that was a fair comment.

"So, no then," Will surmised from their collective hesitation.

"We were killing a demigod before," said Balur. "That is being very similar, and potentially more impressive."

"You told me about that," said Will. "And do we even know what a champion of the gods is?"

Lette again came up short on words. *Champion of the gods* had seemed such a definitive term when Firkin had originally said it. Still, how different from a demigod could it be?

"Well," said Balur, "it is obviously being some mortal warrior who did so well in combat he was being gifted with longevity and strength by Lawl himself. He will be a significant notch in my blade."

He sounded ridiculously sure of himself. And considering the mess with the kobolds, Lette wasn't sure it was a tone he should be striking right now. "Two things," she said. "One, *you* didn't kill the demigod, I did. And two, a champion of the gods is clearly of divine origin sent down here to earth. It's going to be some inhuman beast. You know they have a thing for animals."

Which wasn't necessarily clear, but she wasn't going to take that attitude from him.

"Five gold bulls says it is being a transformed mortal."

"Transformed into what?"

"Into anything. I am saying it was starting here on earth and was being divinely transformed."

"I'll take your money."

Will had wandered away from them. Probably he was looking for another situation for her to save his life in.

"Erm, guys!" he called back over his shoulder. "Guys, I think—"

"It is being a closed bet," Balur called to him. "I am not cutting you in now. Unless you are having a different wager you want to offer."

"You are such an ass," Lette told him. She was feeling unexpectedly protective of Will.

"That is being uncalled for," said Balur.

"I think I found—" Will said.

"Not you cutting him out of the bet," Lette covered. Being protective of Will in front of Balur was likely to lead to awkward questions. "Your whole smug, superior attitude. As if you know what a champion of Lawl is."

"You are being the one who is obstinately insisting it is being a divine creature!"

"Just because you won't stop being such a pretentious prick about it being profane!"

"Well, I am just thinking that it is standing to reason that to be a champion one must—"

"That is exactly the gods-hexed attitude I'm talking about."

And then Will tapped her on the shoulder, and she almost cut his throat.

"Erm," he managed, "so...I think I found the champion."

39

The Champion and the Thief

Lette and Balur brought dual interrogative stares to bear on Will. "Well," he said, "unless you can think of any other golden archways full of light that might be hanging around down here."

He showed them the way. As they drew closer he saw the arch was more ornate than he had initially thought. It was indeed made of gold, and it did indeed ripple with reflected firelight, but he had not seen the delicacy and the detail in the carvings. Gold had been fashioned into branches and ivy, as if an entire bower had been dipped into molten metal and preserved. It was breathtaking in its beauty.

Will couldn't help but reach out and tap a metal leaf as he passed under the arch. But instead of the soft tink of fingernail against metal, it rang out with a sonorous chime, bright and clear, like a church bell on a summer morning.

They all came to a very abrupt halt.

Fucking divinities, thought Will. *They just couldn't let anything be simple, could they? They had to show off. Every pissing time.*

Somewhere in the glow beyond, something rumbled. There was a gravity to the sound, a weight that went beyond human, a rumbling that echoed in Will's gut, and his mind, and... somewhere else too? It was a sound too profound to be wholly of this world.

"Okay," whispered Lette, "that's of divine origin. Pay up."

Balur spat back out into the gloomy dirt of the cave. "Be pissing on that. You are having no proof."

"You know what?" Fear and irritation were both scrabbling at the inside of Will's bowels. "How about you two stay here and piss about, and I go in there and sort it out?"

Balur and Lette looked at each other. Then Balur shrugged. "You are knowing what? I am being fine with that."

Lette slapped him on the shoulder. "You ass. You are meant to be a hulking great barbarian, hungry for blood and glory. You don't let a farmer go to the slaughter."

Balur shrugged. "It is being like a miner bringing a canary below the earth. If the farmer can be defeating it, it is not being worthy of me fighting it."

"You have an ego the size of—"

Will made a decision. And part of it was that he just couldn't take it. He had come too close to death, and now he was too close to victory. This permanent bickering was too much. He loved Lette, he truly did, but right now he just needed . . . gods.

And part of it was . . . he loved Lette. And "a farmer" had stung just a little bit, because even if he thought of himself that way, it was nice that she didn't. And he had caught the look in her eyes when she had caught him as he almost fell to his death among the stairs, and he remembered the look they had exchanged last night. And maybe they could recapture something. But not if he was just "a farmer."

So he stepped through the arch and into the space beyond.

It was less glorious than he had expected. The gold stretched no farther than the arch. The floor and walls were the same rock that enclosed the world outside. But candles and torches had been shoved into the walls, giving the space a soft warm glow, and living ivy grew on the walls, lending it a softness that had been absent from the labyrinth outside.

The space was less imposing than that impossible cavern. It stretched back perhaps fifty yards and was at best half as many wide, and the ceiling was visible twenty yards above his head, vaulting but at least a conceivable distance. Broken columns lined the walls, interspersed with statues worn by age until they were almost featureless. The remnants of a few friezes were on the walls, a few faded figures peering through centuries of collected grime and smoke. Sections of a crumbling mosaic still dotted the floor, brief flashes of red and blue among the dust and dirt.

Will glimpsed all this in a moment, and had the impression of a space more careworn than battered or broken. The place felt redolent with age. This was a home.

And then he saw what it was home to, and he stopped thinking about the space at all.

The champion of Lawl lay slumped at the far end of the hall. Indeed, he was almost all of the far end of the hall. He was vast, far larger than the giants Will had heard of in tales. If he had been standing he must have been twenty feet tall at least. Everything about him was massive. His shoulders were broad the way a grassy plain was broad. His arms were thick the way that trees that had seen the pantheon breathe life onto the earth in the dawn of creation were thick. His breath gusted out, and Will saw all torch flames in the room flicker with it. He felt it blow over his skin like the warm breeze of distant bellows.

The champion was encased in armor, a suit of charcoal gray steel embossed with bright gold filigree. Not an inch of skin was visible. Within the vast helmet narrow opening, where a face might be, there was only shadow. And Will found he was not wholly sure that there was skin beneath that steel. Maybe the steel was the skin. Maybe Lette was right and this was a wholly divine creation.

How did they kill something like that?

And then he heard the deep regular rumble of its breath, and realized that perhaps they did not have to.

He turned back to the archway. Lette and Balur were standing there, staring at him. "It's asleep," he whispered.

He looked back, and now that the initial shock was over he saw the champion more clearly. He was sprawled on his back, propped up by some of the columns, legs spreading across the hall. One arm flopped out down the length of the cave toward him, the palm laying faceup, fingers curling toward the ceiling like the corpse of some vast five-legged spider. And between those fingers, lying on that palm...

A golden chalice.

It was a stunning thing, studded with rubies, sapphires, and emeralds. And it would have looked large in any palm but the champion's. And all Will had to do was to walk down to the end of the room and take it.

"I can see Barph's Strength," he said back over his shoulder. And then with a growing sense of certainty and elation, "I can get it."

He started to shuffle forward, placing one foot before the other as silently as possible.

"Get back here!" Lette hissed. "You're a gods-hexed farmer, and I wouldn't trust you to sneak up on a chicken. Let a professional do this."

But that only spurred Will on harder. Perhaps he could not wield a sword, but he could do this. He would prove his gods-hexed worth to her. He would show her that he was not to be dismissed. That she could count on him for more than a half-thought-out plan formulated in a tavern, with ale to strengthen his resolve. He would take Barph's Strength from this so-called champion, and he would turn the tide of this war. Him. Alone. And maybe, just maybe, she would remember why she had loved him.

He inched forward. He would not rush this. He would do this right.

There was a scuffle behind him.

"Get off me," he heard Lette snap.

"He is doing it now. Just let him get swatted and then we shall be having our great battle."

"Your greatest battle is squeezing your swollen head through most doorways."

Will shuffled forward. He did not remember fifty yards being this far.

"It is being easier to get my swollen head through a doorway than your fat arse."

"Let's see how many doorways you get through while you're trying to hold your guts inside your wilting stomach."

"Shh!" he hissed back at them. Doing this right was hard enough without their squabbling.

Merciful silence fell. Twenty more yards. One foot in front of the other. Scanning the ground for anything that might crunch, or crack, or give him away. Ten more yards. The champion's breath wafting over him now. He could smell it, stale and thick, and he grimaced. Divine champion or not, this creature smelled little better than Firkin did on a hot afternoon.

Just a yard away. He held his breath. The palm laid out in front of him. A snort, half a snore from the champion, and Will almost shat himself. The fingers on the massive hand twitched and the chalice wobbled.

For a moment everything was still. Even Will's heart in his chest. The champion let out another grumbling sound, then farted massively. The chamber rang with the sound. Will threw up an arm to cover his face and tried desperately not to gag as the stench billowed over him. His eyes watered.

Champion of what? Fucking gastric belligerence?

The champion burbled once more, then settled. Will stood, slowly breathing into his elbow, waiting for his eyes to stop streaming.

It did not help that he could hear Balur snickering.

Finally all was still once more. The palm was still laid out before him. It was the size of a dinner platter, and as thick as his thigh. Each finger was as big as his forearm. The chalice, large and ornate as it was, looked fragile in that massive hand.

He won't even notice it's gone, Will told himself. *Its weight is nothing to him.*

He exhaled very slowly, tried to let calm enter him, saturate his mind. It didn't work. He blew out another breath. His nerve continued to fail to show up.

"Get on with it then," hissed Lette from the doorway, which really didn't help because the last thing he needed right now was more sound to wake this monster up.

But the monster didn't wake up, and Will did become more and more aware that the whole point of this stupid, stupid exercise was to impress Lette, and just standing here, desperately trying to keep the shit out of his britches, was probably not going to achieve that objective.

He closed his eyes, realized how stupid that was too, opened them, reached out, and snatched the cup from the champion's massive palm in one quick darting motion.

And he had done it. He held the chalice in his hand. He could feel liquid sloshing inside it. He could feel gems pressing into his skin. The smoothness of its metal. The heat emanating up from the champion's palm. He thought he heard Lette gasp a little.

He had fucking done it.

And then the champion's fist closed like a bear trap snapping shut, and held his arm like a vise.

40

Peace Talks

"So, that was pretty much a shit show."

Quirk looked up and found Afrit looking down at her. She looked away. She couldn't. She just couldn't.

She was sitting in some abandoned ruin of a temple in some abandoned ruin of a district in Vinter. Her arse rested on crumbling sandstone, and her knees were pulled up to her chest, a half-empty wineskin sprawled on the ground between her feet. The other half of its contents had been spilled down her throat. Around her the beaten and bloody members of Firkin's faithful lay slumped in similar states of depression and drunkenness.

Quirk stared at the wilting, flaccid wineskin. It wasn't good wine. The back of her throat burned with its sour bite. Gods, it wasn't even a good wineskin. It was leaking slightly along one seam.

"I feel like such a fool," she managed.

Afrit put a hand on her shoulder. Quirk looked up at her. And there was sadness written across Afrit's face. Not hatred. Not accusation. Not disgust. Sadness. Fucking sympathy.

"No," she said. "That's not right. That's not deserved. I don't feel like a fool. I feel like..." She swallowed. "When I was with Hethren," Quirk said to Afrit, "I killed so many people. Hundreds. More probably. But I don't know if I ever killed as many in one day as I did today. I feel like a fucking murderer."

"Hey. Hey. Hey." Afrit put both hands on her now, holding her by the arms. There were ugly murmurs coming from around them. But Quirk was pretty sure they were deserved too. Hiding from her mistakes... that was just more cowardice. Just another betrayal of these people.

"You're drunk," Afrit said in the same soothing voice. "Let's get you out of here, get some fresh air."

Quirk pulled away. "Not drunk enough," she said. "I still know what I did." She reached down and shook the wineskin. It sloshed lazily. "Useless piss is what this is."

"Come on," said Afrit, steering her gently, and Quirk did not truly have the energy for any more fistfights today. So she gave in and allowed herself to be steered.

The cold air of the Vinter night bit at her after the stifling environs of the temple. Its narrow corridors were packed with bodies. All the dregs of Firkin's supporters had washed up here, at this broken-down temple. All of them had been routed. All had been hacked at, and pushed back, and scattered. No one was sure where Firkin was.

She and Afrit stood next to each other staring out at a city littered with the dead.

"Back in Tamar," said Afrit, not quite looking at Quirk, "back home." She licked her lips. "We talked about power. About how it was good to be nervous about power, you and I, to not truly want it. We talked about how power corrupts."

Quirk opened her mouth. She didn't even mean to. It was simply automatic. Because that felt unfair. Everything she had done, she had done to try to protect these people. Everything she had done had been selfless.

But, no. She was not here to argue her case. She was here because whatever her intentions, this had become an absolute shit show.

"I know." Afrit's words softly spread into the silence Quirk couldn't fill with excuses. "I know." She nodded, but still not quite meeting Quirk's eye, staring into the space over her shoulder, the glimmers of yellow light leaking out of the battered temple. "You had all the best reasons. You weren't doing it for yourself. You hadn't asked for the power. It was given to you. Forced upon you, even. Right?" A smile flickered nervously across Afrit's face. "I'm a student of practical politics, Quirk. I know this story." And for a moment her eyes did meet Quirk's. "It's a pretty common argument really." She shrugged. "History never seems to judge them kindly."

Quirk blew out a breath. And this was a knife that cut very close to the bone. And it hurt. But she would not flinch. She would not.

But Afrit seemed out of words. Quirk, licked her lips. "So…" she said, and then that was all she had. Her mouth was dry. Thought stalled out. And then because it was, in the end, probably better to say it out loud than to just keep it in her head, even if it was harder: "What in the Hallows do we do now?"

Afrit hummed and hawed. "Well," she said after a pause, "historically speaking, typically what happens is the masses turn on you, and some sort of punishment is meted out."

"Oh," said Quirk, discovering she felt rather sanguine about that. "All right then."

Afrit grimaced at the world over Quirk's shoulder. "That's always seemed a bit of a cop-out to me, though." She pushed a hand through her dark curls. They had once been contained in neat braids, but in the months on the road and in the Vale her hair had grown into an unruly thicket. It was a good look on her, Quirk had thought. "The story I always like to teach, instead," Afrit went on, "is about Thadderick of the Vost duchy. The Five Duchies are always such a shit show they're always great for examples. Anyway, at the time we're talking about, the Nettat duchy was the strongman, and it was throwing its weight around a lot. And its favorite tactic was to beat up on the Vost duchy. Nettat was making a threat to the other three duchies. It was saying, this could be you. Piss us off and we'll beat up on you like we're beating up on Vost. And it worked. The Vost duchy was weak, and the other three duchies stayed in line for fear of turning the Nettat duchy's fury on them.

"Obviously for the people in the Vost duchy, this was a pretty bad situation. And so it created a number of resistance groups. And the most successful of these was led by a man named Thadderick. And here I normally give a number of lectures about how he ended up in charge of all the resistance efforts, but just suffice it to say that he did. It's one of the rare cases in history where competence outweighs a lack of ambition. And so he drew up his battle plan, and he led the united resistance forces of the Vost duchy against the Nettat duchy."

She fell silent for a moment. "It was a disaster, by the way" she said. "Thadderick blew it massively. Despite him being ostensibly in charge, the resistance was a fractured mess. The whole attack was terribly coordinated. Thadderick didn't have it in him to command them all."

"This," Quirk commented, "is not the best pep talk I've ever received."

Afrit smiled, her first genuine one of the evening. She even met Quirk's eye. "Academia is not known for encouraging its succinct storytelling." She massaged the back of her neck. "But next Thadderick did something that's almost unique in history. He gave up his power. He admitted to his mistakes, and instead he formed a truly democratic resistance army. Every general he had stood above suddenly had a vote that was worth just as much as his. And what's more, he didn't limit this to just Vostonians. It was open to everybody. It was open to the Corr duchy, the Tull duchy, and the Setow duchy too. All of the duchies could unite. All could be powerful. And just for a moment, for just long enough...it worked. They came together. All of them. And they kicked the Nettat duchy's arse so hard, it's still not able to sit down three hundred years later."

Quirk nodded slowly. "Okay," she said. "I get it."

Afrit reached out and put a hand on her shoulder. "Good." And for just a little while they stayed like that and Quirk felt peaceful for the first time in...gods, how long?

Then Afrit caught her eye. "I'm sorry. I have to check," she said. "I meant that you need to—"

"Yes, yes." Quirk sighed. "I'm going to talk to gods-hexed Firkin already."

He showed up the next morning. He seemed as uncertain as anybody of where he'd been. "I dabble in being located in space and time, all right?" he snapped when Quirk pushed him. "I can't be held accountable for keeping track of both. It's a lot to know. Anyway, where am I?"

Durmitt was with him, with hangdog eyes, a bandage around his scalp, and a pitcher the size of a small child that he was sipping directly from.

They found a quiet room away from the others and all stood around staring at each other. Afrit had her hand on Quirk's shoulder again. Quirk tried to work out how to put everything into words. Then she heard a shout of pain from elsewhere in the temple. A chirurgeon had arrived that morning and was seeing to some of the wounded. And then the words weren't so hard.

"I'm sorry," she said. "I screwed this up. I tried to force my will upon others. I was everything I'm fighting against. I lost my way. I want to find it back." And then she could even say, "I need your help."

Firkin wrinkled his nose, then spat a wad of brown phlegm into the corner of the room.

"I don't *help*," he said with scorn. "I am not helpful. I am...I am...." He rubbed his head violently.

Something really was wrong with him. And Quirk found she still had some compassion left for him. She reached out and held his hand. His skin felt papery and thin. "What do you want, Firkin?" she said.

"Peace," he said to the table. "Peace and fucking quiet." He sounded his age as he said it.

"You know the dragons won't give it to us," she said gently. "Don't you? That there can be no peace under them. Things will only get worse." She waited for him to respond but he just kept his head down on the table. "We have to fight now for peace later. Or else we'll always be fighting. Fighting or dead."

Finally Firkin looked up and spat. "Fucking dragons."

"You want to fight the dragons?" Quirk pressed.

"Authoritarian arseholes," Firkin said. "Deserve to be dick-punched."

This, Quirk supposed, approximated progress.

"I want to help you dick-punch dragons," she told him. Afrit twitched next to her. If it was with laughter they were going to have words later.

Firkin flapped a hand at the door behind them. "So be going and doing it. Leave me to my beverage."

Durmitt picked up on the hint and passed Firkin the pitcher again, albeit with a slightly regretful look.

"That doesn't work." Quirk really wanted him to see. "I can't do this on my own. I need your help. I need Afrit's. I need Durmitt's."

Durmitt looked thoroughly terrified by this prospect.

Afrit shifted her hand from Quirk's shoulder to her arm. Quirk really wished she would stop that.

"How would you stop the dragons?" Afrit said, leaning toward Firkin.

"Dick punches!" Firkin cried. "I finally speak my own words, and no one listens!"

"Okay." Quirk managed to summon a chastised expression. "I'm sorry. You did say that." Firkin appeared to be somewhat mollified. "So," she went on, "we need an army to dick-punch the dragons. And," she added, pointing to the door, "out there you have the start of an army, don't you?"

Firkin looked at her suspiciously. "You want me to say things, don't you?" he said. "You want me to tell them to dick-punch dragons."

"Well…" Quirk hedged.

Firkin gave her a sickly smile. "Talking is…" He grimaced, leaned toward her. "Someone took a shit in my skull," he whispered. "Some skull shitter was in there. And it's a fucking sentient brain turd. You understand? There's a talking shit in my brain."

Quirk, really, *really* did not understand. She tried to put on her most sympathetic face. "I'm sorry," she said. "I just don't understand. What's wrong, Firkin?"

"You want me to talk," he said. "But the brain shit might be waking up and he might not want to dick-punch dragons. Might have some strong moral opposition to dick punches. Might be afeared of them himself. Maybe had a terrible dick punch in his formative years and he can't stand them no more."

Afrit leaned forward and nodded understandingly. "You want peace and quiet," she said. "We want to give it to you. But there's a mile to go before you can get it. And it's not because of us. It's because of the dragons. You understand that?"

Firkin spat. "Fucking dragons," he said again.

Quirk tried to push forward. "You don't want to talk much. You want to give the, erm…brain shit as little chance as possible to talk. We all want that. But that means you need to tell everyone to listen to us. To convince them. If that's what you want."

Firkin stared at Afrit, then at Quirk, then at Durmitt, then at Durmitt's pitcher. He seemed to like the pitcher the most. Durmitt pushed it over with a sigh.

"No offense," Durmitt said, watching with sad eyes as Firkin drained the jug, "but he might have to do a lot of work to sell the pair of you. I don't know if there's much love these days. Not after how everything went."

Again excuses leapt to Quirk's mind unbidden. She breathed. She was listening to other people's advice. "Is there anything we can do to help?" she asked.

Durmitt shrugged. "I don't know. No one wants my opinion. My missus don't even want my opinion."

"I do."

Durmitt seemed caught off balance by her honesty. "I don't know." He grimaced. "I guess to most folk you seem…a bit sober?"

Quirk thought she was going to throw up.

She blinked, tried to focus. Firkin was at one end of what must have once been a large meeting room. A table was serving as a makeshift altar. The roof of the place was gone, and stars winked and flickered in the dark sky above. And she was hammered.

There had to be easier ways to save the world than this.

"—bit of an arse-kicking," Firkin was saying. "Fucked everything up really." He nodded at the crowd. They seemed rather low energy to Quirk. She should probably try to get them more riled up. She whooped. Nobody seemed to respond.

"Bit of an arse that, isn't it?" said Firkin. He was rubbing the side of his head with his palm again. "Hard to kick someone else's arse while they're kicking your arse. You're all the wrong end of the arse, and trying to get your foot round them." He gulped wine. "Arse punching might be a better idea."

"You said we'd tear the city a new arsehole!" someone shouted from the back of the crowd. They sounded belligerent and accusatory. "You said it would be different, that we'd take things back from the High Priests. Now it's worse than ever."

"Well," said Firkin, frowning, "I don't see how that's on me. I was very successful when I told you to rip them a new arsehole. You're the ones who fucked it up."

Which did little to endear Firkin to the crowd. And Quirk realized there was nothing else for it, she was going to have to stand up. When she finally made it to both feet she was sweating and felt nauseous.

"Us!" she shouted, pointing at herself and Afrit, who was still sprawled on the floor. "This is the bit when you introduce us."

But Firkin still couldn't hear her. The crowd was moving now, on their feet, a herd of belligerent beasts, sweating their anger out into the room. There was shouting, the sound of tempers fraying, and furniture breaking.

"Shut up!" Firkin screeched. "You want this city? You nut up and you fight for this city. You don't treat it like a party." His voice screeched higher, wavering at its breaking point. "Oooh, I'm bleeding. I better go home now." He spat. "Of course you're fucking bleeding. They're soldiers. They have pointy bits of metal. So make them bleed. Bring your own pointy metal. You're meant to be anarchists and drunks. Not gods-hexed idiots."

Which seemed pretty much like it was the crowd's breaking point. They roared, a single violent rejection of this new petulant, angry Firkin. This Firkin who had brought them defeat instead of victory. This Firkin who blamed them.

Quirk stumbled forward. She had to get to Firkin. She suddenly really, really wanted to be sober. Her body felt distant and clumsy. She stumbled. She heard the crack of the makeshift altar breaking. Everyone else here was so much more practiced at being drunk than she was.

"SHUT UP!"

Firkin's roar thundered through her. Her whole body quaked with the sound of it. For a second all she was, was the sound. She could feel its echoes thrumming through her blood, her guts. It was a desire transmitted directly into her soul. She could no more deny it than she could will her heart to stop beating.

Absolute silence rang out through the room. There was not

even the creak of people shifting their weight. Not the clink of coin purses against belt buckles. Not a sound.

"GET AWAY FROM ME!"

Breathing rapidly, Quirk found herself backing away from the altar. All of the crowd moved with her, tiptoeing and clutching at any loose clothing that could flap or clank.

Firkin emerged from the locus of the crowd. He held himself differently now, no longer stooped and cowed, no longer clutching at his temples. He shoulders were thrust back, an almost regal expression of disdain upon his face. Quirk couldn't look away, couldn't even glance over her shoulder to see if Afrit was witnessing this transformation.

She had glimpsed this, she knew, back in the cells beneath the High Temple. A momentary look behind the curtain at this thing. But she hadn't understood. She still didn't. What was this? What could this possibly be?

"BLOOD AND WINE, I TELL YOU," Firkin thundered. It almost seemed impossible that he could generate such volume. Blood was trickling in a thin stream from his nose. And Quirk felt ashamed at the scorn she heard in his voice. "AND YOU BRING ME WINE, BUT WHERE IS MY BLOOD?"

And still there was nothing but silence, everyone frozen by the question. And Quirk felt the shame pressing down and down on her like a force.

"I WILL GIVE YOU THIS CITY. I WILL DELIVER ITS QUIVERING CORPSE INTO YOUR GREEDY HANDS. AND YOU CAN FEAST UPON IT. YOU CAN STRING THE HIGH PRIESTS FROM THE SPIRES OF BARPH'S CATHEDRALS. BUT YOU MUST BRING ME BLOOD AND WINE."

Firkin stared out balefully. No one stirred.

"WELL?" Firkin demanded. Both his nostrils were streaming blood now. It sprayed as he spoke. "WILL YOU BRING ME BLOOD WITH MY WINE?"

Another moment's hesitation. And then Quirk found she was

cheering. She had to be cheering. She had to scream that, yes, yes, she would. Of course she would. How could she not? Everyone screamed.

"Good." Finally Firkin eased off the volume. Finally the pressure of his will seemed to lift up off her mind. But she could still feel it buzzing in her like the alcohol she had poured in there. And she was aware of an enormous dryness at the back of her throat, a thirst growing.

"Good," Firkin said again. "And I know you ask yourselves, How? How shall I do this? Well, look at yourselves. See what the priests see. Because they see nothing. You are nothing to them. You are weak and useless and pathetic, and they spit at you."

Again Quirk felt ashamed, but there was anger in the shame now.

"That is your strength." Firkin almost crooned the words. "That is why you will beat them. Because they cannot see the truth. You are invisible. Because you can slip in among them, unseen. Because you can infiltrate and destroy."

And it would work, Quirk realized. Of course it would work. The High Priests were utterly unprepared for such an attack. How had she not seen that?

"Be the piss in their vinegar!" Firkin shouted. "Be the shit in their shoes!"

The energy in the room was rising again, soaring upward. Because they would rise. They would rise, and rip, and tear, and take back this city, just the way Firkin said.

"This woman." Firkin pointed, and suddenly Quirk found herself staring directly at his finger. She felt the whole focus of the room come crashing down on her, assaulting her from all sides. The crowd leaned toward her, as if giving in to some unseen pressure directed by Firkin's outstretched digit. She felt pinned. "She will tell you where to go, what and who to strike. Listen to her." The command was absolute. There was no threat of consequences. There was no need of them. There would be no disobedience.

Then Firkin let out a huge breath, his body sagging backward, almost collapsing. He stumbled a step, steadied himself against the table. He reached for a bottle of wine with a shaky hand.

The crowd hesitated, stared a second. Then they lost their collective mind. They roared, they screamed. They charged forward, grabbed Firkin, and raised him up unto their shoulders. They bore him aloft around the room, bellowing his name. They were, Quirk realized, ready for war.

41

Breakfast of Champions

Oh gods, thought Will, *it's actually going to happen. I'm actually going to shit myself in front of Lette.*

And then he realized he was going to die. Messily, and painfully. First Lawl's champion was going to crush his arm. And then, as he lay bleeding out and screaming on the floor, the rest of his body would be mashed to a pulp by that massive fist piece by bloody piece.

"No!" The champion's voice was like a trumpet blast from the armies of heaven.

"I—" Will heard himself say. "I'm sorry." He tried to let go of the chalice containing Barph's Strength, but his hand was held too tightly.

The champion sat up. And Will truly got to appreciate the size of him as he sat and rolled one shoulder and craned his neck. His hand was so large it swallowed Will's arm above the elbow. He did not relax his grip on Will for a moment, but he did not crush him either. The steel of his armor clattered and clanked. In the impenetrable shadows of his helmet, two eyes of red mist floated.

"No," said Lawl's champion again. "I pour."

And then, with surprising delicacy, Lawl's champion plucked the golden goblet from Will's trapped hand and released him.

Will stood there gasping from shock, still braced for death, for the backhand that would smash him against the rock wall.

Lawl's champion reached one massive hand up and massaged the side of his helmet. "Oh my head," he said. "I got so shitfaced last night."

Will blinked. Something was happening. He didn't know what. He looked desperately back at the golden archway. But Balur and Lette were not in evidence at all. Did he run away now?

The champion reached out and rummaged in some discarded pots and pans. "Here it is," he said, collapsing back and adjusting his codpiece. He held out a hand to Will. In it was a pewter tankard. Again using a delicacy that surprised Will, he poured dark red liquid from the golden goblet, filling the tankard below.

"Bottoms up," the champion said, and he raised the golden goblet to his lips. And poured. And poured. And poured. Will could hear the liquid flowing, splashing down into the confines of that shadowed mouth. It went on and on. Impossibly on.

It never runs dry. Will remembered Firkin's words.

And this was it. This was Barph's Strength. This was what he was meant to deliver to the world above. This was what could save them from the dragons.

And the champion wanted him to drink it?

Was this a test? Would the unworthy be melted from their stomach outward? Was it meant to make him worthy to fight the champion?

He was still staring at his tankard when the champion finally stopped tipping his back. The great creature smacked his lips. "Fuck me," he said in his voice like thunder. "That is better." Then he turned great smoky red eyes on Will. They flickered and billowed in the confines of his great helmet.

"Drink!" he bellowed at Will. "Drink! Drink! Drink!"

Hand shaking, Will raised the cup to his lips. The smell of grapes and alcohol surrounded him, swallowed him. Visions of sunny afternoons spent on grassy hillsides exploded in his head. Of running through a vineyard chasing giggling naked creatures. Of drowsing in the dappled shadows of a tree. Summer, and fruit, and joy.

And then he drank.

"Your thumb is enormous," Will said. It seemed incredibly relevant.

"Like a baby pig," said the champion.

And that blew Will's mind. "Oh gods!" he said. "It's exactly the same size as a baby pig. You have pig thumbs."

The champion wiggled both his thumbs at Will. "Porky," he said.

Will laughed so hard he threw up.

At some point, Will was pretty sure there had been a point to all this. He had come here for something. And he was also pretty confident that if he wanted to he could remember what that thing was. He just didn't want to right now. Why in the gods would he want to? Drinking Barph's Strength was like drinking happiness. Every time he took a sip it was like his mouth was having an orgasm.

He had taken a lot of sips.

"You know," the champion said, and then looked around quickly.

Will looked around too. Maybe there were people here.

Holy shit! Lette and Balur were here somewhere. They should totally try this drink!

Wait...Wait...There was a problem with that. Wait...He almost had it. He...They were *hiding*! He tapped his forehead. He remembered now.

"I don't," Will told him.

"Don't what?" The champion cocked his helmeted head to one side.

"Don't know," Will said.

"Don't know what?" asked the champion.

"I don't know," said Will.

The champion's glowing red eyes blinked twice. "Why are you telling me then?"

"I wasn't," Will told him. "You told me."

The champion thought about this for a moment. "I have thumbs the size of baby pigs," he said after a while.

"You totally do," said Will. "I was a farmer. I've seen tons of baby pigs. Those thumbs are the exact size of baby pigs. We could show them at fairs and win like … a shit ton of gold."

"That's a brilliant idea," said the champion.

"Right?" said Will, nodding vigorously.

"Except," said the champion.

"No!" Will shouted at him. "No! No 'except'! We're going to go to village fairs and show your thumbs and be rich. Rich!" He decided to drink a bit more just in case.

"I can't leave here," said the champion.

Will tried to process that. "Where?" he said eventually.

"Here." The champion pointed to the ground.

"Your fingers are massive," Will told him.

"Like full-grown pigs," said the champion.

"Fuck." Will's mind was irrevocably blown.

"You know," said the champion with another furtive glance.

"Still no," said Will.

"Still?"

"You still haven't told me," said Will.

"Told you what?"

"I don't know," said Will.

The champion sat up slightly, shifted his weight. One of his vast legs swung perilously close to Will's nose. They were propped up on opposite sides of the champion's chamber, facing each other. Will was vaguely aware that too sudden a move from the champion could end his life pretty quickly, but as a counterpoint … moving seemed really hard right now.

"Why can't you leave?" asked Will.

"Where?"

"Here." Will was pretty sure he was right on that one.

"Who says I can't?" The champion leaned forward aggressively. Some warning bell tolled in Will's head, but it had been drowned in a lake of alcohol a long time ago and its sounding was distant.

"You," Will said.

"Oh." The champion leaned back. "Yes. That's fair. Lawl says. He said not to leave. Very strict about the whole thing. He's always strict, he is."

"Why?" said Will again.

The champion shrugged. "His nature I suppose. Though, you know, you know..." He leaned forward. "I wonder, you know, do we worship the gods because of their natures, or do they have their nature because of us worshipping them? I mean, is Lawl the god of law, and therefore we have laws, or do we have laws, and so we have to have Lawl? Did our need create him? I mean, in that case, he's sort of subservient to us, and it's all backwards. Right?" He tapped the side of his head with one pig-sized finger. "Right?"

"No," said Will. "I meant why does Lawl say can't you leave?"

"Oh." The champion sounded disappointed.

"Though," said Will, attempting to rally, "I mean, yeah, that's totally, you know, like, whoa."

"Right?" said the champion again, sounding more satisfied. "But, yeah..." He blinked several times, stared into space. "I can't leave because...He said I can't leave because..." He took a big swig. "Gods, he went on and on about it at the time." He drank again, stared about the room.

"Oh shit!" he exclaimed, so suddenly Will almost fell over. He struck a gauntleted palm to his helmeted head with a sonorous gong. "The cup. I'm even holding it. Have to stay and guard it. Can't let...let it leave." He nodded. "Yeah, has to stay here."

"That's a shit rule," said Will. He felt expansive and capable of criticizing the wisdom of the gods. "You have to rise up!" he shouted. "You have to rebel!"

"Shhh!" The champion placed a finger to the shadows of his helmet. "He might hear you."

"Yeah!" Will shouted. "Hear me, Lawl! You're an oppressor. You're oppressing my friend. He's awesome and you're... you're..." He needed a word. A big word. A damning word. "You're...*not*."

"Shut up!" hissed the champion.

"What?" Will said. "You should, like, stand up for yourself and stuff."

The champion looked about furtively again. "You know"—he leaned forward, so his face was only a few feet in front of Will's—"I'm not meant to drink the wine." The champion pulled back sharply, looking left and right, snapping his head from side to side. Will almost fell into the sudden void before him.

"You're..." He furrowed his brow and tried very hard to understand. "The wine...Why would...? Why couldn't you...?"

"Shh!" hissed the champion, still looking around wildly. "He might hear you."

"Who?" Will was having trouble following all of this.

"Lawl!" The champion ducked his head as if trying to avoid some invisible cuffing hand.

"Is he here?" Will searched around. If Lawl was here, then the god might know Lette and Balur were here. And he was pretty sure no one was meant to know that they were here.

Because...

Reasons. Probably.

"Fuck!" shouted the champion, who flailed in an attempt to curl up in a ball at the end of the chamber with one hand over his head. "I didn't do it!" he shouted. "It was him!" He pointed a massive finger at Will.

"The fuck?" asked Will, still looking around. The chamber was still empty.

The champion looked up and about. "Wait..." he said. "You said Lawl was here."

"I asked if he was here." Will was at least 90 percent sure that was true. There was a fog in his mind that was eating up memories with a voracious appetite.

"Gods," said the champion in a ruffled tone. "If he catches me..." He shook his head. Then they drank some more.

"Have you ever seen him?" Will asked.

"Who?" The champion's head was nodding now. He sounded sleepy.

"Lawl," Will said and yawned.

"No." The champion shook his head slowly. "He just, you know, created me, and dumped me here, and then his instructions rang out in a voice like, you know, thunder and shit. But then, you know, it's been eight hundred years, and a man gets thirsty." He shrugged. "Why?" he asked.

"Oh." Will shook his head. "Nothing. It's just..." He shrugged too. "I was thinking, his fingers must be like cows or something."

The champion nodded ruminatively. "Yeah," he said, but it was clear his heart wasn't in it. Then with a noise like the end of the world he stood up. His armor clanked and clanged as he bounced off the walls, trying to prop himself up on unsteady feet.

"Got to go piss," he rumbled. He still had in his hand, Will noticed, the golden goblet containing Barph's Strength.

Something fought through the fug of inebriation and sleep in his mind. Some mighty lone warrior of a thought battling desperately to make its way to the forefront of his cortex.

The chalice! He had wanted to get the chalice away from the champion. That was why he had come here. That was it! He had known he had known.

"Can I," he said, not making eye contact, and sweating profusely, "grab a sip while you're gone?" He held out a hand for the chalice. "I'm parched."

The champion hopped from foot to foot. "Can't let it out of my sight," he said. "Got instructions. Wait till I get back."

"Aww come on," Will wheedled, but the champion was ignoring him. He squeezed into the shadows between two pillars and Will heard his heavy footsteps retreating away. Apparently there was some tunnel Will had been previously unaware of.

"Pssst!" A hiss came out of nowhere. Will stared about, trying to place the sound in his mental lexicon of noises, as much as in the space around him.

"Pssst!" The sound came again. It was, he realized, coming from the archway through which he had entered the chamber. He stared hard at it, forcing his eyes to focus.

Lette! He could see Lette! Pretty, wonderful, smart, funny Lette.

"Hey!" he called out, waving both hands. "You're here!"

"Shut up, you idiot," came the hissing reply.

Oh, Lette always made him smile. He worked hard and eventually picked himself up off the floor and stumbled over to her.

"Hello!" he said, beaming, holding his arms out wide for a hug. She and he had always used to hug. They never hugged anymore. He should change that.

"Oh gods, you're drunk." If Will hadn't known better he would have thought Lette looked disgusted.

"I know," he said happily. "It's brilliant."

"You drank the…Barph's blood or whatever?" Lette peered over his shoulder.

"Yes!" Will was so happy to talk about that, and to talk about it with Lette. Smart, brave Lette. "You look pretty," he told her.

Lette sighed through gritted teeth. "The Barph's Strength. Did it make you…I don't know stronger? Tougher?"

"It made me feel great." Will put a companionable arm on Lette's shoulder. "You should come in and try some."

Lette shook his hand off. "So it's just made you enormously drunk," she said. "Fantastic."

"No," said Will. "No, no, no. Don't be sad. Don't be sad, pretty Lette. Be happy Lette. Happy, pretty Lette." That felt nice in his mouth when he said it. So he said it again. "Happy, pretty Lette."

"Shut up, you arse," Lette told him. "Do we need to steal this goblet or not? *Can* you steal it?"

"I love you," said Will. She was being very mean to him, he thought, and here he was being so nice, and he loved her. But maybe she didn't know, so he had thought he should tell her so she did.

Lette closed her eyes.

"You're so awesome," Will said. "And you're smart, and you're, like, really good at killing things, which is scary but also awesome. And you're pretty. And you make me laugh. And you make me happy." He grinned at her.

Lette's eyes were still closed. Perhaps she wanted to kiss. Will closed his eyes just in case too. He puckered his lips.

There was no kiss.

He opened his eyes again. Lette was looking at him, but not with her familiar disdain. It was something more akin to . . . sadness maybe? Not quite.

"I love you," he told her again.

"I know, Will," Lette said quietly. "Of course I know. But I'm not going to have that conversation with you here, not when you're in this state. And certainly not when you're unlikely to remember anything I say to you."

"You've got such a great memory," Will told her, full of passion.

Lette made fists. "Gods, I swear, if you weren't good-looking I'd have killed you a thousand times over."

Will wasn't sure what to make of that so he just puckered his lips again.

"Look," Lette said, "I know you're hammered, but can you get that goblet or can you not?"

A thought struck Will. "Where's Balur?" he said.

Lette groaned. She looked over his shoulder, back toward the hidden tunnel where the champion had disappeared. "I don't have time…" She shook her head. "He's gone and had an idea. He's made a plan. And we all know how well that went back in the Vale, but the truth is—and gods, I am only saying this because you have zero fucking chance of remembering it—he is bigger than me, and if he wants to go, I can't stop him without cutting his hamstrings, and as satisfying as that would be, it would be counterproductive at the bottom of a labyrinth of stairs. So, he's gone off to try to stir up the kobolds. He thinks a stampede down through this chamber will be a good distraction. Which it will be, except mostly it will distract us from being alive."

"I like Balur," said Will happily. The big lug was out there, doing what he could for the team. He had great attitude. "Not as much as I like you," he added in case Lette got the wrong end of the stick.

"Just shut up and listen," Lette said, but not unkindly. "I need to know if *you* know a way to get Lawl's champion to give up that goblet fast. And I really need you to come through for me here."

Will tried very hard to concentrate. Lette needed him now. "Did I ever tell you," he said, "that I have always been really into how long your fingers are?"

Lette slapped him. "Focus, you jackass."

"Sorry," he said. "Slipped out."

Will tried. He really, really tried. "You could…when he sleeps," Will managed. "You're all like…" He pantomimed tip-toeing, overbalanced, and crashed into a wall.

"Thank you for that flattering portrayal," Lette said. "But I saw how fast he grabbed you when you tried to take the chalice. I'm not going to hang my arse out for him to swat."

And that made Will think about Lette's arse, and more precious seconds were lost.

There was a noise from the far end of the tunnel down which the champion had disappeared.

"Screw it," said Lette. "He's coming back. Gods, maybe Balur's stupid plan will even work."

Gods piss on it. Will needed this. He needed this plan. He needed Lette to be impressed. He needed to show that she should love him back.

"Lawl," he blurted out as Lette turned away.

She turned back. "What?"

"He's scared of Lawl. Terrified. He shouldn't have drunk Barph's Strength. He wasn't meant to."

"Okay." Lette nodded, looked over Will's shoulder in the direction of the champion. "So…"

"Erm…Erm…" Gods, this was unfair. Will was horribly, horribly drunk. He wasn't meant to think when he was this drunk. He was meant to laugh and sing, and piss his own pants. He was supposed to be a glorious firecracker in the night. Sober things were being demanded of him.

"Be Lawl," he said. "I don't know. He doesn't know what Lawl looks like."

"Trust me," said Lette, "I am not going to pass muster. I've got tits for starters."

"Don't tell me about your tits," Will pleaded. "Not now."

She slapped him again for good measure. It helped a bit. There was a stumble and a groan from the shadows behind him.

"Fuck it," Lette said again. "I'll try and work with—"

"He knows what Lawl sounds like," Will said. "A voice like thunder, he said. Sound like that."

"How…?"

"I don't know."

"Buddy, what are you doing?" The champion's voice suddenly rolled down the length of the hall behind Will.

Lette flinched away. Will fought for control of his bladder.

"I don't know," he said slowly as he turned around. "What are *you* doing?"

The champion's glowing red eyes narrowed within the confines of his dark helm. Will tried to meet the gaze, but focusing his eyes was a very difficult feat right now.

The champion took a slow step toward him and raised an accusing finger.

"You," he intoned, "are drunk."

Will felt his bowels quiver. Then he raised his own finger, pointed. "You're drunk," he said back.

And then the champion threw both hands up and wide. "Come here, you," he said. "Best drinking buddy, ever."

42

Bar Brawl

Glancing quickly over her shoulder, Quirk checked the exits of the Callibian Temple in the Ninth District of Vinter. Her pulse was coming fast now. Sweat beaded her forehead in what she could only assume was the most obviously suspicious way possible. Temple guards wearing the High Priests' colors moved through the crowd of worshippers, eyes searching.

She wished Afrit was there. She hadn't realized how dependent she'd become on the woman's companionship. But ever since things had gone to total shit back in Tamathia, it felt like they'd been together in this. And, true, she had grown a little tired of the academic at times, but right now a familiar face would be reassuring.

But Afrit was not here. Afrit was over in the Sixth District, with her own team of drunken Barphists, slowly slipping into temple slaughter yards. She was, in fact, performing the part of the plan Quirk had come up with. And that left Quirk here, two districts over with a bunch of drunken strangers in tow, about to execute a plan that gods-pissing Durmitt had come up with. Durmitt!

And she knew at an intellectual level that it was a good plan. She had looked it over a dozen times the night before, probing it and testing it for holes. And she had been the one to suggest that she spearhead it. It was a job that fit her skill set. And she knew that working together, combining their ideas and talents, they were stronger.

But gods piss and shit all over everything, this plan was also a paper-thin sack of weasel turds.

She took in a rapid breath, tried to calm herself. This was going to be okay. Everything was going to be okay.

A hand touched her on the shoulder. She whirled round, palm already smoking, ready to melt flesh from bone.

It was one of Firkin's followers. A short, red-faced man called Bebbel. Quirk was somewhat pleased to see that he looked almost as sweaty as she felt. "It's time," he hissed, and then pushed past her and off into the crowds.

Quirk's fear dug deep and found a way to intensify.

The Callibian Temple had the honor of being positioned opposite the main temple guard barracks in the heart of Vinter. Uniforms were everywhere. Even the majority of the worshippers here not in uniform were likely guards, or the family of guards. Or just folk who really, really liked guards, and thought they had good ideas, and were generally of the opinion that anyone attacking them ought to be dealt with fairly severely using pointy bits of metal.

Above her head, the temple bell began to toll. And Bebbel— curse his red, sweaty face—was right. It was time. This was the inciting incident of the whole uprising. She had no leeway to be late.

She checked her position. She was, as close as she could judge, at the dead center of the temple. She looked up. The Callibian Temple had been named after one of Vinland's great generals. A man of great renown and religious zeal, who had significantly expanded their territory several hundred years back. To echo this sense of expansion, the interior of his temple was one massive open space. Pillars dotted it, but as she craned her neck back Quirk had a clear view all the way to the roof. The dome above her had been delicately painted, scenes of battle and drinking intermingling with each other. It was a glorious thing, one of the true artistic beauties in Vinland, one that had largely survived by merit of being out of reach of all the drunken idiots beneath it.

Quirk sighed ruefully. But she had a world to win. She took a breath, looked around.

There were guards everywhere.

Gods.

The bells tolled again. Again. She was running out of tolls.

Were physicians absolutely certain that it wasn't possible for a person to melt entirely into sweat?

The bell tolled one final time.

Gods.

Quirk let her fire out. A rushing, roaring pillar of flame. It rose, thrusting up, up, up. She poured more and more of it up toward that beautiful, holy dome. She watched as her fire tore into it, pressing and pressing, smashing against that masonry. And then her column of fire ripped up through the temple roof and burst out into the Vinter sky.

She was with it for a moment, up there reaching out to the heavens, arms spread wide. She could feel the sun calling out to her, the kinship of fire. She could see the city spread out below her, its thrashing humanity, its seething heat, and sweat, and dreams, and thwarted aspirations. She could see people all across the city turning to stare at this signal fire starting a revolution. For a moment she felt again like she had last night when Firkin had thundered and roared, with his voice roaring in her blood like wine. For a moment she felt the divinity in her magic.

Then the blade struck her shoulder.

She flew sideways, control lost. Fire bloomed and blossomed around her, petals of it unfurling into the screaming, scrambling crowd. She crashed to the ground, felt mosaic tiles crack beneath the heat of her.

But it was too late. She had sent the sign. The rebellion was happening. Even as the guard stood over her, halberd held aloft, grip reversed, ready to punch the blade into her chest, Bebbel was there, red face contorted with rage, hacking and hacking at the man with a rusty old butcher's knife.

There were twenty-five of Firkin's followers there, all scattered through the crowd, all armed. They ripped into the guards with unbridled ferocity.

One man had claws strapped to the backs of his fists, and he tore around him, slashing and screaming. Then a halberd punched into his gut. He roared, smashed the haft with one claw, and tore out the guard's throat. He leapt at another with the shaft still sticking out of his back, spitting blood as he went. The pair went down in a sluicing pour of red.

Shock and awe. That was the goal here. Not death, not destruction, but rather a solid blow to the sternum of the guards' will to fight. Leave them sitting on the ground, unwilling to get back up.

Shock and awe. Yes, that, Quirk knew, she could do. That was what Hethren had bred her for.

Look at you now, he crooned in her ear.

But this was different. She hung on to that still. Hethren's goals had been selfish. Hers were not. *They were not.* She had teetered on that precipice, but Afrit had pulled her back. Violence was a tool. It could be put to other uses than the ones Hethren had held for it.

She told herself that again and again as she melted the face off a man whose only difference from her was that he was dressed in robes of red and gold.

In the sky above, the sun rose, and the sun fell. Quirk fought. And fought. And fought. She left a massacre in her wake. The Callibian Temple had not gone as she had wanted. For long, murderous hours the guards had simply refused to just sit down and shut up. Her twenty-five Barphists had been reduced to three. At the last it had simply been her, holding back a wall of soldiers, with her own wall of fire. She had been trying to weep as she watched them immolate themselves, but her tears simply turned to steam and drifted away.

Chaos and murder were rampant on the streets. And even though the Callibian Temple had been won, she still had work to do. Now she hurried uphill toward the High Temple and the High Priests it held.

All across the city, small independent groups of Firkin's supporters were in temples, all rising up as one, all seizing control, killing guards, barring doors, screaming sermons and Firkin's praises from the rooftops. She passed some of them. On the walls of one both Barph's and Firkin's names had been written in…She prayed it was wine.

The people's dedication to him…It was even more rabid here than it had been in Kondorra. And after his display in the temple the previous night, it was getting harder and harder to dismiss his effect on people as a mere oddity. And this presence in his head he spoke about. What was it? Some buried aspect of his personality? Some dissociative fragment of his self? Was he simply becoming unhinged?

And yet she had felt the power of that other personality. She could see right now everything it had inspired. The passion, yes, but also the violence. She had not wanted that for this revolution. An uprising—in her mind—had been a clean, simple thing, something tactical and precise. This massive upheaval… this had been beyond the scope of her imagination. And yet it had seemed so natural once Firkin had spoken. How had he done that?

She saw signs of the uprising everywhere. Gored bodies lay scattered in the street. Afrit and several others had released the cattle from the temple slaughter yards, then sent a stampede sweeping ahead of them, bowling through the tight streets, mindless and angry.

Some fights still raged. Knots of women and men, screaming and yelling. Quirk ended those where she could. She tried to spare life where she could. Often there was not fighting at all, just crowds screaming and shouting abuse at each other. She left those alone. Nobody *wanted* to die today. She would not risk pushing anything over the edge.

In some places she saw the High Priests' guards just sitting on the side of the street, or leaning against the side of buildings. They looked dazed, staring around, blinking at the sky, as if expecting an answer to fall upon them. They had not seen this coming. They had thought they had won.

The cauterized wound in her shoulder throbbed. She did not have time to figure Firkin out. She didn't have time for half the things she needed to do. She had to focus and prioritize. The dragons were coming. Vinter could become another Birchester—a hollow ruin of fire and burned bodies. She would not allow that. She would help Firkin even if this was the cost.

The fight was going their way, but from the sound of things the High Temple still eluded their grasp. The crash and clatter of fighting grew louder as she got closer.

Gods let her be on the right path.

The front line of the fighting turned out to be a thrusting, shoving mass of bodies two streets from the entrance to the High Temple. They had pushed the guards back farther than she could have dared to hope.

The High Temple guards were armed with halberds, encased in dented bronze armor. They pushed and prodded at the crowd in front of them. Glass bottles arced up, shattering on their helmets and breastplates, glass scouring exposed skin. Some in the crowd had brought genuine weapons, short swords and sickles. They ducked beneath the poking halberd blades, hacking and slashing at exposed thighs and calves. Temple guards were pulled away, howling, clutching at spurting wounds. More than one of Firkin's supporters collapsed clutching at a gaping hole in his or her guts.

There was a sense of frenzy and desperation. This was a brutal, bloody impasse. The smells of blood and shit were mingling in the street. Bodies lay trampled in among the broken glass.

A few yards back from it all, Quirk hesitated. Firkin's supporters would win, she thought. It might take a day, maybe two, but they would win. The tide of sentiment had turned. The guards had no reinforcements coming. Firkin's supporters had a whole city. Eventually the guards would realize that.

Eventually.

She did not have the time.

She was on the right path.

She held on to that thought as she pushed through the crowd.

The little lies we tell ourselves, Hethren's voice whispered in her ear. *Tell yourself the violence is a tool, and your goals are noble, but you're still the creature I made you into.*

She closed her eyes. Everyone around her was thrusting and jostling. Bodies, and blood, and sweat pressing in. The stink and the crush of it.

More lives would be spared this way. Fuck Hethren. Fuck his attempt to own her decisions, even from beyond the grave.

She forced her way forward, eyes open. She screamed and yelled to be let through. And they didn't know who she was, no one recognized her, but they recognized her passion.

She stood in the face of the barking, braying Temple Guards. They were screaming insults and hate. They were threatening to destroy everything these people loved and held dear. They would coat the streets with their entrails, and then hunt down their families and murder and rape until all their line had been extinguished. These were men with all the pretense of civility and civilization slashed away. These were animals, raw and screaming.

Just like the people she stood with now.

She let the fire fill her. Warmth spreading out from her stomach, filling her chest, her loins, her arms and her legs. It was beautiful and blissful. She exhaled. Steam and smoke swirled around her. She let the fire leak out, just a little, feeling it chafe at the bit she placed upon it. Fire wreathed her. It ran lover's fingertips over her body, her face, her hair.

Around her, people fell away. The guards stopped their jeers, hesitated.

This was it. This emptiness. This calm. This was the moment before the storm, perfect and pure. And in it, she was gloriously certain. All doubt left behind, nothing more than ash in her wake.

She slipped the leash from the beast's neck.

Then there was nothing. Beautiful oblivion. Flame, and dancing. She was sweating and panting, commanding the flame to go here, and here, and here. To twist, and kiss, and embrace.

Women and men screamed. They dove free. She sent fire chasing after them. The guards fell back, scattering. One was too late. She gripped his wrist in her hand as he sent a flaming spear past her in a fumbling thrust. He screamed and the skin peeled off his bone. She dropped him. Pushed forward.

The guards tried to use the length of their halberds, desperately hacking at her.

The shafts of her weapons were made of wood. The fools.

All around her people were dying. Their ash-streaked corpses falling to the floor. She could smell cooking meat. She could hear the fat boiling off them, hissing and spitting.

More. The fire whispered. *More*.

It was so hard to hold on to reality. Were the guards broken? She tried to look through the heat haze of her soul and actually assess the situation. *Not yet,* the fire roared in her ear. *Push harder.* But was that real? She didn't know what she wanted to believe.

More. More.

With a gasp she shut down the sluice gate to the ocean of fire within her. She dropped to a knee, tried to take everything in.

The street was a smoking ruin. Buildings were on fire to the left and the right. Wattle and wood crumbled and roared. Thatch went up like kindling. She tried to reach out, to pull the fire back and make it obey her, but she was momentarily spent.

And there were the bodies. So many bodies again. So many screams. And so many not dead. So many just dragging themselves...what was left of themselves...across the blackened cobbles. The wet scrape of their bodies, and the huffing of their ragged breathing. She had done this. She had caused this devastation and suffering.

Gods forgive her.

Then, from behind her, came the sound of cheering, the sound of feet.

The crowd crashed into her, an overwhelming wave of humanity bursting around her, knocking her stumbling forward, forcing her to grab on to thrashing arms as she tried to stay on her feet. Fear joined the mix of emotions swirling in her, and for a moment she almost summoned the fire again.

No! screamed some last vestige of the academic in her. *Never in fear! Never in fear!* That had been drummed into her again and again. That was the moment when she failed, when she became nothing more than a rabid animal once more. Fire *had* to be a tool. She *had* to be its master, not the other way around. Never that way.

She grit her teeth, heaved with aching arms on the belt of someone pushing past, kept her feet. Someone caught her beneath the shoulders, pushed her roughly forward.

Sweat, and blood, and piss, and wine. *Why does a revolution have to smell so bad?* part of her mind burbled. *Doesn't that set things off on kind of the wrong foot?*

They were charging down the streets, up the steps that led to the huge temple edifice. She saw a lone guard running down toward them, a spear in his hands. He managed one thrust before the swarming crowd closed over him. When they moved on, their fists and sleeves were stained red.

Remember what this is for.

Feet pounding up the steps, breath coming fast and hard, Quirk felt the end coming closer. The temple would be theirs. It would be over soon. Everything would come to a halt. They could start to focus on the real enemy. Just a little more bloodshed. Just a little more killing.

The arched temple entrance rose around her, and Quirk was blinking in the sudden shadows. Voices bounced off hard stone. Shouts of anger, and fear. Noises transformed into something unfamiliar.

She was in a corridor, people were spilling left and right. There was no plan now, simply the desire to take, and tear, and punish, even if no one was clear on the actual transgressions. She tried to catch her breath, to take a moment, get her bearings in the maelstrom. But there was nothing to cling to. She was being pushed deeper and deeper in. She glimpsed more fighting, more travesties.

Then before she had a chance to process anything she was back in the main chamber of the temple. There were the three thrones, the three High Priests. There was the last knot of guards standing in a circle around them, bristling with enough weaponry to buy them time, but not enough to buy their lives. People poured into the massive chamber around them, swirling like water poured into a bowl. The moat of open space around the priests and their guards grew smaller and smaller.

Quirk could feel the tension in the room mounting, racing toward its breaking point. The violence and the hatred were about to spill over, and the final atrocities of the day were going to be committed.

"No!" She screamed the word into the crowd. This wasn't how things had to go. They had won. Gods, they had actually won. A small handful of them. In a single day they had taken this city. It had all worked. All of it. There needed to be no more bloodshed. Gods, the High Priests might even be an asset to them in the upcoming fight against the dragons. If she and Afrit handled things right, the High Priests could help unify the city, bring on board hard-liners reluctant to fight for Firkin even if it meant subjugation to the dragons.

Violence was a tool they no longer needed.

But her voice was lost in the echoing screeches of rage that filled the hall. She was just one voice among many and her words were lost.

The crowd no longer swirled. It bulged. She had been pushed to the front line. She could see the High Priests' guards. Young men. All in their twenties and thirties. Younger than her. Sweat dappled their foreheads. They gripped their weapons in white-knuckled hands, working their grips. Their eyes flicked back and forth around the room like flies trapped against glass.

They were going to die, and there was nothing she could do to save them.

Or was there...? What if she surrounded them with fire? A protective barrier...Would the crowd turn on her then instead?

And then suddenly the energy in the room shifted. A moment of stillness. A change of focus. For a moment Quirk thought that this was the breaking point. The moment that violence erupted. But nothing happened.

Then she saw Firkin striding through the crowd. He walked like a king, back straight, shoulders back, and chest thrust forward. Authority oozed out of him. She was leaning toward him, she realized. Everyone was. Even the High Priests' guards.

The volume of the crowd's fury began to ease. A queasy sense of order arrived with him. She could finally make out the High Priests screaming curses and hate.

Firkin could stop this. The thought came in a rush, certainty flooding her. She pulled away from the crowd, dashed across the no-man's-land around the knot of guards, and toward him. One of the High Priests' guards flinched, a spear point twitching toward her, but she didn't have time to worry about it.

Several large men and women had formed an honor guard around Firkin. She crashed into them. They pushed her back easily, as if she were nothing. She pressed against the broad barring arms of two large men. "Firkin!" she yelled. "You have to stop them. We've won." She felt a hand grab her by the scruff of her dress's neck. "We've won!"

Firkin's eyes locked with her. "Stop this!" she screamed at him. "Shut it down. Take the victory. We need them."

Then a huge hand hurled her away. She sprawled into the crowd. They yelled, and pushed, and swallowed her whole.

Scrambling to her feet, she pushed and shoved for a view of what Firkin was doing.

"It's over." His voice boomed out. Everyone in the room heard it. Everyone. And the finality in his voice was undeniable. It was a fact in its purest form. And she saw the fight go out of the High Priest's guards immediately.

"Leave." Firkin waved a careless hand toward the exits.

He saw me, she thought. *He heard me. He must have.*

The guards hesitated, but not for longer than a handful of seconds. Then the first dropped his sword and his ceremonial shield to the ground, pulled off his helmet, and walked toward the crowd. Then the next. Then all of them.

The High Priests were screaming with impotent rage. "Traitors!" shrieked the woman in her mid-fifties. "Cowardly fuckholes!" yelled one of her less eloquent companions.

"Silence!" intoned Firkin. His voice was a weapon. It smashed into the priests. They reeled.

But they were not broken. "Fuck you!" screamed one of the priests. "We have been here for a thousand years. Our order was appointed by Barph himself. We have ruled for a millennia because of his blessing." He spat as he spoke. "No jumped-up street-preaching shit is going to get rid of us. This isn't a victory. This is a blip. A glitch. You will be a footnote in the history of our glorious reign. Barph spits on you. Barph loves us." He looked away, out of the crowd. "All of you!" he yelled. "All of you will drown in Barph's shit, you heathen fucks!"

Firkin's expression barely changed. He just cocked his head to one side. "Kill them," he said.

His voice didn't boom. It did not fill the room. The tone was almost conversational. But everyone heard. Quirk heard. And her heart broke a little bit at that moment. Because for a moment she had hoped. And because she had put this power in Firkin's hands. She had unleashed him. She had forced him past his breaking point. This was, at least in part, her fault.

"I'm sorry," she whispered as the crowd descended and committed their last atrocity.

43

How to Make Friends and Influence Kobolds

This, Balur thought, *was more like it.* Alone in the labyrinth of stairs. Alone with his blade and his enemy. A test of will and cunning. A test of strength and spirit. None of this bullshit about "unwinnable fights," and "obvious suicide."

He truly didn't understand the arguments Lette had tried to mount against his plan. First, she hadn't wanted him to charge in directly and attack the champion because it would lead to Will's death. And Balur was a reasonable Analesian. And so, while he considered this objection revealed a flaw in Will rather than in his planning, he had acquiesced. And he had come up with a new plan that allowed him to attack the champion in a way that would not spell instant death for Will. A plan that provided a distraction so he could clear the path to a serious arse-kicking.

Because what would provide a perfect distraction? Stirring a bunch of kobolds up into a stampede would.

It was infallible.

And Lette's response? To claim that trying to steal a goblet in the middle of a giant stampede was the stupidest thing she'd ever heard.

So then he had said that she needed to unwad her panties and let him go stab things.

So now here he was, belly pressed against the rock, clinging to the wall of the cavern, with the hole marking the entrance to the kobolds' nest only five yards above his head.

His tongue snaked past the blade he held gripped in his teeth. The scent of kobolds was heavy on the air.

He crawled higher up the rugged face of the wall. He could hear small growling sounds, and the click of teeth and tongues. Kobolds talking to each other in their own impenetrable language.

Balur smiled around the blade in his teeth.

And then, without warning, a small red face poked over the edge of the cave entrance and stared down at Balur. For a moment there was taut silence. Then the kobold screamed. Then the kobold died.

Sword dripping blood, kobold body spraying fluids over him, and dangling from the cave entrance with just one hand, Balur scrambled for a firmer handhold. Then he lost it, flailed, caught it again. He grunted a string of curses and heaved himself up into the kobolds' nest.

The wall of panicking kobolds smashed into him like Lawl's fist itself. He was swinging his sword in a flat, two-handed arc, felt the blade punch through fur and muscle, decimating bodies, crushing bones. Then he was swept off his feet, and sent flailing out into space.

He crashed twenty yards down onto the path below. Even through his scales and muscles, his spine screamed. Stars exploded above his head as darkness closed in.

He fought through it, fought through the bodies falling down onto him, biting, and scratching, and ripping. He seized a kobold in each hand, used them like a furry pair of pugilist's gloves. He could feel their organs rupturing as he pummeled them into others of their kind. And it was glorious.

But even as he fought and killed, more and more kobolds swarmed around him. They nipped at his ankles, slashed at his scales, drew blood in long, thin strands.

He kicked, bit, clawed. He snatched up a kobold, and tore the useless fucking thing in two with a roar.

"Be coming on!" he bellowed. And it would be good to stand here against this tide. This was worthy of his strength. To prove that he could outlast them, all of them. That when the last of this pack was on the floor and gasping its last breath, he would still be standing. Clutching his guts, perhaps, dying even. But still standing. That would be a good way to go.

He glanced up at the nest entrance. Kobolds were still trickling out of it. The pathway hacked into the wall's rocky edge was packed with them. He roared. More. He needed more.

And then as if in answer…it was as if the rock pulsed, a huge, orgasmic spray of kobolds launching out of the nest entrance. Out of more and more entrances. Tunnels he hadn't seen. Hundreds of kobolds. Hundreds of hundreds of them.

The crowd of kobolds became a tidal wave, barreling along the path toward him.

Okay, Balur revised in his head, *maybe I shall be going with the original plan of leading them to Will and Lette after all.*

He turned, kicked away a swath of rabid kobolds, and started running as fast as he could.

44

Run, Kobolds, Run!

Will was beginning to think that he had drunk slightly too much. He wasn't entirely sure. He didn't want to be right. But he did keep on vomiting whenever he tried to put new liquid in his body.

"No," the champion was saying. "No. No, you have to choose. That's how it works."

Will made a noise. He wasn't honestly sure what it was.

"A pig's mouth or month-old yogurt," the champion insisted. "You have to choose one."

"I—" Will managed, which he found to be a pretty impressive accomplishment.

"Silence!" A voice crashed massively through the room, bouncing and echoing about them.

Both Will and the champion decided to comply. They looked around. No source for the voice was obvious.

"This is what has become of you? This how you serve my orders?"

The voice had an odd hollow timbre to it.

"Oh shit," the champion whispered next to him. He was on his feet, slowly backing away. "Oh no."

"What?" Will said.

"Stand!" bellowed the voice. "Do not back away from me."

The champion clutched his helmeted head.

"What did I tell you?" boomed the voice. "What was the condition of your service here?"

There was something familiar about the voice. "I think I know—" Will started.

"It's Lawl," said the champion. He sounded on the verge of crying.

"Lawl?" Will managed. That didn't seem particularly likely.

"I told you to guard it," boomed the voice.

"I guarded it," pleaded the champion. "It's still here with me. It's safe. No one has come for it in a hundred years. I've scared them all away."

"You have done *nothing*!" roared the voice. "I created you. I created law and order. You have merely sat here. And you have disobeyed."

If a voice could have flayed the skin from a man's back, Will thought, it was that voice.

It really did sound kind of familiar.

"Distract him," hissed the champion, slowly backing away from Will.

"What?" Will squeaked.

"Distract him," the champion hissed again.

"Lawl?" Will had placed the name now. "The king of the fucking gods?"

"Show him your tits," the champion suggested.

"I'm a bloke!" Will took fairly significant offense to this. They'd been hanging out for the best part of two days at this point.

"You cannot escape me!" Lawl roared.

"Oh shit," the champion moaned.

"Look," Will said, trying to console, "I'm sure you'll be able to explain." Off the top of his head, he couldn't think of any particular stories where Lawl demonstrated any sort of capacity for mercy, but on the other hand he couldn't think of his own middle name right now either.

"I hereby rescind you of your duties!" bellowed Lawl.

"No," moaned the champion.

"I hereby rescind you of Barph's Strength!" Lawl went on.

"No!" The champion's cry was louder this time, harsher. "You can't!"

"You are unworthy!" roared Lawl. And there was thunder with his voice now...

His...? There was something about the timbre that made Will question that.

The thunder grew. A pounding that made the earth shake.

"You can't take it from me!" shouted the champion, waving the goblet in defiance. "It's mine. It's all I've got. It keeps me warm on the cold nights. It bathes my loins with its love! We've got something special!"

"Bathes your..." Despite everything, Will got caught up on that. "What did you and that cup...?"

The champion shrugged awkwardly at him.

"Ew!" Will started spitting.

"The goblet!" Lawl demanded.

"Never!" shrieked the champion.

The whole room was shaking now. Dust was pouring down from the columns. Stacked pots and vases were tumbling. Mosaic tiles were shaking loose.

"Put it down and you may yet know my mercy. Put it down and you shall not be unmade!"

Will wondered why Lawl bothered with the bargaining. It didn't seem very divine. Lawl had always seemed more of the smite-first, ask-questions-later sort of god to him.

"You're not the boss of me!" yelled the champion.

"I think he is," Will noted.

"You're not fucking helping," the champion snapped.

"You will deliver that goblet to me right now," Lawl roared, though he was barely audible over the thunder rattling the room, "or...Oh fuck!"

These last two words were delivered at a significantly different pitch to the other two, and seemed to Will to be a bit of a non sequitur. *Or oh fuck.* What did that mean? Was that some sort of divine punishment?

The champion didn't seem like he wanted to find out. He let out a final defiant, if inarticulate, yell, turned tail, and started to run toward the shadowed corridor down which he had disappeared to urinate earlier.

At that same moment, running at a speed that seemed to suggest her life was in significant danger, Lette entered the chamber from the golden archway that led out to the labyrinth of stairs.

"Lette!" Will shouted, trying to get her attention. "You'll never guess what happened! Lawl actually—"

"Start fucking running, you moron!" Lette screamed and threw what appeared to be a cow's horn at him. Will stared at her.

Then Balur came into the room, also running hard. He appeared to be bleeding from…well, everywhere. His whole being was crisscrossed with cuts and slashes.

"Balur?" Will asked.

"Run!" Lette screamed. She was level with him now, streaking after the champion.

Oh right, Will thought. *The goblet. We should get that before Lawl does.*

And then the kobolds came into the room.

They burst in like water, like a stinking, furry tidal wave of red and teeth. They burst through the golden arch in spray, crashed against the far wall, and then began to flood after Balur.

Will stared. There was a majesty to the sight after all. Something actually divine about it. He was awestruck just by the scale of the madness pouring down upon him.

"Run!" bellowed Balur, and finally, finally the words sank in.

Not for the goblet, he thought. *For my life. I get it.*

And then he turned, and he ran.

Unfortunately, though, Will had just spent two days drinking himself almost comatose, and neither coordination nor speed was within his grasp.

He managed three stumbling steps, and then the kobolds were upon him. Something small, hard, and furry barreled into his legs, flipping him up off the ground. He sprawled backward, landed on a seething carpet of bodies. For a moment he was borne aloft, the world crashing and bouncing around him. He could see Balur, desperately running, arms flailing, the red tide slowly creeping up on him. The pillars and shadows at the far end of the room rose up like a cliff face. Then they were crashing into them, spurring down a narrow channel.

Everything was crushing darkness. Claws ripped at Will's clothes and skin. He smashed into one rocky wall. The kobolds were forcing more and more of their bodies into the narrow channel. They were climbing over each other, over him. He scrabbled to not be buried in the dark, kicking out, stepping on a seething mat of living fur. He heard a yell from Balur suddenly grow muffled.

Then they were out through the passage and into sudden light. Instead of the unnatural twilight glow of the labyrinth of caves, this seemed like genuine daylight, even if its source was distant.

The space beyond was a natural fissure in the bedrock of the world. Will glimpsed its walls stretching almost infinitely up, the tiny slice of white light far above. The passage at the back of the champion's chamber gave out onto an uneven ledge that formed a step on one side of the fissure. A rocky wall rose ever upward to their right. A dark, clawing void descended ever downward to their left. Hot winds rushed up from the abyss, to gust over them.

The towering, surging mass of kobolds teetered on the brink of disaster. Will was balanced near the crest of the wave. He could see the endless black below him. He could see Balur, nearer the base of the stampede, thrashing and tearing to be free. He could see Lette ten yards ahead, still sprinting. And then perhaps a hundred yards away he could see the champion, feet pounding, weaving dangerously, his massive bulk taking up almost the full width of the path.

Kobolds spilled out into nothingness, their swollen numbers too great for the path. Will was crashing down the cresting slope of the kobold wave. Bodies were spilling out into space, plunging down to be swallowed by shadows. Will couldn't even hear their screams over the chattering roar of the kobolds all around him. For a moment he went under the surface, lost track of where he was. He could feel the abyss calling for him. Then he was back on top, somehow astride the back of one of the kobolds, holding on to its sharp, tufted ears, bouncing up and down as it leapt along the backs of its compatriots. They passed Balur, still thrashing, like a drowning swimmer searching for air. Then they were out ahead of the rest of the kobolds, pounding after Lette.

Will's stomach was a churning portal into the Hallows themselves. Something apocalyptic was brewing there. And yet all he could think was, *A racing kobold. I found myself a genuine racing kobold. With this steed, I could be rich.*

They sailed past Lette. She screamed something at him, but he had no idea what. He was laughing, and trying not to vomit, and screaming in terror, sometimes all at the same time.

He was probably not going to drink for a while after this.

The path beneath them was far from even. It spread out, almost as wide as a city street, then narrowed to a country lane. The abyss yawned at them. Air like a god's breath blew over Will, tousled his hair. He screamed again. Beneath him the kobold was letting out a constant, high-pitched, chittering yell. Will wondered if it had been punctured somehow.

The champion was still ahead of them, staggering now,

gripping the side of the wall. Will could just make out occasional shouts of "Noooo!" and "Mine!" over the roar of the kobolds behind them. He risked a glance back, almost lost his seat astride the kobold's shoulders. He had perhaps ten paces on Lette, thirty on the kobolds.

Ahead of them, the champion stumbled to a halt, took his turn to look back. His eyes went wide. What he thought he saw, Will was utterly incapable of telling. A crimson tide. Lawl's punishment. Maybe the champion just really didn't like kobolds. But he let out a shrill scream, took a stumbling step backward, and then, with a yell, tumbled over the lip of the path, and with the goblet still clutched in his hand, fell away into the abyss.

45

Balls

"Balls!"

Lette stared in utter horror as, like a felled tree, Lawl's champion toppled over the edge of the ledge and went pinwheeling into space.

Why? Why was her life always at the mercy of complete and utter fucking idiocy?

It tripped? A divine champion of Lawl? It fucking tripped over its own feet? *And it took the divine goblet holding their one hope for defeating the dragons with it?*

For a moment she almost stopped. Just in sheer awe at how much of an asshole the universe was willing to be. Just so she could stop, throw in the towel, and tell the gods to save their own fucking selves.

Then she remembered the stampede of kobolds that was inches away from her.

She accelerated. Will was just ahead of her, somehow clinging to the back of a kobold that he'd driven into a state of absolute frenzy. Somehow he had stayed on the path and the champion hadn't...

The champion. There was something about his trajectory as he fell...

She was running as fast as she could, breath coming in short staccato bursts. She didn't have time to assess...

His ankle! It was the champion's ankle. There were vines on the edge of the path and his foot had caught in them.

The champion crashed down, his body describing a short, sharp arc. He crashed into the abyss's cliff wall upside down, dangling by his ankle.

She had to think. She had to run. She had to get down to that gods-hexed champion before he dropped that goblet, unless he had dropped that goblet already, and then... Then just piss on everything. Drown the whole world in divine urine.

Ahead of her, Will lurched on his kobold. The teetering pair finally giving way to... honestly just common sense. And then, suddenly Will launched himself into space, hurled himself out at the fallen champion.

Lette's heart stopped. Because this was, surely, a suicide attempt. She could think of no other explanation. Fuck. Life without...

Gods, she *did not* have time for this. And then, whether by intent, or sheer dumb luck, Will collided with the champion's dangling foot and folded in half around it. He clung there desperately as the kobold raced on into darkness.

She would be parallel with Will in a moment. Did she fling herself after him? Rescue him? Was she really that suicidal?

He had said he loved her.

And why? Why did he have to finally say it down here? In the middle of this?

Of course she knew he still loved her. His puppy-dog eyes practically screamed it at her every time he thought she wasn't looking at him. But that was hardly the fucking point. She'd never thought that he'd stopped. She may have hoped it for a while, but she'd never really expected it. Will was the sort who, once he was committed to an idea, had trouble letting go. It was not an unattractive trait. But this had never been about him loving her. If it had been then she would have ruined a lot more shirts with pig shit. And quite frankly, it was a touch insulting for him to assume that she was obligated to him in any way just because of *his* feelings.

To be honest, it wasn't even about whether she loved him or not. She'd given up trying to figure that out. She still found him equal parts frustrating and fascinating. But any future they might have wasn't to do with love, or sex, or any of the stuff the bards liked to pretend relationships were about.

It was to do with compatibility. It was to do with the day-to-day grind that took up most of life between the odd sparks of passion and rage. It was to do with being elbow-to-elbow with each other for hours on end when life was simply...boring.

They were not compatible. Not as they were. He wanted to raise pigs. She, despite her best efforts, wanted to stab people in the guts. She could not stand still watching the seasons grind past. She could not celebrate the numbing repetition of it all. There was not much middle ground between the pair of them. Not unless Will wanted to bury a lot of farmhands. If it was to work, if love was to matter, then one of them had to change, and right now neither seemed on the verge of doing so.

Unless it was Will about to turn into a meat pancake leagues below them. Unless she saved him.

And then it was too late. She was past him. And no matter how or what she felt, it wasn't suicidal.

Still, she had to end this absurd chase. She flung herself sideways. Not at the precipice, but at the wall to her right. There had to be a handhold. Something she could pull herself up on.

She was right. The wall was rough and jagged. Even in the shadows she was able to swarm up, hand over hand. And then she just had time to pull her legs up.

Kobolds barreled past below her. Some leapt at her, trying to grab at her ankles, pull her down. Most carried on, oblivious. Whatever Balur had done he had done it...No, *well* didn't seem like the right word. *Excessively*, perhaps? Kobolds were still spilling off the side of the path, bouncing, howling down into oblivion.

It took five minutes for them to pass. Five agonizing minutes. Her arms throbbed. She could just see the trapped foot of the champion, still dangling. But Will had disappeared. Had he been knocked off? Had he jumped? Fallen down? Climbed to freedom? She had no way of knowing. For five gods-hexed minutes she had no way of knowing.

Finally the outpouring of kobolds slowed to a trickle. A few staggering children and ancients, a couple with broken limbs still struggling on. She dropped to the ground. One kobold growled at her. She stabbed it in the face. The others gave her a wide berth.

Balur was picking himself up off the road. He was smeared with blood, mud, and kobold footprints. Claws had raked through his scales over every exposed inch of his body. He grunted once, then sat back down.

"You stupid, stupid, fucking..." But Lette didn't have the words or the time right now. Why in the name of all the gods she spent time with Balur...

She choked down a shout of pure frustration and scurried toward the fallen champion and his trapped ankle.

"Will?" she called, and the anxiety in her voice almost brought her up short. She did not want to sound like that to him. If she could still sound like anything to him, of course. If he was not still falling down into oblivion. If he was not a red smear halfway down the rock face below.

"Will?" she called again, and this time, if anything her voice sounded even more tremulous.

"Hey!" came a slurred shout from below, and Lette felt as if her legs had melted. "I..." came Will's voice. Then, "Whoa!"

"Will!" And all Lette's temerity was burned off in the flash heat of her sudden anger. "You fucking moron!"

She leaned out over the edge of the precipice, lying flat on her belly to get the most balance she could. The champion was dangling upside down beside her, swaying slightly. His free limbs were splayed limply. The back of his helmet had an enormous dent in it, and black blood was bubbling out of a crack in it, dripping down into the abyss below.

"I think he's pretty much, you know...dead," Will said. He was perched halfway down the champion's massive torso, one foot wedged into a joint in his breastplate, one hand gripping the man's belt. He was beaming up at her.

"What in the Hallows are you doing?" she snapped at him.

"The chalice!" Will was still beaming. He pointed with his free hand. Then the body rocked back and forth with the shifting weight, and Will grabbed for the champion's belt with both hands. "Whoa!" he cried again. His free foot whipped back and forth wildly.

"That keeps happening," Will said when death seemed slightly less imminent.

Lette would have been slightly more tempted to fling a knife into his throat had the champion's rocking not revealed a glint of gold still clutched in the loosely curled fingers of his limp right hand. It was hanging down below his head, dangling over an absolutely enormous amount of nothing.

Will followed her gaze. "I'm going to get that," he said. He attempted to puff out his chest while maintaining his death grip on the champion's belt. "Impressive, right?"

Lette tried to process that. "Impressively stupid," she told him. "You're going to kill yourself. Get back up here."

"No!" Will pouted. "I am doing this. It is manly, and impressive, and I am going to do it, and you are going to be impressed by my manliness that, is..." He searched for a word. "Impressive," he said. And let go of the belt.

"No!" Lette screeched as Will plummeted down the length of the champion's torso.

Will crashed into the champion's helmet, almost flipped himself backward into oblivion, scrabbled desperately for a handhold, and only managed to snag one at the last moment. Lette's stomach lurched sickeningly as he swung back and forth from his fingertips, feet dangling in space.

"Whee!" Will cried, swinging back and forth.

Beside Lette the vine gripping the champion's massive weight groaned.

"Stop it!" Lette snapped. "Stop it, you drunken arsehole."

Beside her she felt Balur sit down heavily. "What is it that is going on?" he asked with a grunt.

"This." Lette couldn't even bring herself to describe the debacle. Balur leaned over and peered down. Blood dripped off the end of his snout.

Will had managed to wrap both legs around the champion's right elbow and was slowly transferring his hands over.

"Impressive," rumbled Balur.

If Lette had been sitting up she would have thrown up her hands. "What?" she snapped. "What is impressive about doing something this fucking stupid?"

"I am not sure I could be doing that when I am being that drunk," said Balur.

"Something that nimble, or that stupid?"

Will was now fully astride the champion's upper arm and shimmying down toward his wrist. Lette felt like her heart was in her mouth. The champion's arm swayed back and forth, pitching Will left, then right. If it pivoted into the rock face, it would crush his grip and send him flying...

"Hmmm..." said Balur. "I am wondering what he is going to be doing now."

"Get up h—" Lette started.

"Don't worry," Will interrupted. "I've got it!"

And he let go with his hands. He flailed backward, arms pinwheeling. Lette screamed. It was a high-pitched, shrill sound.

An awful sound. She hated it, but she had no time. Because Will…

Because Will…

Will was hanging upside down, gripping the champion's wrist with his knees. He casually reached into the champion's slack palm and plucked the goblet out.

"Got it!" he called up, cheery as a spring fucking lamb.

"Fuck you!" Lette yelled back. Gods, if he didn't die on the way back up here, she was going to kill him when he arrived.

Slowly, Will started trying to work his way back up into a sitting position. Lette stared at him angrily, finding her eyes unexpectedly blurry.

"Be being a shame if he fell," said Balur quietly.

"Of course it'd be a fucking shame!" Lette snapped.

"Because of the chalice that he'd be dropping, right?" said Balur heavily.

She turned to look at him. The look he was giving her from behind the scrim of blood oozing out of a hundred cuts could not be entirely described as innocent.

"Yes," she hissed through gritted teeth. "Because of the motherfucking chalice."

She knew what he was implying. And there was no way she was giving the lizard man ammunition like that.

Slowly, carving years off her life as he came, Will scrambled back up the champion's body. When he was within arm's reach, she seized his wrists and heaved him up onto the ledge.

From his knees he grinned up at her, and held out the goblet. Blood-red wine sloshed back and forth inside it.

"Impressive, right?" he said, grinning.

And gods hex him from now until the end of his days, he was right too.

46

Unprepared

Quirk stood on the walls of Vinter and watched the horizon. Clouds of black smoke smudged the sunset. Three days was not enough time. It was just not enough.

They had barely cleared the corpses out of the High Temple when the first reports of the dragons' army had started to come in. It was finally on the march, pushing deep into Vinland's heartlands, roasting and slaughtering as it came.

"How long?" Quirk had asked. She had thought that the events of the coup had left her too exhausted to care about anything, but she had been wrong. Her heart had hammered against her ribs like a frenzied prisoner behind bars.

"They'll be at our walls in three days' time."

And it had not been enough time.

But she had done her best. At least she could go to her grave knowing that. She had been the best and done the best she could. It was just it didn't matter.

In some ways the organization they'd managed had been miraculous. Especially considering this was Vinter. Words of events had spread through the sluggish city like fire through thatch. The military had mobilized like a herd of spooked centaurs leaping to their feet. Within a day they had press-ganged every able-bodied man and woman into a uniform. Combat drills had been run. They had been building defenses. Smithies had forged blades, arrow- and spearheads, bossed shields, and breastplates. Water had been gathered for putting out the inevitable fires. Food had been stockpiled in underground facilities. Farmers had been forced to collect crops as early and as quickly as possible. The fields had been emptied of workers. She had commissioned teams to build her ballistas.

And of all people, Firkin had been almost single-handedly instrumental in pushing all their plans toward completion. He had marched through the city, bare-chested, bellowing orders and abuse in his thunderous voice. Quirk had followed, dazed in his wake, nursing a headache, and a wineskin she had found herself carrying around almost constantly. Firkin's boundless rage and enthusiasm were exhausting. She was almost always thirsty in his presence, and she trusted the wine here more than she trusted the water.

Wherever he went, people had fallen into a frenzy of activity. "More!" he had bellowed at them, and they had done more. She had had to ask him to ease off when reports started coming in of people collapsing from exhaustion as they tried to do everything he asked of them. She could not risk him thinning their numbers further.

And still, despite all their efforts, it had not been enough time.

More information about the oncoming army had filtered into the city. Three dragons were at its head: Diffinax, her old foe who had conquered Tamar and destroyed Birchester; Theerax, who had foiled Will, Lette, and Balur in Batarra; and Gorrax, a massive brute who had apparently laid waste to most of Salera's capital city, Essoa. Quirk wasn't looking forward to telling Lette about that when she returned. If she remembered correctly, most of Lette's family were meant to be from that city.

When Lette returned... That was it now. That was the last hope. She stood on the walls of Vinland, watching the smoke rise, knowing she had not done enough, knowing that their only hope was distant and in someone else's hands.

What if Lette failed? What if Barph's Strength was just a

nonexistent myth? What if she, Balur, and Will were all dead? What if they simply came too late? What if the effects of the wine were an exaggerated rumor?

Then she and everyone else in this city had nothing, and they would die. Vinter and Vinland would fall as one, and take the last outpost of hope in Avarra with them. That was it. That was the simple truth.

She looked over to the others on the wall—Afrit, pacing back and forth, muttering to herself; a line of recently conscripted soldiers, gripping a mix of old swords and new pitchforks, some with hands gnarled by arthritis, others with palms too young to be worn rough by calluses; and Firkin, standing a little in front of her, pressed against the wall's makeshift battlements, beard whipping back over his shoulder in the evening's still-warm breeze.

"They're coming," he said, turning to grin back at Quirk. "They're stomping their little feet, all eager and excited. Like virgins on their wedding nights. Tender and sweet." He licked his lips. Quirk suppressed a shudder. As efficient as this new iteration of Firkin was, he was no more pleasant than the last. "They want to throw themselves upon our steel. To hack at us while their guts spill out sweet and slick. An intermingling. A sacrifice." He grinned. "There's a sort of beauty in that, I think."

Quirk tried hard to remember all the help Firkin had been. She tried to remember that she had done nothing to help heal his encroaching madness. Listening to this drivel was a direct consequence of her decisions.

"Have another drink, Firkin," she said, holding out her wine-skin for him with what she hoped passed for a smile. He was quieter at least when he was really drunk. As he approached her, her headache spiked. She really had to cut back on her own wine consumption. Cutting back on the stress wasn't really an option right now.

Firkin grabbed the wineskin greedily and guzzled it down. Quirk stared back out at the Vinland landscape. The dragons' army was burning everything before it. No attempt was being made to sway the hearts and minds of the Vinlanders anymore. They had defied the dragons' bid for worship and love for too long. Clearly, now the only fit fate for them was to be destroyed.

Two hundred and thirty thousand strong. That was what she had heard. An army unlike any other seen before in Avarra. Something epochal. Two hundred and thirty thousand fanatical troops come to punish the heathens who rejected their new gods. New living gods, who stood at the head of their army, spewing fire and hatred.

What was left of the academic in her couldn't help but think of the history books that would be written about this time, about that army. The superlatives that the future's historians would fall over themselves to use.

She felt a hand on her arm. She knew without looking that it was Afrit.

"I'm okay," she said. She knew what question was forming on Afrit's lips without looking too.

"You don't look okay. You look like you've got a hedgehog wedged in your under garments."

Quirk gave that a thoughtful nod. "That's a very specific metaphor," she said finally.

"Well," said Afrit, lowering her voice, "I thought it might be better than just saying it looks like you're spending a lot of time thinking about how royally fucked we are."

Quirk winced.

"I mean," Afrit kept on whispering, "I know we are, but I'm not sure looking that way in front of the troops is the best idea."

Quirk glanced over again at the line of soldiers standing on the wall. She made sure she looked away before grimacing.

"Maybe a pep talk?" Afrit suggested.

"Isn't that why we have Firkin?" Quirk whispered.

"He just talked about the glory of intermingling guts," Afrit pointed out.

Quirk sighed. "Why do *you* never make inspiring speeches?" she asked, which was petulant but not necessarily unwarranted.

"Because I didn't tame the dragons in Kondorra," Afrit said. "Because I didn't lead rebellions in Tamar and the Vale. Because if history remembers me at all, it will be as a sidekick. Sidekicks don't make the speeches. We've both studied history enough to know that."

"That's not—" Quirk started.

"Just make the fucking speech already."

Quirk decided another sigh would not necessarily be well received, so she choked it down, turned to the troops, and plastered something approximating a smile on her lips.

"Try to make it look less like the hedgehog is now trying to nest in your arsehole," Afrit whispered.

Quirk chewed back the retort, and readjusted her smile. She took a breath. "They will come tomorrow," she said, trying to make sure her voice carried to as many people as possible. "They will bring forces beyond counting. They will bring dragons. And they will bring flame to burn us to the ground."

"Not where I would have started," Afrit whispered.

"They will look fearsome," Quirk went on. "They will look fucking terrifying actually." She took another breath. There was a young man, perhaps sixteen summers old, staring at her, face as white as a sheet. He was gripping a pitchfork that was shaking in his white-knuckled grip.

"They will stand before these walls and they will roar their hatred, and their rage, and their flames at us. And we shall be afraid." She paused. "I shall be afraid."

"Okay, okay, I get it," whispered Afrit. "Next time I'll do the pissing speech."

"They shall expect that fear to break us," Quirk went on.

"They shall expect it to rob us of our will to fight. They will expect us to be brittle with fear. So that when they push, we break. And when we break they will spill in here and burn us all."

She looked up and down the line of soldiers. Glared at them.

"I will be afraid," she said. "But I will not be brittle. I will not break. Because I will also have hope. Because I will have all of you at my back. All of your rage. All of your hate. All of your faith in Barph. All of your history and your skill. All of your guts. Because I know that fear is okay. Fear is just one emotion. Fear is not as strong as the love we bear each other, and that we bear Barph. And our strength will face them down, and our strength will be greater than theirs. And all their rage, their hate, their belief...it will come to be eclipsed by *their* fear. The fear we shall put in them. Together. As one. Because we are stronger!"

She thundered the last words as loud as she could. She looked into the young soldier's eyes and saw a little more color in his cheeks now.

"In Barph's name!" she cried.

"In Barph's name!" they roared back, up and down the line.

Quirk smiled as warmly as she could and headed toward the steps leading down into the streets.

"Okay," said Afrit, following after her. "I concede that you finished strong. Now you just have to give that speech at every other wall on this city, and we should be okay."

"Right up until the dragon's army actually shows up and proves how full of shit I am," Quirk said.

"Yes," Afrit agreed. "Until then."

It really did seem to be going well until the dragon's army showed up. Morale had been strong through the night. Fires had burned bright, songs had been sung.

And then the sun had gone and ruined it all by rising.

The dragon's army had marched on through the night. There was bloodlust in those troops now. They were clearly visible barely three miles away. Behind them the ground smoked—a charred ruin. The scent of grapes roasting on the vine was a faint tang at the back of the smoke slowly drifting over the city. Light reflected off polished steel. Faint shouts could be heard. The ground trembled slightly under their collective feet.

But what everyone gathered on the walls was truly looking for was the dragons.

"Where are they?" Afrit was pressed up against battlements made of scavenged wood and broken furniture tacked on to the crumbling stone parapets beneath.

Quirk swigged from her wineskin. She'd started early this morning. Tent after tent stretched out across the landscape. Knots of men scurried back and forth, but of the dragons there was no sign.

"Maybe they can't be bothered with us," she said. "Maybe it's an act of disdain."

"Do they do that?" Afrit looked at her hopefully.

Quirk shrugged. "How in the Hallows am I supposed to know?"

"You're the leading expert on dragons!" Afrit, it seemed, was a little tense this morning.

Behind them, down in the city, the buzz of industry was still alive. Runners brought more wood, and more chunks of iron to add to the battlements. Nearby a carpenter was banging six-inch nails through the makeshift crenellations. In the streets below, a group of men had spent all night drinking and failing to figure out how to build a catapult. They were still hard at work.

Quirk felt a plucking at her shirt sleeve. She turned. Firkin had appeared once more. She'd lost track of him that night, but she'd stopped worrying about that. He seemed eager for this fight.

"Where are they?" he asked.

"The dragons?" Quirk asked. "I was just telling Afrit, I really don't know. I never had enough time to observe them in—"

"Not the fucking dragons!" Firkin interrupted. "Who gives the slightest shit about poxy dragons?"

Quirk stared at him. "Probably," she suggested, "all the people about to be attacked by them."

"Fuck the dragons." Firkin waved a dismissive hand. "What about Will. The other two. With the drink. Where are they?"

Quirk shrugged again. "You mean Barph's Strength? The gods alone know. Maybe they're all with the dragons having cups of tea. How am I supposed to know?"

"We need them." Afrit had glanced back from her search for the dragons.

"I know that!" Quirk snapped. "I am nothing but aware of that. They are..." She broke off, lowered her voice. "They are pretty much our only hope. But I cannot magic them here."

"You do magic!" Firkin shouted, affronted. "Do the magic! Do the magic! Do it! Do it!"

"I can roast you alive, if you want," Quirk hissed. "That's my magic. Do you want that?"

"Roast my nuts for a saint's day?" Firkin spat over the wall as if that were somehow a response. He seemed to be back to his old self this morning.

"Are you feeling better?" Quirk asked. "You seem—"

"I will be fucking better"—Firkin wheeled on her—"when we have Barph's Strength. I told them how to get it. I laid it fucking out. They should be here with it. Now. I said now. I want it now."

So...not really better then. Quirk felt the headache buzzing behind her eyes again. She really had meant to drink less today.

But there was an army coming.

Suddenly a shout rose from the soldiers to her left. She spun to stare at them. People were pointing out into the fields.

"There they are," Afrit gasped.

"Will and Lette?" said Quirk, squinting out at the fields, trying to work out what the pair was doing out there beyond the city walls.

Then she remembered that the regular city soldiers didn't give two shits about Will, or Lette, or Balur.

Then she saw the dragons.

They must have taken to the sky in the night. They must have been above her while she slept. They could have rained fire down upon them at any time. They could have taken this city at any time.

But they had not. Instead they had waited. For this. This moment of revelation.

They swept down out of clouds and smoke. Their wings sent curling pillars of gray wafting through the air. They roared. The clouds and the earth trembled. Their army roared.

They were titans of flesh, and scale, and fire. They were a refutation of reality. They were simply too large to truly comprehend as a whole. It was as if great geologic tracts of rock and soil had wrestled free of the earth, and risen writhing into the air. One was a slab of slate-gray horns and muscles, wings spreading like night falling upon the earth. He sent streamers of red fire howling up into the night as he arced and roared. His mouth opened like the gates to the Hallows, a yawning herald of inevitable death.

To his right, a creature of pure gold spun up toward the heavens. It glinted and glittered, like some great testament to death raised up by loving and insane hands. Its eyes were red jewels studded in a face that was a nightmare of scales and spines. Teeth protruded from its elongated mouth at all angles, fine as Lette's stiletto blades and long as Balur's tail. Its own tail was a contusion of bone and spikes. Razorlike fins stitched their way down its back.

And finally, battering and bludgeoning its way through the sky on wings like spreading stains—Diffinax. A mottled orange and brown creature. The ragged edges of his wings fluttered in the air. He came crashing down to earth. Talons that seemed to stretch all the way from the fields of Vinland into Quirk's nightmares tore up massive tracts of earth. He reared up on his hind legs, broad as two great oak trunks, and sent a column of fire smashing toward the heavens.

Part of her, the part she thought she had left behind in the Tamathian University, reveled in it. It was glorious. The dragons were purposely intimidating them. They had waited all night, so they could do this: dominate their foe. It was a fascinating glimpse into their natural instincts, their psychology.

Except she would never write a paper on that subject. Instead she would die here, a victim of those stupid, hateful instincts.

"A victim of the thing I study," she muttered to herself. "Just like a good, self-respecting thaumatobiologist."

"What?" said Afrit, looking over.

Quirk shook her head.

"They're here! They're here!" A frantic voice came hurtling up the stairs behind them. Quirk looked over her shoulder. It was Durmitt, red-faced and panting. He stared at them all wildly.

"They're here!" he shouted again despite the fact he was only a few yards from them now.

"I know," said Quirk gently. "Everyone knows. They're quite large and they're spitting flames."

"No!" bellowed Durmitt. "Down here." He pointed back down the stairs. "In the city."

Quirk's eyes went wide. Dragons? In the city? A fourth... How had they...

"The ones you sent down to get Barph's Strength," said Durmitt, interrupting her panic. "Will and . . . and . . . the other two."

It was too much. Too much information too quickly. Quirk whipped around, looked out at the dragons roaring and howling outside the city. She saw the army behind them starting to march. She looked left, saw the line of troops stretched out along the wall. Looked back to Durmitt.

So much hung in the balance.

"Did they have it?" she asked. Her voice held a calm she didn't feel. It was as if the emotions were too big, had log-jammed in her throat and left her voice untouched.

"Had what?" Durmitt stared at her with his wild eyes.

The logjam broke.

"The motherfucking chalice!" she screamed. "Barph's fucking Strength!"

Durmitt took a step back, almost went over the edge of the wall and down into the city below. "I . . ." he said. "I don't . . ."

Quirk took a step toward him. She knew she should have stopped drinking. If she was less drunk and hungover, she would probably feel a lot less murderous.

And then, before she even had the chance to kill the impulse to wring Durmitt's stupid neck, there they were, stomping up the steps. Will. Lette. Balur. The trio gone to get their only hope. And against all the odds they had held up their end of the bargain just as she, against the odds, had held up hers. Because there, in Lette's hand, she saw it. A chalice studded with jewels. Red wine slopped over its sides.

She looked out again at the oncoming army, at its titanic leaders . . . She, Lette, Will, Balur, Afrit, Firkin—they had already beaten the odds. Maybe—just maybe—they could beat these odds too.

She turned back to the trio, and she thought her smile might split her skull.

She ran forward, seized Lette in a massive hug. "You did it," she heard herself saying. "You actually did it."

"I swear," said Lette to her, "if I have to climb another set of fucking stairs, I am going to start chopping people's legs off just on principle."

Which didn't make any sense, but Quirk didn't care.

Balur was looking down at her. "I was doing it as well," he said. "Where is my moment of awkward affection?"

Will was just rubbing the side of his head and groaning.

Quirk just didn't have time for all of their usual bullshit. She was happy...no, she was overjoyed to see them. And still she didn't.

"Does it work?" she asked instead, reaching out for the goblet. "Does it do everything Firkin said it would?"

She glanced over at the old man, to see how he was taking all this. He was staring at the chalice, jaw slack. She supposed it was a fairly unbelievable sight. At least he was being quiet.

"I don't know," said Lette. "Only Will drank it, and he..." She shrugged. "He was cataclysmically wasted, almost instantly. But I did see him pull off some improbable shit that should have got him killed."

Quirk thought about it. "Doesn't that describe most of Will's life."

"Hey," grumbled Will. "That only happens where you're around."

"It does something," said Lette. "Even if it's just getting people really wasted really fast and making them overly confident."

And that was not exactly what Quirk wanted to hear. And yet... And yet... The chalice was real. Its contents were sloshing right in front of her. And it had to work. The dragons would be here in an hour. It had to.

"I will take confidence," she said. "Gods if that's all it does, well, at least that way our lines might not break before the enemy gets here."

She took the chalice. As she moved, she considered drinking from it herself. But she could not afford to lose control yet. She had to get this to every soldier. She would be the last to drink. Instead the first would be... She held it out to the sixteen-year-old from the night before. He had upgraded his pitchfork to a sword. It looked a lot like an oversized butter knife.

The youth looked at her, a question in his eyes. But he didn't voice it as he took the chalice, raised it to his lips, and drank.

And drank.

And drank.

Quirk pulled the chalice away from him. The boy gasped, wine running down his chin. "Oh," he gasped. And then, "Bugger me." He staggered, planted his sword for support, reeled. "Oh. Can I have some more? That's... Barph's balls. Wow."

Quirk tried to assess. Was he stronger? Was he invulnerable? If she tried to burn him now, would he live?

He just seemed very drunk.

She looked back at Will. He had a graze down one cheek, a bruise on his lip. Were those the marks of someone invulnerable? She didn't think so. But he *was* alive. Was that enough?

There was not enough time. There was never enough.

She passed the chalice to the next man in line. It was still as full as when she had given it to the first man. And that was magic, wasn't it? That was a sign surely. "Here," she said. "Now you."

The man took a deep gulp, staggered, stared at the chalice, and tried to push it back to his lips. Quirk grabbed it out of his hands.

The man stared cross-eyed into space. "Oh that's lovely that is." He laughed. A sound of pure joy. "Oh, that's perfect."

"Your turn." She gave it to the next man in line.

The man raised it to his lips.

Then from behind her, Quirk heard a cry. It sounded like a kettle reaching the boil at the very moment it orgasmed and also happened to lay eyes upon its most mortal enemy. A high-pitched animal squeal that scraped through her brain and grated against the roof of her skull.

She spun around to see—arms outstretched, fingers hooked like claws, lips pulled back against his teeth in a rictus of the purest, most unadulterated rage she had ever seen—Firkin charging toward her.

47

And a New Day Will Begin

Firkin watched as Will, and Lette, and Balur walked up onto the wall surrounding Vinter. He watched as they held out the chalice containing Barph's Strength. He watched as Quirk fawned over them and it.

And he knew. He knew that this was...this was...the end.

Of...

Of what?

He knew that he knew. He knew that all of this—everything that had happened here—made sense somehow. He knew that it was all part of some grand plan, some strategy. But he didn't know what it was. He couldn't...

Remember?

There was a memory in his head. Something hidden. But who had hidden it there? Was it him? And if he had...then what? Did answers matter now? He was no longer sure where he ended and the memory began. His headache was a constant throbbing behind his eyes. Like an earthquake in his mind. And things kept clambering out of the fissures. Words, and thoughts, and plans. And he knew that somehow they were all connected, all important. But he didn't know how. He didn't...remember.

Maybe the memory wasn't enough, or wasn't complete, or was the wrong memory. Maybe the memory was keeping secrets.

Maybe that was what was coming to an end. Maybe he wouldn't be confused anymore.

As he watched, he felt something in his head moving. He felt it aligning. And he waited. He watched Quirk take the chalice. And he did nothing. Because that was all that was left to do. Just wait. The memory was whispering to him. He could hear his own lips crooning the phrase. "Just wait."

Dragons were at his back. An army was marching. But none of that mattered. All that mattered was the glint of the light shining from the goblet, the sound of the wine sloshing inside of it.

Emotions were starting to shake loose inside his gut. They felt distant, as if they belonged to somebody else. Perhaps they did.

The first of the soldiers drank from the cup. Firkin watched him almost curiously. The way the wine spilled from the edges of the cup, ran down his chin, through his peach-fuzz beard. There were stories in the ripples of that wine. There were untold histories. He could see them right there, almost his for the grasping. They were his stories. His histories somehow. Or the memory's. Or he had a memory of them belonging to the memory …

He watched. He waited. He waited for things to make sense. Because they would. The memory in his head was stirring now, growing. There was no stopping it. He knew that. He had given up trying to resist. He had given up trying to ignore it. It just was. So Barph's Strength spilled down the youth's chin and the memory grew.

The pressure in his head doubled, tripled. He dropped to one knee. No one was paying attention to him. He was strangely aware of the dragons roaring. Those sounds seemed louder to him than anything else. They were important somehow. And the reason why … Gods, it was so close.

He pressed his hands to his head, trying to stop it from splitting wide open. And the bubble of memory had to burst soon, had to rupture and break into his thoughts. He knew it would. It always did. Just wait. Just wait.

A second man was drinking. And he was so close to … to …

He tried to get up off his knee, found himself down on the other one as well. He thought maybe he was screaming, but maybe that was the dragons, or maybe he just remembered screaming.

He just...just...just had to wait...

Everything was a roar now. A howl of rage. His rage. And... and someone else's. The memory in his head. That was it. It was a memory of rage. Of blood. Of wine. He almost had it now. The memory wasn't bursting. It was crushing his thoughts, his memories, it was forcing him to become part of it. This was no longer an invasion, it was his mind being co-opted, recruited...

The second soldier was clutching for the cup.

The memory was a memory of flailing fingers. Grasping, gasping.

Quirk took the cup away from the man.

And yes, that was in the memory. In the rage. That denial. That the cup would not be his, could not be his.

But there was the cup. There was Barph's Strength. The wine and the blood.

He almost remembered now. He was so close...

Emotions in him. Memories of emotions.

Memories of rage.

Quirk moved as if in slow motion. All the world in slow motion. The dragons' wings spreading. Their skin rippling. Muscles stretching taut. Their teeth stained yellow. Their tongues bright red. Quirk's teeth. Smiling. Uncertain. Unsure. Proffering the cup. Proffering it to...to...

He tried to focus on the soldier. Tried to bring him into focus. But the pain in his head was too great now. The world was splintering. Sharp fragments of light and madness. He grasped desperately at the pieces, tried to put them back together.

Quirk moving like molasses. Almost still.

Proffering the cup.

Proffering it to...

To...

Not him.

Denying *him*.

Turning away from *him*.

His wine. *His* blood.

And the rage tore through him like a knife through flesh. He was eviscerated by rage. His was left hollow and gasping by it. By the scale of it. Years of rage. Decades of rage. Centuries of rage. All of it at once. Too much of it, bursting through his seams. Too much to hold. Too much for his mind.

He moved. Maybe he had already been moving, his body slightly ahead of his fracturing, fragmenting mind. His body holding together just a little longer. But he could feel it coming apart. Trying to hold the rage was too much for it. It couldn't take it. The skin at the edges of his mouth was tearing. His grimace was too large for this paltry frame of flesh and bone.

A sound was coming out of him. Not a scream or a howl. Just sound. It was being expelled. He could no longer hold it. The integrity of his being was coming apart.

With nerveless fingers he seized the cup, tore it from Quirk's hands. His arms were shaking. His bones felt like rubber. And he was so close. But this was it. This was the moment he had been waiting for. The memory had been waiting for. This stupid fucking body would not fail him now. It could not.

He was on his knees, trying to lift the goblet. And it was so heavy. As if it held an ocean of wine. Of blood. He tried to get his mouth beneath it, tip it. Wine was spilling from the cup, a great torrent of it, splashing over his stomach and knees. He wanted to paw at it, to put just a fingertip in it and put it to his lips. But he couldn't let go of the cup. Not now. This was it. This was it.

He was shaking, and shaking, and shaking. He fell backward. The goblet was an anchor weight crushing down on his chest.

He screamed. He heaved. A roaring screamed in his ears.

A drop of wine splashed upon his lip.

It was as if he had never tasted wine before. It was as if he had never drunk before. It was as if he had never breathed before. It was as if the world was dirty, and rotten, and infected and he had never known before, as if he had forgotten what purity tasted like. And now he tasted it. He tasted beauty. He tasted joy. He tasted love. It was white heat in his veins. It was summer sun sluicing through leaves. It was lightness.

He rose. It was so easy. So easy. All the aches and pains and petty frailties sloughing away. The concerns of physicality were a discarded coat, cast into a corner to be forgotten forever. He rose, and he rose, and he rose. He grew. He swelled.

People were staring. All around him they were staring. They were dropping to their knees. They were crying out.

And he laughed, laughed even as he drank, as he drained the chalice to its very last impossible drop, braying and spraying as he did so. Because it had worked. Everything had worked.

Because he remembered.

48

WTF?

Will stared. He didn't understand. He didn't understand anything.

He had walked upstairs for three days. He had been drunk for one of them. He had been hungover for the next two. He had actually begged Lette to kill him at one point. She had thought it was funnier to not do it. He had arrived in Vinter. He had discovered that against all the odds, Quirk had held up her end of the bargain. She had helped Firkin win the city. He had heard that the dragons' army was marching. That it was almost on them.

So, as much as his knees had begged and pleaded with him not to do it, he had run for the city walls. He had yelled at the top of his lungs that he needed to find Quirkelle Bal Tehrin. And he had been sent to her. He had given her Barph's Strength. She had given it to the army. It had all worked.

Except he knew that Barph's Strength didn't.

It couldn't. If it did, how could he feel so bad? And the men he watched drink Barph's Strength became…drunk. That was it. There was nothing else. And Will simply couldn't believe that if you ran them through, they wouldn't still fall, wouldn't still bleed out, wouldn't still die.

And then, out of nowhere…

No. He didn't understand at all.

He tried to piece it together. Firkin had been over by the makeshift barricades at the top of the wall. He had been…

what? Will really hadn't been paying much attention to him. There had been too much else going on, and Firkin, for once, had been being quiet. He thought Firkin might have grabbed his head perhaps. Another headache?

And then... Then he had been running at Quirk, screaming like a banshee. His face had been full of hate. But as he got to her... He had gripped the goblet, but he'd been in some kind of fit. He'd collapsed, pouring the wine all over himself. And the cup never ran dry so it had just poured, and poured.

And then...

And then...

Then shit just got weird.

Firkin had... he had...

He'd stood up. Will had seen that. He'd stood up as if everything was fine, and he had drunk more. That was definitely one thing Will had seen.

But he'd seen something else as well. Something layered over that image of an old man picking himself up, and grinning, and taking a long, long drink from a jewel-studded goblet. As if the images from his left and right eyes had not agreed.

He'd seen...

What the fuck had he seen?

Firkin had... grown. He'd grown... younger? Or more... virile? Will wasn't sure that was a word he particularly wanted to associate with Firkin. But in that second image there had been an undeniable sense of energy to the old man. A youthfulness, even while his body... Well, it had not exactly stayed the same. Because he'd also grown... and... well, just grown. Up. Wider. Broader. Beyond six feet. Beyond Balur's towering eight feet, he had grown. Twelve feet. Twenty feet. He stood as Lawl's champion had stood. He was massive, and laughing, and drinking. And everyone was staring. Everyone had their neck craned up at that massive second image stuck on the world over the first. So it wasn't just Will going mad. It was everyone.

And there he stood. Firkin. Massive. Towering. He had flung the goblet away. It had bounced, and even as it had glittered and spun, Will had seen that it was empty. All that infinite river of wine was gone.

Firkin had laughed. It had been a massive, booming sound. Will had felt it as much as he heard it. Not in his sternum, where he expected it, but in his head, his thoughts. It had been a wild, capricious laugh that seemed to infect him, to make him want to run and scream naked through the night, cackling as he went. It had been a mad, mad joy. It had reminded him of the way he had felt drinking Barph's Strength.

Was that what the wine was meant to do? Was that what Firkin had promised them it would do? Why in the name of all the gods would it only work on Firkin?

Now, looming over all of them, Firkin turned to look out at the oncoming army. The hundreds of thousands of men. The dragons that still dwarfed him. Both Firkins turned, the massive one and the small one together in perfect harmony. And both of them laughed.

Will clutched at his head. There was a buzzing behind his eyes, and pain in his head.

And then Firkin gripped the edge of the makeshift battlements with both his normal and his massive hand, and like a man hopping a fence, flung himself over the wall. Just casually leapt down thirty feet of brickwork, like it was nothing.

And maybe it was. Maybe the massive Firkin was the truth. Maybe the Firkin whom Will had always known, was a lie.

Will rushed to the edge of the battlements. They all did. Every man, woman, and child standing there clutching whatever scavenged weapon they had found surged forward. They all looked down. And Will half-expected to see Firkin's broken corpse lying spread-eagle on the ground. To see it was all some mad illusion...delusion.

But no. No, there was Firkin. Straightening up. And up. Taller now than ever. Thirty feet tall. The height of the wall. His lank hair was blowing in the breeze that buffeted up against the great wall. Faintly, down below, Will could also see the smaller Firkin, still there, but fainter now, less present than that strange, vast version of his old friend.

Then Firkin was striding away, taking huge steps through the surrounding fields, leaving footprints that would later collect water like small ponds. And with each massive stride it was harder and harder to see that smaller version of Firkin, and the massive version became more and more true, until it was all Will could see. And it was still growing. Forty feet now. He had hands that could rip a man in half. And the dragons were still massive, massive creatures, but a little less massive now.

The dragons' army seemed to hesitate as Will watched, as all of Vinter watched. And this was but one man come against them, and they could swarm him and kill him with ease. But still... such a man. His beard like a waterfall down his chest. Sixty feet tall now, still growing.

The three dragons howled challenges to this creature that had come to defy them. Even from two miles away, Will could feel the air thrum with the volume of their scream. But Firkin just laughed. Seventy feet tall now.

What was going on? How could this be true?

He should be doing something, Will thought. All of them gathered here in Vinter—they should be taking advantage of this somehow. But all they could do was watch in wonder.

The dragons swept toward Firkin. All three of them. Like arrows loosed from bows. Massive heads held out straight on massive necks. Massive wings beating at the air. Massive claws poised to eviscerate.

The slate-gray Theerax was in the lead. Will remembered him from the camp in Batarra. Remembered the scale of him up close. Remembered the heat of his flame scouring through the world. Remembered knowing that he was death. Just the way he'd known Diffinax was death in the Vale.

The dragon swept out, a mile before his troops, and smashed into Firkin, claws outstretched.

Firkin caught Theerax about the neck as the beast closed, his two huge hands closing about the dragon's throat. He pivoted on his back heel, even as the dragon's claws slashed and hacked at his chest and guts. He whipped the dragon round in a massive arc and brought him crashing down to earth.

The ground quaked. Battlements tore loose from Vinter's walls and fell crashing down to the earth. Men fell to their knees. Will's jaw fell along with them.

He couldn't...What...What was happening?

Firkin stood over the fallen dragon. It writhed on the ground, twisting around. Its jaws opened.

Firkin delivered a hammer blow to the side of Theerax's head. The long neck whiplashed to the side. The huge head struck the dirt, kicking up clouds of dust and sod.

Firkin was still laughing. Ribbons of flesh and blood ran down his chest, but he was laughing.

Then his back was bathed in flame as the other two dragons arrived. Diffinax. The beast from the Vale. Clouds of his fire coated him. The gold—surely Gorrax, who had tamed Salera—raced through the fire, claws extended, raking Firkin's back.

Firkin's laughter turned to a howl. He staggered forward. Theerax's gray head darted forward, tore at his ankles. Firkin went down.

Will gasped. He felt tears at the corners of his eyes. Firkin could have sat astride one of the three dragons and ridden it as a steed, but it was not enough. When one man faced off against three lions, you did not bet upon the man.

The dragons' army came to the same realization. They roared. They began to charge once more.

Firkin was on the ground, grappling with Theerax, trying to get on top of the beast. Its claws ripped and ripped at his skin.

The pair was occluded by another storm of fire.

The moment, whatever it was, whatever it had been, was slipping away. Firkin had bought them a few minutes of time. For what, Will had no idea. But they had wasted them.

"Battle stations!" he roared.

Everyone stared at him.

"A fucking attacking army is coming!" he screamed. "Get ready! Get in your battle stations!"

They had to have battle stations, right? That was what they were called, wasn't it? He wanted to glance at Lette, but he didn't have time for her to roll her eyes at him if he was wrong.

"Ready weapons!" It wasn't him this time. It was Quirk yelling, Quirk starting to run up and down the length of the wall. "The attack is coming! The attack is coming!"

The soldiers began to shake themselves, to form up in lines. Will took off in the opposite direction from Quirk. "Form up! Form up!" He grabbed a sluggish soldier by the shoulders. "They'll take your city from you while you stare!" The man stared after him. Will moved on. Time was slipping away with every footstep the oncoming army took.

Out in the field, Firkin was back on his feet, had one dragon by the tail while it clawed at the air and his face. Will could see his friend's back, remembered seeing the flame and claws scraping it. It was hard to tell at this distance, but the injuries appeared remarkably slight. His clothes were ragged, yes, but there was only a fine tracery of red line, and pink skin exposed. None of the brutal damage Will would have expected.

Did Firkin have a chance? Was it Barph's Strength? If only they'd drunk more, would it have worked? Was that the secret of Firkin's success?

Though, right now it didn't look exactly like success.

A dragon dug its claws into Firkin's back, picked him up, carried him two or three wing beats through the air, then sent him plowing face-first into the earth.

The dragons' army was spilling around the wrestling, writhing knot of bodies. Firkin lashed out with a massive hand. He kicked and stomped his way to standing. Around him, soldiers' lives ended in bloody ruins. But the others didn't stop running. They didn't try to swarm him, or stab him. Their gods were fighting this unexpected champion of Vinter. It was a conflict that was out of their league. And they had faith after all.

A dragon landed on Firkin's face, roaring fire, scrabbling with claws.

Maybe, Will thought, *the army was right*.

A troupe of men near him on the wall seemed more organized and less obscenely drunk than some of the others. Will paused in his madcap dash down Vinter's walls.

"What…" he managed, sucked down air. "What defenses do we have?" The lead soldier cocked a head at him, glanced at the other soldiers, clearly puzzled why someone would ask when they were arrayed before him.

"Archers?" Will managed. "Catapults? How in the Hallows do we stop them coming up these walls?"

The soldier looked down at the sword of his hand. "We stab them when they get to the top."

"That's it?" Will was incredulous. Quirk had always given the impression of not being completely fucking useless after all.

"There are archers strung out along the wall as best as we could manage, sir," said a taller soldier, one bearing a mustache on his upper lip the size of a baby seal pup. "But the bow isn't a popular weapon in the city, sir."

"Not a…" Because popularity was so important in defending your city from ravening hordes. "You see that giant oncoming fucking army?" Will double-checked.

The soldier shrugged. "Sorry, sir. It's just it's hard to hit something with an arrow after your fifth or sixth drink in the morning."

If the city could have spared the defenders, Will would have had a go at flinging the man off the wall to his death. Why did it have to be a city of Barph worshippers? Why couldn't it have been Lawl worshippers? Discipline-loving death worshippers. An army made of the cult of Lawl's black eye, with a bunch of white-eye healers packing the streets behind them? Then at least when they all died, Will wouldn't have had the nagging doubt that it was actually of stupidity.

Out in the fields Firkin had torn the dragon off his face. He had it by the neck and was flailing it into the earth again and again. Theerax was angling in, bathing his side in flames. Diffinax wheeled above, ready to descend.

The army's vanguard was only a few hundred yards from the walls. Long ladders were balanced on their shoulders. A few desultory arrows flicked down from the walls, mostly going well wide of their targets.

The time for preparing was no longer upon them. If the army wasn't ready, there was no way Will could get them there at this point.

"Shit," he swore. He looked down. He really needed to start carrying a weapon with him. "Someone give me a sword."

A large number of soldiers looked at him with very little sympathy.

"A knife," he yelled at them. "A dagger. A club. Any-fucking-thing!"

"Here." Someone shoved something at him. He grabbed it, felt the weight of it, looked down.

"Is this a fucking ladle?" he managed.

"I'm not the one who didn't bring a sword to a giant battle," said the soldier.

Will didn't have much of a comeback for that one.

49

Sour Grapes

The ladder crashed down against the battlements. Hastily tacked together wood and nails gave way.

"One of these days," said Lette, "I really am going to have to learn how to use a crossbow properly."

"I am always thinking that a crossbow is being a bit of a Nancy's weapon," said Balur. He grabbed hold of the ladder's top rung, heaved. With a grunt he tipped it backward. From below, a scream drifted up.

"Would you care to explain that?" Lette leaned down over the battlements, spotted another man hefting a ladder, and flung a knife. The man stumbled, then fell.

"I think I would be being feeling more charitable about the crossbow," said Balur, starting to move toward the spot where another ladder had landed, "if the longbow didn't exist. But it does. And it is requiring great skill and strength. It is making the crossbow seem lazy in comparison." He shrugged. "I am being an archery purist, I suppose."

Lette kicked aside some drunken ass of a Vinter soldier and prepared her broadsword. "You're not a purist. You're a snob."

The first of the dragon soldiers poked his head above the height of the battlements. Lette poked him in the face with his sword. He fell back, flailing and screaming.

"I am always thinking," said Balur, breaking the top rung of the siege ladder with his own sword, "that *purist* and *snob* are meaning the same thing, and are just being used depending upon which side of an argument you are falling."

"There's a very distinct difference, you arse." Lette grunted as she thrust her blade into another man's face. "And it's to do with how reasonable the expectations are. If your opinion was reasonable then you'd be a purist. But a longbow is really fucking hard to use." To mix things up she slashed her sword at the next soldier's arm. He pitched sideways. "It's unreasonable to expect everyone to use them. You're a snob."

Balur grabbed the next soldier up by the face. "There is being quite a lot of subjectivity in that argument," he said, raising the soldier above his head in both hands, "but I am willing to concede the general point. I am a snob. I can own that." He took careful aim and threw the soldier he was holding into the next one perched on the ladder below.

"I don't need to demonstrate my skill with a bow," Lette said. "I have no pride at stake in this. I just need to be able to hit something at range. There's only so far I can fling a knife."

Someone crashed into her from behind. She spun around. It was a soldier of the dragon army. Two Vinter soldiers lay dead at his feet. Behind him dragon troops were boiling up a ladder and onto the wall. She cursed.

"That," said Balur, grunting as he swung his sword in a great arc, "I think, is why this whole purist thing is not making sense to you." He gutted one soldier, beheaded another. "You are already having a realm of expertise. You have mastered the knife."

"I wouldn't say 'mastered,'" Lette cut in, just as she cut into another man's throat.

"False modesty is having no place in a warrior's arsenal," Balur said loftily.

Lette rolled her eyes, and ducked a series of blows from an incensed dragon soldier armed with a fairly prodigious morning star. "Quoting that doesn't make me think of how smart you are," she told Balur. "It just reminds me that you've only read one book."

"You are knowing that this is not my native tongue. One book is very impressive." Balur actually sounded wounded as she ducked behind the morning star–wielding lunatic and slashed his hamstrings. The soldier collapsed screaming, and Balur delivered the coup de grâce.

"Okay," Lette conceded, "your reading achievements are not totally underwhelming." She looked about. "Also, I think we've lost this section of the wall."

The Vinter soldiers had given a good fight, but they were outnumbered on a scale of three or four to one. People were being flung down the walls to the left and right. Blood was misting the air and spilling around their feet.

"To the stairs?" Balur asked.

"After you."

"Oh no." Balur shook his head. "Ladies first."

Lette grit her teeth. "Fine, but only because you're such a big bastard."

"Actually," said Balur, planting a massive foot in the back of one dragon soldier and sending him flying down off the edge of the wall, "I have been trying to lose a little weight recently."

Lette looked at him askance. "Seriously? There's like, no fat on you."

"I put it on in my tail. It is hard to notice." Balur snapped the aforementioned tail around, slammed it into the neck of one of the dragon army soldiers. The woman's neck jerked at an acute angle and she dropped bonelessly.

"Seems like a little extra weight back there might be helpful," Lette said. "And anyway, you're being ridiculous."

"The weight is having some advantages, but I am disliking the speed it is costing me. It is throwing me off my game." Balur leaned down, punched a soldier into unconsciousness. "Note how I have not been eating any of my foes today. That is being self-restraint."

"I was wondering why you hadn't done that."

She was on the steps leading down from the wall into the city, darting and stabbing around Balur's legs, cutting at ankles and hamstrings. As enemy soldiers dropped, she pulled their bodies clear so Balur didn't trip. She could do nothing about the viscera and blood making the stonework slick beneath their feet.

"So," she said after a few minutes' work, "Firkin went and turned into a giant and went off to fight the dragons."

"Yes," said Balur, caving in a man's skull. "I was not expecting that."

"A bit fucking weird," Lette said.

"Very much."

Lette glanced down. Dragon soldiers were starting to swarm up the foot of the stairs. "Time to head into the streets," she said, tapping Balur's back.

"Already?" He grabbed the throat of the soldier he was fighting and held him aloft as a human shield so he could glance backward. He rolled his eyes. "Fine."

They hacked their way down into the street below. "Bit of hit-and-run then?" Lette said to him.

"That is always being fun," he said, as they dropped back looking for a good ambush spot.

"As far as siege defenses go," Lette commented as they went, "this is fucking terrible, isn't it?"

"Awful." Balur sounded disgusted. But then he shrugged. "Fucking Barphists," he said.

Lette nodded in agreement. "Fucking Barphists."

50

Falling Down

The stones around Quirk's feet glowed white-hot. The corpses of the soldiers who had tried to defend this wall alongside her were nothing but ash. She was alone. She was at the limits of her control. But the wall had not fallen. It would not fall. Vinter would not fall. She would not allow it. This was, by necessity, her final stand. And so she would stand here, and the world would burn in front of her, until it finally submitted.

The dragons' army was still pouring into the city, she knew. She could see them to the east and west surging up their ladders. She knew they were behind her in the streets. But this wall—this section of wall beneath her feet—had not fallen. And while it stood, and while she stood, then the city would not fall. This island of defiance would always beat at its heart.

She tried to breathe. She was losing herself. The torrent of power and flame was scouring through, threatening to sweep her away. But she had to hold on to herself. She had to hang on to the why of it all. The fire had to be her tool. Never the other way around. Never again.

So she planted her feet, and she burned. And she burned. And she burned. She sent tendrils of fire to slap away ladders. She sent it spinning down the stairs as soldiers tried to climb up behind her. She sent balls of it arcing into the ranks of soldiers who were within her range.

And out of range…the dragons. They were still out in the fields outside the city. Still battling…

They were battling *Firkin*.

She didn't know what had happened. She couldn't afford to try to work it out. Maybe it was the Barph's Strength. Maybe it was something else as well. Something had been happening to him here, in this city. The memory he'd been talking about…

But whatever had happened, he was out there, eighty feet tall, pummeling and tearing at the dragons, and somehow far less injured than he should be. She had seen the dragons tearing at him, savaging him, she had seen him bathed in flame, but still he kept fighting on.

She felt fire snaking out from her, a widening corona, slashing back toward the wood and thatch of the buildings. She snatched it back. She had to focus. She had to keep her mind on the present. She had to fight.

They were sending arrows at her again. She burned the shafts, used sudden thermals and blasts of superheated air to knock the arrowheads aside.

Distantly she was aware that her legs were trembling. Her mouth was parched. Her eyes burned. But she would not submit to any weakness of the flesh. She was fire. She would burn eternal.

Firkin was on his feet. He was seizing great clods of earth from the ground, flinging them at the dragons. They beat at the air, sputtering and roaring. Firkin was laughing as he snatched up a small tree and flogged Gorrax in the mouth with it.

Gorrax howled in rage, curled his tail around Firkin's throat. Firkin kept on laughing even as Gorrax brought him to his knees. Diffinax and Theerax saw their opportunity. They slashed into his sides, barreling him backward, dragging him kicking and choking through the dirt, claws deep in his sides. They smashed through their own ranks, soldiers scattering out of the way. Lives were smeared bloody red across the Vinland landscape.

They were coming toward her. Only a quarter mile away. She could almost reach them with her flames.

Firkin managed to get his fingers around Gorrax's tail. He twisted. There was a crack like the earth itself splitting. Gorrax howled, flinched, lurched away through the air. Firkin collapsed back, still laughing and choking. Gorrax's tail hung limply and he came crashing to earth.

Quirk wondered briefly what had happened to Afrit. Was she dead out there in the city? Had the dragons' forces killed her?

Flames roared all around her. An approaching soldier became nothing more than a stick figure of blackened bone. She breathed heavily, staggered, pulled the fire back.

Firkin was back on his feet, but Theerax and Diffinax were coordinating their attacks now. They both came at him, both breathing fire, one slashing at his front, the other at his back. Firkin was pinwheeling his arms like a child caught in the throes of a tantrum. One of his oversized fists came crashing down on Theerax's neck, snapping his head up, jackknifing it against his body. The dragon flailed into the ground in a spray of stones and dirt.

But even as Theerax fell, Diffinax slashed the backs of Firkin's calves. Firkin let out a shrill scream, dropped to his knees.

Theerax was back up before Firkin, but Diffinax was ahead of both of them. The dragon had wheeled around, was diving out of the sky toward Firkin's head, rear claws outstretched. Firkin threw his hands up, but too late. The massive talons closed around his head.

Diffinax's wings smashed at the air, fighting for lift. With a snarl of effort, Diffinax hauled Firkin's massive frame up into the air, dragging him, legs kicking up, and up. With a final burst of speed, the dragon flung Firkin away.

Quirk watched as, hurtling through the air, Firkin came flying toward her for the second time that day.

51

Defeat of the Total Variety

"Okay, this time I am being pretty sure she is losing it."

Lette looked over to where Balur was pointing at Quirk. Flame was spilling off the woman in waves, rolling down the wall and splashing out into the street beyond. It boiled away to nothing a few yards from the houses that bordered the wall, perhaps fifteen yards from their hiding spot.

"You are being an old maid," Lette said to Balur.

"That is being fine as long as I am not being an old maid who is being burned to death by a half-crazed mage. I have been being very clear for a very long time, I am not wanting to be killed by a mage. It is unnatural. Something with teeth and claws, or at the very least with a sword."

"You want me to stab you now?" Lette asked him. "Because I'm willing to do it."

Balur gave her an insultingly pitying look. "You are just saying that because I am in the lead right now."

"Oh for..." Lette took a breath. "I am not competing with you in body count."

"Only because you are losing."

Lette sighed. She honestly had not been keeping count. Though she did suppose their combined body count was horrifyingly high. Quirk was providing a wonderful distraction. Enemy troops would stare at her as they approached, making it very easy to spring into their midst and gut them all. Honestly it was getting to the point where finding somewhere to stash all the corpses was becoming difficult.

It was drops in the ocean, of course. They were more passing time than actually affecting the outcome of the battle. The majority of the dragons' army was already deep in the city, killing, looting, and pillaging.

"When do we fall back?" she asked Balur.

He looked at her. "Right now. I was literally just saying we should. Quirk is going to lose control and burn half this block."

"No." Lette shook her head. Balur's head was as thick as his muscles some time. "I meant, when do we fall back from this entire city? It's lost. The whole fucking war is lost. The dragons have won. We need a contingency plan."

Balur looked at her for a moment, appearing genuinely perplexed. "We have lost?"

Lette rolled her eyes. "Do you honestly think we can retake this city?"

Balur looked at her as if she were asking him whether the dukes of the Five Duchies would shit in each other's beds at night. "Well of course not."

"And so where else do we go? Where else do we find an army?"

"Erm..." Balur's confidence faltered. "Wait," he said. "Really? We have been totally losing?"

Lette clawed at her face. "How did it escape you that this was our last stand?"

Balur scratched at his jutting lizard chin. "I was just figuring that there would be some...I am not knowing...That we would be being underground resistance fighters or something. That there would be being leaflets, and meetings in secret rooms, and underground passageways and such."

Lette weighed that. "Well fine," she said. "There will probably be some of that."

Balur nodded to himself, looking more comfortable. "Well okay then."

"How many resistance movements have you seen be successful, Balur?" asked Lette. She wanted him with both feet planted in reality.

"Well, there was Kondorra," Balur said.

"That was an exception," Lette answered, feeling reality stepping just out of reach again.

"It was also being the only resistance movement we have been being part of," Balur said. "We are having a good track record with them."

"You're an idiot."

"Hush," said Balur. His thin tongue snaked out. "I can taste people coming."

Lette sighed. They would pick this up later. For now she ducked away, waited until the tramp of boots was parallel to her, then stepped out, her sword raised.

"Gods be pissing on it," said Balur. The soldiers spinning around in surprise wore the red and gold of the Vinland military.

"It's all right," Lette said to their startled expressions and raised blades. "We're on your side."

"Says you," said one man, lowering himself into a fighting stance.

Lette was about to draw her knives and teach this bastard a lesson just on principle when she heard someone shouting her name.

"Lette! Lette! It's me."

Both she and the soldier peered.

Will emerged from the crowd. He was soaked in blood from head to foot, and for a moment something that just might have been her heart lurched. But she could see no obvious wounds, and he had a manic grin upon his face.

"Lette!" he said again. "Come with us! We're going to make a raid toward the District Seventeen gate!"

Lette licked her lips, taking a moment. "Is that," she asked delicately, "a ladle that you're holding?"

"Skullcrusher!" yelled Will, swinging the ladle wildly around his head.

The soldier had lowered his sword. He shrugged. "He's enthusiastic," he said with a vaguely apologetic tone.

"You know the city is lost?" Lette asked. She felt both Will and the soldier could use a reality check.

"We're still fighting," said the soldier.

"Skullcrusher!" Will whooped again.

"Are you willing to die here?" Lette asked.

"Yes." And the soldier was completely sincere, she saw.

She blew out a breath. And perhaps self-sacrifice was the noble thing to do. Maybe even the right thing. But she would always rather find a way to fight another day than lay down her life for a principle.

"Sorry," she said. "We're not coming."

"Really?" said Balur next to her. He gave her a crestfallen look. "It was sounding kind of fun to me," he said lamely.

"We need to work out an exit strategy from this city, and we need to—"

She was cut off by another roiling wave of flame that Quirk sent blasting out into the street. All of them ducked away, casting up arms in paltry defense.

"Oh gods, I am thinking she really is…" Balur started. Then his voice died.

They were all looking now. They all saw.

Firkin reeled into sight. He was pinwheeling his massive arms, flailing. He was traveling too fast, out of control. A dragon could be seen in the sky before him, roaring in triumph, sending gouts of flame spilling up into the sky. Firkin stumbled back, teetered. Then with all the majesty of a collapsing midden heap, he crashed into the city wall just where Quirk was standing.

The effect reminded Lette of the time she had set a bomb in a gunpowder factory. Except when that bomb had gone off, she had been half a city away.

Quirk seemed to detonate. Flame, masonry, and bodies were everywhere. Sound and heat blasted down the street like a god's sweeping hand. Soldiers flew head over heels, spilling down the street in a tangle of limbs. Lette caught glimpses of men bent at acute angles, faces distorted in pain. She ripped down the street on her chest, feeling the hardened leather of her breastplate shred and tear. Her chin scraped on the rough cobbles and the skin tore away. She rolled to a bouncing stop, shook her head, tried to blink through the pain and disorientation.

Firkin was still falling. The wall was crumbling beneath his enormous weight. He sprawled into buildings, crushing roofs, collapsing walls, bringing bricks pouring down upon his head. Clouds of smoke and dust wreathed his torso, slowly enveloping him. The whole thing played out in silence before her. All she could hear was a faint high-pitched ringing.

Slowly, dizzily she picked herself up. Her left arm didn't seem to be working well. She looked around. Half the soldiers were dead, broken rag dolls spilling their stuffing across the street. Others were lying, clutching broken limbs, coughing blood. She reached a hand up to her ears. Her fingers came away bloody. Her chin and nose were dripping more blood. Balur was on his knees. He reached up a hand, wrenched his jaw back sideways. He must have dislocated it in the fall.

Will. Where was Will?

Strange thumping pressure from above drew her eye upward. A dragon was soaring over her, its mouth open wide. Flame fell in waves from it, crashing into the houses. She felt the shock waves thud through her.

Someone grabbed her shoulder. She whirled around, reaching for a sword she'd lost in the explosion. Balur was there. He was trying to say something, but his jaw was fucked and so were her ears.

She shook him off. She needed to find Will.

She found him in a bundle of three other figures. Two of them were dead, their spines snapped into a series of irregular angles. Will was curled up on top of the third. A bone was jutting violently out of his shin, but apart from that and what she took to be his screaming, he seemed okay.

She made hand gestures at Balur until he understood enough to grab a broken spear shaft. She tore strips of cloth from a dead man's shirt.

Will passed out as they set the bone. That was good. Balur held the bone and splint in place while she bound everything as best she could.

Then she sat back on her haunches, looked at Balur. He shrugged at her again.

She used her finger to scribble a word in the dust that lined the floor.

Firkin?

Balur nodded. They should try to find out what was left of their friendly giant at least. Balur heaved Will up onto his shoulder, and together they stumbled toward the slowly dissipating cloud of dust and debris. Lette held her hand over her mouth, peered into swirling shadows. Firkin shouldn't be too hard to spot; he was larger than most temple spires.

And yet, as the cloud grew thinner and thinner it became harder and harder to deny: He was not there. Lette turned to Balur, brow knit, trying to telegraph her confusion.

And then she saw two figures lying in the dirt. One lay in a small circle of flame.

"Quirk," she said. She could almost make out her own voice now.

The academic lay on her back, head lolling back on broken stone. Her lips were cracked and bleeding, and her palms looked raw, but aside from a few other scrapes and cuts she appeared whole and hale.

And beside Quirk...beside her lay Firkin. Not gargantuan, titanic Firkin. Not the Firkin who had fought three dragons to a standstill. But regular old, repugnant Firkin.

"Looks okay." Balur's voice sounded like a faint whisper as he toed Firkin's body.

Lette nodded. "I don't know how," she said. "I don't know any of this. I'm pretty fucking sure that Firkin was a giant fighting dragons a minute ago. And now...Now..." She honestly didn't have words for what was going on. "Weird shit."

The street shook beneath her feet. With the crushed city wall at her back, she looked out onto Vinter. The buildings were burning, thatch and wood going up like so much kindling. Dragons were visible in the sky above, launching fireballs like catapult stones. The explosions thudded through the ringing in her ears. The ground shook again, and again.

"This is over," Lette said. "We've lost."

Balur nodded. "Tactical withdrawal?"

Lette nodded. "Very tactical."

Balur bent, hoisted Quirk onto the shoulder that Will wasn't draped across. Lette knelt, and awkwardly heaved Firkin's dead weight up.

"You think that gate they were talking about is still a good way out?"

Balur shrugged. "I was just going to be walking through the big gap in the wall."

Lette looked. She nodded. Then she started picking her way through the rubble. And slowly, carefully, they slunk away as the dragons won their war.

PART 3:
DRAGONS DESCENDING

52

By Way of an Explanation

As much as Will still loved Lette, he was also pretty certain that she was shit at making splints. He bit down harder on his belt as she carefully bound the broken spear shaft back against his broken leg.

"Of course it hurts," Lette said, catching his reproachful look. "You bust a bone out of your leg. If you can walk properly after this, you'd better pour libations in my fucking honor."

"Also," said Balur from where he was lying at the base of a tree, "you are being a total pussy."

Will didn't even bother looking at him. He was in too much genuine pain.

They were about five miles from Vinter now, taking refuge in a copse of startled-looking trees standing in the middle of a trampled field. The city was still visible on the horizon, a broken, smoking ruin. A few dazed cows and sheep, escaped from their pillaged farmsteads, wandered about.

"I was in an explosion," Will pointed out to Lette instead. "The same one you were. This was hardly my fault." He couldn't help but feel that there had been an accusation hidden in her words.

"I wasn't the one running around waving a ladle in the air and shouting 'skull splitter.'" Lette looked at him pointedly.

"So I took some blows to the head early on in the fight," said Will. It was hard to act nonchalant with his leg throbbing as if Lawl himself were pissing on the wound.

"Can we not talk about blows to the head right now?" Quirk was propped up next to Balur with a makeshift bandage wrapped around her skull. It turned out she had taken a decent chunk of flesh out of the back of her scalp in her fall from the city walls.

Firkin was still unconscious. Will was trying not to fret about that. Unconscious was a lot better than dead, which is what by all rights the old man should have been. In fact he had the fewest obvious injuries of all of them. The scrapes in his skin were shallow and clean. His burns were minor. They had all seen him roasted, impaled, and clawed half to death, and yet he seemed little worse than he would have done after a bad day on the farm.

None of them were talking about Firkin. They were not talking about a lot of things. They were not talking about the fields of ash they had walked through all day. They were not talking about whatever had happened to Afrit. They were not talking about the future. They were not talking about the fact that they'd lost.

Lette gave Will's leg an appraising look. The sun was just below the horizon now. The sky was still a watercolor wash of pinks and yellows staining into midnight blue, turning the copse of trees into a series of stark silhouettes.

"I'll go see if I can rustle up some supper," Lette said. "Bound to be some rabbits around somewhere." She slipped away.

Will looked over to Quirk and Balur. "How are you feeling?" he asked neither of them in particular. It was easiest to talk about the immediate now.

"Like I could use a drink," said Quirk with feeling.

"Me too." Will rubbed his head.

Quirk shook her head. "I don't want to drink."

"You just said..." Will pointed out.

"I've been drinking for days," said Quirk. "Normally I'll have a glass of wine, perhaps two, perhaps none. I water it usually.

But in Vinter, the past few days…Gods…I cannot remember the last day I didn't have a hangover."

"I don't think needing a drink when…" Will hesitated. They were not describing their current situation. "I don't think needing a drink now," he amended, "is totally unreasonable."

"Well, if someone had not been wounding his leg and been requiring that we are sterilizing his wound with all my hard liquor…" Balur started.

"You were in the same explosion as me!" Will pointed out.

"Hush," Quirk whispered. "We are supposed to be in hiding. Shouting kind of undermines that."

And there she was again, talking about things that everyone else seemed to think were better left unsaid.

"Oh," said Lette, reappearing suddenly, "if there were soldiers about, you'd be dead already." She smiled cheerfully and looked over her shoulder. "Isn't that right?"

Will almost had time to look perplexed when Afrit walked out of the lengthening shadows behind Lette. Quirk let out a squeal like a kettle undergoing a major revelation, and was suddenly shooting across the copse toward her. And through all the ash and grime and dirt that covered it, Afrit's face lit up like the sun.

Then Quirk screeched to a halt in front of Afrit and stood there awkwardly. She reached out, seemed to abort the hug, and then just held Afrit by her shoulders. Afrit seemed unsure what was going on now.

"You're okay," said Quirk, then released Afrit's shoulders. "That's erm…" She turned away. There was a look like panic on her face.

Afrit blinked. She seemed even more disoriented by Quirk's quicksilver emotions than Quirk was.

"Where were you?" asked Will, mostly out of a sense of social decency, trying to cover the awkwardness.

Afrit turned to him slowly. She blinked again. "The, er... Vinter. It's fallen, by the way, though I suppose you know that. Most of the soldiers I was with...well, they're all dead." She took a shaking breath. "And I've just been walking, and...you know..." She sent a plaintive look in Quirk's direction. "I'd lost you. But then I heard voices. And..." She shook her head. "You're hiding, aren't you? I mean, we lost. We're on the run. Aren't we? But you were all shouting." She bit her bottom lip. Will thought she was going to cry. "And then..."

"I've got supper," Lette cut in loudly. She held up two dead rabbits.

They risked a fire. Lette had come across no one else wandering in the fields around them. Soon Will's stomach was rumbling as the smell of rabbit roasting on a spit over a small fire of leaves and twigs started to wind between the trees.

"That smells fantastic."

They all froze. Balur's hand, turning the spit, clenched so hard that the wood splintered to pulp.

They all turned and looked.

Not to the fringe of trees. Not to a group of dragon soldiers. Not to another tired fight to the death. To Firkin.

He was sitting up. He was grinning at them. He yawned and stretched luxuriantly. Somehow he managed to keep grinning the whole time.

"That," he said, ignoring all their stares, "was a brilliant nap. Best one ever." He still wore that same shit-eating grin.

There was something different about his voice, Will thought. It sounded...deeper perhaps? More resonant? *Richer.* That was the word. It was still the same voice, shrill and grating, but it somehow seemed more important, as if Will should listen to it more closely.

Why in the Hallows should anyone listen to Firkin? Wasn't that part of how they'd ended up in this mess?

Balur certainly seemed to be of that opinion. He had crossed the small corpse and had Firkin in the air, holding him by the throat. "Your magic drink was not working," he said simply. "So you had better be giving me a reason to not be squeezing."

"Because," Firkin said, still managing to keep his grin in place, "that won't be working either."

Balur looked puzzled. "You are knowing what normally happens when someone's throat is being crushed, right?" he said. "Because this threat is only working if you are knowing about the whole thrashing around, and dying in convulsions while your bowels give way thing."

"Yep." Firkin did his best to nod. "Won't work."

"Don't try it!" Lette shouted just as Balur's bicep flexed.

"But he was saying," Balur grumbled.

"He's a drunk arsehole who blathers stupid shit constantly," Lette pointed out. "Do not listen to him. Ever."

Balur huffed in disappointment.

"Can we please just put him down," Will said, "and find out what in the Hallows happened?"

"He really can squeeze," said Firkin, feet still dangling in the air.

"Shut up, Firkin!" Will snapped.

"Shut up or talk about what happened?" Firkin cackled. "Which is it?"

"I think I'm just going to squeeze," said Balur.

"Don't!" Lette barked.

"I need a fucking drink," Will said. His throat felt parched and his headache was getting stronger.

"I don't even think you could do it," Firkin said to Balur amiably. "I think you've got the arm strength of a six-year-old girl."

"Now I have to do it," Balur rumbled, without much malice.

"Put him the fuck down, Balur!" Lette yelled.

"Why is this you people's answer to everything?" Afrit looked utterly bewildered.

"Yeah," said Firkin. "I doubt you can hold me up much longer, what with those shrimpy little arms of yours."

"Are you actually fucking insane?" Will was almost tempted to let Balur try at this point.

"Actually," Quirk cut in, her voice quiet, "I don't think he's Firkin at all."

"What?" Will, Lette, and Afrit all said at once, turning to look at the former thaumatobiologist.

And then the sound of clapping drew their gazes back to Firkin. He still dangled from Balur's fist, and he was still grinning.

"Clever girl," he said.

"I am not being a g—" Balur started.

"I don't understand," Afrit said.

"I should have worked it out sooner." Quirk was shaking her head and ignoring the lizard man. "Right when you drained the cup. That was when I should have seen it."

"Oh," said Balur. "You were talking to…"

"What are you talking about?" Will said, also ignoring Balur.

"In Vinland," Quirk said to Will, "Firkin was acting differently. Complaining about a voice in his head."

And yes, of course Will remembered that.

"Look, is this meaning I can throttle him or not?" asked Balur, sounding slightly annoyed at all the delays.

"Put him down," said Quirk. She sounded very tired.

"No," snapped Lette, who was apparently in full contrarian mode. "If he's not Firkin, who is he?"

Firkin just kept on grinning.

"I think…" Quirk hesitated. She leaned briefly into the diffuse light of the fire glowing up above the screen she had made. Her brows were knit right. "Well, if I'm right, then he was never Firkin."

This, Will was fairly sure, was the worst explanation ever.

"Of course he's Firkin," he said. "I grew up with him."

At the same time, Lette said, "He's a shapeshifter? Throttle him."

"Thank you!" said Balur.

"No!" shouted Will. Firkin had metaphorically asked to be throttled several times in their shared past, but Will had managed to run interference. He didn't want to compound all the day's failures now.

But he was too late. Balur's muscles bunched.

"Fuck!" Will tried to get to his feet, but his broken leg betrayed him. He staggered, fell, screamed. Lette just sat watching carefully. Quirk didn't look from the fire. Afrit seemed caught between horror at Balur's actions and confusion at Quirk's indifference. Balur had a look of grim satisfaction on his face. Firkin for his part didn't do much. He just looked vaguely bored.

Balur's look slowly changed to one of puzzlement. Then frustration. He squeezed so hard his arm started to shake.

"Have I proved my point yet?" asked Firkin.

"Okay," said Lette. She was on her feet now. "I am officially full of what the fuck."

Will satisfied himself by rolling around on the ground, clutching his leg, and whimpering.

"Put him down," said Quirk in a voice as tired as her expression.

"Oh!" Afrit said suddenly. "Oh no."

Balur hesitated, then finally opened his fist. Firkin dropped to the ground. For a wonder he did not trip over himself. He barely even staggered.

Lette was pointing a dagger back and forth between Quirk and Firkin. "Someone," she said, "explain what in the Hallows is happening right now." Her knife settled on Firkin. "If he's not Firkin, who is he?"

"He was never Firkin," said Quirk again.

"What the fuck does that mean?" Lette demanded.

"That's not really true," said Firkin, cricking his neck first to one side and then the other. His voice sounded no worse for the damage Balur had done to his throat. "Firkin was very real for a while."

"The same way a mask is real?" asked Quirk. The first hint of something beyond resignation had entered her voice. A touch of academic curiosity, Will thought.

"Any more cryptic bullshit," Lette hissed, "and I shall feed you a broad assortment of your own organs. Probably starting with the spleen."

"Always be starting with the spleen," said Balur, who seemed to want to recover some ground after the whole throttling debacle. "That is being pretty much what it is for."

"It's not so much a question of who," said Quirk, "but what."

Lette threw up her hands. "What did I just say?" She looked at Balur. "I just said the spleen, didn't I?"

"I was even commenting upon it," said Balur with a nod.

"That's it," Lette said to Quirk. She shrugged. "It's your fucking spleen."

Quirk held up her hands. "I am desperately trying to get you to see what I see. Because you're not going to believe me if I just say it."

"Try me."

"She's right," said Afrit, who seemed to have finally settled on horror as the emotion du jour.

"Shut up," said Lette whipping around to point the knife at her. "I'm not talking to you."

"You want a drink," Quirk said calmly, "don't you?" She looked at each of them in turn. "We all want a drink. You've wanted one ever since you got to the wall in Vinter."

And…Will thought about that. Yes. Yes, he had. But surely that was pretty much to be expected when you were facing imminent death and then saw all your dreams go up in dragon smoke.

"I have been in a constant state of wanting a drink since I was being about six years old," said Balur.

"I always liked the Analesians," said Firkin.

"You're not helping," said Quirk.

Firkin raised both hands. "Very sorry, I'm sure." But that mocking smile was still on his lips.

"Remember the story he told?" Quirk said, turning back to the rest of them, ignoring Firkin. "The story of Barph's Strength. Barph angers Lawl. Lawl collects Barph's blood. And he tells." She pointed at Firkin. "He *tells* us that whoever drinks it is given powers. *Divine* powers. That they're stronger, invulnerable. That they can face dragons. Except does it work on us? No. It only works on him."

"Yes," agreed Balur. "That was being weird."

"*Barph's* Strength," Quirk almost shouted. "*Barph's!*"

"Yes," Balur said again. "That is being the name of it."

But Lette said, "Ohhhh," long and drawn out, and with just enough horror in it to make Will's skin start to creep, because he felt like he almost saw. Almost.

"Right?" said Afrit. "Right?"

"Lawl always was a precious fucker," said Firkin. "Never could take a joke."

"No," said Will. He shook his head. Because it couldn't be that. It could never be that. It was too big, and too wild, and too utterly devastating.

"But why now?" said Quirk, still talking a step ahead of Will. "Why—"

"Because of the champion," Lette cut in. She had apparently caught up. "Because Lawl rules the Hallows. If he'd gone down to get it himself and he'd gotten himself killed . . . then he would have ended up in the Hallows. And Lawl would have been in charge of him. That was the true punishment, right?" She pointed at Firkin. "He stole your strength and he put it within arm's reach, but if you fucked up . . . then you'd be stuck in his domain. You'd be under his thumb. So you send us dumb shits down to get it for you."

"I don't…" Will started. But he did. He really did. He just didn't want to.

Barph's Strength. Not anybody else's.

"Never could take a joke," said Firkin.

Except Firkin didn't say it. Will knew that now.

Barph said it.

53

The Chapter of Revelations

Barph. Firkin was Barph. Okay. Okay. Lette took a breath and kept her cool.

Will didn't. "No," he said. "Just…No." He shook his head. "Really just no. That's absurd. That's just…no. That defines no. That stands in opposition of all that can be said to be yes. That's no in its purest, most unadulterated form. Complete no. No, and no, and no, and no again. So much no." He held his hands as if to ward the idea off. "It's a tidal wave of no. A no that could trample through the countryside destroying small towns and breathing fire upon the landscape. An epic no. The sort of no bards will compose song cycles about. Absolute no. Infinite no. A divinity? Firkin? *Firkin?* No. No. No. No. No. No. No."

"Look," said Firkin, "it's not like I'm any happier about it than you are."

Which, given the enormous shit-eating grin he was wearing, didn't necessarily seem to be the truth.

"There is being," Balur said, "one way to be sure." No one paid him much attention.

"But it fits," Quirk was saying. "Everything fits. He drained the cup."

And as much as Lette wanted to agree with Will, she agreed with Quirk.

"I know," Will said. "I know. I know. I know. Everything fits the way you've explained it. It makes sense. But, I mean…it's impossible. The sequence of events as we see it has to be flawed. We have to have made a mistake. Something's wrong."

And then, with a roar, Balur smashed his sword into Firkin's midriff.

The little man flew. His legs left the floor. They trailed behind him as he sailed through the air, flying out behind him like streamers on a child's kite. He smashed into a tree with enough force to see splinters and bark flying. Then he slumped to the ground.

"Holy fuck, Balur!" Lette shouted.

"Shit!" Will yelled Firkin.

"Gods!" Even Quirk seemed to have forgotten this hiding they were meant to be doing.

Afrit let out a short, sharp laugh, then clapped her hands to her mouth and went back to looking horrified.

"What did you just do?" Will was running at Balur, fists balled impotently. "What the fuck did you just do?"

Lette wondered if she would have to intervene, but Balur barely paid any attention to Will, focused on the spot where the old drunk or new deity had landed.

"I was testing," said Balur. "Someone is claiming to be a deity, so I am seeing if he is invulnerable to harm. Obviously."

"You fucking killed him, you maniac!" Will's fists pounded against Balur's waist. "He was a sick man!" Balur watched Will distastefully.

"That was perhaps a bit much," said Lette, advancing on Firkin's collapsed corpse.

"He was the one saying—"

And then Firkin stood up. He rubbed his stomach with one hand, then cracked his back. "Now that," he said, "is what I'm talking about."

There was a lot of shouting and yelling after that. And a lot of denials. And Balur had to stare down Will when he suggested that Balur had used the flat of his blade.

"Just admit it!" Quirk almost shouted finally, apparently oblivious to the fact that if she was right, she was chastising a being powerful enough to smite her like she was a small and particularly irritating bug.

Lette took a step away from the Tamathian academic.

"It's how I told you all back in the Vinter cells," said Firkin. He sat down next to the fire as if he didn't have a care in the world. "Lawl couldn't take a joke. He cut me. He collected the blood in that goblet. And all my divine power ran out with it. He hid the goblet in the city dedicated to me, because he thought *that* was funny. Then he put a divine guard over it.

"The idea, as you surmised, was that I go and try to get it back. The only thing he hadn't been able to take from me was my life. And he knew I wasn't going to go and just die for his convenience. So he had to tempt me to get into trouble. And so I was meant to go and face off against the champion, have my arse handed to me, go to the Hallows, be utterly at his mercy, and learn my lesson."

He spat into the fire. "Well, fuck that."

"What," said Lette, who was curious now despite her skepticism, "could you have done to piss him off that much?"

"I got him drunk," said Firkin with a shrug.

Balur thought about that. "That is not seeming—"

"Fine!" said Firkin with an exaggerated sigh. "I got him blind drunk, and told him that this mortal he was seeing on the side was about to dedicate herself to a temple of Betra, at which point my grandmother would know all about his latest series of indiscretions and castrate him. He was always worried about that from her. Anyway, he was in a panic, and I sort of egged him on and got him to smite this temple. But then I told him he missed, and he did it again. And then I told him he missed again. Told him he almost got her that time. So he smote another bit of town. And then I got a bit carried away."

"Smote," said Will. "As in thunderbolts, people dying, that sort of thing?"

"In my defense," Firkin said, "I was just as drunk as he was."

"How carried away?" asked Balur.

The lizard man was loving this, Lette knew. He'd always loved stories about Barph's antics.

"Well…" said Firkin, looking a touch embarrassed. "You know the Tharkian Waste?"

The Tharkian Waste was a nation-sized desert of blasted, inhospitable land that lay over the Broken Peaks, which formed the easternmost wall of Kondorra.

"No way," Lette found herself saying. "You're saying you really are responsible?"

"No!" said Firkin. He sounded put out. "I am saying very distinctly that Lawl is responsible." Then more sheepishly, "I am just responsible for him being responsible."

"No," Will said again. He put his head in his hands. "No. Just no. You were my friend. All my childhood, you were my friend. You fought against the dragons with my father. You helped raise me. You were a good man. This is bullshit. This is all bullshit."

There were tears bright in the corners of Will's eyes.

Firkin smiled sadly at Will. "I know," he said softly. "I know." Then he brightened. "But the truth is," he grinned, "it was all bullshit, and I was never your friend. So there's that at least."

And that was how Lette found herself peeling Will's fingers off a divinity's neck.

"Fuck you!" he shouted, though whether he was shouting it at Firkin or at her, Lette wasn't entirely clear. "Fuck you!"

"I wasn't done, piss on it!" Firkin snapped. "Touchy little fucker." But he was still smiling to himself. "Firkin was a construction. A mask." He grimaced slightly. "That's not quite it. He was more than that. He was a personality I put on. I *was* Firkin, for my own sanity. Just only for as long as I needed him to be. And when I was Firkin I didn't know who I really was."

He reached out a placating hand toward Will. "Firkin really was your friend. That was real. But when we got to Vinter. A lot of things I'd put in place in my mind...contingencies." He shook his head. "It was hard to come back to myself. But I had to try. I had to try to get my real life back. You understand that, right?"

"But...But..." Will just couldn't take it. And Lette's heart went out to Will. It really did. "You practically helped raise me. I mean...Not with any of the important staying-alive parts. Or anything hard. But you were....You were there. You helped teach me how to smile. How to be angry.

"And I thought...I thought...when you lost your mind to drink, it was like you were dying. It was like pieces of you were dying right in front of my eyes."

Tears were running straight down his face.

"And then in Kondorra, there were...glimpses...moments. I thought I saw you in there. I thought maybe..." He put his head in his hands.

"Firkin's really dead now, isn't he?" he said into his palms.

"Pretty much," said Barph without missing a beat.

"Fuck." It was like Will took a blow to the gut, and he took it badly.

"On the flip side," said Barph, still without any indication that he gave much of a damn, "the good news is that now I'm back to being me, I know how we can defeat these stupid dragons."

And that, right there, in the middle of every disaster that had befallen them, in the wake of the loss of a world to the dragons, in the wake of everything, that casual claim that now it could be fixed? Really? Fucking seriously?

Lette found it was her turn to lose her cool.

"Oh bullshit!" she yelled. "Fucking bullshit! You show up here, all divine, just as everything goes to shit, and all of a sudden now things can be fixed? Now? Fuck you. *Fuck* you."

"I didn't know before," said Firkin, or Barph, or whoever in the Hallows he was meant to be. "Before, I wasn't myself. It was only after you rescued me that I knew what was going on. But I can see it now. And I know the pattern of it. And so I know how to interrupt the pattern."

He looked apologetic, which as far as Lette was concerned was pretty much a pure admission that some shit was awry.

"Shit is not that convenient," she said. "It's not." She pointed at Will. "I'm with him," she said. "There's a mistake in here."

"The dragons," Firkin—or Barph—cut in, "are trying to kill me and my brethren. They want to kill the gods. I don't need a ploy or an angle. This is self-preservation. And not much of the world is left on my side."

"Your side," Lette spat. "Who said we're on your side? I'm on my side, which is the side of not being oppressed by dragons or anybody else."

She was breathing hard. She tried to get a rein on her temper but it was bucking hard, trying to break free.

"How can someone kill the gods, anyway?" Quirk asked. If Lette could have thought of a reason to shout her down as well, she would have done so. This was not a moment for quiet academic interest.

Firkin opened his mouth.

"Stop!" It was only after Lette said it that she realized she had a knife in each hand. She found that she was pointing them at pretty much everybody. "We're saying . . . let me get this straight. We're saying Firkin is Barph, the god of drunken carousing, the god of anarchy, the trickster god, the god of hedonism. We're saying that he pretended to be a village drunk and Will's childhood mentor for five or six decades, and that we just woke him up . . . and . . . okay, I can actually believe that. I can get on board with that. I saw what Balur did. But now he has a plan and we're just going to be like, "Oh great, please tell us more about that"? We're not questioning *anything*?"

She looked desperately at Will. She so needed him to be Will at that moment. To be kind, and nice, and reassuring, and sweet, and also angry, and pissed off, and to have a plan.

"I don't see another option," he said to her. He looked utterly defeated. He looked exactly like what she didn't want to see. "I think we have to hear him out at least," he said.

"Do we?" she said. "Really?"

"Even I am thinking we should at least hear him out," said Balur. "Even if it is just so I can be having longer to figure out how to try and kill him again."

Firkin met her eye without hesitation. And he *could* kill her. Suddenly she knew that very clearly. She had seen that smile before. She had worn it herself. He could kill her, and he knew it, and he knew she knew it too.

But also, he wasn't killing her. He made sure she saw that too. So in the end she just collapsed. It was easiest just to let her legs go out and slump to the ground.

"Fine then," she said. "Just fine. Lay it on us. Tell us how to kill the dragons. And at the end I'll see if I think it's better to kill them or you."

Barph smiled. The self-satisfied fucker. "The question," he said, "is how to kill a god."

"Be stabbing it very hard," suggested Balur.

"No," said Barph.

"Dropping something on it." Balur tried again.

"No," said Barph.

"What if it was *really* big? Like a mountain."

"No," said Barph.

"Blowing it up." Balur was relentless.

"It wasn't a fucking multiple-choice question," Barph snapped.

Sometimes, Lette found herself reminded of exactly why she liked to be around the big Analesian.

"Well, it was sounding like a question," Balur said quietly to himself.

"Rhetoric!" Firkin snapped. And there was an echo of the command that had been in his voice in Vinland. But this seemed to Lette like a less forthright version of Barph than the one that she had glimpsed there. Those had been violent outbursts. Something calmer was in their place now. And was it simply control? Now that Barph had all his faculties, could he be civilized? Or was this calmer face another mask? She wished she knew more about the myths of Barph.

"How do you kill a god?" Quirk asked. Her calm seemed a little forced now.

Barph smiled, settled back. "You weaken him," he said.

"How?" the academic pushed.

Barph nodded appreciatively. "I can tell you're the smart one." He looked at the others. "Where does a god get his strength?"

There was a long pause. Lette was fucked if she knew.

"Was that being a rhetorical question?" asked Balur. "Because I honestly could not be telling."

Lette tried not to laugh. She really did.

Quirk and Afrit were looking at each other, as if shocked they didn't know this. Barph was looking at them. "Something you want to say, Quirk?" he said, but then he shook his head. "No," he said quietly. "You don't know either, do you? Too much head and not enough heart in you."

Quirk apparently took offense at that. "That sounds like the way things should be to me. The world could use a little more logic in it."

Lette enjoyed watching Afrit's face during that little exchange. She thought Barph probably did too.

Barph turned to smile at Will. "Maybe you have it," he said. "My old friend."

Will twisted on the end of that particular blade. It was a cruel thing to say, Lette thought. But she also saw that he did know.

"It's people, isn't it," Will said. He pointed around the group. "It's us."

Barph beamed. "Yes, Will," he said. "It is. It's you. And Lette. And Balur. And Quirk. And everyone else on this world."

"You are eating people?" Balur said, sounding confused. "I am not remembering those stories. I am thinking I would be remembering stories that awesome. And would maybe have been going to temples a bit more often."

"How about," Lette said, "you shut up for the rest of this conversation?" Her affection for Balur only stretched so far.

Balur snorted indignantly.

"You believe," said Barph, taking charge of the conversation once more, "in us. In the gods. You believe in our power. In our right to rule. You have faith in us. You"—he licked his lips—"worship us."

Quirk thought about that. "How would you even measure—"

"No!" Barph snapped. And again there was that undertone of command. A steel bar rapping her will on the knuckles. "Do not put limits on it. Do not define it and control it. Do not put it in a neat little box and make a prisoner of it. Let it be. Let it be the thing it is and needs to be."

"They've been taking it away." Will was staring into the middle distance. And Lette thought she understood, and a little part of her was amused to watch Quirk flounder with these ideas. "The dragons have been making people worship them instead of the gods," Will glanced at Barph for confirmation. "They've been taking away the gods source of power. They've been weakening them."

Barph gave a small sad nod. "Yes," he said. "And very soon, almost no one will believe in us at all. We will be old, forgotten things. Broken toys. And the dragons will ascend to the heavens, and will be worshipped as we were. They will assume the powers of the gods, and then, I think, the chances of them manifesting only rarely are very slim indeed."

"Shit," said Lette. Because it really did all make sense. No matter if Barph was a trickster or not. Everything added up.

"But," said Will, who managed to dredge up a hopeful expression from the gods only knew where, "you said you have a plan."

And with that Firkin's face lit up like a fire in a war chieftain's hall. And his smile beamed like the sun, and he said, "Yes." He licked his lips. "Yes I do. But in order to do that, I very much want to introduce you to some people."

And Lette knew, she just knew they shouldn't have trusted the slippery bastard.

"Who?" She had a knife in her hand.

Firkin gave her a little bow. "My family."

54

Deus Ex Machina

Family? Will's mind honestly couldn't figure it out. Too much had happened too fast. Firkin didn't have a family...

No...not Firkin...

Lette apparently wasn't going to wait for Will's brain to get its shit sorted out. "We are hiding," she said, waving a knife around wildly. Will wasn't sure she even knew she was holding it. "If you summon anyone here—"

Firkin arched his eyebrows, but still didn't say a word. Will saw muscles bunch in Lette's neck.

All of a sudden lightning lanced down out of the sky. Thunder tore through the trees, a cataclysmic boom that made the world quiver. Loose branches and leaves rained down in a storm of debris. Will's leg was shaken hard enough that he had to bite down on a scream.

Twenty yards away, through the tangle of the copse, a broad swath of the landscape was reduced to ash. The stench of charred soil and foliage filled the air. Will could see small flames dancing on the periphery of the impact crater.

"Ha," said Lette, with a note of satisfaction. "You missed."

Firkin rolled his eyes. "No," he said. "That's not what I do."

Honestly, thought Will, *I could really do without all the dramatics.*

All eyes went in the direction of the crater. And for a moment there was nothing. But then they heard the crunch of feet on dry branches. Then they could just make out the silhouettes of figures moving toward them.

Walking unhurriedly, they came into the light of the fire. There were six of them. The one in the lead was a man who was perhaps in his fifties. His age was difficult to judge. His long, flowing beard and hair were white as fresh fallen snow, but they were both thick and luxurious, and his body rippled with more coiled muscle than an eighteen-year-old griffin wrangler. A step behind him was a tall, voluptuous woman, all spilling curves within a loose-flowing dress of purple that seemed to swirl around her. She also lay in that nebulous fifties range, with a soft ample face that housed curiously hard eyes, and an incongruous nose that jutted out like a hawk's beak.

Behind this pair were two men, close enough in their features that they could be twins. They had smooth tanned skin, and cheekbones you could cut lemon slices on. Their loose curled hair was well oiled, as were their well-trimmed beards. Their choice in clothing, though, was markedly different. One wore slick silks trimmed with soft white fur. His fingers, wrists, neck, ears, nose, and lip were all adorned with heavy golden jewelry studded with bright jewels. He danced a coin along his knuckles as he walked without appearing to have any idea he was doing it. His twin, however, was dressed in the garb of the fields, dirty brown garments of cotton and wool, hems stained with mud and sweat. His hands, in contrast to his brothers, were heavy and gnarled with thick calluses.

Two women followed these two men, as different as they were alike. The first was...Will felt his mouth fall slightly open no matter that Lette was right there. Balur was letting out a low moan. She moved like silk. Her dress covered her like an oil slick covered a lake. She was soft everywhere a woman needed to be soft, hard everywhere she needed to be hard. Her body... gods, how it moved. The subtle shift and sway of her body as she walked was a dance Will could have lost days watching. Her companion, on the other hand, seemed to have gotten dressed by stumbling into a closet while holding a book. White robes had accreted around her in a shapeless mass. She still held the book, and her head was down, tangled hair dangling in front of her face, reading as she came toward them.

Will heard Quirk make a noise that might have been the start of a question, or a gasp, or just inopportune gas.

The well-built man who stood at the front of the newcomers fixed Firkin with a stony gaze. "You," he said.

There was an ocean of emotions contained in that one word. Will felt them roll through him, as if the word was forcing them into his skull with a blacksmith's hammer. He felt disgust and regret, fondness and disappointment, hope and anguish. He grunted, closed his eyes, tried to focus. Hadn't he had his own thoughts once?

"Grandfather," said Firkin. He had definitely ratcheted up the smirk several notches in its intensity.

Foreign washes of emotion were still swirling through Will. Lust. Rage. Boredom. The curious desire to start plowing a field. He felt caught in a storm of unexpected conflicts. He tried to focus.

"Barph." Unexpectedly it was the woman who had become the target of most of Will's unwanted lustful thoughts who spoke. She nodded her head toward Barph just slightly, an echo of his own smile on her lips.

"Lover," said Firkin. If he grinned any further he was going to do some serious damage to his cheeks.

"Why you—" said the twin in stained workman's clothes. His fists were balled. And while Will wasn't an expert on these things, he looked of a scale to kick Firkin's arse.

Except Firkin was Barph.

Except . . .

"Oh gods," said Lette, clawing her face. "They're the gods." Barph's family.

Barph's.

And that was Lawl, Will realized. Lawl, king of the gods. Lord of law and order. Ruler of the Hallows and arbiter of men's fate in that realm of death. Lawl with one white eye of justice and mercy and one black eye of rage and misfortune. And he had his hand on the chest of his son, Toil, god of hard work, champion of farmers, smiths, and craftsmen. Toil who made sure a hard day's work was rewarded, and to whom Will had poured ten thousand libations day after day.

All of them. They were all gods. The soft woman with hard features was Betra, mother of the gods, or…mother of Toil, Knole, and Klink. Holy shit. Toil's richly robed twin—that was Klink, god of coin and merchants. God of the rich. And the woman with her nose in a book was Knole, goddess of wisdom, wit, and knowledge. Which would explain why Quirk and Afrit were looking at her with such ardent longing.

And the woman that was causing such a disturbance in his loins…That was Cois. Which meant she wasn't exactly a woman. She was…he was…Between *hir* succulent legs was more meat than Will was usually looking for. And yet…gods. Gods. Cois god(dess) of love, of fertility, of life. Cois, son and daughter of Lawl and Toil. Wife and husband of Toil. Who were in turn parents of…of…

Of Barph.

And gods, could this day not be done with him?

The gods were, he supposed, right there. He could just ask them.

But he didn't. He just…he couldn't. They were the gods. You didn't just pipe up and say, "Hey, arseholes, how about you mess with me less?"

"So," said Lawl, and Will felt all of his attention forcibly ripped away from his own thoughts, and focused upon the god whether he wanted it or not, "you return to power." The head of the pantheon looked pointedly at Barph.

Will wanted to look and see if the others were being similarly compelled to watch, but he couldn't even achieve that.

"I do, Grandfather," said Barph. He had eased back on his smile finally.

"You did not come to see me in the Hallows." Lawl's voice was perfectly civil. Will had the impression of tidal waves of emotion battering against the seawall of his calm.

"You made me powerless, Grandfather," said Barph. "Not stupid." The smile twitched but then stayed at its dimmed brightness.

Lawl took that head-on, and stared impassively at Barph. Strange torrents of feeling washed through Will. For a moment he was sure he was about to leap forward and tear out Barph's throat. And he wasn't sure why he was going to do it.

Then abruptly Lawl laughed. And then Will was laughing. He could hear Lette, and Balur, and Quirk, and Afrit all laughing along with him. He didn't want to laugh. He wanted to weep. Firkin's body sitting there, talking with Lawl as if it were nothing. Ignoring him, as if he were nothing but a fly that had alighted on a nearby leaf.

Lawl stopped laughing, but he was still smiling. Will could feel the rictus smile on his own lips.

"It is good to have you back, Grandson," said Lawl in booming tones. "We can use your insights at a time like this."

"His *insights*?" Toil stalked forward, and Will felt the smile ripped forcibly from his face. "You don't find all of this just a little convenient? We are at our lowest ebb, and suddenly from nowhere Barph returns to us?" He jabbed a finger at Barph. "This has the stink of your shit all over it."

Barph did a very good job of looking mortally wounded by the accusation.

Inside Will, a spark of genuine emotion flared among the oppressive weight of other people's thoughts. How many times had he seen Firkin perform that pantomime of outrage? How many times had he made Will laugh, when Will was just a child, with that same performance? It was all so familiar, and so very foreign at the same time.

"Come now," clucked Betra, her matronly tones belied by the death stare she angled at Toil from behind her jutting nose. "He's your son, after all."

"He fucked my wife!" shouted Toil, who was apparently not inured to this offense, no matter that it must have been more than eight hundred years old. "His own mother!"

Will did suppose that was a lot to get over. There again, given that Cois was Toil's child via the medium of divine rape by Lawl—Toil's own father—Will wasn't entirely sure if this was actually considered transgressive among the gods or not.

"To be fair," muttered Klink examining his manicured fingernails, "your wife—"

"Say another word," bellowed Toil, whirling upon his twin, "and there won't be much left of you for the dragons to kill."

"Toil." The word dropped into the conversation like oil sliding over water. Cois gave both Toil and Klink looks that Will could only describe as silky. Dramatic things happened in his loins. He heard Balur moan. For that matter, he heard Lette moan as well. Which he realized wasn't her fault, but he couldn't help but be a little disappointed about.

"Yes, wife," said Toil through gritted teeth.

"Be kind to our son, love," said Cois.

Will found the sound of hir voice made him go almost cross-eyed.

Knole yawned, and turned another page in her book, apparently oblivious to all the drama. Will thought that if somehow, he emerged from all of this with both his sanity and his body intact, he might worship Knole more enthusiastically.

"Yes, dear," said Toil, still grinding his teeth. Cois sank back into the background. Will felt the weight of her presence on his willpower slacken, and almost gasped in relief.

"So," said Barph, "not too much has changed then?"

Lawl considered that. "It has been"—he cocked his head to one side—"quieter without you."

"Less interesting, you mean."

Whatever mirth Lawl had been feeling disappeared like the sun before a rainstorm. "Do not presume that because time has eroded my animosity, you are yet in my good graces, trickster." His voice rolled out like thunder. Will was fairly glad that he managed to keep his britches clean.

Barph bowed his head. "Sorry, Grandfather," Will heard him mutter.

And it was so...so very not Firkin. And yes, he totally got that pissing off the king of all the gods was a very, very, very bad idea, but...he couldn't help but want to see Firkin piss in this god's eye.

"I understand," said Barph, not lifting his head up, "that you've been having some trouble with dragons."

"As if you know nothing of them," barked Toil.

This was a challenge that Barph seemed prepared to meet. "You accuse me, Father," he said, finally standing up. "Yet I have been down here, let me remind you, *powerless*"—he spat the word—"for *eight hundred* years." He looked directly into Toil's eyes. "You have sat in your golden throne, fucking mortals behind my mother's back for eight hundred years. And now the world rebels. Whose fault is that? I finally return to power and I am likely to remain that way all of five minutes. Whose fault is that? The people turn to the dragons and strip you of power, and you accuse me? Because I have been down here with them unable to do anything. Able to do *nothing*!" He roared these last words. He had been slowly advancing on Toil and now stood no more than two feet from him. His spittle sprayed the air. "At whose feet does this blame lie, *Father*?" The name became a bitter joke in Barph's mouth.

He turned and looked at all the gods. "You have come here

as beggars, and you know it. You have come here because you are desperate. You have come here because you felt my power reach out across the land for the first time in almost a millennia, and you felt hope flare in your hearts." He turned to look to Lawl. "Even you grandfather." He turned back to Toil. "Even you, Father. You are here because you are out of ideas, and you know the only chance of someone coming up with one that works is me."

He spat upon the ground. "Now I can be graceful about that. I was not planning to lord it over you. But do not come here after what was done to me, after none of you aided me, after you abandoned me... Do not come here and rub my face in your accusations." He took another step toward Toil. "My desire to survive is only a hair's breadth ahead of my desire to laugh as we all burn together. And you, Father, you could so easily alter that balance." He smiled a shark's smile. "So tread carefully."

Toil's face was almost purple. He clenched and unclenched his fists. But he said nothing as Barph turned his back on him.

"So..." It was Betra who spoke now, and Will felt a strange sense of calm roll over him, a muting of emotion under misplaced motherly affection. "...underneath all this bluster and bullshit, do I detect that you *do* think you can do something about our current conundrum?"

Barph hesitated. His back was still to them all, and Will couldn't see his expression. He tried to pick up on the god's emotions through the mess of his own feelings and those of the other divinities. He had no idea what he was feeling.

"Yes," said Barph, nodding as if to himself. "I do. I do. I do have a plan, and—" He turned around. His smile was wider than ever. It looked almost painful. He swept an arm at Will, Lette, Balur, Quirk, and Afrit. "And these fine mortals are it."

Now that, thought Will, *doesn't sound fantastic.*

"Them?" Klink looked at Will and the others with barely disguised distaste. "What use could there be in them?"

Will would have liked to take that little cultured piece of distaste and cram it so far up Klink's arse that he would taste it at the back of his throat for a week. But that was about as likely to happen as all of this ending well.

"Yes," said Barph. "I shall be using these precise mortals." Will's heart continued to sink.

"Even that one?" Cois was pointing at Will again. He glanced over at Lette. It sounded like she was growling.

"Even him, Mother dearest," said Firkin. There was a lascivious look in his eyes.

And she…he…*zhe* was Firkin's lover. Not just his mother, but…Zhe looked like…Gods the heavens were messed up.

"You'll like the plan actually, Mother," Firkin went on. "Because you're going to have to sleep with them." He turned to the other gods. "All of you are, actually. There's going to have to be a lot of sex."

There was a very distinct pause during which Will tried to work out if he really had heard what he thought he'd just heard.

"Sex?" Betra said loudly. Her voice sounded scandalized in a way that was, in Will's estimation, utterly false.

"Lots, Grandmother," said Barph, nodding to himself.

Toil spread out his arms. "He's messing with us. He's always messing with us." He wheeled on Barph. "You are small, and petty, and false." He shoved his finger into Barph's face.

Barph shrugged, but his eyes were on Lawl. "I cannot force you to do anything. I can only talk and let you decide. That has always been the limit of my power, Father."

"You mix your words like you mix your drinks." Cois did not sound as if she minded this, though. From Barph's expression he didn't mind the accusation either.

"Let me put it to you simply then," Barph said. "The dragons are going to kill you. They are going to take your powers. They are going to cast you into the Hallows, which they shall rule." He looked directly at Toil while listing this fate.

Besides his twin, Klink was nodding. "This plan is up there with your best, Barph," he said, barely able to talk around the vast wedge of sarcasm in his mouth. "I can see why we were so anxious to come to you."

Cois laughed. Will sighed against his own wishes and better judgment. He heard Barph, and Lette let out little moans of their own.

Barph shrugged. "I cannot change these things. I cannot change the world as it is. I can only plan around it."

"You plan around our deaths?" Lawl's voice crackled like a thunderhead.

Barph smiled, ducked his head in submission. "You and I both know that death is not the end, Father. Life goes on in the Hallows. As things stand, however, your death at the hands of the dragons will mark the moment when all your powers pass over to the reptilian usurpers. No one believes in a god they have seen defeated. No one worships them. All will believe in the dragons. All will worship them."

"I have to say, I am glad we have you back, Barph," said Klink, who was clearly just playing to Cois now. "Otherwise things would be looking very bleak."

Cois laughed again, and there was another round of sighs. Klink looked terribly smug, and Toil equally sour.

"You mentioned sex," said Betra, doing an even worse job of sounding scandalized.

"I said," Barph went on, "that the dragons would steal your powers. But what if you didn't have them when the dragons killed you? What would they have to steal?"

Confused expressions rippled out through the copse of trees. "Not have them?" Lawl asked. The storm was closer now.

Even Knole, Will noted, had looked up from her book. She had a finger on the edge of her page, holding the covers open, but her gaze, sharp and hard, was fully upon Barph.

"What if you hid them?" said Barph. "What if you stored

your powers somewhere else? What if the dragons killed you and stole nothing. What if you then retrieved your powers and worked against them? Undermined their power? Eroded their worship?"

Barph looked around the group significantly. "It is far easier to criticize those that rule, than it is to rule. I simply propose we change the rules of the game. The dragons will oppress the people of Kondorra. It is in their nature as much as is their love of gold. The people will grow to resent and hate them. And so there we shall be, in the place the dragons are now. There we shall be with platitudes and kind words. And we shall change the course of this war. We shall steal back our rightful places in the heavens. We shall rule, and the dragons will be but a fading ripple in the memories of a few. A warning to any who dare oppose us."

His voice rang out at the last. And Will remembered all the times he had seen Firkin preach. The old man's voice strident and cutting. The people curiously fascinated by all he had had to say. And here was all that strange magnetism with its mortal pretenses stripped away. And a few things about the past began to make sense.

He could see the familiar effects happening here as well. The gods trying to surreptitiously catch each other's eyes. They wanted to believe Barph. Even he wanted to believe him.

And then Knole, the goddess of wisdom and knowledge, closed her book. "Betra's right," she said. You definitely said something about sex." She pushed her hair out of her eyes.

Will sighed. Because even in this moment, even trying to save themselves, and indirectly the rest of Avarra along with them, the gods were a bunch of horrendously self-centered pricks.

"Ah," Barph said. "Yes. The sex." He was looking directly at Toil. "I thought you'd like this part."

Toil demonstrated restraint that had previously eluded him, limiting himself to coiled fists and ground teeth.

"Sex and these mortals." Barph swept his hand around. "Vessels. A repository for your divine powers. A place to keep them while the dragons kill you. And then, when the time comes, these mortals will return them to you."

This was greeted with silence. Everyone quietly working through the implications. Will felt like his brain was struggling to run in the waist-deep water of divine beings' emotions. Sleep with... A repository for divine powers. He would have...

Cois interrupted his flow. "We sleep with these mortals and deposit our divinity in them?" zhe asked. Zhe even managed to make it sound delicate.

Barph bowed.

"Oh, you are clever." Zhe laughed again.

"He's a fucking imbecile!" roared Toil. "Deposit our divinity in...in..." He stared at Will, Lette, Balur, Afrit, and Quirk in utter horror. "In *these*?" The word sounded as if it had been embalmed in disgust.

"I don't know..." Cois shrugged. "Some of them have...certain appeals." One finger played with hir lower lip.

"Wife!" roared Toil, in full outrage.

"There do seem to be...questions," said Knole. Will watched her pace in a circle. She reached into a pocket in her dress and pulled out an apple. She bit into it deeply, chewed. The others watched her.

"They are weak." Knole had paced around to Will and prodded him in the back. He staggered a step, though the touch had been slight. He looked slightly dazed.

"They are, by definition, mortal." Knole chewed her lip. "It would be easy for the dragons to kill them, to take their powers. Easier than it would be for them to kill us."

"That is true, Aunt," said Barph, with another of his subservient nods. False nods, Will was beginning to call them in his head. There was an element of performance to all of this. Will just didn't see the third-act reveal yet.

"However," Barph went on, looking up, a gleam in his eyes. And Will realized he had an answer ready for this. When had he prepared it? "There are many, many mortals. Even if the dragons knew which mortals were serving as repositories for our power—and a lot will have to go wrong for them to know that—then they still will not know where they are. They could kill people at random, of course, hoping to get lucky, but how much do they erode their power base before they get that lucky?"

"Who keeps them in line?" asked Lawl. He was watching Barph as carefully as Will was. "Who makes them give their divinity back? Who says that they do not run off with their new-found powers and make merry with the world while we languish at the dragon's pleasure?"

Another false nod. "I think, Grandfather, someone has to stay behind. Someone has to keep them in line."

Cois's smile was broad as a river mouth. "Someone risks everything," zhe said. "Someone risks losing their divinity. They risk having nothing to come back to." Zhe made it sound like foreplay.

"Oh!" Toil threw up his hands. "Now I see it! This is your petty revenge. You have me stay. You have me killed. You come back and take my place, like the ungrateful shit you always were."

Was that it? Will tried to think through all the buzzing in his head. All the foreign emotions and desires. He almost prayed to Knole for wisdom, but... with the goddess in front of him. No, he could not.

"Actually, Father," said Barph, "I was thinking it should be the one god that the dragons might not expect to face. The one god that there has been no evidence of for the past eight hundred years. The absent god."

"Oh," breathed Cois. "My clever boy."

"*You* stay?" Toil was suspicious still.

"It is my plan," said Barph. "It is only fair that I take the risk."

Klink snorted. "As if fairness mattered to you."

Barph shook his head, and with a sincerity that shocked Quirk said, "If my time among the mortals has taught me anything, Uncle, it is the value of fairness."

And Will had a hard time believing that, except when he was looking straight at Barph.

"We die," said Lawl. "You live?"

"I *remain*, Grandfather," said Barph with another false nod. "I keep the mortals in line. I ensure we come to you to return your powers."

"And who is there to make sure you keep your promise?" But there was give in Lawl's voice, Will thought. He was coming around.

"The dragons," said Barph simply.

It was the smart play. To leave it simply at that. It was not a strong argument, but it was delivered with confidence, as if it were obvious. This whole encounter had the feeling of something rehearsed. But Barph had been back with them...an hour perhaps? So that could not be.

The gods were hesitating. For once, Will couldn't blame them.

Again Cois was the first to speak. "Do we..." zhe said, fingering hir lower lip once more, "happen to get to choose the vessel in which we deposit our divinity?" Zhe was looking straight at Will. He could feel hir eyes boring into him. He could feel his willpower dissolving. He could feel his desire to do whatever zhe commanded overwhelming him.

Desperately he tore his gaze away and looked for Lette. He did not want this. Well...he did. He desperately, desperately did. But that was not a desire native to his own soul. It was a desire planted there by another, a virulent weed that was choking out his own thoughts. And he needed her to know that.

He caught Lette's eye. And he saw sadness there. He saw

hatred. Revulsion. Heartbreak. Glee. Bitterness. Excitement. And he didn't know which of them was her true emotion.

Behind him, the gods were haggling, bickering. They were so small in some ways. So petty. And he had struggled for them. Bled for them. His leg was shattered in two for them. To preserve their rule. It felt like such a mistake right now.

Then he felt Cois's fingers run thin trails across his shoulder blades. His willpower was water, running away into dry ground. His eyes rolled back. He tried to hold on to himself.

"Her." Another god's voice penetrated the cracked shell of his consciousness. He looked up. Knole was pointing at Quirk. Quirk looked like a bug speared by a needle upon a corkboard. She looked around desperately.

"I am really thinking Cois would be better with me." Balur leaned into the proceedings.

Will felt twin stabs of jealousy and hope. Perhaps somehow he would escape this.

"I shall take the Analesian."

But it was not Cois who said it. And not Knole. And not Betra.

Lawl pointed a finger at Balur. "My divinity is strong, and shall deserve a powerful container. This one is mine."

"Erm…" said Balur. "That is not exactly what I was having in mind."

Muscles rippled all over Lawl's quite frankly magnificent body. Veins bulged and moved. Joints cracked. "You reject me?" thundered Lawl. "You question my favor?"

"Erm…" Balur managed in a strangled voice. Will suspected that under the force of Lawl's will it was a struggle to get that much out.

"If…erm…" Afrit raised a tentative hand into the awkwardness. "If we're making requests…" She was blushing furiously. "If Knole and Quirk needed a hand then I'd be…you know… I could…erm…" She was studying her feet with the kind of ferocity that Will usually associated with Balur mid-battle frenzy. "If that's...Well..." Afrit worked her hands like she was trying to unscrew them from her wrists. "You see...I just thought..."

Quirk was staring at Afrit with a look of absolute bafflement.

Which meant she was the only person there who was shocked.

He looked around, did some quick mental math. Three gods remained, Toil, Betra, and Klink. Facing them were Afrit and Lette. It did not seem like the equations were in Afrit's favor.

Toil got there too. "There are two women and three of us," he pointed out, still sounding pissed.

"Well," Barph shrugged, and looked at Betra and her twin boys, "I just assumed you three would want to share someone again."

At this point, Toil finally ran out of words. He opened his mouth, closed it again. He gawped, gasped. He looked at Quirk's feet.

Klink shrugged. "Well, it doesn't really seem like it's worth denying at this point."

Betra said nothing, but she did sidle closer to Lette.

"Fine," said Barph, looking at Afrit. "Go with Quirk and Knole. Knock yourself out."

"Really?" Afrit probably couldn't have sounded more excited had she actually been in bed with her one true love at that actual moment. Her mouth hung slightly open.

Quirk's reaction was significant in its disparity. Shock mingled with betrayal.

"Don't we get a say?" said Will as loudly as he could. Cois was a good step from him at this point, and Will felt he might have his wits about him right now, albeit briefly. But even without seeing it, he could feel Cois's arched eyebrow like a whip crack across his back.

"Yes!" said Balur just as loudly. "If Betra wished to join her husband even—"

"Ew," said Klink, shaking his head. "Don't be vile."

"These are our bodies," Will managed, despite Cois's will crashing into his head. The rampaging beast of desire screaming at him to shut up. He wanted Lette to know his objections here. He wanted to save Quirk from a fate she clearly did not want.

"It's okay, Will." Quirk flicked a slightly tortured glance in Afrit's direction. "It's okay."

Will ground his teeth. But...was this their best shot? He had no better plans. Was his objection simply that this mockery of what Firkin had once been had come up with the plan?

"Excellent," said Barph, clapping his hands together. "Now let's lower our britches and save the world."

55

The Two-Backed Beast

Balur just wanted to murder dragons. That was all. That was why he had gotten involved in all this. When he had been doing it before, it had been being the greatest moment of his life. It had been being the most brutal and wondrous murder. It had been being the very edge of life. He had been standing on the cusp between existence and death. He had been teetering between the greatest height and the greatest abyss. Life had been flickering between the two. His heart had been thrumming like a plucked harp string. His muscles had been burning. Agony and ecstasy mixing in him like a divine cordial.

And now...

Now...

Lawl, muscles rippling, looked up at him. "Come on," he said, eyes approximately as coquettish as a stable door, "put it in me and let's get this over with."

56

The Four-Backed Beast

Lette had assumed that she would enjoy this more. She liked sex. She had practiced it enough to believe she was quite good at it. She had certainly received compliments to that effect. And in her experience, men were poor at faking their pleasure.

Will had certainly seemed to enjoy his time.

Gods, Will.

If he just hadn't looked so gods-hexed happy about Cois picking him. And yes, he had argued against it, but Lette had seen his expression when Cois had stroked his back. Gods, she had seen the circus tent he had erected in his britches.

And, yes, she knew that Cois had a certain... effect on people. The state of her own underwear after receiving Cois's attention was perhaps better left unmentioned. And yet... still Will's idiot smile played in front of her face again.

That was *her* idiot's smile, gods curse it. *She* put that smile on his face. Not some whore god(dess).

And now here she was with two strapping young men—twins no less—and a woman who had clearly been around the block more than a few times, and yet... all she could see was that idiot smile.

And it pretty much ruined the whole foursome experience for her.

57

The More You Know...

Quirk, Knole, and Afrit stood and regarded each other. They had remained close to the fire while the others found their own private spots. They could already hear them going at it. Quirk rather wished they had found a more secluded spot. This might be easier if she couldn't see the others' faces.

Afrit looked so eager...

Had she known that Afrit would want this? She supposed in some ways she had. Or she could have known. It would not have been so hard to add up all the small touches, all the little glances. She remembered Afrit as she had been back in the Tamathian University, eager and anxious. Waiting for her like a puppy awaited its master to come home. And she remembered her in Vinter, staring at her, so disappointed.

No, it would not have been so hard to work it out. And yet she, who claimed to prize knowledge and wisdom, she had remained willfully ignorant of this.

She could not blame any of this on Afrit.

But...Knole. She could still be disappointed in Knole. She could still rage against her goddess.

"You were meant to be better than this." Her voice sounded pathetically plaintive in her ears.

Knole had taken a first step toward her. She stopped and cocked her head.

"You were meant to be above this." And now that the words had started, Quirk couldn't stop them. And she couldn't stop the horrible wheedling tone. "You were more than flesh, and sweat, and…and…juices. You were…" She waved a hand at the heavens. Why did her vocabulary have to abandon her now? "You were elevated," she managed. "Above this."

She looked away from Knole. She couldn't bear the sight of the goddess anymore. Unfortunately she made the mistake of looking at Afrit for support. And the look of sadness on her friend's face was almost unbearable. But she still could not stop the words.

"No!" she snapped. "No! I do not want your sympathy. This is not a plea for comfort. This is a demand for an explanation. I have been down in the flesh and the sweat. I have had flesh in my hands. I have taken, and taken. And you…you…" She thrust an accusing finger at Knole. It trembled like a branch in the grip of a summer storm. "You rescued me," she accused. "You saved me from all of that."

She pulled in a ragged breath. "Why are you dragging me back down?"

"Oh, Quirk."

Quirk felt a hand on her shoulder. And the touch was so familiar now. Afrit was there. And when Quirk looked at her, there was such sympathy in her eyes. Such wells of sadness. And, gods piss on it, so much gods-hexed love.

"No," she said, but Knole was advancing on the other side of her. And she knew this was the way forward for Avarra. This was her sacrifice.

"Why did you leave the university and go out into the field?" asked Knole. She had a quiet, lilting voice. Her hair was back in her eyes again and she did not push it away. "When you first went in search of dragons. Why was that?"

Quirk was caught off guard. She stumbled over her hurt.

"You...You know about that?" And she did not want to be in awe of this goddess. She did not want to feel pride that she actually knew her. But she did.

"You have prayed to me," said Knole. "And I have heard you even if I have not answered. I remember." She looked away into the distance, smiled to herself. "I remember everything." Her gaze flicked back to Quirk. "So tell me. Why did you leave?"

Afrit was stroking her arm, and she wanted to pull away, but Knole's gaze pinned her as certainly as any wrestler's hold would have done.

"I wanted..." Quirk's mouth was dry. She licked her lips. "I wanted to see dragons with my own eyes. I wanted to know them truly. I didn't want it to simply be writings in books. I wanted it to live and breathe."

Knole nodded. And she understood. She truly did. Quirk knew that. She was only a few steps away now.

"This is like that," she said. "This is closing the distance between you and knowledge." She reached out a hand toward Quirk. "Not all flesh is burned. Not all of it rots. Do you not deserve to know that?"

And there was a promise there. Even a kindness. But Quirk felt something else behind it. She could not help but be aware in this moment, with the goddess's psyche pressed up against her own, that for Knole there were no limits to the search for knowledge. The goddess would know everything if she could. She would want to know how a beggar would feel if she poured a million golden bulls into his lap, just as she would want to know how a mother would feel as she twisted her infant's head from its body. And this moment, right here and now, was just the same thing. It was a chance to learn, to add another drop to the infinite ocean of information that lived within her.

But there was some comfort in that thought too. And Quirk felt that, despite the clear inhumanity of the woman before her, the offer of intimacy was meant with that spirit. There was a concept of kindness within her goddess. Knole understood it even if she did not experience it.

Knole's hand was on her wrist. Afrit was still stroking her other arm.

And, yes there was comfort here.

Slowly, Quirk sank to her knees and allowed them to teach her.

58

In the Afterglow

Well, thought Will when it was all said and done and he had pieced back together most of his sanity, *that was a lot better than I thought it might be, but I'm still not going to tell a single gods-hexed soul about it.*

59

Changing Plans Like Diapers

The sun filtered slowly into the copse of trees. Birds called back and forth to each other. On the horizon, Will could see the ruined city of Vinter smoking gently. Disheveled and disarrayed, the gods of Avarra and his dazed-looking companions gathered around the dead remains of a campfire.

"So!" Barph clapped his hands. Of all of them, he looked by far the best. His beard was groomed for the first time that Will could ever remember. His hair was slicked back, and braided. "Morning, everybody." He beamed.

"Fuck you, Barph," Toil muttered.

"Ready to die, Father?" said Barph, the force of his smile not wavering for a second.

"I believe," said Betra, voice haughty despite the fact that her dress was torn almost to the point of indiscretion, "that some breakfast might be in order before we address the necessities of the day."

Will wasn't sure where the sausages came from. Or the potatoes. Or tea. Or even the plates and cutlery. But he didn't complain.

Nobody said much.

When they were done—Barph the last to finish, licking his plate clean with his tongue—the gods stood, looked at each other.

"The dragons are in Vinter," said Barph helpfully. "I'd suggest trying there." He smiled.

"You don't have to enjoy it so much," Cois said to him. Zhe looked surprisingly dreary to Will this morning. There was nothing physically different about hir that he could tell, but whatever had lit a fire in his britches was absent now.

Will watched them walk away, stumbling slightly, a little unsure of themselves. Toil stubbed his toe, bent and rubbed it.

"Shit," he heard the god say. "Never done that before."

And then they were out of earshot, and the five mortals and one smug deity were standing watching as they slowly trudged back toward the ruins of Vinter.

Did he feel divine? Will wondered. Mostly he felt like shit. His broken leg was throbbing fit to burst. The rigors of the previous night had not been good for it. That didn't seem very godlike.

"Did it work?" he said, turning to Barph. "Are we...? Did they...?" He really, really wanted to avoid anyone using the word *deposit* again.

"Did you cause Cois to..." Barph waggled his eyebrows at Will.

"Erm..." Will spluttered. He tried really, really hard not to look at Lette. He failed miserably. "Well..."

Barph was grinning almost as much as when he sent Toil off to Vinter. "If your evening's pleasure was successful then the magic I wove should have been as well."

"Pleasure," Quirk muttered to herself, almost contemplative. Afrit turned away.

Will looked at the pair. But he didn't have time for the vagaries of Quirk and Afrit's ever-more-complicated relationship. Instead he turned back to Barph and asked, "So, what can we do?"

"Okay," said Barph. "You'd like to heal your leg, wouldn't you? So...think about your leg. How you want it to be. Close your eyes. Picture the ideal state of your leg. Think of bone knitting, and skin meshing. Think of pain floating away."

Will was dubious, but he also wanted his leg to feel better. He closed his eyes. He pictured things. His leg still throbbed. He opened his eyes. Barph was grinning at him.

"Fuck you," Will told him.

"I just wanted to know what you'd look like," said Barph.

"So we are not being divine?" asked Balur. "I was…I was… Last night I…for nothing?" His fists were balled.

"Oh stop crying," said Barph. He sounded bored. He pointed at Will. "Just put your hand over the wound and tell it to heal."

"Tell it to heal?" Will looked at him skeptically. "If you're messing with me…"

"Then you'll be able to do nothing, because I'll still be divine and you won't be. But if you are then we can have a much more interesting conversation."

Will still hesitated. Firkin had always enjoyed a good practical joke, but there was a streak of cruelty in Barph's humor that had never been so prominent in the old man's jests.

Still, what did he have to lose but pride? And he had precious little left of that this morning anyway. He bent awkwardly, put his hand on his leg. He winced as he did so.

"Heal," he told it through gritted teeth.

Nothing happened.

"Not like that." Barph sounded slightly disgusted. "Mean it."

"Mean it?" Will hoped someone besides Barph was enjoying this. Sighing, he reached down to his leg once more. "Heal," he said, more forcefully this time.

Barph's slap caught him entirely off guard. It was a full palm to his cheek. He reeled, stumbled on his injury, bellowed.

"Mean it!" yelled Barph. "Believe it!"

Will looked up at him, and thought about murder. But even if he was divine he still had no way to actually back up his threats until he mastered this.

"Heal," he said.

Barph's slap was no less hard the second time. "Mean it!" shouted the god.

"Heal," he said.

Another slap.

"Gods, is this really—" Quirk started.

"Heal!" shouted Will.

And then he felt it. Warmth and liquid pleasure rolling through his leg. Bone knitting together. Skin meshing over the wound. The relief was incredible. He stood up with a gasp, tested his weight on his leg. The others stared at him. He stood one-legged before them. He hopped. He laughed.

"Gods," breathed Afrit.

"Yes," said Lette. "That's actually right."

"What can I be smiting?" asked Balur. He was almost jumping up and down. "I am wanting to smite something!" He pointed at a lone cow that had wandered into the half-burned field that surrounded the copse. It was picking at odd stands of grass that had survived the passage of the dragons' army. "Smite!" he yelled. Nothing happened. He turned to Barph. "How am I smiting things?"

"Oh good," said Barph. "It worked. I wasn't sure it would. I've never taken the divinity from another god and shoved it into a mortal before."

"You...?" Will managed. "You weren't sure...?"

Barph shrugged again. "What was the worst that could happen?"

"Smite!" Balur shouted.

"We all die horrible messy deaths," Lette hazarded.

Barph nodded. "Yes. But that was probably going to happen anyway."

"But you said..." Will couldn't believe it. Except he could. Of course he could. Take Firkin's bullshit, and mix it with a divinely cavalier disregard for human life...Gods. Fucking gods.

His jaw worked. And now that he did have divine powers he could teach Barph a lesson. He could...

Have a much more interesting conversation. That was what Barph had said.

"Are we immortal?" he asked. Because suddenly his anger was drowned out by all the questions shouting in his head.

"Why don't you have Balur smite you and find out?"

Balur beamed. He pointed at Will. "Smite!" he yelled.

Will leapt back. "Gods, Balur!" But lightning did not strike. Life did not end.

Balur grunted, evidently disappointed, and went back to pointing at his cow. "Smite!" he shouted. The cow continued to quietly chew her cud.

"You seem to know very little," said Quirk. She, of them all, seemed the calmest this morning. A little more detached perhaps, but calm. Will wondered why Afrit had such a sour expression.

"Oh good," said Barph. "Did Knole deposit her supercilious condescension in you as well? That's fantastic."

Quirk narrowed her eyes. "You have a plan, though," she said. "You weren't sure if this would work, but you had contingencies for either scenario."

"I plan," said Balur, "far less than people seem to imagine. I merely improvise well."

Quirk shook her head. "No," she said. "That's not it." She sounded quite sure of herself.

Barph rolled his eyes. "There is no getting through to some people," he said with a sigh.

"Smite!" shouted Balur to no avail.

"What is next in the plan anyway?" asked Lette. "And why isn't Afrit saying anything?"

Afrit shot Lette a look that Will would have expected on a cornered and injured badger. "I'm fine," Afrit barked.

Quirk, Will noticed, didn't even spare Afrit a glance. She stayed intent on Barph.

"You said we'd go to the Hallows," she said. "You said we would return their divinity."

"I did," Barph admitted.

"But that's not it," said Quirk. There was the hint of a smile etched on her lips. A look of slight satisfaction.

Will totally got what Barph had been saying about supercilious condescension.

"Smite!" shouted Balur.

This was abruptly followed by a violent cracking sound, a wet splat, and the sound of thunder. A hundred yards away, lightning struck, and a tan-colored cow burst apart like a sack of wet meat. Blood and offal sprayed, and bone fragments rained down, little yellow hailstones smashing through the grass.

"Oh," breathed Balur. "Oh, I could be getting used to that."

For a moment, Will stared in horror. And then, slipping through his thoughts, the question...Could he do that now? Could he turn his enemies to...

The possibilities stretched out before him. But had he ever heard a story of Cois smiting anyone? He had assumed divine powers were a rather uniform package, but the gods each had their own realms, their own areas of influence. Did having Cois's divinity within mean that he was attuned to...to...fertility? Could he make crops grow? Could he encourage farm animals to breed?

Could he make someone feel desire?

Could he make Lette...

No. Gods, no. A thousand times no.

"When do we go to the Hallows then?" Lette asked, and Will almost jumped. "If that's still the plan."

Gods, Will hoped she couldn't read minds now.

"Tomorrow," said Barph. "Once the gods are dead." He reached behind the spot where he was sitting on the grass and produced a vast wineskin from nowhere. He unstopped it, spilling fluid liberally over his hands, and took a long slurp. "Anyone else?" he asked.

"Where will we be finding the entrance to the Hallows?" asked Balur, taking the wineskin.

"The Atrian Waste," said Barph nonchalantly.

Which caused Will to pause. "That's four hundred leagues north of here," he pointed out. "As the crow flies. And we have to go through the Spatters and likely the Osten Jungle to get there. Not to mention that every inch of ground between here and there is now controlled by the dragons." His voice, he noticed, was getting a little high-pitched.

"Yes," Barph sighed. Then he added, "Tomorrow," as if that somehow magically solved everything.

"Except," Quirk said, "tomorrow the gods will be dead, and the dragons will be divine. Won't us working miracles draw them like flies?"

All eyes fell upon Barph, who was, for better or worse, the closest thing they had to an expert on these matters.

Barph cocked his head. "They are not gods yet," he said. "They will need to ascend to the actual heavens first. There is ritual to these things. It is based upon worship." He stroked his chin thoughtfully. "They'll need the will of the people to take them there."

"I think they have that," Will said. "I still don't honestly know why, but they have almost three hundred thousand supporters gathered in Vinter now."

"And more are still coming," said Lette. On the horizon they could all see the dust of carts and foot traffic as people slowly came in pilgrimage to the site of the dragons' final victory.

"That might be enough to do it," Barph said, nodding slowly. "They all gather in Vinter. The people worship them. They ascend." He nodded more definitively. "Yes, I imagine we'll be seeing all the other dragons assemble here soon enough."

"So that's our grace period then," Will said, his brain churning furiously. "That's how long we've got to safely travel...gods, four hundred leagues." His heart sank. He turned to Quirk. "How long do you think it'll take the dragons to get here?"

Quirk puffed out her cheeks. "Well," she said. "The Fanlorn Empire is probably the farthest from here. She cocked her head to one side. "From there...if my estimations of their airspeed velocity hold true...perhaps four or five days."

"Gods," breathed Will as his heart went into a nosedive, dragging all his hopes along with it. "Is that all?"

"Could we be beating one of the dragons in Vinter into submission and riding it as a steed into Atria?" Balur asked, eyes gleaming.

"No, you jackass." Lette spoke for the group. "We could not."

"Wait," said Will, because what Balur said was clearly the product of balls too large and thoughts too small, but there was perhaps a nugget of an idea hidden in there. "We can smite things now...Or..." He considered. "Balur can anyway." He looked at Barph. "I don't know about the rest of us." Barph gave him a poker face that Firkin would never have been able to sustain. Will moved on. That wasn't the crux of his concern now. "But what if Balur smote a dragon? What if lightning reached down and slammed into one? We saw magicians do that in Kondorra and it hurt that dragon. Hurt it badly."

"I think I should do that," said Balur, nodding sharply. "That should be being part of all our plans going forward. Regardless."

"So," said Quirk, "you think we should attack the dragons now?" She had her disapproving schoolmarm face on.

Will ignored her. He wasn't ready for that step yet. "What would happen, Barph?" he pressed.

Barph shrugged. But Will called bullshit on that shrug. Barph knew something. "What would happen?" he pressed.

Barph shook his head. "It wouldn't work. People believe in

the dragons and their invulnerability too much. They're not gods yet, but they're very close. Remember when you saw me fight the dragons. You saw me in the heart of my own city, in the heart of my worshippers. You saw me shrug off wounds that should have killed me a thousand times. It would be the same with them." He gave a sour smile. "One does hate being the bearer of bad news all the time.

"Belief protects them?" Will asked.

"Why are you asking about attacking the dragons?" Quirk said again, a hard edge to her voice now.

"You have a plan," said Lette, catching on. She looked at Will. "Don't you?"

"And I smite dragons in it?" asked Barph.

"No," said Afrit, but no one was really paying attention to her.

"That isn't what you agreed to do, Will," Barph said. But his smile was back.

"Oh?" said Will. "Like you're the god of keeping your word? Like you don't have some sort of betrayal in your heart? At least this way it's *our* betrayal."

"No," Afrit said again, louder this time. "We have a plan. We stick to it."

Lette gave Afrit a look that Will thought was far more offended than he would have expected. "Hear him out," she said. "You might even get to fuck Quirk again."

Will's eyes flew to Quirk. But the academic-cum-resistance-leader hadn't even batted an eyelid. All her attention, it seemed, was on Barph. Afrit, though, when Will looked, was white-faced and pink-cheeked. There was a look like murder in her eyes. And, of all the people in the group, it was Balur who was subtly shaking his head at Lette.

Will tried to work out if he had time for all the social undercurrents and personal politics whirling around in the aftermath of the gods' visit, and decided he didn't. A plan was forming in the back of his head, and for the first time in a long time he felt like maybe, just maybe he was in control. He wasn't going to let go of that.

"Think about it," he said. "All this time we've been trying to save the gods. Because of the two shitty options available to us, they're the ones that stink just a little bit less. But when we met them last night...were they really worth saving? Or were they just another set of arseholes? Little people with a lot of power. Just like every other arsehole in charge we've found. What if there's another way? What if there's a way so that no one is in charge? No one is forcing—"

"You are meaning anarchy?" said Balur. "Right?"

"Well..." Will had been in midflow and he felt a little like Balur had just shoved his foot out and tripped him.

"Fucking anarchy." Lette rolled her eyes.

"I'm not talking about anarchy." Will managed to elbow his way back into the conversation.

"It was sounding a lot like anarchy," said Balur. "Wasn't it sounding a lot like anarchy?" he said to Lette.

"Let's give him the benefit of the doubt, shall we?" Lette was being oddly reasonable.

"Everyone has power," Balur rumbled on even as Will opened his mouth. "No one in charge. Chaos, murder, rape, pillaging. Bully warlords rising to power. What else was it sounding like?"

"I didn't say anything about warlords," Will protested.

"What were you imagining would happen?" Balur looked amused.

"Look," said Will, "I haven't figured out the third step of the plan yet. But I'm not advocating anarchy."

"Then your word choice is being very poor," huffed Balur.

"I don't think anarchy is necessarily as bad as you are making it sound," said Quirk. "Afrit, wasn't there that example from Teppu?"

"Do not drag me into this. I'm entirely opposed to it."

"I," Will tried again. "Am not. Advocating. Anarchy." He looked around. There seemed to be a momentary gap in the idiocy of his friends. "I am advocating us being a little bit hesitant handing back the reins of power to the arseholes who traipsed through our lives last night. We have more power than any other mortals have ever had on this planet. And our plan is just to give it up? Think about all the good we could do first."

"Okay," Afrit said. "You know what, on second thought, I am getting involved because that is basically Dictator 101. You get given a little bit of power and you plan to do just a little bit of good with it. And then a little bit more. But then someone objects to what you've done, because while it's good and fair in your eyes, it's not in theirs. But, you think, that's okay, once they really see your grand design, then they'll stop complaining. After all, you're just trying to help them.

"Except they don't stop complaining. Instead more people join them. And a lot of them don't even have legitimate complaints. They're just there because perhaps there's some power to be had. And unlike you, all their plans are self-serving and foolish. So you have to crack down, just so you can make things better for everyone.

"But then these jackals start demanding you share power. And yes, that's your plan eventually, but that plan is going to be derailed if you just give power away to all these self-serving imbeciles. And so on and so forth, and then you're sitting on a throne made of your enemy's gold-plated bones while the populace crawls through squalor to do your bidding. Because that is the oldest fucking pattern in history." She actually spat at him.

"See," said Quirk mildly. "I told you she would know about all of this."

"Gods." Will shook his head. And he briefly wished he was the sort of strong-arm thug that Afrit was accusing him of being, because that would certainly make shit like this easier. "I am not talking about anarchy. I am not talking about dictatorship. I am talking about buying time to make a better decision than the one we've felt we've been stuck with. I am talking about"—he pointed at Afrit—"involving you in a decision to put into place whatever power structure you think might be best."

"I have not," said Barph, commenting for the first time, and Will braced himself, "actually heard a plan in all of this. Just the threat to break a promise."

"It's simple," said Will. "It's easy."

Barph arched an eyebrow.

Will shrugged. "It's your plan. We rob the people of their belief in the dragons. We take away that power. We undermine it. And then when the dragons are weak and unprotected, we make them nothing more than a footnote in history."

"And there is being no anarchy?" Balur asked.

"Not unless we decide that's how life should be."

And then they sat with that for a while. They all sat as the sun mounted to the sky, and wondered about taking power for themselves. And no one suggested making for the Hallows now. No one said anything. Afrit did wear her judgmental face, but Lette seemed to have misplaced hers for once. Balur mostly spent a lot of time looking at the crater where the cow had been.

The day got late. Barph stood up. "It's going to begin soon," he said. He was looking out at Vinter.

They all turned to stare. Will was so involved in his own thoughts, he wasn't sure what he was looking for. Then something moved in the skyline of Vinter. Lette squinted. And then one of the city's few remaining towers—silhouetted by the distance—spread its wings and flapped up into the sky.

"Gods," Quirk breathed.

"I thought that was—" Will started.

"Yes," said Lette, cutting him off. "We all did."

Another dragon flapped up into the sky. Then the third. Will tried to see if he could figure out which was which from this distance. He thought he caught the gleam of gold on Gorrax's scale but he couldn't be sure from this distance.

"It's happening," Barph said softly. "I honestly didn't think they'd go through with it."

"They're desperate," said Quirk.

"Yes." And Barph's voice was almost emotionless, but Will thought perhaps, just maybe he heard a smile. He looked over at him. Lette was looking too. Their eyes met. She looked away before she could tell what was written in them.

"You hate them," he said, as much to distract himself from the unexpected images of Cois's athleticism that had risen unbidden in his mind as anything else. "You hate the other gods, for what they did to you."

For a while Barph said nothing. The dragons flew in an ever-tightening circle around the center of the city. Their roars were audible even from the copse of trees.

"Yes," Barph said after a while. "I do."

The dragons had stopped circling. They thrashed their wings, hovering in the air.

Barph held Will's eye for a moment, then looked away. Will stayed looking at Barph's profile. The set of his jaw. The tension at the corners of his eyes. And he knew that if he wanted to hold on to power, Barph would not stop him.

Above a city, three dragons bathed the world in fire. Below them, gods died.

60

Make War, Not Love

In the face of a bold new world, there didn't seem to be much to do except make supper. Barph summoned dishes and food from nowhere. Lette made a fire.

Quirk sat back and watched. So many things seemed different since last night. So many things that had been unclear now lay bare. Barph's false glibness, for example. Even Will had seen the hurt lying clearly beneath it, yet still the god persisted with the lie. Why?

"You want us to keep the gods in Hallows, don't you?" she said to him. "That was Lawl's punishment for you. You think it's poetic."

He ignored her. She found she wasn't surprised. She turned to Will. "That doesn't bother you?"

He at least had the grace to think about it. "If we want the same things," he said, "even if it's for different reasons, I can live with it."

"From a professional standpoint," said Afrit, her voice full of an acid that Quirk truly didn't understand, "I suppose I should be glad to see a dictator in this embryonic stage, rather than just reading about it."

"Hey," Will snapped, his temper fraying, "I did not ask for this power. I have never asked for power. But I have had it thrust on me again and again. And I've tried giving it up, but that never seems to work out. So this time I'm going to use it. I am going to try to do the responsible fucking thing. And I am going to do it regardless of whether Quirk was a shitty lay or not."

And that caused Quirk to blink several times. Because she had not…Knole had not…She looked at Afrit. "I was…?" she asked. Then she regretted asking.

And then Afrit let out a sound that made her realize Will had landed a barb far closer to Afrit's heart than anyone seemed to have expected. Balur was actually face-palming.

"Oh," Will said. "Oh, I didn't…I'm sorry. I got…Shit."

But Afrit was running away, stumbling into the night.

"I was…?" Quirk said again. And of all the things that had become clear, that was not one of them at all. She looked to Lette, who was for better or worse the only other woman here. "She's…Because…?"

"I should go after her," said Will. "I feel like an ass."

"No." Lette caught his shoulder. "*You* shouldn't."

Which Quirk was pretty sure she disagreed with.

"Quirk should." Lette spoke as if dealing with particularly obtuse children.

"I should?" All of Quirk's sanguine calm was fleeing her. All her reassurance about the world, about her newfound insights…She was floundering wildly. She felt a little bit like she was drowning.

"She *loves* you," said Lette.

And Lette couldn't have hit her more solidly if she had used the hilt of a sword. Because…Because…No. But yes. Oh gods. Suddenly everything played out again in front of Quirk's eyes. *Everything.* Her whole history. And suddenly so much made sense. And so little did. "She…" Quirk felt as if her eyes were as round as saucers.

Lette shook her head. "And you think you're so smart."

Quirk stood. She stared around, looking for an escape route. There wasn't one. "I'll go after her?" she said. She hadn't meant to make it into a question.

"Yes," said Lette. "You will."

Quirk took a few steps after Afrit, hesitated. Lette nodded encouragingly. Quirk didn't feel encouraged. But she went anyway.

She had rationalized things by the time she caught up with Afrit at the far side of the copse. Lette had exaggerated. It wasn't love. It couldn't be love. She put a hand on Afrit's shoulder.

"Hey," she said. She wasn't sure if she was trying to calm Afrit or lecture her. She wasn't sure about anything. "Don't... Don't run away from me."

Afrit wheeled on her. "I am not running away!" she yelled. "I am storming off in a rage."

Quirk stared at her. The moon was rising behind her, full, and yellow as Barph's teeth. And Quirk had been feeling so serene. She and Knole had talked for hours the previous night. They had discussed many of the intricacies of the act of love. They had spoken of its historical and political importance. Knole had revealed secrets of chemistry and alchemy. They had talked about its cultural relevance and variations. Knole had been a constant fount of minor revelations. There had been so much to process. So many new ways to look at the world.

And now this. Unseen. Another way of seeing that she'd still been blind to.

"How was I supposed to know?" she said. She sounded more plaintive and less forceful than she'd hoped.

"Oh," said Afrit, voice so laden with sarcasm, Quirk was surprised it could make it all the way through the air to her, "I don't know. Maybe it was the way I *made love to you* last night?"

"But..." Quirk tried to process all of this. "That was about..."

"What?" Afrit stared at her. "Look, I know... trust me, I really, really do know how hard this is for you. I am intimately aware of that. But I would still really love for you to tell me what you thought I was doing there last night. What could it have possibly been about?"

And the truth was of course that she had barely thought about Afrit at all. She had thought about Knole. And about herself.

"I just…I thought you were my friend," Quirk said. And it sounded so very pathetic. And also just a little like an accusation. Which was unfortunately exactly how Afrit took it.

"Oh," she said. "I am sorry for having emotions. I'm sorry that they're an inconvenience to you."

"They're not inconvenient!" Quirk said, but apparently exasperation wasn't the way to go either.

"Just this conversation?" asked Afrit. "Am I imposing on your important time sitting around enabling Will becoming a dictator?"

"He's…" Quirk started. She closed her eyes. She was reacting. She wasn't thinking. This was why Barph was so wrong with his heart-over-head thing. Too much heart led to nonsense like this.

"This isn't about Will," she said. "This is about me taking you for granted."

And finally, finally that was the right thing to say. Or at least she thought it was. Afrit was glowering at her now, instead of biting her head off.

But Afrit was expecting something in addition to that, of course. Some follow-up thought that made a cease-fire possible. Quirk flailed around for ideas.

"I…" she managed, waving a hand in the space between herself and Afrit. "I am not good at this." She shook her head as something flared in Afrit's eyes. "You know that. I know you know that. You said that. But…it means that I think I have missed some obvious signals. Or maybe I've ignored them. Or not allowed myself to be conscious of them. Or maybe I'm just a self-centered arse. I don't know. I don't. And I…You have been a better friend to me than I ever deserved. And that should be repaid, rewarded. In the epics... that's how it is, isn't it? There's a moment of revelation and reward."

She hung her head. "I can't stop being me. I can't make a piece of myself appear."

Afrit licked her lips.

"I..." Quirk started.

"You don't love me."

And there it was. That was the truth of it.

"I like you a lot," Quirk said, and then wished she hadn't. It was the worst of consolation prizes.

"I know," said Afrit. She looked away.

"You..." said Quirk. She hadn't expected that.

"Shut up," said Afrit, but without the anger of a moment before. "You are terrible at this."

"Okay."

"I had hoped," Afrit said carefully, as if picking her way along a treacherous ledge, "that after last night I might change your mind. But I didn't. I know I didn't. And, yes, part of me is upset because I didn't. Because I don't think I ever can change your mind. And that hurts." She made sure Quirk met her eye when she said that. "That really hurts. I want you to understand that. Not all the time. But often."

Quirk wanted to look away but she didn't truly dare.

"But that's okay," Afrit said. "I can live with that. If I couldn't, I would have left a long time ago. But I would ask... in the name of friendship if nothing else, please just acknowledge that the pain is there. Be just a little sensitive. And I know I don't have much right to ask that. It is my love, after all, not yours. But, please... for friendship."

There was something desperate in her eyes. And Quirk wanted to tell Afrit that what she was describing didn't sound like a healthy lifestyle. She wanted to say it was too much to ask of her. She wanted to say that she wasn't sure that a friendship with so much at stake would really survive. But Afrit was, in the end, her closest friend.

"I can try," she said.

Afrit sighed. "That's probably the best I can hope for, isn't it?"

Quirk shrugged. "I'm sorry."

Afrit laid a hand on her shoulder. It didn't feel quite so unwanted now. "Also," she said, "if you ever fall in love with anyone else, I'm going to kill you both. Just so you know."

61

Lette and Will Sitting in a Tree

The next few days were spent in preparation.

Barph refused to help them when they asked him for it. "I'm no drill sergeant," he told them. "And I do not think that I endorse your plan to betray my fellow divinities." But he made no move to stop them. Instead he lay back, drinking from his enormous wineskin and eating grapes that had appeared from nowhere.

And then, when Will made a hash of trying to command the plants to grow beneath his feed, and when Lette could not command the birds to wheel in the sky, and when Balur struggled to make the weather bend to his dictates, and when Knole could not force a whisper to crawl through the camps outside Vinter... Barph was there. He may have chastised, or mocked, but there was information hidden in his words. And the four of them got better.

And five days became four. And then four became three.

More and more people streamed toward the smashed ruin of Vinter. A second city of wagons and tents gathered around the Vinland capital's tumbledown walls. Lette could hear singing at night. There was a sense of defiant joy among those coming here. Even the sanctimonious Vinlanders had fallen to the dragons. Even a nation that had the rapt attention and sworn protection of one of the old pantheon. The dragons were triumphant.

And there were not just three dragons roosting in Vinter now.

Each night as the sun fell, and each morning as it rose, Will could see the shapes of their slumbering bodies dominating the city skyline. Horned, ridged, covered in spikes the way a Saleran noblewoman would cover herself in jewelry; wings draping like cloaks, bunched up in tumorous knots, slicked back along their bodies; gold and gray, brown and blue, shades of green from grass to mud, they came crawling, and flapping, and roaring into Vinter. The city heaved with serpentine bodies.

And yet despite this, a sense of calm seemed to descend on their little copse. They had a plan. They had time. And if Quirk had not entirely quenched the flame in Afrit's britches, then the pair had at least found some sort of comfortable resting place.

Which just left her, and Will, no distractions. Not a single gods-hexed one.

She loved him. Of all the stupid times to make peace with that fact, it was now. When she had just slept with three divinities. When he had just bedded the god(dess) of love and lust hirself. When Avarra was lost and their lives looked even shorter than they usually did.

She loved him. And they had no future.

How did she even start that conversation? They had to have it. She felt sure of that. She wasn't sure why, but there was a compulsion that was strong within her.

And so, as three days became two, she seized the bull by the horns. It was not hard to send Afrit and Quirk away to spy on the encampment outside Vinter. It was not hard to tell Balur that he needed to go and practice smiting things farther away from the trees. It was hard to live with Barph's knowing wink and the mocking sashay of his hips as he wandered off to do the gods alone knew what, but she lived with it.

"So…" said Will, looking around the empty camp and then back at her. "We should, erm…"

Why in the name of all the gods did she find his blabbering adorable?

"You love me," she said. That seemed a safe enough place to start. They both knew that.

She tried to hold the shape of the conversation in her mind the same way she would hold the shape of a swordfight. He would bluster. She would be firm. She would override him until the facts were all laid out on the table. She also loved him. They were incompatible. They had tried before and failed. Neither of them had changed. Then she would ask him for a plan. That was what he was good at, after all. He would prevaricate. She would say there was no rush, but there had to be a plan, a legitimate plan if they were to move forward.

Gods, she hoped he had a plan.

Will was giving her a startled look. "Oh," he said. "This is...?" He stared at the space between them.

"Yes," said Lette. And that was good. She was sticking to the facts. "So—" she started.

"I think that's getting better," said Will.

Which brought her up as short as an unexpected parry in the flow of a fight. Some technique she had not expected to see in her opponent's library of maneuvers. "What?" she said.

"Well." Will gave her a sad smile. "I know you don't love me. And I kind of feel bad about everything I said back in the labyrinth below Vinter. It wasn't fair of me to put all of that on you."

"Will—" Lette started.

"I just wanted to say," said Will, who then caught her irritated expression, "it's just, I wanted to say sorry, and to let you know that that night with Cois helped."

Lette bit her lower lip with force. But not enough to bleed. Because apparently bleeding was the thing Will wanted to do tonight.

"Helped?" she said as calmly as she was able. Which was not particularly calmly.

"Yes." Will was of course incredibly earnest. "I mean, I didn't think it would. I hated the very thought of it." He seemed to read disbelief in her expression, which proved that despite the evidence before her, not every ounce of his brain had turned to cottage cheese. "I mean obviously zhe has…or had a rather overbearing effect on my libido. But that was externally forced upon me. Inside, I was…" He pantomimed horror. "I hadn't been able to imagine…" His hands fluttered in midair like two distressed hummingbirds. "You know. With anyone. But then it happened, and it wasn't actually as unspeakably awful as I thought it might be. And, you know, I still have what might best be called very strong feelings for you, but also I think I can finally imagine moving on some day."

Lette stared at him. And of course. Of all the infinitely possible things that could be said, he would say the worst possible one. That was how the world worked. Regardless of whether the gods were alive or dead, they were still shitting on her.

"So," she said, feeling the weight of every dagger secreted about her person, "what you're saying is that after a decent roll in the hay, you're not as hung-up on me as you once were?"

Will hesitated. Apparently even the shriveled lump of rancid cheese he used for achieving his deep thoughts recognized that just maybe he had gone astray somewhere.

"Wait," he said. "I just…Lette…I mean…I just…I thought, you know, that I'd be less of…" He looked around. "An imposition?" he tried.

An imposition. A fucking imposition. If Will had been in an orphanage at that moment, Lette might have actually been tempted to burn it down.

She felt so fucking stupid. That she'd been about to pour out her heart to this stinking, mud-swallowing, base, Cois-fucking pig. That she had considered letting him inside her guard. Inside more than that.

"Yes," she said. "Yes, that sounds wonderful." Her voice could have cured a world shortage in acid.

"Wait," said Will, still several leagues behind the actual purpose of their conversation. "Is that not...?"

"It's perfect, Will," she said, standing. "It's fucking perfect. I hope you and the girl you move on to are very happy, fucking in straw and pig shit for the rest of your lives."

She stood up. She needed to find Balur. She needed to take out her frustration on his hide.

"Thank you?" Will tried.

She hadn't meant to throw the knife. But it was an instinct that died hard. She managed to pull the shot at the last moment. It landed in the soft earth between Will's legs, burying itself up to its hilt, which quivered slightly.

Will squealed.

For her part, Lette wasn't sure if she was actually sorry she had missed.

62

Wolves in Cows' Clothing

"All right then," said Balur. "Let us be doing this." He clapped his hands. The sound boomed out from the little copse of trees and Lette gave him an annoyed look. They were, he knew, supposed to be being quiet and sneaky. And he appreciated that. But he was excited. After a week of sitting on his hands he was to finally be putting a plan into action. There were only so many farmyard animals an Analesian could be smiting before he was wanting to try out bigger fare.

He still did not understand why he was not allowed to be smiting the men and women around the city. That, to him, was seeming like the most obvious plans. Their belief made the apotheosis of the dragons possible? The dragons were impervious because of that belief? Then kill all the people so there were no believers left. And then kill the dragons. But, when he had been suggesting that...Oh the condescension and the mockery.

Fuckers.

But now. Now. Balur grinned, and licked the air. He tasted sweat and humanity, excitement and fields, bricks and blood.

The plan was, of course, trickery. Deception was always being Will's plan. That was Will's way. But much to Balur's satisfaction, Will's plans always broke down. Bloodshed always happened. So Balur nodded to himself. Chaos would come. Barph was with them, after all. And the god might not be good for much, but he was surely good for mayhem.

The god in question was looking at them all. "I still do not hold with this," he said, which was absolute bullshit and they all knew it.

"Who is it you are thinking is watching you?" Balur asked. Because they were all wondering it, he knew. "Be fucking enjoying your revenge, already."

Barph licked his lips. "I have no—" he started, then stopped. "Lawl's hairy balls to it." He grinned. "Let's go enjoy not giving that prick his powers back, shall we?"

"And then?" asked Afrit. "What then?"

Balur wished she would be giving it a rest. Someone had to be in charge. Why not them? And if they fucked it up—like Afrit was so afraid they would—well then, what would separate them from any other bastard with a crown in the annals of history?

"This is going to work," said Will, as much to himself, Balur suspected, as to anyone else.

"I don't know if you know this," said Lette, giving Will amounts of side-eye that Balur had not known she was capable of, "but actually saying it out loud doesn't make anyone feel more confident."

"I feel slightly more—" Will started.

"Just shut up and do what the big lizard man said," said Barph.

And that was enough for Balur. He wasn't waiting any longer. He closed his eyes and concentrated. He held the image in his mind.

"Become," he said. Not just with his mouth, or his tongue, or his lungs, but with his heart, and his mind, and his soul. He said it with all of himself, the way Barph had taught him to. He felt the word reverberate through his being.

And he became. He felt his skin flow like water, his bones become rubber. He felt his muscles shifting, his joints dislocating. He felt warmth running through the length of his whole body.

And then he stood on the ground, on all fours. And he lifted his great shaggy head. And he mooed.

"Gods," he heard Afrit mutter. "Subtle as a fucking brick."

Balur did not care what Afrit was saying. Will had been telling them that they would be getting into the city disguised as cows. He had said they would divinely transmogrify themselves. And Balur had divinely transmogrified himself, and he had become a cow. Nobody had been saying what sort of cow. Nobody had been saying he could not be a prize bull with horns the width of a wagon cart. Nobody had been saying that he could not ripple with muscle.

"More than a little Lawl in you, isn't there?" Afrit muttered.

Balur did not think he had left any doubt about the use of the words "Lawl" and "in you" in front of him. He objected loudly. Even to his own ears, an affronted moo didn't seem to do much.

Afrit rolled her eyes at him. "Oh give it a rest."

Of all of them, she had not transformed. Instead she held a long stick of wood, with which she would pretend to drive them toward the city. That was the extent of the role she was willing to play, and only after much cajoling from Quirk. The others were in their bovine disguises. Will looked like a young bullock, the others—including Barph—finely shaped tan cows.

And so they traipsed slowly down the road, kicking up dust as they went. The sun slowly rose before them. Birds sang. Elsewhere, dragons roared.

More than a little unexpectedly, Balur found himself admiring the curves of Quirk's bovine hips as he went. It was a slightly unsettling feeling. He had never before given the arse-end of a cow much thought. Afrit, he noticed, was stroking Quirk's new fur almost incessantly. Was Quirk perhaps a curiously good-looking cow? Was she somehow more desirable with udders?

That was a confusing thought.

He considered checking out Lette's bovine derrière, and couldn't quite bring himself to do it. Maybe it was being a cow. Maybe when he was being a cow, he was...liking cows. He was liking human women after all, and many Analesians would consider than an interspecies kink. Though at least humans were being sentient. For the most part anyway.

He shook his heavy head from side to side, feeling the satisfying weight of his horns, and pushed to the front of their small herd. Afrit called and clucked her tongue at him. But he honestly could not take the view of attractive cow hips anymore.

Out at the front he was able to settle into a more peaceful frame of mind, letting the weight of his body carry him forward, wondering at the curiously dull senses, the surprising range of vision.

Others were on the road with them now, marching toward the city. They were singing and cheering. Many had wineskins out. More than a few, Balur began to notice, were falling into step with Afrit, exchanging pleasantries, though few were meeting her eye.

He felt a hand fall upon his side.

"He's a fine-looking beast," he heard a woman say, her hand slapping his flank.

He flicked his head trying to get the bovine's eyes to focus properly on the woman. He wondered idly if he could parlay his beefy allure into something more serious. The gods did it all the time in myths, after all.

At the movement of his head the woman shied away, but with more of a coquettish giggle than a startled squeal.

Someone else was stroking the tuft of hair on the top of Lette's head. And glancing at her now, Balur did have to regretfully admit that in her bovine form she did have deep and soulful eyes.

He shook his head again. What in the Hallows was going on?

"I bet she's a fine milker," said the man stroking Lette's hair.

"Fine." Balur was forced to conclude there was being a distressingly sexual lean on that last word.

Balur huffed and took a stride toward the man with Lette.

"Oh look out!" squealed the woman who'd been patting him. "Look at his muscles."

And come to think of it, there actually was something sexual in the way she said that. And as nice as it was to receive positive comments from the opposite sex, perhaps someone with a thing for cows was not what he was into after all.

"Okay," said Afrit, "that's enough handling the merchandise."

More people were starting to gather. "They like it!" said someone else, putting a hand on Balur's flanks.

"Fucking fine-looking animals."

"That's a tasty side of beef."

"Like to taste her milk, I would."

All right, that was being downright creepy.

They were getting into the camp of tents and wagons, and a crowd was starting to form. Balur lowed again, swung his horns from side to side. What was it that was getting into people? There were being all sorts of stories of the gods getting into places disguised as animals without a problem. Admittedly, they were only getting into those places so they could have an awful lot of deviant sex with an awful lot of…

And then it hit him.

And gods, he had expected the plan to fall apart, but already?

The stories of the gods disguising themselves always ended in the gods getting laid. Which had never made much sense to him. Why had Lawl become a goose when he wanted a bit on the side? And why was Betra a horse when she permanently boned the Batarran monarchy? But those were the stories and so you just nodded and smiled.

Except now here they were using abilities borrowed from those same sexually deviant gods…

He tried to explain to the others, but his mooing did nothing but draw a lot of the wrong kind of attention. People were all around him, pawing at him.

Will was right. They truly did have to find some way to make sure the old gods never got back in power. Because he was a cow. A sexy cow. All of them were sexy, sexy cows.

He could hear Quirk's shrill moos of distress, Lette's snorts of anger. And maybe he could be using his horns to skewer a few of the bastards first.

He lowered his head.

There was a loud crack, and a squeal of pain. Then another.

"I said," he heard Afrit roar, "hands off my cows, you perverse bunch of arseholes." She wielded her walking staff above her head like a two-handed blade and brought it cracking down on the shoulder of a man who seemed to be trying to climb up on Will's back.

There were shouts and cries, bellowed curses.

"These cows are to be sacrificed to the dragons themselves!" Afrit yelled. "Touch them again and you bring down their wrath!"

Which put paid to a lot of the grumbling and made their passage a lot easier, but rather kicked Balur's plans to smite everyone in the nuts.

Soon enough, though, even Afrit's tactic of standing out in front, whirling her walking staff, was not enough to help them make much more than a grinding forward progress. At least now the touching from the crowds was not inappropriate. Instead it was the grunt and shove of people desperately heaving toward what was left of Vinter's gates. It felt like half of Avarra was clamoring to get into the city.

Banners were waved. Names were chanted. Gods were mocked. Dragon roars were imitated. Stories of fire and destruction were swapped. Prayers were improvised. Merchants stood at the sides of the roads trying their best to take advantage of the crowds. They sold toy dragons, dragon kites, ashes of those who had opposed the dragons suspended in holy water. Who exactly had blessed the water was left unclear. There were apothecaries selling cures, ointments, and oils made from the ground bones of the dragons who had died in the Kondorra uprising. There were street preachers telling new myths of these new gods. There were mad men screaming, and screeching, and loving every moment of it.

Avarra was celebrating. Avarra was alive with passion. Avarra had new gods this day. Better, and stronger than the old. The fact that these new gods were totalitarian arseholes bent on stealing every last copper from the people come to worship them seemed of only peripheral concern.

As the broken walls of Vinter loomed closer, Balur could see more and more guards perched upon them. The three hundred thousand troops the dragons had brought with them had not given up their weapons or armor. They kept a watchful eye on proceedings. Balur saw more than one party try to mount the walls in their more run-down sections, only to be beaten back with enthusiasm by the soldiers.

Rather than dampen anyone's spirits, though, these displays of brutality only seemed to egg the crowd on to new heights of worship.

The reasons for the guards' enthusiasm became clear as Balur finally reached the gate. There the soldiers were in heavy force, using spear butts to force people into line. Their grim expressions were a marked contrast to the citizens around them. Balur saw one vendor, a dozen yards ahead of them, offer the guards some dumplings. It was a clumsy attempt at bribery, to be sure, but even Balur wasn't sure it warranted the beating the man received.

"Golden bull each," said one of the guards as Quirk approached.

Balur let out a grunt of surprise that his bovine anatomy translated into a spray of bile into the back his throat. He gagged and coughed.

"That a sick bull?" asked another.

"Looks pretty majestic to me," said a third with what could only be described as a leer.

A golden bull each? Each of these families was paying a golden bull a head to get into Vinter? It could take a family of farmers a month or more to earn a single golden bull. And here they were spending four or five to enter the city, sometimes more if they had been particularly enthusiastic in their worship of Cois.

"I am not here as a bystander," Afrit insisted. "I am here to deliver cattle to be sacrificed for the dragons during the ceremony. I am as much a part of this as you."

The guard spat. "One golden bull each," he repeated.

"Sacrificed" said another. "That seems a shame."

"Each?" Afrit sounded outraged. "You are charging me an entrance fee for my animals?"

"Pay up," said the guard, without even the flicker of a smile or a conscience, "or step aside so you can start picking your teeth up off the floor."

This was good, Balur thought. There was no way Afrit would be carrying six golden bulls on her. Violence was definitely going to happen.

"How about," said one of the guards peripheral to the discussion, nudging his more authoritative friend, "we say we'll skip the entrance tithe if you give us half an hour alone with your cattle?"

The first guard looked at his companion with genuine disgust in his eyes. It was the first appropriate emotion Balur thought he'd seen all day. Possibly longer.

"The fuck—" he started.

"Look, fine." Afrit cut him off. She reached into a pouch at her belt, and much to Balur's surprise retrieved a fistful of coins. She shoved it into the guard's hand, and was then pushing past him, through the gates.

The guards stared after them, grumbling slightly as Balur and the others finally entered the city of Vinter, where they would make their final attempt to rip Avarra from the clasping grip of the dragons.

63

Buckling Under the Pressure of Thinking Up Funny Chapter Names

Of all the things Will liked about returning to a human form, the one he liked the most was that he regained the power of speech.

"Attractive cattle?" he shouted at Barph. "Cows that give people hard-ons? What in the Hallows is wrong with you?"

Barph spread his arms, all innocence and affront. "I thought you knew. That's how the gods do it. It's written into us. We are always desirable."

"You," said Will with considerable feeling, "are an arsehole of a deity. And I rather get where Lawl was coming from when he banished you."

For just a moment, there was a flash of something cold and hard in Barph's eyes. And despite it all, it was easy to forget that of all of them he was the true deity. He was the one born to these powers, who was as familiar with them as Will was with breathing.

"Sorry," Will said quickly. "Eight hundred years was a dick move by Lawl." He rubbed the back of his head. "But you're still an arsehole."

Barph's smile was already back in place. "I never professed that I was not."

Lette shrugged. "It wasn't that different from being in a tavern for me."

Balur made a scoffing sound.

Lette wheeled on him. "Oh, like you don't paw at every girl who comes within arm's reach after a few ales."

"Maybe," said Quirk, leaning in between the pair, "we should try to attract less attention?"

They were at the shadowed end of a blind alley they had ducked down to shed their bovine forms.

"It's okay," Afrit called back to them from where she stood at the alley's entrance, keeping a weather eye out on the crowds passing by. "At this point you could all start having an orgy and I don't think anyone would notice."

"We could always be trying to have an orgy and testing the hypothesis," Balur said.

"You aren't helping," Quirk called back to Afrit.

"Look," said Lette, "this being the moment when we really do have to save the world from a bunch of arsehole dragons, maybe we can skip the whole banter bullshit and just move on to the next step in the plan."

"Oh," Balur grumbled. "I am always liking the banter part. It is sort of being a way to let off steam."

Which was, oddly enough, perhaps the most personable thing Will had ever heard Balur say.

"How about," he said to the lizard man, "I just call you a prick and then make sure we all know what's happening next?"

"Fine," Balur groused, but then he cracked a smile. "Arsehole."

"Thank you," said Will graciously, "you lover of leprous whores." Balur's grin widened and Will had to admit, he did feel better.

"Okay," said Will, taking a breath and trying to project a confidence he didn't feel. "This is where we split up. Remember, we need to get good views of the ceremony. We need to be where we can see what everyone else is seeing. So we're on the lookout for vantage points. And once everything gets going then we're going to want to be hard to find. So we try to make our vantage points as discreet as possible. Inside buildings and behind windows. Hidden in crowds if necessary."

Barph nudged Lette and winked. "Don't you just love him when he gets all bossy?"

Will half-expected a lightning bolt to smash into Barph's body in that very moment.

"All right," Lette said instead, "let's get back out there and fuck some shit up."

64

Live from the Vinland Bowl

Quirk knew she was about to risk her own life. She was indeed probably risking it at this very moment, in the crowded streets of Vinter. Eddying pools of guards swirled in the streaming crowds of dragon worshippers. She was a well-known agitator in the resistance that had...well that had essentially buckled and been crushed. Still, it was well within the realm of possibility that they should have descriptions of her, and of the others. Balur was hardly a subtle figure.

And even if they did survive their passage to wherever the dragons were having their ceremony, then the plan was for her to directly antagonize the creatures that had killed the gods of Avarra. Actual gods. And with some of their power inside her now, she knew exactly what the gods had been capable of. And they had been utterly defeated. Utterly. And now she was going to attempt to do what those divinities could not. Based on a plan Willet Fallows had concocted. Possibly while under the subversive guidance of a god who could best be described as a vengeful dickhead.

And yet, despite all of this, what she was actually thinking about was transmogrification.

She could be anything. She could appear as anything at all. She had seen Barph treat the physical limitations of his body as if they were negligible concerns. She could grow. Could shrink. She could be...gods...a dragon. A wyvern. A giant. An ogre.

A chimera. Any megabiofauna she wished to be. She could insert herself into their societies, their social structures. She could move through them unnoticed. Not just an observer, but a participant.

The knowledge she could reveal. The papers she could write...

It always caught her off guard...the realization that that world was gone. That she had no one to publish her papers. No one to read them.

That was why, she supposed, she was here in the end. Stupid as it was, she was fighting to recapture a world where she could stand in a room and share her passion for large magical animals with poor, unsuspecting students. There were other reasons, like decency, and goodness, and a basic sense of what was morally right, mixed in there, but in the end, what it was all about was getting back to the university.

If Ferra hadn't messed with her all that time ago, back in Tamathia...if he had just left her to her studies, would she be here now?

She hoped so, but she wasn't entirely sure.

The crowd was getting tighter and tighter. It was becoming harder and harder to maneuver. They were still at least a mile from the city center. Banners were flying in the streets. People were hanging from their windows, shouting and cheering, throwing loaves of bread and sacks of wine down to the crowds below. Children were perched on rooftops, dancing and spitting on the passersby.

She felt someone take her hand, looked over, half-expecting it to be some pickpocket or another, but it was just Afrit. Her friend made apologetic eyes. She said something but Quirk could hardly hear her over the increasing roar of the crowd. She leaned in closer.

"I don't want to lose you."

It was an innocent enough thing to say, and Quirk had to admit she was glad to hear it. She still wasn't entirely sure how she felt about Afrit's recent romantic revelation, about the emotions caught up in this friendship, but she saw the advantages of companionship more clearly now. Whether it was the divinity within her, or something Knole had said, or just…time, she wasn't sure. So much had changed in such little time. She squeezed Afrit's hand, but she turned away before she saw the smile she knew would come. She wasn't ready for that yet.

They had not seen any dragons, she realized. The lizards had dominated the skyline for days. She had sat, writing notes when she could. Group behavior was something she still knew so little about. But this morning the beasts were absent. Where were they hiding? Could it be a calculated move to build the crowd's anticipation?

They hardly seemed to need the help. Quirk could see some people visibly crying with excitement. One young man was letting out occasional screams, loud enough to cut through the hubbub of the crowd. Everything smelled of sweat and straw, shit and burned street vendor meat. Quirk was no longer making headway voluntarily so much as she was moving with the sway of the crowd.

Slowly she and Afrit forced themselves to the edge of the street.

"Where to?" Afrit was sweating, panting slightly. The heat of the crowd in the sun was immense.

"Up," said Quirk, nodding at the rooftops.

They tried the first door they found. To her surprise, it was open, leading onto a cool dark corridor. Stairs lead up. Multiple families it seemed were living in the building. They could hear them shouting to each other from deeper within the rooms. They pressed up quietly. When someone caught sight of them, Quirk tensed, but the man just gave a friendly nod. He beckoned them and they followed him to a window where someone had lowered a rope for easier rooftop access.

They scrambled up onto tile roofs, the heat of the clay

baking up through the battered soles of their shoes. What Quirk wouldn't give for a new pair of shoes. She should have asked Barph about how he conjured things from nowhere. That knowledge, though, she suspected would have a price. The god still had clearly not told them everything. She would piece it all together though. Sooner or later.

The roofs were a little clearer than the streets, and the going not as hard as she had suspected. Makeshift bridges of planks and rope had been erected, providing access across the streets.

There was a makeshift quality to these celebrations. Homespun bunting dangled from windows. People were belting out hastily scribbled songs set to old tunes. They were genuinely excited, Quirk thought. They truly thought things were going to be better.

The willingness of the people to swallow the dragons' lies should have been a clue, she thought. Will was right that they had to be cautious returning power to the gods.

She had just finished navigating a bridge that was nothing more than two ropes stretched taut—one to stand upon, the other to grip for balance—when finally she saw it. What the dragons had done.

The old High Temple still stood, crumbling upon its hill, looking down on the city. But everything beyond that had changed.

The dragons had systematically leveled every block in a half-mile radius of the temple, creating a vast, rubble-strewn bowl on all sides. Homes, livelihoods, statues, monuments, history—all of it had been erased. The dragons had no respect for what had been here. They simply needed space for their audience, for those they would dominate.

And how their audience had come. Every inch of space was covered with a vast, seething pack of humanity. And still more and more people streamed into the space. The crowd heaved and shrugged, sprawling and restless beneath them. Quirk could feel the building they stood upon shaking as the crowd moved.

She could feel more than that, she realized. She could also feel the power coming off them. Their desire. Their worship. Their desperation to believe in a savior. It was something palpable in the air, like a heat shimmer, like an elusive scent at the back of her throat.

"Gods," Afrit breathed beside her.

"Yes," Quirk agreed, "they will be soon."

Some sort of critical mass was approaching, she knew. Whether it was divine knowledge or not she couldn't be sure. But it felt as if a thunderhead were building somewhere just out of sight. Something she could almost glimpse out of the corner of her eyes. The moment—whatever it was—was almost upon them.

They were almost too late.

And then a roar came. Not from a dragon's throat, but from a hundred thousand human ones. From half a million souls perhaps. All of them giving tongue to their joy, their rapture, their ecstasy. The building shook. Tiles slid loose. Afrit grabbed hold of Quirk, both of them fighting for balance.

Out of the heart of the old High Temple, the first of the dragons rose up. Then the next. Another, and another. They crawled up, like snakes boiling from the earth. Some slithered over the ruins. And slowly, looming over them all, dragons filled the sky.

65

Ready, Aim, Fire

Lette watched the dragons mount to the sky from her vantage point, hunched beneath the window ledge of an apartment overlooking the dragon's most recent civic works project. The inhabitants of the building, along with an assortment of family members, friends, and overly forward strangers, were perched on the rooftop. She could hear the beams creaking as they moved about overhead. It would be in keeping with her general luck, she thought, if the whole structure gave way under the weight and she was literally buried in idiots before she could do her part in what was to come.

The sky was alive with lizards now, their vast bodies undulating through the air, their leathery wings clapping out long, slow beats. She shuddered. There was so much power out there. In the crowd and in the sky. She could feel it, like a physical presence, like electricity in the air pressing against her eyes and her sinuses. She took a long breath. It was far from being as calm as she would have liked.

She thought now that perhaps she had mishandled things with Will. He had been trying to be kind. He had, admittedly, done a fucking awful job of it. And he had deserved her scorn that night, had deserved more perhaps, the back of her hand or the taste of her steel to remind him to be a more mindful fucker with his words, perhaps. But after that...

Maybe she should have made up with him at the end. Smoothed the air.

She had been going to tell him she loved him, for fuck's sake. And now they were likely going to die without her having said it to him.

She looked down at the crowd. It was their fault. She was going to die without admitting her feelings to Will because of these people.

Would that mean that she had finally achieved her goal? Would she finally be a better person if she made that sacrifice? That was how all this had started, in the end. That one, stupid goal.

Of course, if she did, none of these people would care.

Except for Will, she supposed. Will thought she was a good person.

Will thinks I am a good person.

The thought caught her off guard. She went to throw it away, but she couldn't dismiss it that fast. And the more she examined it, the truer it felt. Will really, truly believed she was a good person. Even when she had two blades in the guts of a man, deep down Will fundamentally believed she was trying to do the right thing. Even as she had scorned him, she knew he had assumed that the fault had been his own, not hers. He'd been right, of course, but there were not many men she'd known who would have thought that way.

Plus, she could probably have got a good lay out of the whole thing if she'd just swallowed her pride.

She sighed. Regrets. The only way to beat them was to outlive them. If there'd been any gods left, she would have said that that was in their hands. Now...she supposed it was in hers.

Outside the dragons were flying in an approximate circle around the whole bowl. A second circle of figures in black robes had emerged from the High Temple. They were chanting something, but she could only just make out the murmur of it over the roaring of the crowd.

There was an ominous feeling in her gut. Why did people always choose to color-code their moral decisions with their robes? If it had been white robes she might have felt a little more confident about everything.

The crowd didn't seem to care. They were in paroxysms of delight, hands and voices raised, writhing with joy. Every head was craned back, staring up at their new lords. Every mouth was open. Every hand grasped at the ineffable. The sound of the robed figures' chanting rose.

Lette closed her eyes. It was time to begin.

Birds. She would start all of this with birds.

She pictured them, the way Barph had taught her. She pictured their beaks and feathers, their legs and claws. She felt the texture of them in her hands. She heard their cries. She smelled their musk, their shit drying in the sun. She tasted their feathers in her mouth. She felt their desires to soar, and to eat. She felt their fears, their joys. Everything in her mind was of birds. She was almost a bird herself. All that maintained the boundary between mental image and reality was her will. Because she did not want to be a bird. She wanted something else.

"Come," she said. She said it with all her being. She said it in the language of the birds, though exactly how she did that escaped her. She said it and she knew every bird in the city heard her.

"Come," she said.

And they came. She could feel them coming. She could feel them leaping off roofs, fence posts, perches beneath bridges. They left their food scraps and their young. They left their prey. They left everything. For her. For her command.

She was with them as they swept over the crowded streets,

over the unfamiliar thermals of the crowds. She was with them as they ignored the scents of food and danger. She was with them as foxes launched themselves out of hidey-holes and snatched them from the air. She was with them as their bones crunched. She was with them as they soared. She was with them as they raced toward her, toward her command.

"Hold," she told them as they drew close. They arced and wheeled. They flocked in the streets just beyond the bowl. More were still coming, racing to catch up. Vinter was a vast city. It had many birds. Pigeons, and hawks, ravens and crows, sparrows, starlings, kestrels, owls, even a few harpies and one lone phoenix. They came for her.

She could hear the disturbance they were causing growing on the far side of the building she was crouching in. She could feel too the birds' awareness of the people looking up. Some of them wanted to flee. But they could not. Her will held them.

Was this how Quirk felt when she commanded fire? This heat flooding her? This power welling up? How did she ever let go?

They were still coming, birds from beyond the outskirts of the city. Birds who had roosted in the fields and the farms beyond the city walls. But she was also still aware that her small, paltry body was squatting uncomfortably in a dingy apartment, and that it could hear the chanting rising. There was no more time.

"Now," she told the birds. And, "Obey."

They swept over the roofs and into the sky above the bowl like nightfall. The sound of their wings drowned out even the crowd. They saw the dragons and they wanted to flee but still she would not let them.

"Obey." She was the word, and the word was her will, and her will was the birds' will, and they obeyed. They shit themselves in terror, but they obeyed.

The crowd gasped. They thought this was part of it. But through the ears of the birds, Lette thought she heard a slight quaver in the chanting of the figures in robes. A slight tremor of uncertainty. And they did not know, she thought, those men and women out there. This was magic not performed in the living history of Avarra. Indeed, if it had ever been performed it was lost in the origins of the gods. How had the dragons even gotten a hold of such a thing?

But now was not the time for such musings. Now demanded all of her attention. The birds were wheeling, struggling against her. There were eyes everywhere, and the birds wanted to flee from them. The eyes of the crowd stretched wide, staring up at them. And the eyes of the dragons, fiery and terrible, flashed in the skies. The birds' hearts hammered in their chest. A few came to stuttering halts—the combined pressures of fear and her divinely reinforced will too much for them to bear—and dropped from the sky like macabre rain. Dragons clawed at others in irritation.

"Higher," Lette willed, and the birds wheeled up, past the barking, snapping jaws of the confused dragons. The crowd gasped.

Lette closed her eyes tighter, screwing them up. She could feel sweat standing out on her skin, her breath coming ragged. The power thrumming through her was becoming hotter, more abrasive. She felt as if she were chafing her mind. She grit her teeth.

The birds didn't want to do what she told them to do. It was unnatural behavior. Their instincts screamed against it. And so she bore her will down upon them. She stamped their resistance out with her heel.

And as the crowd gasped, slowly the whirling cloud of birds formed letters in the sky. Milling, squawking bodies fluttered back and forth caught in the prison of Lette's will. And grunting as she did so, Lette forced the bodies of birds to form the message she and the others had agreed upon. And written in the sky, for all of the people gathered below to see, was a single, simple message.

Written in the sky, in the bodies of living birds were the words, "What the fuck, people?"

66

Dangerous Subversives

"We can't beat them in a fair fight."

Five days ago, that was what Will had said to them all. And Lette, still waiting for him to kick all her passion aside with idiot words about Cois, had hung on everything he said.

"So we are making it unfair," said Balur.

Will shushed him with a hand motion. He was obviously getting to that.

"People have to lose faith in the dragons," he said. "That's how the dragons defeated the gods. They made people lose faith, then they stole their power, forced a fight, and took the heavens." He was pacing in a circle. "Except it was easy for them. The gods had pissed on the people for millennia. Nobody truly wanted to worship the gods. We just didn't have any choice. The dragons, whatever their other faults, gave people a choice."

He looked around the little copse of trees. They were gathered in a circle around the charred remains of last night's fire. Barph was lying on his back feigning sleep.

"We don't have that luxury," Will went on. "The dragons are new. People are excited. They saw the dragons kill the gods. They *know* deep in their bones that the dragons are powerful."

"Are your pep talks always this good?" asked Afrit.

"Give him time," Lette said.

"It just means," said Will, "that if we're to break people's faith in the dragons, we can't do it by physically attacking them. And we can't do it by pointing out what cruel arseholes they are. The gods tried the first of those two, and we've tried the second. It doesn't work. So we've got to think of something different."

Afrit looked to Quirk. "Okay, I know I'm supposed to be patient, but how much stating the obvious do we have to get through before we move past this preamble?"

Quirk patted Afrit's knee indulgently.

Will pointed to Balur. "Why don't you respect me?" he said.

Balur puffed out his cheeks. "There are being so many reasons. You are being so weak and fleshy. You are not aware of at least five different ways I could be killing you without even standing up. You cannot be lifting more than I would be expecting of small girl child. You are complaining almost incessantly. You are not being half as funny as you think you are." He took a breath. "You—"

"Okay." Will cut him off. His smug grin had evaporated. His eyes rolled up, as if he were searching his eyebrows for inspiration. Then a sly look sidled onto his face.

"Okay," he said to Balur. "What do you do when I tell you to do something?"

Balur shrugged. "Mostly?" he said. "I am laughing in your stupid face."

Will's grin was very broad indeed. "Exactly," he said. "Exactly that."

The crowd was not laughing. They were staring up at the birds in confusion. There was angry muttering in some quarters.

Lette grit her teeth harder. A headache was mounting in her temples, like hot blades pressed into her mind. She forced the birds into the next message.

"I mean, seriously?" the birds spelled out.

The dragons were still circling below. But there was disorder in their ranks now. Some were flapping wider, arching their necks up. They were wondering what was going on. They didn't know this magic either, Lette thought. They had thought perhaps this was part of it. But now they were catching on.

She only had limited time.

The next change of words brought a cry from her lips. The birds were fighting this. The brutal force of her will was killing some of them, overriding their need to keep their hearts beating, their lungs pumping. The letters were growing thinner. Though it would be nothing to when the dragons' indignation and rage finally caught up with them.

"You chose these fat fuckers," spelled out the birds, "over us?"

And there it was. The first big lie. The first big swipe at the dragons' power base. The first suggestion that the true gods of Avarra were not as dead as advertised.

The dragons roared, screamed their rage.

Lette released the birds with a gasp, collapsed backward into the cool, dark space of the abandoned apartment. It felt like Balur had punched her directly in the temple.

The dragons broke ranks, billowed up into the sky, screaming great exhortations of flame. The birds fled, shrieking, scattering in all directions. A few fell flaming down into the crowd below, tiny parcels of cooked meat, but to most people, Lette knew, it would be as if the dragons were clawing impotently at so much smoke that eluded their grasp.

67

Flora and Fauna

Will watched the crowds desperately. He was perched up in a temple tower a few blocks back from the dragons' bowl of devastation. He wished he could be down there in the thick of things. He wished he could feel the pulse of the crowd's thoughts. So much of this depended on nuances.

He thought the people were all looking at each other. He thought they were confused.

Ask questions, he prayed. Though who he was praying to, he no longer knew. *Be skeptical. Please.*

It was his turn now. Lette had struck the first blow well, just as he had known she would. He had to be quick. There had to be no breaks.

Still he hesitated. So much depended on this. If he screwed it up...

Gods, he was screwing it up already by taking this long. He closed his eyes and took a breath.

"Grow," he said. And with everything he was, he committed to that thought.

He could still hear the sounds of confusion down in the crowd. He could still hear the roaring and snapping of the dragons up in the sky. But order was slowly returning. The people had come here with certain expectations. They didn't know what had happened, but perhaps it was just some strange aberration. Maybe? Perhaps. They could find a way to excuse this.

Will pushed harder. The timing of this had to be so precise. He had to catch them just as they thought it was over. He was moving too slowly. "Grow, you fuckers," his whole being yelled.

Then there was a shout from the crowd. A group near a building directly opposite him. A group at the periphery of events. It was a shout that became a scream. Will risked opening his eyes.

Dust was exploding out from the building behind them. Chunks of stone spattered down. A shutter crashed to the ground. The façade was lost behind a cloud of dust.

And everyone was staring. Everyone was holding their breath. Even the dragons hesitated.

The dust began to clear. People saw.

Vines were racing across the surface of the building, darting shoots of green curling up around windows and doors, spreading in great sheets across the stonework. Leaves were slowly spelling out a message in letters thirty feet high.

"These overgrown iguanas?" they said.

The sound from the crowd was not quite a gasp. It was close, but the initial shock of outrage was ebbing away. The crowd was slowly realizing that something very strange was going on. And it was not what they had come here to see. But it was not as solemn and po-faced as what they had come here to see either.

If he was lucky, thought Will, if he had gauged this just right, then people were realizing that they were here to see a show.

"Bloom," he said.

In a field of green letters, white and pink flowers erupted. A thousand tiny blooms opening their petals as one. A golden mist of pollen sprayed out.

"Even that bloated blubber monkey, Theerax?" the flowers spelled out.

Will was going to twist the knife in Theerax's side very specifically if he could.

There was a roar from the heavens. Will smiled. From the dervish of dragons spiraling above the crowd, a single lithe shape peeled away. Flame trumpeted from its vast jaws. *Take it personally*, Will whispered to himself. *Take offense.*

It suddenly became apparent to the people standing in the crowd below the wall, and to those on the roof above, that Theerax was about to collide with considerable force into the wall that was busy insulting him. They screamed, tried to thrash away from it. There was nowhere to go. The crowd was packed in too tight. Some of those perched on the roof tumbled out of sight as the crowd gathered there rippled and spasmed.

With a bellow of rage Theerax smashed into the wall. The building disintegrated. Stone and bodies flew. People howled. Theerax screamed hatred, his heavy head snapping into the ruins, coming back out with a mouthful of brick and vines.

"Grow," said Will to the world.

The crowd gasped almost as soon as he had finished the thought. They were catching on faster now. And there, spelled out in leaves on a wall directly opposite the first piece of offending graffiti, were written the words, "Missed me, you dullard."

The silence of the crowd was almost a palpable thing. The reality of the situation was beginning to sink in. Someone was truly mocking these dragons. This great and serious ceremony had become something else entirely. It was not an aberration, and it was not a mistake. This was a design. There was a hand guiding this.

Theerax became aware of the crowd's focus, spun around. His bulk was vast. People were scrambling and screaming to get away. *That's right, you bastard,* thought Will, *become the villain.*

Theerax roared, and launched himself at this new offense. The crowd screamed and scrambled away.

Now, Will thought, *it really starts.*

"Go," he said to the world, to its plants. "Grow. Bloom. Blossom. Spread." He willed the words into being.

And the vines grew. Even as Theerax raced across the open bowl, his wingbeats sending bodies crashing to the ground, Will sent the vines racing off around the walls surrounding the bowl. They ripped up through brick and stone, clutching desperately to ancient mortar, spilling words and insults as they went.

"Catch me if you can," he spelled around the circle.

Theerax bellowed, smashed into Will's first insult, saw the new words, and went howling after them. He bathed the wall in fire, scorching the leaves to ash even as new ones grew ahead of them.

"Looks like you could use the exercise," Will forced the leaves to spell. He was sweating now. He was at the limits of his control. He wanted to close his eyes but he had to keep on top of what was happening, keep the timing right.

Theerax howled, beat his wings faster.

"A real god could do this," Will managed. He was barely ahead of the dragon. His vision was starting to blur. He couldn't afford to lose this. It had to be perfect.

Theerax's roar flattened bodies to the ground. They rolled clutching bleeding ears. The dragon ripped through the air like a shaft from a bow. Flame washed up and over the walls of the buildings. People were running, screaming, yelling, diving for cover.

"Now," Will said to the world. "Now. Grow you bastard."

Theerax wiped the last words from the walls, howled in bitter triumph.

The tree exploded from the ground ten yards in front of him, lanced for the heavens. The dragon's howl of victory became a screech of surprise. He tried desperately to pull up, straining with his neck, his vast wings fluttering.

It was not enough. His massive head smashed into the branches that were still spreading out into the sky. He ripped halfway through them before his body bucked, and his massive scaled arse was flipped up into the air by his own colossal momentum. He described an ungainly, squirming circle, then landed on his massive back on the tree's far side.

Silence. Not even the yells of the people running for cover could be heard. Not the calls of the dragons above. Not even the billowing of the dust in the wake of the fall. The silence was perfect.

And then Will heard it. And it was the greatest sound he had ever heard. Greater even than his own name, whispered on Lette's exhaled breath as her body embraced his.

It was the sound of an idiot braying out a single laugh.

Whoever it was, he tried to stifle it almost as soon as it was out. But then it came again. A bright snort of merriment. Because Theerax—laid out on his back, legs clawing at the sky, wings tangled and twitching—looked like an absolute ass.

For a moment that was it. Just that one man. Everyone else was too stunned and too horrified. And Will's heart, up in his throat, fell down toward his toes, and it was looking to drop-kick his balls on the way down.

And then someone else laughed. And another. Not many, and not loud, but a little. Chortles, and smothered snickers. And it was enough. It was a start.

It was, Will knew, the beginning of the dragons' end.

68

Insults and Injuries

Balur blew out his breath slowly. Theerax was just lying there.
Just lying there. The dragon was out cold. This could be being
his moment...

He knew what the plan was. He knew what he was supposed
to do. "Taunt the dragons," Will had said. "Make them look
ridiculous." *But*, Balur thought, *what is looking more ridiculous
than me spilling your guts upon the ground?*

Anyway, he was being pissed at Will. "Find high ground,"
Will had said. "Hide somewhere out of sight," Will had said.
Not once had Will said, "And once you find a nice place, for
example in the buildings surrounding the large amphitheater the dragons have been creating, then I shall be sending a
dragon to smash it all and bathe it in fire." If he had been saying
that, then Balur was pretty sure he would be having a lot fewer
burns than he had right now.

He pressed a hand to his side. "Heal," he said. And yes, he did
know that he could heal his wounds now, but still...

So fuck Will, and fuck his plan.

Balur gripped his sword in one hand and the lip of the win-
dowsill in another, preparing to fling himself down into the
fray.

And then he reconsidered.

Gorrax landed in the center of the crowd. And when the golden
dragon had been fighting Firkin—Barph, he supposed—outside

of Vinter he truly hadn't gotten a sense for the scale of the beast. Gorrax had to be at least as large as the red brute that Balur had killed in Kondorra. The sun glistened off his scales like liquid fire. His eyes blazed. Bodies twitched beneath him where people had failed to get out of the way. He turned and his great barbed tail obliterated lives.

Balur's tongue tasted the air. There was fear in the crowd, yes, but not as much as the slaughter might suggest. There was... anticipation also. People were waiting for what came next. They wanted to know what would happen. There was eagerness even. They were excited.

"Taunt them," Will had said. "So we can kill them all."

Kill Theerax now, or kill Gorrax, and Theerax, and all the others later?

Balur cursed and closed his eyes.

"Who?" Gorrax roared. His words were hurricane blasts of sound ripping through the crowd. "Who does this?" He turned about. The crowd ducked his spinning tail. One daredevil even turned a cartwheel in its wake. "Show yourselves!"

Sparks spat from his mouth as he spoke. He was furious. A living testament to impotent rage. The anger almost crackled off him.

Balur concentrated. "Wind," he said. "Cloud. Weather."

"Who?" Gorrax bellowed once more. "Cowards!"

There was a fluttering of wings. The crowd gasped. Lette was playing her part. He knew the birds would be sweeping upward through the ring of still-circling dragons, spiraling up, drawing the crowd's gaze.

And then he heard the second gasp. Louder. He heard the mirth at the edges. They had seen what he had done.

Far above Vinter, spelled out so all could see for miles around, written in clouds, were the words, "Up here, dumbarse."

Gorrax roared. He leapt up into the sky. Birds shrieked and scattered.

"Wind. Water. Condense." Balur did not know how he had been ending up with the weather portion of things. Stupid Lawl and his control of thunderbolts. There were so many commands to be remembering.

"Oh," said the clouds, "you shall be smiting the clouds now?" The others had argued about syntax for a long time, though not for quite as long as Balur had been ignoring them.

"Weather. Wind. Blow." Balur panted.

"Such a powerful little dragon, aren't we?" said the clouds.

Gorrax strove higher. Balur could hear the roar of his flame. The other dragons were bellowing. But beneath it all, the robed figures around the temple were still chanting.

But there was another sound too. Muttering in the crowd. And yes, there it was, laughter.

"Wiggle that arse for the crowds," said the clouds. "Give them a thrill."

And then the crowd broke. The first big laugh. It ripped out of them, almost reluctantly. A snickering, snorting sound, given volume through the hundred thousand throats that gave it tongue.

The world laughed at the dragons.

Balur felt it almost immediately. A sudden rush of power. An electrifying, galvanizing crackle, like electricity down his spine, tingling in his limbs. And gods, he could be doing anything. He could be smashing these dragons. He could be tearing their heads from their limbs.

He could be losing his concentration completely. The clouds he had been carefully gathering above Vinter were evaporating. He cursed, redoubled his will. And suddenly this felt easy.

"Come on," the clouds said. "You can do it. You can make it." Clouds flexed and flashed, bustling across the sky. "A real god could do it," mocked the heavens. "Though not the misbegotten spawn of weak iguana ejaculate."

Gorrax was still struggling upward. But the clouds Balur had summoned were a mile up. They were great towering ziggurats of dust and water vapor. They rolled and whirled up in the sky. And they were emphatically out of Gorrax's reach.

The dragon screamed in frustrated rage. "Bye-bye, little dragon," said the clouds. Gorrax swept down. "Don't let the door hit your arse," said the clouds.

"Spark," said Balur with all his body and mind.

The lightning lanced down, a little piece of punctuation that smashed into Gorrax's hind limbs and sent him howling and spiraling down.

The dragons roared. And the crowd roared right back. Fear sublimated into mirth. Laughter tumbled out of them. Unstoppable. A dam bursting.

The dragons screamed. Power danced through Balur.

One last thing. One last message Will had insisted upon. "You think you killed us?" the clouds demanded of Gorrax's tumbling body. "We're the fucking gods."

And as the crowd roared, Balur believed that it was actually true. It felt as if a heat shimmer was coming off him. Power evaporating out of his pores, his body trembling to contain it.

And yes, yes, some dragons were going to die today.

69

Hilarity Ensues

Balanced on the smoking ruins of a roof, Quirk surveyed the scene. The dragons triumphant ascension to the heavens was in disarray. Instead of shock and awe, there were dead bodies and laughter. Something like hysteria was gripping the crowd. With each fresh insult the gales of their laughter grew ever more desperate.

Somewhere beyond the view of the Vinter bowl, Gorrax crashed to earth. A great cloud of dust and ash rose up. How many lives had he just smashed, Quirk wondered? How many people just died that we do not care about?

The clouds of dust Gorrax's body had kicked up swirled in foreign winds. The word *Parp!* floated off into the skies. Giggles chased it upward.

The energy being given off by the crowd was changing too. When Quirk had arrived there had been a sense of imminence in the people. The dragons' ascension had been almost palpable. An inevitability. Now it was different. The energy was swirling about wildly. She could feel the power she wielded growing inside of her, heady and potent. It was like when she took hold of her own magic, but the sluice gate was so much harder to control. She could feel her body filling with power that was desperate for an escape. She felt like she could do anything she wanted. She could reshape the world, make it the better place she always knew it could be.

"Gods," she said.

"What?" Afrit was still beside her, still balanced on the roof. A lot of the people who had not been dealing with serious burns after Theerax had passed by had scrambled for freedom in the aftermath. Those who had stayed were dealing with a distinct reduction in the building's structural integrity.

"This power," Quirk gasped. "It's toxic." She could imagine the whole bowl burning. She could imagine this whole city as a university. She was inches away from trying to force one of those futures into being. "No one should wield this."

Afrit flashed something that could have been mistaken for a smile. "We'll make a practical politician of you yet."

Quirk dropped down, squatting on her haunches, resting her hands lightly on the roof tiles beneath her. She wanted to stay grounded, to not be too caught up in this. But there were tides in the power surrounding her, ripping at her, pulling back and forth. Power filled her, lifted her high above reality, then ebbed away, sending her crashing back down.

And still at the old High Temple, the robed figures chanted. Was Ferra in among them? Her old foil from the Emperor's court back in Tamathia. Was he full of fear now? Did he wonder at the might of his masters? Did he fret it had all been for naught?

She had her part to play now, she knew. And she could do it. Easily, she suspected, as another tidal shift of power flooded through her.

People would die because of this, but she had made her peace with that a long time ago. Many people had died, and only a handful at her hands. And she had been fighting for something she still believed in when they had.

No, what worried her was that she would enjoy it.

Violence is a tool.

Except power was just a tool as well, and she could feel the corruption of that tool scouring at the edges of her morality already.

Afrit put a hand on her shoulder. "The one thing I ever really wanted to teach my students back at the university was that they would all make mistakes, and they'd all have regrets," she said. "But," she went on, catching Quirk's look, "that they'd only ever truly fail if they let those failures define them. If they stopped fighting to be better. Better than themselves. Better than the systems they were operating within. They always had to be fighting."

Quirk felt something swelling in her chest. Something more than gratitude. But she didn't have time to work out what it was. Instead, she took a breath and committed herself.

"Fall."

The crowd felt it before she did. She heard them react. A cry caught between eagerness and fear. What was next? they wanted to know. Would it make them laugh or scream? Then the rumbling earth reached Quirk's own building. Tiles fell from the already damaged roof. Afrit yelped, crashed down to all fours beside Quirk. Precariously perched though she was, Quirk kept her eyes open, fixed on the spot where her will became reality.

The dust cloud came from the center of the bowl this time. It obscured the central temple. People in the crowd started to spot it, pointed, and yelled. Quirk could see their arms gesticulating.

An unexpected breeze caught the clouds and blew them away up into the sky. Balur doing his bit to help. To reveal that the façade of the temple had partly collapsed and that a message written was now in masonry.

"Shut up, you pricks," it said.

She had objected to the cursing, but Will had insisted. "It's funnier if you swear," he had said.

Apparently he was right. The crowd were chuckling to themselves.

But far, far more important, the chanting was beginning to quaver. It droned in and out. Some of the robed figures were fleeing. Some were lying dead and buried beneath piles of masonry. Others were merely injured, clutching at their wounds and screaming.

"Explode," Quirk told the world.

She saw the detonation a moment before the sound reached her. It was like a thousand kettles reaching the boil at the same moment. The sound, though, was a sharp, flat crack that ripped through her abdomen.

Some people in the crowd, she could see, were actually clapping at the carnage.

When the smoke cleared the temple was barely standing. The façade was gone. Most of the structure was gone. Only a few internal walls were standing. And the message they spelled was clear.

"Roses are red, violets are blue, this is our city, and we say fuck you."

If she was going to curse, Quirk figured, she was going to do it in style.

Some people laughed. Some people clapped. A few actually whooped and threw up their hands. A few shouted the gods' names. Some were shouting angrily that the gods' time was over, that they were here for the dragons now. A handful had even dropped to their knees and begun to pray to Lawl, and Betra, and the rest of them. But, Quirk noted with a satisfied smile, not a single gods-hexed one of them was chanting.

70

Oh My God

"Gods," Will breathed. Because it had worked. It had actually worked. He had had a plan, and it had actually fucking worked. Everything he had suggested, it had played out as he had imagined it. Every nuance. Every consequence. The dragon's ceremony was a shambles. He could feel the shifting tides of the crowd's loyalty washing into him faster and faster. They had ruined the day. He had ruined this day. On purpose.

And none of them had died. Not even once. It was incredible. More than the power of the gods thrumming through him, it was that knowledge that left Will hardly able to breathe.

He had beaten the dragons. His plan had laid them low. *His.*

He wanted to shout obscenities at them. He wanted to lord it over their heads. He wanted them to know it was him, just him. This poor farm boy from Kondorra that they'd shit on since the day he'd been born. He'd seen dragons die in Kondorra, and now he'd see them all die all over Avarra. They could not stop him. Fuck them.

But, of course, if he did start shouting, then they would find him, and then all his plans would be naught. So he kept his mouth shut.

And yet... he could not just slip away. Not now. He could not let this moment become a memory just yet.

Will closed his eyes, hesitated, and then for just a moment, he committed all his will to the world.

"Belief," spelled the clouds.

"Worship," spelled the branches of the tree he had grown next to Theerax's comatose body.

"The dragons demand it," spelled the birds swirling in the sky.

"If it is not given willingly," spelled vines sprouting around the bowl, "then they take it by force."

"But," spelled the clouds.

"Worship cannot be demanded," sang the birds, alien sounds being forced into their throats; "it is earned."

"We," said the branches of the tree, "are your gods."

"We," said the vines, "serve you."

"For so long you have believed in us," said the clouds.

"But now," sang the birds, "we believe in you."

"Avarra does not belong to tyrants," spelled flowers bursting out of the vines on the house fronts.

"It belongs to you," the birds spelled in the sky.

"Don't give it to bullies," said the clouds.

"Even if they do breath fire," spelled the tree.

"Hold on to it with both hands," sang the birds.

"Because it's yours," said the flowers.

"And you deserve it," said the whole world. Everything within Will's span of control singing and spelling it out. Cats in the streets, rats in their jaws. The wind howling down streets. Piles of trash in the streets. Dust clouds. Scattered roof tiles.

"Avarra is not for them," said the world. "It's for all of us."

71

Lette There Be Blood

Lette had been called a cynic many times in her twenty-eight years upon Avarra. She didn't mind the name. She had been called worse. When pressed on the matter she had occasionally admitted that she would prefer the term *realist*, but people seemed to just take this as further evidence of her cynicism.

And, having heard the term bandied about so much, Lette was willing to admit that she was perhaps a little more willing than most to declare a cup half-empty, and the fluid within tainted by piss. She knew what degenerates she was forced to share this world with. But for her that just confirmed she had a greater grasp on reality than most people. And for its part, the world rarely took the opportunity to prove her wrong.

And so, Lette was not entirely prepared for the moment when Will broke from his script. Because they were not simply words in the sky, and voices in the throats of animals. They were emotions. They were ideas writ into the psychic landscape of the earth. They were a plea, a hymn, a prayer. They were a desperate pledge to the best parts of humanity.

And she was moved. She was unprepared for the experience, for the sheer genuine wave of emotion that went through her. Because in that moment, she did so very desperately want to live up to everything that Will asked of her. She wanted to be the person he wanted everyone in the world to be. She wanted to be a better person with her whole heart. And more than that, right now, it actually seemed possible.

She felt dampness on her cheeks, reached up. She expected to find blood. The echo of Will's psychic plea, she supposed, must have caused something to rupture. But no, it was simpler, and somehow far more startling.

She was crying.

"Oh, Will," she breathed.

Then she realized that there was absolute silence from the crowd below. All the mirth and rebellious joviality of a moment before was gone. All that was left was a collective inhalation. A sucking in of breath. A wondering.

"Oh," she said again, putting a hand to her temple, wonder sublimating to exasperation. "Will. You just had to—"

Outside the window of the apartment where she was hiding there was a sound like the world exploding. She grimaced, put her hands on the hilts of her knives. Then she realized what she was hearing.

Everyone was cheering. Everyone was bellowing out their worship and their praise. Everyone was screaming, screaming for Will and for his message. They were screaming their support for the old gods.

Power slammed into Lette like a sledgehammer. She was physically lifted off the floor by it and flung backward across the room. She smashed through furniture, leaving tattered chairs and tables in her wake. Her body slammed like a rag doll into the wall behind her. Stone cracked.

And she barely felt it at all. She stepped down. Dust blasted away from her, blown back by the power coming off her in waves. She could feel it crackling at the back of her mouth. She could taste it, like a copper shek in the back of her throat. She gasped and the air felt ice-cold in her mouth. When she exhaled, the world seemed to bend around the heat of her breath.

A face appeared at the window. A startled-looking figure peering into the room. "Hey!" he shouted at Lette and scrambled in to face her.

Lette was studying her hands. They felt so...so...powerful. She thought she could...what? Anything? Everything?

"What the fuck you doing in my house?" yelled the man. "What you been doing to my furniture?"

Lette made a brushing motion with her hand, as if sweeping aside a cobweb. The man flew through the air, crashed through an open doorway, and disappeared with a scream and a thud. She barely paid him any heed.

She could feel something happening outside. She couldn't see it. But it was important somehow. Sounds...it felt like they were taking place at the periphery of her awareness. She couldn't quite focus on them. The power was...gods, there was so much of it. She could barely hold on to herself. She blinked, found herself at the window, staring out. How had she...

Chaos. She saw chaos. She saw murder. She saw the city running red.

The great, tangled knot of dragons in the sky had broken apart. Vast silhouettes were distant no longer. They were plunging, roaring, screaming fire. They were rage, and fear, and frustration writ in flesh, and when the gods had made the dragons, they had been using their broadest brushes.

Because the dragons knew. Because they were fully aware of what was happening. They had felt the power ebbing, abandoning them and returning to...

They didn't know. She, and Will, and Quirk, and Balur, and Barph were too well hidden. So the dragons lashed out indiscriminately at the crowds.

She saw one massive brown brute slam into the ground, his vast jaws smashing through the crowd. He scooped up five or six bodies, bit down. Blood, bone, and viscera sprayed out in great sloppy arcs. A woman was struck full in the face by her husband's severed leg, was sent sprawling and screaming. Another creature, a sinuous red, writhing in a great red tantrum through the sky, breathed fire and immolated thirty more lives in an instant.

Even if they were not attacking Lette directly, the dragons were killing the people powering her. This surge in people's faith in the old gods was a local event, Lette knew. As vast as the crowds were, they were but a thimbleful in relation to the ocean of people who stood upon the surface of the entire world.

But there was still time. With every bite and bludgeon and murder that the dragons brought down upon this crowd, they also turned more and more people away from their own worship and more and more back to the old gods. The tide of power flooding into Lette was not yet diminishing but instead seemed to grow ever more strong. She felt full to bursting with power. Her guts hurt from holding it all in.

Two dragons slammed into the buildings surrounding their bowl of devastation. One was only a few houses away from her. Its claws tore through stone and mortar, through shutters and door, through lives. People tumbled screaming from roofs. She saw the dragon—a beast of charcoal gray—reach out and snatch one body as it fell. Its throat convulsed massively as it swallowed.

Another dragon, a blunt powerhouse of muscle sketched in yellow and green, was flying along the rooftops, raking its claws through tiles. People were screaming, leaping, tumbling, diving down for windows and attics. Bodies dangled from balconies. Blood dripped down through great tears in beams and pooled on garret floors below.

Other dragons were dive-bombing the crowd, snuffing out lives with flame and talon. This was, Lette knew, more than just a failure for them. It was an embarrassment. This was to be their glory, and instead all of these people had witnessed their shame, their humiliation. They were trying to scour the witnesses from the earth.

The dragons weren't the only ones doing the killing, though. The crowds were doing their own part to kill each other too. The number of people gathered here was vast; the number of exits from the bowl were not. Some people were trampled, others crushed. People screamed and fought to get away. They clawed at each other with no less ferocity than the dragons who sent them running.

There were other, less self-serving murders as well. Other men and women were caught up in the tussle and tangle of emotions and powers, and now they killed for a cause. For a belief. Some screamed the name of Barph, or Lawl, or Klink, or Toil, and others howled for the dragons, for flame and authority. They clawed at each other, bit and gouged, throttled and smashed. And for every drop of blood that fell, for every breath that came as someone's last, for every life that became nothing but a memory that day—Lette felt herself grow yet more powerful.

She wasn't sure if she was breathing anymore. She wasn't sure she needed to. The power of divinity was burning inside her, a limitless well of energy that mocked the petty constraints of mortality. The power was transforming her into something else, something greater. It ran through her like a wild horse through a field, begging to be broken and bent to her will.

She looked out of the apartment window, over the seething chaotic bowl, and saw a dragon flying straight toward her. It was teeth, and claws, and flame, and hatred. It was a thunderbolt of rage launched straight from the Hallows, and aimed at her heart. It was death, stripped of all beauty and pretense, all ceremony and wonder. It was pure in a way, almost perfect. It was everything a dragon was meant to be. The grimmest, most brutal statement of finality that the gods and nature could devise.

She reached out, raised up an arm to fend it off. It was an automatic gesture, and if it had been one she'd had the time to think about, she would have dismissed it as futile and ridiculous. The creature outweighed her by a factor of what surely must have been a thousand to one. Not only was her demise guaranteed; so was that of the entire building surrounding her.

She felt her hand collide with muscle and scale. A cold, hard impact that shook her whole body.

And her arm held.

She had closed her eyes at the last, at the inevitable moment. She opened them slowly.

The dragon was caught just short of her building. Its silver body dangled, writhing and thrashing, claws raking the air. Its tail whipped back and forth. And it was held. Held by the neck.

She held it by the neck.

It didn't make sense. The physics and biology of it didn't make sense. Here she was, inside the room. There it was, hanging... ten... fifteen yards outside the apartment window. She couldn't reach that far.

And yet she felt it in her hand. A neck too broad for her grasp. She could feel the muscles in it working. She could feel the scales biting into her skin. She could feel her palm starting to bleed.

It made no sense. But she began to squeeze. She watched the dragon convulse and twitch. She felt the strength of its neck muscles fighting her.

The silver dragon's throat bulged, its jaws opened. Flame filled her vision. She threw up an arm, smashed the dragon sideways, felt the whole structure of the buildings quake as the beast impacted with the building to her left. Flames boiled over her, enveloped her, became her entire world. And this was death, had to be death. She knew it, clear as she knew that the sun rose and that humanity made an ass of itself beneath its withering stare.

But the crowd below did not know. The crowd below knew only their gods. And they poured all their hope and belief into her. And so she felt the scalding, unending heat of the flame, felt it, and screamed in fear and regret at all that she had left unsaid, and undone... And then it was over, and she was alive. Her skin smarted, was red perhaps, but she was not the twitching pile of ash and charred sinew she expected to be.

Gods...she was...she was a god.

She could feel the belief of the people outside flooding into her, rejecting the injuries and the harm. She could feel them defending her.

She could feel the dragon still held in her hand.

With a savagery she thought Balur would be proud of, she slammed her fist back toward the building, hauling the dragon with her. Over and over she smashed its body into the building façade. Over and over she saw the walls facing her quake and crack. Plaster and stone fell away. The building started to tilt. And still she beat the dragon against the wall, feeling the blood running down over her knuckles, making her grip slick. Until she no longer held a dragon, only the corpse of one.

72

Goddess Among Us

Lette unfolded out of the window of the apartment. She felt her body expanding to accommodate the power pouring into it. She could feel herself growing even as she emerged, standing over the broken body of the dragon she had dropped onto the crowd. She towered over them all, head level with the rooftops, feet upon the ground, the world suddenly having become a smaller, pettier thing.

This was not the plan anymore, but she didn't care. This moment had become something else, something greater, something more profound. She had blood on her hands now. And she wanted more.

Around her ankles, people dropped to their knees, spoke in tongues, screamed the names of Betra, and Cois, and Knole. They didn't know who she was. They didn't care. She was simply there, and thus they worshipped her.

They were not the only ones who noticed.

A contingent of the dragons hurtled through the air toward her. Three of the beasts. Flame heralded their charge.

She caught the first in her right hand, the second in her left, abbreviating their desperate charges.

Diffinax ducked beneath her guard, then slammed into her gut with all the grace and subtlety of a battering ram.

The air whistled out of her. No matter that the power of three gods was in her. No matter that she was at least as tall as it was long. No matter that she had slain one of the dragon's compatriots. It was a blow with the force to knock the people around her to the ground. She staggered back a step, sprawled into another building. She could feel people tumbling down around her shoulders. She tried to grab at them but she still had a fistful of dragon.

One of the beasts twisted the free part of its head and sank its teeth into her wrist. The pain was bright and sharp. She howled with what little breath she'd regained. She brought her fist up and around, plunged it into the ground, using the dragon's body as a glove.

She felt the creature's bones break, its ribs bursting through its skin. She felt the tremor of its heart rupturing. She felt its life tear out through the back of its smashed skull.

But even as one dragon died, Diffinax tore and tore at her chest. His claws slashed through her leathers and her shirt, scored deep, ragged gashes down her chest. His fire enveloped her. She howled in pain. And she felt the belief of the crowd quiver. They had seen this fight before. It was one the dragons had consistently won.

Diffinax's head lanced up, striking like a snake. She felt his teeth close on her throat, felt his body begin to twist and tear. With her free hand she grasped at the back of his neck. The other dragon, still caught in her left hand, jackknifed and clawed, shredding the skin of her arm like so much paper.

She danced down a knife's edge of belief. The crowd's commitment wavered. A clown they could clap for. A heartfelt sentiment they could cheer for. But this...flesh and blood, dirt and grit. This stomping, screaming, fighting, bleeding monster that had come stampeding into this chaos...There was a reason Will had asked them to hide in the shadows, to show their hands but not their faces.

The pain was excruciating. She flickered between two realities, one where she was impervious to these ridiculous wounds, and one where she was lying on the ground gasping out her final breaths. She collapsed, still grappling with Diffinax.

"You almost killed my friend, you fucker," she gasped into its hate-filled, snapping face. Jaws slammed shut inches in front of her eyes. Flame snorted out of nostrils. Somewhere, and some-when, her hair was on fire.

"We've both got teeth, fuckwad." She lunged forward, bit down hard on the dragon's snout. She felt it try to howl. She felt fire blast down her throat. In some version of reality, in the heads of some people in the crowd she was dead then, her head nothing more than charred stump. She could feel that reality clawing at her, sinking talons into her as savage as any beast.

And she did not give one single fuck. She would not succumb to that or this dragon. She would define her own gods-hexed reality. She would not be dictated to by beast or man.

She reached up with her spare hand and gouged at the drag-on's right eye. It howled as the orb burst under her pressure, as she rooted around in the oozing socket for a better grip.

Its blood was filling her mouth, bitter and scalding. She bit down harder.

And then, with a great wrenching bite, she tore the snout right off Diffinax's face.

The dragon fell away, a gushing, twisting fountain of blood. Its screams of pain were lost in the deluge. It twisted back, wings flapping, clawing at the air for what little purchase on life was left to it.

And Lette felt the crowd's faith surge back to her. She felt the wounds on her chest knitting together. She felt the burns in her throat healing. She grabbed at the dragon, still savaging her left arm. She seized its tail and ripped it away from her arm while still desperately clinging to its neck with her other hand.

The dragon's vast muscles contracted against her, but the momentum of the crowd was with her now. Blood still poured from her wounds, but this was about will now, not muscle and sinew. She felt the dragon's spine pull straight. She held it tight as a bowstring. Heaved, with a scream as pain exploded through her chest, half-closed wounds bursting open under the pressure.

There was a ragged, booming crack from the dragon's back, and suddenly all resistance was gone. It squealed in her hands as she yanked it down and pressed its body like a garrote across the throat of the gasping, twitching body of Diffinax.

Slowly, and with great pleasure, she throttled the life out of the beast.

She stood and roared at the crowd. They would know her fucking name. Because she had saved them. And perhaps, just perhaps in doing so, she might have saved herself.

"For Will!" she shouted at them. "For you! For us! For fucking humanity!"

Another dragon lanced down out of the sky toward her, a thunderbolt of flesh and claw. She whipped out with the limp body of the dragon whose neck she'd broken. It flailed through the air, smashed into the plummeting dragon. Its tail wrapped around the newcomer's body like a well-weighted whip. Pivoting on her back heel, Lette slammed the massive weight of the beasts into the ground. She heard bone snaps.

"Fuck the gods!" she bellowed, stamping down again and again on the bodies, feeling skin and blood squish beneath her heel. "And fuck you too!"

The crowd was in chaos. This was something else. This was anarchy in the heavens. They did not know what to believe. They did not understand. Their faith tore back and forth through her, and each time it left, the pain of her wounds was fresh again. She was weeping, howling, roaring all at once. All in different people's heads. She felt like she was being torn apart.

"For Will!" she yelled again. "For all of you ungrateful bastards!" She held on to that, whatever that was, whatever core piece of her that she wouldn't let divinity touch.

I'm human, she told herself. *I'm here for humanity.* That was the rallying cry. Not gods. Not dragons. Not lords and fucking ladies. Not hierarchies and power structures. Humanity.

She felt something crash into her back. Somethings. Claws tearing at her. She was bowled forward, crashed into what was left of a building, felt it give way beneath her massive bulk. And then she was falling, gasping into blackness.

73

About That Victory . . .

Lette was bleeding. She was trying to work out if she was dying. She thought perhaps she was. She'd almost died before, a couple of times. This felt a lot like that.

She was in darkness and smoke. Rubble was scattered all around her. She could hear sounds of fighting. Massive, epic fighting. It was hard to take much else in beyond her own pain. Her chest was slashed to a ruin. Her left forearm was virtually gone in its entirety, not much left beyond the bones. She closed her eyes.

She had dreamt she was a god, fighting dragons . . .

She tried to heave herself up, dazed. Something was buzzing inside her, an energy she couldn't quite place, something carrying her forward despite her wounds.

She was in a room, or . . . no . . . A room had collapsed on top of her. The surviving corner of it formed a pyramid above her head. There was a door up there just out of reach. She thought perhaps she could pull some rubble beneath it. At least she could if she had a left fucking arm.

She looked down at the ragged stump. Gods . . . She was . . . Fucking . . . Gods . . . A sob tore its way out of her.

And yet still she kept moving, couldn't keep still despite her desire to fall down, curl up, and see if she woke up in the morning.

Movement above her made her look up. There was a figure

perched over the doorway in the wall above her head, a black shape in a field of gray smoke.

"Will?" In other circumstances she might have been ashamed of the desperation she heard in her voice. But she needed help now. Help out of here. Help to deal with her wounds. With her missing fucking arm. Help with whatever the hell was going on in her head.

She had fought a dragon. She had curb-stomped one to death. Crowds had cheered her, had hated her, had worshipped her, had feared her. She had stood like a giant upon the world.

"Not quite," said the figure above her, and dropped down.

It took her a moment to place the voice. "Barph?" she said.

It was hard to pick out his bow in the darkness. He straightened, appeared to regard her.

"Oh," he said, "look at you."

She couldn't quite keep the second sob down. "It hurts," she said. "So fucking much."

"They are a fickle bunch," Barph said. There was such a depth of sympathy in his voice. "You just tore the life from four dragons in front of them. You just destroyed their faith in those beasts utterly, and then you are knocked out of sight and..."

He shook his head sadly.

Lette pressed her right hand to her temple. "I can't take this. It's doing my head in."

"Once they see you again," said Barph. "Once you make them remember." She could hear something mocking in his voice, but something affectionate too. "Fickle arseholes."

"I..." Lette gestured with her stump of an arm, grit her teeth against the pain. "I can't."

"You still have divinity within you," said Barph, stepping closer. "More now than ever." There was a note now in his voice that she couldn't so easily identify. Something like hunger, perhaps? "You can heal yourself."

And he was right. She knew what the force keeping her

upright and moving was. It was the will of the people at her disposal. She tried to place a hand on her wounded arm, but the pain made her cry out again.

"I can't." She felt so fucking stupid. She had been so defiant, so powerful, and now here she was, begging for help.

"I can." Balur stepped toward her, put a hand on her shoulder. His palm felt warm against her cold skin. She was shivering, she realized. Shock and blood loss taking their toll. But she would be whole soon.

"I really killed four dragons?" she asked. She could hold on to pieces of it now. She had been knocked into the collapsing building. She must have taken a serious blow to the head. Along with the blood loss, and the unfamiliar pressures of the crowd's desires in the back of her head...

"You were like a fucking storm of death up there," said Barph. He was smiling at her. "You taught them how to have faith."

Lette wasn't sure she had meant to tie those two sentiments together, but she was honestly too punch drunk to give too much of a damn.

"Just fucking heal me already," she told him.

"Your wish." She could just make out Barph's smile in the dark. "Now close your eyes and concentrate with me. It'll be easier that way."

She complied. And she felt warmth.

But...not in her arm. In her...her neck.

And then warmth was fire, was pain, was a slash across her throat. She gasped. But no air came. Warmth flooded down her chest. A bright red arterial gush of heat flooding out of her. She dropped to her knees.

She could see Barph standing over her. She could see his smile, like a crescent moon in the heavens, like a knife wound in the sky. And she could see the knife in his hand. She could see the blood on the blade. She gasped again. There was no air. No breath.

"There," said Barph. He reached into a pouch hanging from his belt and pulled out a jeweled chalice. "I've taken all your pain away."

He knelt down in front of her, pressed the chalice to her neck. Her blood gushed into it, splashing and gurgling.

Stop, she tried to tell it, but she had no strength, no breath, no will left. The world was racing away. It was shrinking down to that terrible white smile.

"You want to ask me why," said Barph, and he was right, but she didn't have the air. She was so cold now.

"But I am a god," said Barph, "and you are not." He leaned in a little closer. "And I don't have to explain myself to you."

He dropped her. She barely felt the impact on the floor. She could hardly feel anything anymore. Only the cold. Only the dark.

And the last thing she saw was Barph standing over her, putting the goblet to his lips, drinking deeply, her own blood running down his chin.

74

Cutting the Puppet Strings

Barph looked down at Lette's body and thought he was going to weep. She looked so fragile now. So weak and broken. Everything she had been in life was gone from her. She had become a mockery of her own existence, the antithesis. What was left of her blood was pooling around her head, soaking her hair, matting it with the dirt and dust.

He had done it. He had finally fucking done it. After all his planning, it was actually happening.

He could feel the others now. Feel the power within them, reverberating through the world.

Could they feel him yet? He wondered. They were new to their powers, weak and foolish as newborn babes. But perhaps still they could feel *him*.

The power of Betra, and Klink, and best of all Toil, his stupid, absurd father, swirled in him, fresh supped from Lette's veins. He felt almost drunk on them. He felt like he could do anything.

Who next?

Lawl. It had to be Lawl. If he could have taken the old fuckhole first he would have done. For everything that had been done to him. For every insult laid at his feet. For every injustice. For his grandfather being the sanctimonious prick he always had been.

How it had hurt, to bend, and scrape, and pretend he shared their desperation. How he had wanted to spit and scream in their faces. But he was glad now. This was better, playing the prodigal son, and then tearing it up behind their backs. Knowing that his betrayal would sink into them slowly, like poison in their bones that would never relinquish its grip. To know that this would pain them forever.

He had needed to take Lette first. She had been the most powerful, with the divinity of three gods held within her. But now. Now it was Lawl.

He lost his focus on the physical world, chased lines of power, traced them to the locus that was Balur.

The world resolved around him once more. And he was somewhere else.

He was in an attic apartment, perhaps five hundred yards from where Lette's corpse now lay. The apartment's roof was gone, the floorboards exposed to the skies. Rain had started to fall, fat droplets soaking into floorboards, into ruined sheets and smashed furniture.

Balur stood by the shattered edge of the room, looking down over the bowl of panicking dragons and worshippers. The lizard man had his arms spread and his head thrown back. He was laughing at the sky, laughing as rain pelted him. Lightning lanced down from the heavens, illuminating him. Every muscle appeared to be flexed, every sinew tight, veins standing out beneath his skin. Barph snorted quietly. Balur was so much like Lawl he could almost taste the bile at the back of his throat.

Balur still hadn't noticed Barph, standing ten yards behind him, materializing out of nowhere. The Analesian was too focused on what was happening below, too deafened by the peals of thunder ringing out in one continuous symphony of discord.

Barph grew. He increased his height, his weight. Just a little. Just enough. This would need to be quick. He wanted the right angle. He stepped lightly toward Balur. As he drew closer he glimpsed how events were progressing in the bowl.

Lightning slashed down, striking dragons, smashing them to

the ground. One beast lay writhing, as bolt after bolt left black welts on its skin and the stink of burned flesh in the air. Balur cackled as each one hit home.

Not every thunderbolt flew true. Some struck mortals, and houses. Lives ended in shivering, twitching moments, and for each drop of blood that was shed, Barph felt the power in his body grow.

Barph looked down at the knife he still held. No. This would be better with his hands. Tooth and claw. Balur would want it that way.

He put one hand on Balur's shoulder. The lizard man barely even twitched. He was too lost in his own power, in the destruction of the storm.

Barph casually reached over the lizard man's shoulder and tore out his throat.

Barph let go. Balur reeled. The lizard man staggered around drunkenly. The spray of blood made Barph think of someone pissing red out of the Analesian's neck, and he laughed. The lizard man stuck out a hand and pointed at him.

Barph nodded, and bowed. He enjoyed these moments. Had always enjoyed these moments, until for eight hundred fucking years he had been condemned to walk this earth without them.

"Do you hear me in there?" he couldn't help but shout at Lawl across realities. "Do you hear me, you old fucking man? I have beaten you. I have consigned you to your own Hallows to rot forever at my leisure. This is my world now. Mine!"

Balur tried to say something. Blood burbled from his neck. Barph grinned.

Then lightning lanced down, smashed into Barph, ripping through his body. Balur's desperate attempt to go down swinging.

And Barph laughed right into Balur's face. Because it was too late. He was too powerful. Even as the lightning poured through his muscles, he reached down, pulled out the chalice that had once held his own blood, and held it up in front of Balur's increasingly glassy eyes.

"Do you see this?" he spat. "Your own goblet. You gave me the tools to do this to you, old man." He collected the last dregs of blood dribbling from Barph's neck, sucked them greedily down.

The power hit him like a gallon of wine injected directly into his brain. He reeled. And gods, gods, gods this was so very good. He dropped to his knees laughing.

Two left.

Quirk was trying to flee. Barph couldn't tell if she knew what was afoot. Of all of the mortals, she had been the closest to working it all out. Knole had always been suspicious of him too. But the Tamathian was too locked up in her own head. The passions of revenge were a mystery to her cold heart.

Quirk was down on the street, hand in hand with her stupid mooning friend. That one knew about the heart. Knew far too much. But she was nothing to him.

People were running pell-mell through the rain, running for the lives. Their terror was a palpable tickle at the back of his throat, making him grin. He tried to touch them as they ran past, to luxuriate in their emotions. Humans always seemed to experience things so shallowly. They couldn't appreciate the full depth of experience, with their brief flickering lives.

Quirk and Afrit stumbled through the crowds, fighting forward, trying to keep their footing in the mud and rain. Trying not to be knocked to the floor and trampled.

Quirk saw him first. She skidded to a halt. Afrit pulled at Quirk's arm, but she wouldn't move. She was rooted to the spot. Afrit looked up, saw him too. The woman's brow creased. But there was only realization in Quirk's eyes. *Now you see*, Barph thought. *Now you know.*

The crowd broke around her like a river around a rock. They

spilled to either side of the divinity they felt instinctively inside her. The mad dash closed once more behind him. A little oasis of calm. The eye of this particular storm.

"How long?" asked Quirk. "How long have you been planning this?"

Barph had no answers for this curious little mortal. He just slowly closed the distance between them.

"Before the copse in the trees?" Quirk said, only half to him. "Back in Vinter?" She cocked her head to one side. "When you sent Will and the others looking for Barph's Strength? Were you in control then? Pulling the strings."

He was only a yard away. "The sad thing is," he said in a conversational tone, ignoring the people scrambling for their lives only a hand's breadth away, "that you could probably figure it all out, even how to stop me, if only you had the time."

He would use the knife this time. He bore Knole little ill will. She was barely aware of anything going on outside of her precious books. She would die for her ignorance, but she didn't have to die in pain.

He brought his arm back—

Something crashed into him screaming. A whirling dervish of teeth and fists. It didn't hurt, but it caught him off guard, sending him spilling sideways into the stampeding crowd. Someone was on top of him scratching, and clawing at his face. Afrit, he realized. The two-bit Tamathian professor who was forever panting after Quirk. The mortal did not want to see the object of her unrequited love reduced to nothing more than a meat carafe holding the blood he wanted.

How touching. How futile.

Still lying sprawled in the mud, he reached out a hand, and she went rigid, sitting astride him, arms still raised, immobile, frozen by his will.

Then someone kicked him in the forehead, tripped over him. He grunted, feeling his head snap sideways. Someone trampled over his midriff, another tripped over his ankle. He growled. More and more people, stepping over and onto him, stubbing their toes on him.

He roared, stood, bodies flew.

A boot hammered into his nose. He felt the bone break, the cartilage smear across his face. Quirk was standing before him, brandishing one of her boots like a weapon. He threw Afrit at her. The two women fell in a tangle of limbs. He spat after them. "Not so smart now." He pulled out the goblet, held that in one hand, his knife in the other.

He was a yard away when one of the women sprang at him. He couldn't tell which one. It didn't really matter. And then suddenly there was a lancing pain in his crotch. He looked down. A stiletto. She was holding a fucking stiletto. She had speared him in his fucking balls.

With a bellow he grabbed the woman, dangled her aloft by the ankle. She was all falling fabric and hair, fluttering like a bird with a broken wing. He was tall now, growing as he needed to. She swayed above the earth. He reached down, tore the blade out of his body. He roared again. The other one was down at his feet, grabbing and clawing. He kicked her hard, was vaguely aware of her crashing into the crowd, going down beneath their stampeding feet.

He heaved the woman's body up with a shout, closing his wounds even as the blood started to pool in his shoes. He held on to the stiletto they'd used against him, imbuing it with new powers even as he did so, feeling it thicken and elongate in his hand. There would be some poetry in this after all.

He swung the newly made sword. Its blade bit into the woman's neck, tore her head from her shoulders. He punted the tumbling skull before it even hit the floor. Then with another roar he heaved the decapitated body up into the air, growing as he did so until he held what was left of her over his head. Her blood splashed down over his chin. He reached up, held the cup so the blood splattered against its golden sides, swirling around before falling into his open mouth.

He felt the power crackle through him. Less than he'd hoped. But Knole's worshippers were thin on the ground here. And power was power, after all. And soon it would all be his. Not a dragon's, not a god's, not a mortal's. His.

He stepped out of the physicality of the world, and went to find Will.

75

Even Heroes Fall

Will couldn't wipe the smile off his face. No matter how hard he tried, it remained there. And, yes, people had died. And yes, this was a mess. But…but…

The dragons lay dead! This wasn't just his plan working. This was his plan blowing all expectations out of the water. Half the dragons lay dead and bleeding on the floor. Lette had torn the life from four of them. Balur's lightning bolts had taken another five. He had managed to mob one more with every flying beast in Vinter he'd been able to find. It had fallen in a black cloud of wings, feathers, and chitin. Then the foxes and rats had come. Now half the natural wildlife of Vinter also lay dead, but so did the dragon.

His plan. *His* plan.

The moment was passing, he knew. The crowds were fleeing. He still felt flush with power, but soon he would need to break off from this assault. Then he could meet up with the others, and they would take the next step toward reclaiming Avarra, returning it to its people.

A creak on the floorboards startled him, made him turn. He had thought he was alone. But it was just Barph. And, in that moment, the god looked so much like Firkin, so much like the old man who had helped raise him as a child, that Will couldn't help but run to him and grab him by the shoulders.

"Did you see?" he shouted. "Did you fucking see? They fell!"

He was almost dancing. He was half-drunk on divine power, he knew, but he didn't care. This was worth it. He shook Barph. "We did it!" He whooped.

"Yes, Will," said Barph. "I saw. We did."

Will was laughing. And he suddenly, desperately needed Barph to see the scale of this achievement. Because whatever he was now, he had been Firkin, and Firkin would have loved this. "And...And..." He struggled to get the magnitude of it out. "It wasn't for any poxy, pissing gods. It wasn't for any king, or any country. It was for us. It was for the people. It was a victory for all of us. This could be the beginning of..." He cast about trying to imagine it. "I don't know," he said after a second of achieving nothing. "But something different. It starts here."

"Yes," said Barph. "Yes it does."

"When I was kid"—Will couldn't stop himself from gabbling—"we used to talk about rescuing all of Kondorra. This was *all the world*, Firkin. I mean...I'm sorry. Barph. I meant Barph. And I know you're a god, so I'm sorry, but gods...We did it." He grabbed Barph again. "We did it."

"And what will you do with it, now you have it?" asked Barph.

Will was caught wrong-footed. He stared at Barph. "What?"

"The power," said Barph. "What will you do with all this power now that you have it."

And that was the whole reason Will was in such a good mood. "I'll give it away!" he said, grinning. "I'm going to give it all away. Give it back to everybody. Everyone will carry a little piece of divinity within them. Everyone a god. Everyone with power. Everyone in charge. No dictators. No kings. No dukes. No earls. No emperors, or chieftains, or warlords. I'm going to give it to everyone."

Barph put both hands on Will's shoulders, and there was such a smile upon his face. "You know," he said, and the sincerity washed through Will like a balm, "not much of my time as Firkin is left to me now. But I do remember...he always thought of you as more than a child, Will. You were never his employer's son. And you were more even than a friend, Will. A kindred spirit. That's how he thought of you. Someone cut from the same cloth."

Will was so touched he honestly didn't have the words.

Barph nodded to himself. "Firkin," he said, sounding almost amused. "He was such a fucking idiot."

Will still looked confused when Barph killed him.

76

Hail to the King, Baby

Barph strode out into the center of the bowl. The wind played with his hair and his beard. Birds swirled around his head. He stood astride the world. Massive. A titan. A fucking god. *The* god. The people of this shithole of a city were but ants to him. They were paralyzed. Their fear was absolute, an obliterating totality in their thoughts, pressing down, holding them still. But they believed in him. Oh by all the ghosts in all the Hallows, they believed in him.

The remaining dragons were swirling, just so many confused beasts, looking to escape. He reached out, snagged one from the air. It curled around his fist, snapping, biting, achieving nothing. He squeezed and its life ended.

One tried to flee from him. Twenty lightning bolts reached out and batted its corpse from the skies.

He simply made the insides of another boil. It exploded before it hit the ground.

One by one, he killed the dragons of Avarra. They were nothing to him now. No longer was he the weak stripling they had left for dead on the walls of this city. No longer could three of them hold him to a standstill. Now he held the power of seven gods within him. Now the whole world worshipped him, and him alone.

The last two dragons came and knelt at his feet. The blood of their brothers and sisters dripped from his knuckles, fell upon them like red rain.

"We worship you," they told him. "You are our master. This is our obeisance."

He trod upon them, ground them beneath his heels.

There would be no more dragons in Avarra. He had not lied about that. History would forget them. History would forget whatever he told it to. He was history now. He was the future. He was the present. He was everything. He was the one god. The only god.

This was his revenge.

"People of Avarra," he said, and the whole world spoke with him. Every bird, and every beast spoke with his voice. The wind howled it. The tree branches creaked it. Babies breathed it, pressed against their mothers' chests. "People of Vinter. I am Barph, and after eight hundred long years I am returned to you. After eight hundred years, my rule begins once again. After eight hundred years, I am your god. Bow to me, and know your place."

And every single head bowed. And every knee was bent. Mortals, and beasts alike.

"You came here," he told them, "to watch dragons ascend to the heavens. To see pretenders to my throne." He let the violence build in his voice, felt them quake. He fought to keep the smile off his face. "But I shall be merciful, and today you shall watch me take my rightful place instead."

He breathed in their worship, felt it swirl heady in his head. Felt it lift him up. He felt the call of his old home, stolen from him for so long. He could feel the high of it rushing in his veins. And he was laughing uncontrollably. It was his, all his. The heavens. The world. The people. Everything they had tried to take from him. He had outsmarted them. He had seized it. He had taken it back. He was going home.

It was good to be king.

CODA:
WHAT IN THE
HALLOWS WAS THAT?

77

Soul Survivor

Standing alone, in a street full of mud and corpses, Quirk stared up at the skies above Vinter. The clouds were whirling, whisked upward in an inverted tornado. A tiny spot of impossibly distant sun was visible...or perhaps it was not the sun. Perhaps it was the heavens themselves. Perhaps it was where Barph had just disappeared to.

Rain still fell. Quirk was soaked to the bone. She felt numb.

Afrit was dead.

The others were too, she supposed, but that didn't seem to matter as much. Afrit was dead.

She didn't know how Barph had made the mistake, but he had. He had kicked her away into the crowd, grabbed Afrit by the ankle, and...and...

She broke down crying. Perhaps she was not so numb after all.

She had searched for Afrit's head. She couldn't tell yet if she was glad she hadn't found it or not. The crowd either had kicked it away so far she could not find it, or had simply trampled it into oblivion.

Sacrifice. Afrit had sacrificed herself for Quirk. Barph had grabbed her instead of Quirk and she could have screamed out, could have howled that the god had the wrong woman. But she hadn't. She had lain still and waited for the blade to come. She had tried to buy Quirk the gift of anonymity.

Quirk had thought that, in the moment of death, Barph would

know it wasn't her. She had thought he would be able to tell when Knole's power hadn't flowed into him. But he had seemed satisfied. And then Quirk had realized. Because Afrit had slept with Knole too. Perhaps the god's divinity had not come to her alone, but had instead been divided between them both. Afrit had been quiet about it, but she had also been horrified at the thought of using the god's power.

And now she never would.

Another sob went through her.

They had all been such fools. Such utter fools.

It had all been so obvious to her when she had seen Barph standing there in the street. Their deaths had been the god's plan all along. But he had played so carefully at making it seem like their plan. He had only given them the very slightest of nudges. So that they had always felt in control. So that when they looked back at the chain of decisions, they felt that they had guided their own fate.

But of course he had wanted them to reject the gods' offer. He had set it all up so that of course they would make that decision. Barph had known what arseholes his fellow gods were. They could not have endeared themselves to her, or to Lette, or to anyone. And Barph had known too the corrupting influence of power. He had known they would not give it up.

And Will had known how to steal the faith from the dragons. And gods, oh gods, they had been so close. She had been so excited. And Afrit had been beside her, cheering her on. They had been hand in hand. And even though they had been fleeing in a crowd of panicked strangers at the end, it had somehow felt as if she was finally experiencing the childhood she'd never had. She had felt giddy, and carefree, and...

And Afrit was dead. And that feeling, that lightness in her bones, was gone.

Around her, the crowds were starting to emerge from the smashed houses and piles of rubble where they had been sheltering. They blinked as if dazed, as if the nightmare were somehow over. Quirk knew it was not.

Barph had taken all the gods' power. Lawl's. Betra's. Toil's. Klink's. Knole's. Cois's. All the power of all the gods resided within him. He was the sole deity. The others were trapped in the Hallows, which now, thanks to his capturing of Lawl's power, he controlled. The gods had walked into the jail, and Barph had calmly picked the pocket of the key keeper.

And the situation was no different for the mortal populace of Avarra. All of them now sat in a jail of Barph's making. When Lawl raged at the world, then Betra raged at him. When Klink was a miser and spendthrift, then Toil rubbed largesse in his face. The gods balanced each other out. It might be dangerous and petty, but it was balanced.

Barph had no balance. Whatever he demanded, they must obey. No one would come to their rescue. Barph's deification was absolute.

And he had killed Afrit. He had killed…what? How had he killed Quirk's hope? Her joy? How had he killed her passion?

Standing in the blasted ruins of Vinter, Quirk knew that just like Knole, Barph had taught her something. He had taught her that though it might take time, though it might take planning beyond all conceivable measure, though it might take murder and bloodshed on inhuman levels…despite all these things, revenge was possible.

And she would have hers upon Barph.

78

Time for a New Plan

Down.

Down.

Down.

Through earth and soil. Past roots and worms. Down beneath the clay and stones. Beneath rock and burrowing things. Beneath geological strata. Beneath the shambling, crawling things the gods had discarded at the making of the world. Down. Deeper and deeper. Traveling to the very core of the earth.

And deeper still. Deeper in more than physical dimensions. A sinking into the reality of the world. Past despair. Past pain. Past death.

Deeper.

Down.

Down.

Down.

And there at the bottom, beneath all other things, a blasted plain of rock and scree. A dead land. No plants. No creatures. Nothing lived. Wind was the only thing that moved across that place, slowly etching a landscape of pain. The sky was the flat, dead purple of a corpse left weeks too long in the sun. But there was no sun here. No birds. No clouds. No weather. Not even hope.

Mountains rose from this landscape. Teeth that tore impotently at the impossible sky. And set into the face of one of those mountains, lost in among a million other identical mountains, were two doors. They were made of a wood that had never grown in this place, or anywhere else. They were black as pitch and hard as iron. Studs of a metal whose ore was not found here, or anywhere else, stitched the outside of that door. And the doors never opened, and no one ever, ever came out.

But souls entered. Souls entered all the time.

These were the gates to the Hallows.

Down. Inside. Past the doors' guardians, all lined up one after another. Down farther still. Into the bedrock. Into a steadily rising heat. Down past infinite fields of infinite labors. Into unchanging plains that slowly broke the will of women and men over the course of eternity.

Down. Through layers of these fields, these wastelands of futile activity. Down to where the memory of the sun was a memory itself.

There. There stood four figures.

A mercenary, face etched in hard plains, her red hair pulled back in a ponytail. An eight-foot-tall lizard man, scales like fist-sized cobblestones. A Tamathian professor, delicate hands worrying in front of her like a pair of blackbirds. And facing them, a farmer. A farmer with a face full of fury and a heart full of revenge.

"Okay," Will said. "So this is how we're going to con our way out of death."

The story continues in …

BAD FAITH

Book three of the Dragon Lords

Coming in August 2018

extras

www.orbitbooks.net

if you enjoyed
THE DRAGON LORDS: FALSE IDOLS

look out for

KINGS OF THE WYLD

by

Nicholas Eames

*Clay Cooper and his band were once the best of the best –
the meanest, dirtiest, most feared and admired crew of
mercenaries this side of the Heartwyld.*

*But their glory days are long past; the mercs have grown
apart and grown old, fat, drunk – or a combination of the three.
Then a former bandmate turns up at Clay's door with a plea for
help: his daughter Rose is trapped in a city besieged by an
enemy horde one hundred thousand strong and hungry for blood.
Rescuing Rose is the kind of impossible mission that only the very
brave or the very stupid would sign up for.*

Chapter One

A Ghost on the Road

You'd have guessed from the size of his shadow that Clay
Cooper was a bigger man than he was. He was certainly
bigger than most, with broad shoulders and a chest like an
iron-strapped keg. His hands were so large that most mugs
looked like teacups when he held them, and the jaw beneath
his shaggy brown beard was wide and sharp as a shovel
blade. But his shadow, drawn out by the setting sun, skulked
behind him like a dogged reminder of the man he used to be:
great and dark and more than a little monstrous.

Finished with work for the day, Clay slogged down the
beaten track that passed for a thoroughfare in Coverdale, sharing smiles and nods with those hustling home before dark.
He wore a Watchmen's green tabard over a shabby leather jerkin, and a weathered sword in a rough old scabbard on his
hip. His shield—chipped and scored and scratched through
the years by axes and arrows and raking claws—was slung
across his back, and his helmet ... well, Clay had lost the one
the Sergeant had given him last week, just as he'd misplaced
the one given to him the month before, and every few months
since the day he'd signed on to the Watch almost ten years
ago now.

A helmet restricted your vision, all but negated your hearing, and more often than not made you look stupid as hell. Clay Cooper didn't do helmets, and that was that.

"Clay! Hey, Clay!" Pip trotted over. The lad wore the Watchmen's green as well, his own ridiculous head-pan tucked in the crook of one arm. "Just got off duty at the south gate," he said cheerily. "You?"

"North."

"Nice." The boy grinned and nodded as though Clay had said something exceptionally interesting instead of having just mumbled the word *north*. "Anything exciting out there?"

Clay shrugged. "Mountains."

"Ha! 'Mountains,' he says. Classic. Hey, you hear Ryk Yarsson saw a centaur out by Tassel's farm?"

"It was probably a moose."

The boy gave him a skeptical look, as if Ryk spotting a moose instead of a centaur was highly improbable. "Anyway. Come to the King's Head for a few?"

"I shouldn't," said Clay. "Ginny's expecting me home, and..." He paused, having no other excuse near to hand.

"C'mon," Pip goaded. "Just one, then. One drink."

Clay grunted, squinting into the sun and measuring the prospect of Ginny's wrath against the bitter bite of ale washing down his throat. "Fine," he relented. "One."

Because it was hard work looking north all day, after all.

The King's Head was already crowded, its long tables crammed with people who came as much to gab and gossip as they did to drink. Pip slinked toward the bar while Clay found a seat at a table as far from the stage as possible.

The talk around him was the usual sort: weather and war, and neither topic too promising. There'd been a great battle fought out west in Endland, and by the murmurings it hadn't gone off well. A Republic army of twenty thousand, bolstered by several hundred mercenary bands, had been slaughtered by a Heartwyld Horde. Those few who'd survived had retreated to the city of Castia and were now under siege, forced to endure sickness and starvation while the enemy gorged themselves on the dead outside their walls. That, and there'd been a touch of frost on the ground this morning, which didn't seem fair this early into autumn, did it?

Pip returned with two pints and two friends Clay didn't recognize, whose names he forgot just as soon as they told him. They seemed like nice enough fellows, mind you. Clay was just bad with names.

"So you were in a band?" one asked. He had lanky red hair, and his face was a postpubescent mess of freckles and swollen pimples.

Clay took a long pull from his tankard before setting it down and looking over at Pip, who at least had the grace to look ashamed. Then he nodded.

The two stole a glance at each other, and then Freckles leaned in across the table. "Pip says you guys held Coldfire Pass for three days against a thousand walking dead."

"I only counted nine hundred and ninety-nine," Clay corrected. "But pretty much, yeah."

"He says you slew Akatung the Dread," said the other, whose attempt to grow a beard had produced a wisp of hair most grandmothers would scoff at.

Clay took another drink and shook his head. "We only injured him. I hear he died back at his lair, though. Peacefully. In his sleep."

They looked disappointed, but then Pip nudged one with his elbow. "Ask him about the Siege of Hollow Hill."

"Hollow Hill?" murmured Wispy, then his eyes went round as courtmark coins. "Wait, the Siege of Hollow Hill? So the band you were in . . ."

"*Saga*," Freckles finished, clearly awestruck. "You were in *Saga*."

"It's been a while," said Clay, picking at a knot in the warped wood of the table before him. "The name sounds familiar, though."

"Wow," sighed Freckles.

"You gotta be kidding me," Wispy uttered.

"Just . . . wow," said Freckles again.

"You *gotta* be kidding me," Wispy repeated, not one to be outdone when it came re-expressing disbelief.

Clay said nothing in response, only sipped his beer and shrugged.

"So you know Golden Gabe?" Freckles asked.

Another shrug. "I know Gabriel, yeah."

"Gabriel!" trilled Pip, sloshing his drink as he raised his hands in wonderment. "'*Gabriel*,' he says! Classic."

"And Ganelon?" Wispy asked. "And Arcandius Moog? And Matrick Skulldrummer?"

"Oh, and . . ." Freckles screwed up his face as he racked his brain—which didn't do the poor bastard any favours, Clay decided. He was ugly as a rain cloud on a wedding day, that one. "Who are we forgetting?"

"Clay Cooper."

Wispy stroked the fine hairs on his chin as he pondered this. "Clay Cooper . . . oh," he said, looking abashed. "Right."

It took Freckles another moment to piece it together, but then he palmed his pale forehead and laughed. "Gods, I'm stupid."

The gods already know, thought Clay.

Sensing the awkwardness at hand, Pip chimed in. "Tell us a tale, will ya, Clay? About when you did for that necromancer up in Oddsford. Or when you rescued that princess from . . . that place . . . remember?"

Which one? Clay wondered. They'd rescued several princesses, in fact, and if he'd killed one necromancer he'd killed a dozen. Who kept track of shit like that? Didn't matter anyway, since he wasn't in the mood for storytelling. Or to go digging up what he'd worked so hard to bury, and then harder still to forget where he'd dug the hole in the first place.

"Sorry, kid," he told Pip, draining what remained of his beer. "That's one."

He excused himself, handing Pip a few coppers for the drink and bidding what he hoped was a last farewell to Freckles and Wispy. He shouldered his way to the door and gave a long sigh when he emerged into the cool quiet outside. His back hurt from slumping over that table, so he stretched it out, craning his neck and gazing up at the first stars of the evening.

He remembered how small the night sky used to make him feel. How *insignificant*. And so he'd gone and made a big deal of himself, figuring that someday he might look up at the vast sprawl of stars and feel undaunted by its splendour. It hadn't worked. After a while Clay tore his eyes from the darkening sky and struck out down the road toward home.

He exchanged pleasantries with the Watchmen at the west gate. Had he heard about the centaur spotting over by Tassel's farm? they wondered. How about the battle out west, and those poor bastards holed up in Castia? Rotten, rotten business.

Clay followed the track, careful to keep from turning an ankle in a rut. Crickets were chirping in the tall grass to either side, the wind in the trees above him sighing like the ocean surf. He stopped by the roadside shrine to the Summer Lord and threw a dull copper at the statue's feet. After a few steps and a moment's hesitation he went back and tossed another. Away from town it was darker still, and Clay resisted the urge to look up again.

Best keep your eyes on the ground, he told himself, *and leave the past where it belongs. You've got what you've got, Cooper, and it's just what you wanted, right? A kid, a wife, a simple life.* It was an honest living. It was comfortable.

He could almost hear Gabriel scoff at that. *Honest? Honest is boring*, his old friend might have said. *Comfortable is dull.* Then again, Gabriel had got himself married long before Clay. Had a little girl of his own, even—a woman grown by now.

And yet there was Gabe's spectre just the same, young and fierce and glorious, smirking in the shadowed corner of Clay's mind. "We were *giants*, once," he said. "Bigger than life. And now . . ."

"Now we are tired old men," Clay muttered, to no one but the night. And what was so wrong with that? He'd met plenty of *actual* giants in his day, and most of them were assholes.

Despite Clay's reasoning, the ghost of Gabriel continued to haunt his walk home, gliding past him on the road with a sly wink, waving from his perch on the neighbour's fence, crouched like a beggar on the stoop of Clay's front door. Only this last Gabriel wasn't young at all. Or particularly fierce looking. Or any more glorious than an old board with a rusty nail in it. In fact, he looked pretty fucking terrible. When he saw Clay coming he stood, and smiled. Clay had never seen a man look so sad in all the years of his life.

The apparition spoke his name, which sounded to Clay as real as the crickets buzzing, as the wind moaning through the trees along the road. And then that brittle smile broke, and Gabriel—really, truly Gabriel, and not a ghost after all—was sagging into Clay's arms, sobbing into his shoulder, clutching at his back like a child afraid of the dark.

"Clay," he said. "Please . . . I need your help."

Chapter Two

Rose

Once Gabriel recovered himself they went inside. Ginny turned from the stove and her jaw clamped tight. Griff came bounding over, stubby tail wagging. He gave Clay a cursory sniff and then set to smelling Gabe's leg as though it were a piss-drenched tree, which wasn't actually too far off the mark.

His old friend was in a sorry state, no mistake. His hair and beard were a tangled mess, his clothes little more than soiled rags. There were holes in his boots, toes peeking out from the ruined leather like grubby urchins. His hands were busy fidgeting, wringing each other or tugging absentmind-edly at the hem of his tunic. Worst of all, though, were his eyes. They were sunk deep in his haggard face, hard and haunted, as though everywhere he looked was something he wished he hadn't seen.

"Griff, lay off," said Clay. The dog, wet eyes and a lolling pink tongue in a black fur face, perked up at the sound of his name. Griff wasn't the noblest-looking creature, and he didn't have many uses besides licking food off a plate. He couldn't herd sheep or flush a grouse from cover, and if anyone ever broke in to the house he was more likely to fetch them slip-pers than scare 'em off. But it made Clay smile to look at him (that's how godsdamn adorable he was) and that was worth more than nothing.

"Gabriel." Ginny finally found her voice, though she stayed right where she was. Didn't smile. Didn't cross to hug him. She'd never much cared for Gabriel. Clay thought she probably blamed his old bandmate for all the bad habits (gambling, fighting, drinking to excess) that she'd spent the last ten years disabusing him of, and all the other bad habits (chewing with his mouth open, forgetting to wash his hands, occasionally throttling people) she was still struggling to purge.

Heaped upon that were the handful of times Gabe had come calling in the years since his own wife left him. Every time he appeared it was hand in hand with some grand scheme to reunite the old band and strike out once again in search of fame, fortune, and decidedly reckless adventure. There was a town down south needed rescue from a ravaging drake, or a den of walking wolves to be cleared out of the Wailing Forest, or an old lady in some far-flung corner of the realm needed help bringing laundry off the line and only Saga themselves could rise to her aid!

It wasn't as though Clay needed Ginny breathing down his neck to refuse, to see that Gabriel longed for something unrecoverable, like an old man clinging to memories of his golden youth. *Exactly* like that, actually. But life, Clay knew, didn't work that way. It wasn't a circle; you didn't go round and round again. It was an arc, its course as inexorable as the sun's trek across the sky, destined at its highest, brightest moment to begin its fall.

Clay blinked, having lost himself in his own head. He did that sometimes, and could have wished he was better at putting his thoughts into words. He'd sound a right clever bastard then, wouldn't he?

Instead, he'd stood there dumbly as the silence between Ginny and Gabriel lengthened uncomfortably.

"You look hungry," she said finally.

Gabriel nodded, his hands fidgeting nervously.

Ginny sighed, and then his wife—his kind, lovely, magnificent wife—forced a tight grin and reclaimed her spoon from the pot she'd been tending earlier. "Sit down then," she said over her shoulder. "I'll feed you. I made Clay's favourite: rabbit stew with mushrooms."

Gabriel blinked. "Clay hates mushrooms."

Seeing Ginny's back stiffen, Clay spoke up. "Used to," he said brightly, before his wife—his quick-tempered, sharp-tongued, utterly terrifying wife—could turn around and crack his skull with that wooden spoon. "Ginny does something to them, though. Makes them taste"—*Not so fucking awful*, was what first jumped to mind—"really pretty good," he finished lamely. "What is it you do to 'em, hun?"

"I stew them," she said in the most menacing way a woman could string those three words together.

Something very much like a smile tugged at the corner of Gabe's mouth.

He always did love to watch me squirm, Clay remembered. He took a chair and Gabriel followed suit. Griff trundled over to his mat and gave his balls a few good licks before promptly falling asleep. Clay fought down a surge of envy, seeing that. "Tally home?" he asked.

"Out," said Ginny. "Somewhere."

Somewhere close, he hoped. There were coyotes in the woods nearby. Wolves in the hills. Hell, Ryk Yarsson had seen a centaur out by Tassel's farm. Or a moose. Either of which might kill a young girl if caught by surprise. "She should've been home before dark," he said.

His wife scoffed at that. "So should you have, Clay Cooper. You putting in extra hours on the wall, or is that the King's Piss I smell on ya?" *King's Piss* was her name for the beer they served at the pub. It was a fair assessment, and Clay had laughed the first time she'd said it. Didn't seem as funny at the moment, however.

Not to Clay, anyway, though Gabriel's mood seemed to be lightening a bit. His old friend was smirking like a boy watching his brother take heat for a crime he didn't commit.

"She's just down in the marsh," Ginny said, fishing two ceramic bowls from the cupboard. "Be glad it's only frogs she'll bring home with her. It'll be boys soon enough, and you'll have plenty cause to worry then."

"Won't be me needs to worry," Clay mumbled.

Ginny scoffed at that, too, and he might have asked why had she not set a steaming bowl of stew in front of him. The wafting scent drew a ravenous growl from his stomach, even if there were mushrooms in it.

His wife took her cloak off the peg by the door. "I'll go and be sure Tally's all right," she said. "Might be she needs help carrying those frogs." She came over and kissed Clay on the top of his head, smoothing his hair down afterward. "You boys have fun catching up."

She got as far as opening the door before hesitating, looking back. First at Gabriel, already scooping at his bowl as if it were the first meal he'd had in a long while, and then at Clay, and it wasn't until a few days after (a hard choice and too many miles away already) that he understood what he'd seen in her eyes just then. A kind of sorrow, thoughtful and resigned, as though she already knew—his loving, beautiful, remarkably *astute* wife—what was coming, inevitable as winter, or a river's winding course to the sea.

A chill wind blew in from outside. Ginny shivered despite her cloak, then she left.

"It's Rose."

They had finished eating, set their bowls aside. He should have put them in the basin, Clay knew, got them soaking so they wouldn't be such a chore to clean later, but it suddenly seemed like he couldn't leave the table just now. Gabriel had come in the night, from a long way off, to say something. Best to let him say it and be done.

"Your daughter?" Clay prompted.

Gabe nodded slowly. His hands were both flat on the table. His eyes were fixed, unfocused, somewhere between them. "She is... *willful*," he said finally. "Impetuous. I wish I could say she gets it from her mother, but..." That smile again, just barely. "You remember I was teaching her to use a sword?"

"I remember telling you that was a bad idea," said Clay.

A shrug from Gabriel. "I just wanted her to be able to protect herself. You know, stick 'em with the pointy end and all that. But she wanted more. She wanted to be..." he paused, searching for the word, "... great."

"Like her father?"

Gabriel's expression turned sour. "Just so. She heard too many stories, I think. Got her head filled with all this nonsense about being a hero, fighting in a band."

And from whom could she have heard all that? Clay wondered.

"I know," said Gabriel, perceiving his thoughts. "Partly my fault, I won't deny it. But it wasn't just me. Kids these days... they're obsessed with these mercenaries, Clay. They worship them. It's unhealthy. And most of these mercs aren't even in real bands! They just hire a bunch of nameless goons to do their fighting while they paint their faces and parade around with shiny swords and fancy armour. There's even one guy—I shit you not—who rides a manticore into battle!"

"A manticore?" asked Clay, incredulous.

Gabe laughed bitterly. "I know, right? Who the fuck *rides* a manticore? Those things are dangerous! Well, I don't need to tell you."

He didn't, of course. Clay had a nasty-looking puncture scar on his right thigh, testament to the hazards of tangling with such monsters. A manticore was nobody's pet, and it certainly wasn't fit to ride. As if slapping wings and a poison-barbed tail on a lion made it somehow a *fine* idea to climb on its back!

"They worshipped us, too," Clay pointed out. "Well *you*, anyway. And Ganelon. They tell the stories, even still. They sing the songs."

The stories were exaggerated, naturally. The songs, for the most part, were wildly inaccurate. But they persisted. Had lasted long after the men themselves had outlived who (or what) they'd been.

We were giants once.

"It's not the same," Gabriel persisted. "You should see the crowds gather when these bands come to town, Clay. People screaming, women crying in the streets."

"That sounds horrible," said Clay, meaning it.

Gabriel ignored him, pressing on. "Anyhow, Rose wanted to learn the sword, so I indulged her. I figured she'd get bored of it sooner or later, and that if she was going to learn, it might as well be from me. And also it made her mother mad as hell."

It would have, Clay knew. Her mother, Valery, despised violence and weapons of any kind, along with those who used either toward any end whatsoever. It was partly because of Valery that Saga had dissolved all those years ago.

"Problem was," said Gabriel, "she was good. Really good, and that's not just a father's boasts. She started out sparring against kids her age, but when they gave up getting their asses whooped she went out looking for street fights, or wormed her way into sponsored matches."

"The daughter of Golden Gabe himself," Clay mused. "Must've been quite the draw."

"I guess so," his friend agreed. "But then one day Val saw the bruises. Lost her mind. Blamed me, of course, for everything. She put her foot down—you know how she gets— and for a while Rose stopped fighting, but..." He trailed off, and Clay saw his jaw clamp down on something bitter. "After her mother left, Rosie and I . . . didn't get along so well, either. She started going out again. Sometimes she wouldn't come home for days. There were more bruises, and a few nastier scrapes besides. She chopped her hair off—thank the Holy Tetrea her mother was gone by then, or mine would've been next. And then came the cyclops."

"Cyclops?"

Gabriel looked at him askance. "Big bastards, one huge eye right here on their head?"

Clay leveled a glare of his own. "I know what a cyclops is, asshole."

"Then why did you ask?"

"I didn't . . ." Clay faltered. "Never mind. What *about* the cyclops?"

Gabriel sighed. "Well, one settled down in that old fort north of Ottersbrook. Stole some cattle, some goats, a dog, and then killed the folks that went looking for 'em. The courtsmen had their hands full, so they were looking for someone to clear the beast out for them. Only there weren't any mercs around at the time—or none with the chops to take on a cyclops, anyway. Somehow my name got tossed into the pot. They even sent someone round to ask if I would, but I told them no. Hell, I don't even own a sword anymore!"

Clay cut in again, aghast. "What? What about *Vellichor*?"

Gabriel's eyes were downcast. "I . . . uh . . . sold it."

"I'm sorry?" Clay asked, but before his friend could repeat himself he put his own hands flat on the table, for fear they would ball into fists, or snatch one of the bowls nearby and smash it over Gabriel's head. He said, as calmly as he could manage, "For a second there I thought you said that *you sold Vellichor*. As in the sword entrusted to you by the Archon himself as he lay dying? The sword he used to carve a fucking doorway from his world to ours. *That* sword? You sold *that sword*?"

Gabriel, who had slumped deeper into his chair with every word, nodded. "I had debts to pay, and Valery wanted it out of the house after she found out I taught Rose to fight," he said meekly. "She said it was dangerous."

"She—" Clay stopped himself. He leaned back in his chair, kneading his eyes with the palms of his hands. He groaned, and Griff, sensing his frustration, groaned himself from his mat in the corner. "Finish your story," he said at last.

Gabriel continued. "Well, needless to say, I refused to go after the cyclops, and for the next few weeks it caused a fair bit of havoc. And then suddenly word got around that someone had gone out and killed it." He smiled, wistful and sad. "All by herself."

"Rose," Clay said. Didn't make it a question. Didn't need to.

Gabriel's nod confirmed it. "She was a celebrity overnight. Bloody Rose, they called her. A pretty good name, actually."

It is, Clay agreed, but didn't bother saying so. He was still fuming about the sword. The sooner Gabe said whatever it was he'd come here to say, the sooner Clay could tell his oldest, dearest friend to get the hell out of his house and never come back.

"She even got her own band going," Gabe went on. "They managed to clear out a few nests around town: giant spiders, some old carrion wyrm down in the sewer that everyone forgot was still alive. But I hoped—" he bit his lip "—I still hoped, even then, that she might choose another path. A better path. Instead of following mine." He looked up. "Until the summons came from the Republic of Castia, asking every able sword to march against the Heartwyld Horde."

For a heartbeat Clay wondered at the significance of that. Until he remembered the news he'd heard earlier that evening. An army of twenty thousand, routed by a vastly more numerous host; the survivors surrounded in Castia, doubtless wishing they had died on the battlefield rather than endure the atrocities of a city under siege.

Which meant that Gabriel's daughter was dead. Or she would be, when the city fell.

Clay opened his mouth to speak, to try to keep the heartbreak from his voice as he did so. "Gabe, I—"

"I'm going after her, Clay. And I need you with me." Gabriel leaned forward in his chair, the flame of a father's fear and anger alight in his eyes. "It's time to get the band back together."

Enter the monthly
Orbit sweepstakes at
www.orbitloot.com

With a different prize every month,
from advance copies of books by
your favourite authors to exclusive
merchandise packs,
**we think you'll find something
you love.**